Heidi Swain lives in Norfolk with her family and a mischievous black cat called Storm. She is passionate about gardening, the countryside and collects vintage paraphernalia. *The Summer Fair* is her fourteenth novel. You can follow Heidi on Twitter @Heidi_Swain or visit her website: heidiswain.co.uk

Also by Heidi Swain

The Cherry Tree Café
Summer at Skylark Farm
Mince Pies and Mistletoe at the Christmas Market
Coming Home to Cuckoo Cottage
Sleigh Rides and Silver Bells at the Christmas Fair
Sunshine and Sweet Peas in Nightingale Square
Snowflakes and Cinnamon Swirls
at the Winter Wonderland
Poppy's Recipe for Life
The Christmas Wish List
The Secret Seaside Escape
The Winter Garden
A Taste of Home
Underneath the Christmas Tree

Heidi Swain

The Summer Fair

SIMON & SCHUSTER

London · New York · Sydney · Toronto · New Delhi

First published in Great Britain by Simon & Schuster UK Ltd, 2022

1 3 5 7 9 10 8 6 4 2

Simon & Schuster UK Ltd
1st Floor
222 Gray's Inn Road
London WC1X 8HB

Simon & Schuster Australia, Sydney
Simon & Schuster India, New Delhi

www.simonandschuster.co.uk
www.simonandschuster.com.au
www.simonandschuster.co.in

A CIP catalogue record for this book
is available from the British Library

Paperback ISBN: 978-1-4711-9586-0
eBook ISBN: 978-1-4711-9587-7
Audio ISBN: 978-1-3985-1289-4

Typeset in the UK by M Rules
Printed and bound by CPI Group (UK) Ltd, Croydon, CR0 4YY

MIX
Paper from
responsible sources
FSC® C171272

To darling Lia
Thank you for your infinite patience and insight

Chapter 1

Falling asleep to the soothing sounds of Ella Fitzgerald and Billie Holiday had been a well-established childhood habit and one that stayed with me until I was in my early twenties. When I was little, I used to lay in bed, my eyelids drooping as I listened to Mum's sweet voice as it accompanied the music she always had playing in the house.

It comfortingly carried up the stairs and into my room, lulling me into a peaceful sleep, but when she died shortly before her fortieth birthday, after her second stroke in as many years, the music stopped. I banished the melodic back-drop, unplugged the radio, packed away the vinyl and took an oath that I would never listen to music or sing another note. At that point, my heart had been broken twice over a song and I was adamant that it wouldn't happen again.

I had more than one reason for taking the self-imposed vow of silence but as a result, I found falling asleep nigh on impossible. I generally stared at the ceiling until, just a couple of hours before I had to get up, I pitched over the edge into a disturbing nightmare-filled haze. Consequently, I had downloaded the RSPB birdsong app to help rouse me before I was ever anywhere near rested. It was nowhere near as soulful as Ella or Billie, but it just about did the job.

On the eve of June the twenty-third, I sat on the edge of the narrow single bed in the house I shared with three other people, still mostly unknown to me even after months of co-habitation, and considered not setting my avian alarm. Of all the days of the year, this was the one that would guarantee no sleep at all.

'Better to be safe than sorry,' I murmured nonetheless, keying in the time I needed to be ready for another busy shift working at the Edith Cavell Care Home.

Just as I had known I would be, I was still awake before the alarm the next morning and much earlier than any lark. I swept my hair into a ponytail, pulled on my cotton floral dressing gown and padded down to the kitchen, willing myself not to play through events as they had unfolded minute by minute exactly two years ago.

'It won't ever go away,' a well-meaning neighbour had warned me during the excruciating weeks which had followed Mum's fatal stroke, 'but time will rub away the sharpest edges of it.'

It was a mercy that they had been right about that, but sometimes if felt like time was ticking by at an extraordinar-ily slow pace. Last year, June the twenty-third had seemed to last for three days rather than just one.

Functioning on automatic pilot, I blinked at the haphazardly stacked piles of unwashed dishes and spotted my favourite mug right at the bottom of the detritus and covered in something that looked solidly dried on. In spite of my attempt to calmly breathe through what I was feeling, a technique that usually served me well, I felt my annoyance bristle.

How was it possible for the almost-thirty somethings I shared a house with to still be living like first-year students? No boundaries, no hygiene, no consideration for anyone other than themselves. The bin was overflowing, the milk I'd picked up after my shift the day before was almost gone and, to top it all off, there was an ominous scurrying sound coming from under the sink.

I focused with more intent on my breathing and separated myself from the infuriating sight by walking through to the sitting room. Unfortunately, things looked no better in there. If anything, they were worse.

Aretha, my colossal and much-loved cheese plant, the one specimen in my treasured houseplant collection that was too big to squeeze into my meanly proportioned room, had not one but two ground out cigarette butts in her pot. Tears sprang to my eyes and I felt my chest tighten as I picked them out and dropped them into one of the takeaway containers congealing on the coffee table.

I realised I needed to get out of the house. Not just to go to work, but for good.

*

'Good morning, early bird,' was the greeting I received when I signed in at reception almost an hour ahead of my shift.

Being so early meant the bus which usually crawled along with the rest of the traffic had positively sped around the ring road.

'Morning Greta,' I responded, trying to raise a smile. 'You've got your nightie on back to front.'

'I thought it felt tight around my neck,' my octogenarian friend muttered, stretching it out to look at the label which must have been scratching her throat.

At least at work, with a band of mischievous, and mostly merry, elderly pensioners to look after, I wouldn't have too much time to dwell on the events of the past. Last year I had taken a day off and given in to it completely and that hadn't helped at all. This year was going to be all about the other end of the spectrum and powering through. Wallowing hadn't worked, so perhaps immersing myself in work would.

'Here you are, Greta!' puffed Phil, another carer, who was just coming to the end of his twilight shift, as he raced down the corridor, 'I've been looking all over for you.'

'You can't have been.' She sniffed importantly. 'I've been here, manning the desk, all night.'

Phil looked at me and shook his head. The dark circles under his eyes implied that the usual suspects had been giving him the run-around for hours.

'You're early, Beth,' he said to me.

'That's what I said,' tutted Greta, as she eyed me again, suspiciously this time. 'Couldn't you sleep either?'

'Something like that,' I swallowed, making for the staffroom. 'I'll come and give you a hand in a minute, Phil.'

'Go to the kitchen first,' he said, leading Greta back along the corridor, while wrestling to stop her pulling her nightie over her head. 'It's full English Thursday. You're going to need some extra calories to get you through the day. I don't know what's got into this lot but they've been running rings around us all night!'

And they were on form to continue doing so all day. I'd barely settled into my uniform and swallowed my last mouthful of breakfast before I was called into action to track down Greta who'd gone AWOL again.

'What's she up to now?' asked Harold, as he nodded towards the door where a rumpus could be heard coming from Greta's room once she'd been found and which was next to his. 'Actually no,' he said, settling back in his chair, 'don't tell me. It's too early in the day.'

I couldn't help but laugh. Harold was always able to make me smile, no matter what the date on the calendar. We'd joined Edith Cavell Care the same week. Me, because I needed to earn more money than was on offer from stacking shelves part-time and caring was the only other thing I could do, and him because he'd had a fall and needed more support than the team running the assisted living units next door to the care home could offer him. He was completely recovered now, but had enjoyed the company and camaraderie in the home so much, he had decided to make the move a permanent one.

'Red or mustard?' I asked, holding up two pairs of socks.

'What about one of each?' he twinkled.

'No way,' I said, returning the mustard pair to the drawer and kneeling down to put the red ones on for him. 'Not after all that confusion in the laundry room last time.'

'Fair enough,' he relented, with a grin.

'How's that?' I asked, once I'd slipped the socks on and his feet into his slippers.

'Cracking,' he beamed, wriggling his toes. 'Thanks, my love.'

'Just doing my job,' I said, standing back up.

'I think we all know you go above and beyond your job,' he smiled with a nod to the clock next to his bed.

It was still a while before my shift was supposed to officially start.

'Have you told her?' came another voice, before I could wave away what he'd said.

It was Ida. She had a room on the floor above, but like Greta, she also refused to stay where she was supposed to. I was beginning to wonder if the tagging system Phil had jokingly mentioned at the staff meeting the previous week might not actually be a bad strategy to contain certain residents.

'Not yet,' said Harold, beckoning Ida in.

'What's this?' I frowned.

Ida came in, tottering slowly with her frame. For someone who could only move at a snail's pace, she could cover a remarkable amount of ground unseen.

'You missed a treat yesterday,' she chuckled.

6

'I'm not sure I'd put it quite like that,' said Harold, with a shake of his head. 'You want to think yourself lucky you had to accompany Walter to the hospital and were late back, Beth.'

'Why?' I frowned. 'What did I miss?'

'Macaroni,' Ida guffawed.

'Macaroni?' I repeated. 'For dinner, you mean?'

Harold shook his head again.

'No,' he said, rolling his eyes. 'She means macramé, not macaroni.'

'That's it,' said Ida, ineffectively clicking her arthritic fingers. 'Macramé.'

I was still at a loss.

'Who in their right mind would have thought that knotting multiple strands of cord together to make plant pot holders was a suitable craft for a bunch of arthritic pensioners, most of whom are losing their marbles?' Harold scathingly said.

The penny suddenly dropped.

'Karen,' said Ida, slapping her thigh and verifying what I'd worked out. 'That's who.'

'It was a rhetorical question,' Harold reacted.

'A what?' frowned Ida.

'Never mind,' I quickly said.

'That was the so-called activity that the so-called activities manager came up with for yesterday afternoon,' confirmed Harold, while I bit my lip and imagined the carnage.

I had nothing against macramé. In fact, I had quite a few

of the plants in my collection hanging up in cleverly knotted holders, but it wasn't a craft for the less dextrous and easily confused.

'George nearly lost a finger,' Ida gleefully said.

I looked at Harold.

'He got the cord wrapped so tight around his pinkie,' Harold elaborated, waggling his own little finger to demonstrate, 'it was cutting his circulation off. Karen had to cut him free. She had a right panic.'

'And I thought Greta was going to strangle Bob,' Ida added excitedly.

Clearly, she'd had a whale of a time. I felt my lips twitch into a smile, in spite of my determination to remain impartial and professional. It was working. Immersing myself in my work, was stopping me thinking about . . . well, almost stopping me.

'Disaster,' said Harold. 'Another total disaster and now we're seeing the result.'

'What do you mean?' I asked.

Harold pointed to the door, cocking his head to listen to Greta still objecting to everyone's attempts to keep her safe.

'Everyone's bored witless,' he said, spelling out what deep down I already suspected. 'That's why the likes of Greta are acting up. That Karen never asks us what we want to do and half the stuff she comes up with, most of us can't manage.'

'And it's months since we've had a trip out,' Ida said sadly, her former excitement banished. 'We're going stir crazy.'

I knew the pair of them were right. I'd experienced

first-hand the hash the current activities manager was making of keeping the residents entertained, interested and stimulated.

'We want you back doing it, Beth,' Ida wheedlingly said. 'That week you were in charge was the best we've had in ages. We want you in charge of activities again.'

There had been a few days when Karen had been unwell and Sandra, the care home manager, had asked me to step in. I'd had a great time coming up with things to do every afternoon, but it had only been a very temporary arrangement. To be honest, I'd assumed everyone had forgotten about it. However, the hopeful looks on Harold and Ida's faces suggested otherwise, not that it would make any difference. I was employed as a carer, not an activities organiser; I didn't have the qualifications for that.

'We're rallying the troops,' Harold then said conspiratorially, tapping the side of his nose. 'We want Karen out and you in.'

I shook my head and edged around Ida's frame towards the door, determined to nip whatever scheme they were concocting in the bud. If they started rocking the boat, they could get me in trouble as well as themselves and right now, all I wanted was a quiet life. My home life was already a catastrophe, I didn't want my work life turning calamitous too.

'That's not an option,' I therefore sternly told the pair. 'Karen's a bona fide qualified activities manager and I'm just a carer. Don't either of you start stirring anything up. You could get me in trouble and I need this job.'

'You're not *just* a carer,' Harold kindly said.

'And they wouldn't get rid of you,' Ida chimed in. 'They couldn't.'

'They'd be buggered without you, Beth,' added Harold, looking a little bright-eyed. 'None of us would be able to cope without you. We need you. I need you.'

I took a deep breath and tried to swallow away the lump in my throat. Just as I had been thinking I was going to get through the day dry-eyed, he'd uttered those fateful words.

'What is it, Beth?' Ida frowned, gently laying her liver-spotted hand lightly on my arm.

In my mind's eye, I saw Mum propped up in a hospital bed, pale, weak and damaged after her first stroke. She had aged in an instant and looked far older than her thirty-something years and all thanks to an undiagnosed heart condition.

'I need you,' she had hoarsely said. 'I need you, Beth.'

With just those few words, the course of my life had been altered forever. Had she even an inkling of what the consequences of them would be, I know she would never have said them, but it was too late to think about that now.

'Nothing,' I swallowed, placing my hand over the top of Ida's and giving it a gentle squeeze. 'It's nothing. Now, let's get you back upstairs before someone sends out another search party.'

Meek as a lamb, she followed me out of Harold's room.

'Come back if you get a minute, would you, Beth, love?' Harold called after us. 'I've got a favour to ask you.'

'Will do,' I responded, leading Ida towards the lift.

As I worked through my shift, my head was awash with countless thoughts. For the most part, and even though I tried to stop it, my mind kept tracking back to the date, my eyes roving to the clock, as the moment I'd arrived home and found Mum collapsed and unresponsive on the hall floor ticked closer.

I hadn't wanted to leave her that day, but she'd insisted I needed some time out and even though every single health professional I'd spoken to since had said my being with her wouldn't have made any difference to the outcome, it didn't stop the guilt eating me up.

The second stroke might have been destined to be huge and fatal, but she shouldn't have endured it alone.

'Penny for them,' said Harold, when I checked in with him as my shift finally came to an end and I grabbed a minute to speak to him again. 'I was hoping you'd spent the last twelve hours thinking about mine and Ida's plan, but the look on your face suggests otherwise.'

I hoped it hadn't been obvious to everyone that I hadn't been quite as present as usual.

'What's up, my love?'

'Nothing,' I said, shaking my head. 'I'm fine. What was the favour you wanted to ask?'

Harold looked at me and narrowed his rheumy eyes.

'I've told you before, I'm not smuggling in whisky and cigars,' I quipped.

My attempt to divert his attention didn't work and he fixed me with a more intense stare.

'Today is the anniversary of my mum's death,' I said, knowing he wasn't going to let it drop. 'I lost her two years ago today, so it's been a tough day.'

'Oh, Beth,' he said, making my eyes fill with tears again. 'I'm so sorry, my love, I didn't realise.'

'There's no reason why you should,' I said, blinking.

Having joined the home at the same time, Harold had known a little of my sad history, but it wasn't something I'd ever dwelled on.

'It's okay,' I said stoically.

'No,' he sighed, 'it's not. Of course it's not and it never will be.'

'Oh thanks,' I hiccupped, his bluntness taking me by surprise and pulling me out of my rapidly declining mood. 'Tell it to me straight, Harold.'

He shrugged his shoulders.

'No point lying,' he said.

'No,' I agreed, feeling surprisingly grateful for his honesty, but also sad because I knew it came from a place of understanding, 'I suppose not. Now,' I sniffed, straightening out his bed cover and checking his jug was full of fresh water, 'out with it. What do you want me to do?'

'I know it's your day off tomorrow,' he said, thankfully letting the subject of my loss drop, 'so I'll completely understand if you have other things planned. Perhaps there's somewhere you need to visit.'

Not completely dropped then. I knew immediately what he was hinting at.

'No,' I said, 'there's no grave to tend. Mum was cremated.'
Harold nodded.

Mum had been very specific about that, along with details of how quickly she had wanted her ashes scattered. She hadn't been able to say much immediately after her first stroke, but one thing she had been increasingly clear about was that. I'd said she was being maudlin and that she was going to be fine. She maintained that she was being practical and I should do as I was told, otherwise she'd come back and haunt me, whenever she went.

'In that case,' Harold carried on, 'I was wondering if you might be able to escort me somewhere.'

Harold's accident had involved his mobility scooter. The only way he was allowed to use it now was if he had a chaperone.

'It would be an honour to step out with you, Harold,' I smiled.

Truth be told, I had been dreading being stuck at the house on my day off. If I was home alone when the others were at work and the place was a mess, my resolve inevitably crumbled and I ended up cleaning and tidying.

There was never any thanks for my efforts and I realised everyone was beginning to take my inability to live in squalor for granted. Dogsbody wasn't a personality trait I was keen to adopt. I could have gone out, of course, but that most likely would have led to spending money and I needed to save every penny I could. I was determined I would be moving out at some point and that would inevitably be an expensive business.

13

'Well, that's grand,' said Harold, looking pleased. 'Can you be here at one?'

'I can,' I told him. 'Where are we going?'

'The Grow-Well Garden,' he said loudly. 'I haven't been for a few weeks and I want to see how it's all coming on.'

I felt my heart race, then sink in my chest. The well-known community garden in Nightingale Square, which Harold loved, was the last place I wanted to go.

'But I thought you usually went there with Sara,' I stuttered. 'Can't she take you?'

Sara was another carer at the home and she was also a volunteer in the garden of the Victorian manor house, Prosperous Place, which was where the Grow-Well site was located. Harold had told me on more than one occasion that he had lived practically his entire life in a house in Nightingale Square and how thrilled he'd been to meet Sara, who had found the Square, the big house, the garden and all its associated connections through a festival being held there to celebrate winter.

'We do usually go together,' Harold confirmed, not noticing my change of tone, 'but she's away on holiday and there's a bit of a gathering happening tomorrow. I really don't want to miss it.'

Having been so willing to help, I could hardly back out, but I wasn't a fan of gardens and gardening. Mum had been a keen and accomplished amateur horticulturalist, who spent every moment she could in the great outdoors, until the stroke robbed her of the ability to dig, sow and mow. To help aid her recovery, I'd encouraged her to adapt her skills to embrace my passion for houseplants, but I knew she didn't get the same amount of pleasure from the scaled-down pursuit.

Given the timing, I really wasn't in the mood to work my way up to paying my first visit to a green space, which would doubtless further remind me of the woman I'd loved and lost. Just like music and song, I'd banished gardening too, but then I noted the look in Harold's eyes and remembered the house-share from hell, which was fast turning into a health hazard.

'And you won't have to,' I said, swallowing away my reluctance. 'I'll be here at one on the dot.'

Chapter 2

I kept my eyes front and centre and focused on the stairs when I got back to the house, so I had no idea if the kitchen looked better or worse than when I'd left it that morning. It certainly didn't smell like anyone had bothered to take the bin out.

'Hey Beth,' said a man's voice when I emerged from the bathroom after a restorative soak. 'I didn't hear you come in.'

'Hi Aaron,' I nodded vaguely at my housemate, my gaze firmly fixed on my bedroom door.

The bath had helped my muscles relax after my busy shift and I had no desire to get drawn into a conversation that would doubtless make them tense up again.

'We're all heading into the city if you fancy it?' Aaron offered. 'Kangaroo Jacks has cheap beer on a Thursday.'

I knew only too well the real motivation behind his invitation. I'd been out with him and the others a couple of times when I first moved in and, immediately labelled as the responsible one, it had been down to me to look after wallets, keys, coats and bags. I'd only gone the second time to see if it got any better. It didn't. I'd been the mobile cloakroom again and the thumping music had proved far too much for me and so I'd been turning their invitations down ever since. They could carry on finding their own way home. And I knew they noisily would. Complete with burgeoning hangovers and greasy kebabs.

'It's kind of you to ask,' I told him, acting out my part in the familiar exchange, as I took a step towards my room, 'but I'm going straight to bed. I've just finished a block of twelve-hour shifts, so . . .'

'Does that mean it's your day off tomorrow then?' Aaron cut in.

'It does.'

'That's handy,' he grinned, before heading down the stairs.

'Is it?' I frowned, after him.

'Yeah,' he said, stopping to look back up at me. 'The agency called. The landlord is coming to do an inspection tomorrow afternoon.'

Usually, that would have put me in a tailspin and Aaron, the scheming sod, knew it. He might have been dense enough to think he'd dropped it casually into the conversation, but I was well aware of his not-so-hidden agenda.

He was banking on me now spending the evening tidying and washing dishes and then being there, in full hostess and model homemaker mode, to reassure our landlord that his house was in safe hands, the next day. Well, he was out of luck.

'Oh right,' I said lightly. 'Well, I hope he remembers his key.'

'It won't matter if you're here, will it?' Aaron smugly said.

'But I won't be.' I took immense pleasure in telling him.

'What?'

'He'll have to let himself in because I won't be here. I've got plans.'

I would have loved to have lingered long enough to take a mental snapshot of the look on Aaron's face, but considered it more impactful to walk away.

He must have relayed my out of character reaction to the others, but it didn't stop them heading out and the second the front door slammed, I reached under my bed and slid out the box I'd been telling myself all day I wouldn't delve into.

'Oh Mum,' I swallowed, as I spread the envelopes of ageing photographs I'd had printed out over the duvet and tried to focus on them through a gathering torrent of tears.

Along with Mum's treasured records, which I couldn't have played even if I wanted to because I'd had to sell our turntable, there were dozens of photos, scribbled notes and childhood drawings. Little mementos that would have meant nothing to anyone else or held any financial value, but were the world to me.

I picked up a photograph of the two of us standing with Moira Myers, the woman who ran The Arches, which was a creative refuge for local kids. That place had been like a second home to me when I was growing up and Moira had been a friend to Mum even before she had found out at seventeen that she was pregnant with me and her parents had disowned her.

With Mum working two jobs to make ends just about meet, and unable to afford childcare, I had spent endless hours at The Arches watching Moira, my surrogate nanna, nurture the talent of city kids who loved to sing, dance, act and perform but whose parents couldn't afford the fees for private lessons. My being there had lessened some of the guilt that Mum felt for not being able to take long holidays and regular weekends off.

With music playing at home, in place of a television constantly blaring, and under Moira's watchful eye, it was little wonder that all I wanted to do when I grew up was sing. I was barely ten when I took to the stage at The Arches and I had been hooked on making a career out of performing from that moment on.

I put the photograph down and picked up another, sobbing with utter abandon as I remembered that not only had I lost Mum and sold practically all of our possessions, but Moira, my best friend Pete, and my long-held dreams and ambitions had been banished too.

And to add insult to injury, I'd also had to leave mine and Mum's last home. The council had had another tenant lined up for the adapted bungalow almost before the funeral, and I had swiftly found my life changed again and myself very much alone in the world.

*

I didn't expect to sleep at all again that night, but I did. I had no idea whether it was standing up to Aaron or allowing myself the cry out I so obviously needed which helped, but I woke the next day feeling the benefit of the few uninterrupted hours' rest.

Safe in the knowledge that I'd counted my housemates out of the house, I pulled on a pair of rubber gloves and went down to the kitchen. It took some careful manoeuvring, but I managed to extricate my dirty dishes, or should I say, the crockery and utensils which belonged to me and that the others had used without asking, and carried it all up to the bathroom.

To the untrained eye the kitchen looked just as rancid as when I'd gone in, which was exactly what I had been aiming for. I already kept my cutlery in my room so, after soaking and washing everything they'd used in the bath, I packed it all in a lidded plastic crate and pushed it under my bed, next to my box of treasures.

'This worm,' I said, smiling at myself in the mirror, 'has well and truly turned.'

I hadn't forgotten my thoughts about 'getting out' the day before. I had no idea when or how it was going to happen, but happen it would. I'd had enough of my housemates and their filthy ways. It was definitely time to move on.

'Right then, you lovely lot,' I said to the many pots lining my bedroom shelves and the windowsill. 'Now it's your turn.'

It took the best part of the morning to give each of my

houseplants the care and attention they deserved and I imagined Mum looking down on me and smiling as I did a thorough and careful job.

I watered some of the plants in the bath, washing their glossy green leaves and giving them a fine mist spritz, while top-dressing others with grit and snipping off any less than perfect leaves. It was the ultimate soul soother and I wondered if I might dare suggest to Sandra, my permanently stressed-out boss, that a few houseplants dotted around the home would enhance the ambience and potentially lift a few spirits.

'Just you now, Aretha,' I cheerfully said to the cheese plant that had suffered the humiliation of having cigarette ends dumped in her pot the day before. 'And don't worry, I'm going to get you out of here. We're all going to get out of here.'

Harold was already waiting for me in reception when I arrived a few minutes before our arranged time. Wearing a checked cotton shirt, a rather battered straw trilby and an eager expression, he was clearly keen to get going.

'Look at you,' he beamed when he saw me. 'Don't you look lovely?'

'Do I?' I said, as he joined me outside and I looked down at my well-worn Converse pumps, floral print tea dress and short denim jacket.

'Yes,' he said. 'You do.'

I waved his compliment away. I'd never been any good at

accepting them and besides, he wasn't used to seeing me in anything other than the lilac Edith Cavell Care Home polo shirt and scratchy trousers, so that no doubt accounted for his kind comment.

'Where are your wheels?' I asked him.

'Right here,' said a voice behind me. 'Fully charged and good to go.'

'Thank you, Philip,' said Harold, practically trotting up to and hopping onto his beloved scooter. 'Don't wait up!' he cheekily added, before zipping off along the path, skimming the laurel hedge in his haste.

'I hope you're in the mood for a jog,' laughed Phil, as I rushed to catch up with my charge.

'Ah,' Harold chuckled as he slowed down a little and I fell into step on the edge of the pavement beside him. 'The thrill of the open road!'

As we wove our way towards Nightingale Square, along lanes I never knew existed, he kept up a running commentary about how the city had changed since he'd been born, pointing out certain buildings and landmarks, before asking me what I'd been up to that morning.

He was mightily impressed by the description of my colossal houseplant collection, but I didn't fill him in on my living conditions or the impending saga with the landlord. I knew he'd worry if I told him how unhappy I was with my houseshare and it wasn't as if he could do anything to help solve the situation.

'Here we are then,' he said, coming to such a sudden

stop I almost tripped over him. 'Welcome to Nightingale Square, Beth.'

My tummy felt like it was on a spin cycle, thanks to thoughts of visiting a green space for the first time since Mum had been denied the pleasure of working in one, but its unsettling motion was forgotten as I took in the sight of the seven pretty houses built in a horseshoe shape around a central green. They were absolutely lovely and the grassed area, surrounded by metal railings, looked like the perfect spot for sunny picnics and parties. I couldn't believe I had never seen the place before, but then it was a little tucked away and not in a part of the city I usually visited.

'What do you think?'

'It's beautiful.' I smiled, taking it all in. 'Which one was yours, Harold?'

He'd already given me a potted history of the place, explaining how Victorian shoe factory owner, Charles Wentworth, had built the houses for his workers along with Prosperous Place, across the road, for himself and his family. Looking at the design and solidity of the houses, Mr Wentworth had clearly thought a lot of his staff.

Harold had told me that his family had been gifted their home generations back and how now one of Mr Wentworth's ancestors lived in the family pile with a family of his own. True to his ancestors' generous and philanthropic credentials, his successor, Luke, had helped turn the outdoor walled garden into the Grow-Well for Nightingale Square residents and opened the rest of the gardens up to the public throughout the year but with specific emphasis on the winter months.

'And this lovely house,' said Harold, with a flourish as he stopped again, 'was mine.'

'It's lovely, Harold,' I said, admiring the well-maintained exterior while he told me how the inside was set out and how the property was now back in the original family fold.

'Luke and Kate, who now live in Prosperous Place, bought it together,' he told me, 'and very generous they were too. And Kate also owns that one,' he added, casting a look behind him.

'But she doesn't live there now?' I asked.

'No,' he said, 'not since she moved into the big house with Luke.'

I was about to ask who currently lived in Kate's house, but didn't get the chance.

'Well, now,' said Harold, 'aren't you a sight for sore eyes?'

I followed his gaze up the path of his former home and spotted a tall woman, with impossibly long hair, stepping out of the door accompanied by a timid-looking lurcher.

'Harold!' she beamed, shutting the door behind her and rushing over. 'Finally! We've been wondering where you'd got to. Luke said only yesterday that he'd been expecting to see you here before now.'

'He's a good lad,' Harold nodded. 'Been to see me in the home every week, regular as clockwork.'

If I'd got the right person, then I knew he was a handsome

visitor as well as a regular one. I'd never been on shift when he'd called, but I'd heard from colleagues that he'd set pulses racing, and not just among the staff.

'And you're not alone,' said the woman, smiling at me.

'Sorry,' apologised Harold. 'Where are my manners? Freya, I'd like you to meet my friend, Beth.'

I was touched that he had introduced me as a friend.

'Pleased to meet you, Beth.'

'Likewise,' I said, feeling a little shy.

'She drew the short straw today,' Harold expanded. 'It's her day off, so I goaded her into chaperoning me as Sara's away and I'm not allowed out on my own.'

'You didn't goad me at all,' I scolded him, but with a smile. 'I was more than happy to come.'

It wasn't completely true, but I wasn't about to go into the why's and wherefores of the situation.

'I know,' said Harold, reaching for my hand. 'You're good to me, you are.'

'I take it you work at the Edith Cavell Care Home, too?' Freya asked. 'I know Sara loves it there.'

'For her sins,' said Harold, answering on my behalf. 'Now come on, let's get over to the Grow-Well.'

'Yes,' said Freya. 'let's. There's quite a crowd over there today and I really need to get back to work.'

My tummy starting doing crazy acrobatics again.

'Freya's the head gardener,' Harold informed me.

'And this is my assistant, Nell,' she added, patting the head of the dog, standing just behind her. 'She's a bit shy.'

'I know how she feels,' I said, my nerves increasing as I thought of the crowd gathered in the garden.

We crossed the road and then, once Freya had typed in a security code, slipped through a gate set in a high brick wall, which looked as though it ran all the way around the perimeter of Prosperous Place and its grounds. Freya and Harold had moved ahead while I stopped for a moment to look around.

Suddenly we weren't in the centre of the city anymore and the circuitous ring road wasn't just a couple of streets away. We were in a green haven, complete with birdsong, winding paths and hidden spaces. No wonder Sara waxed lyrical about the place. It was The Secret Garden and Rivendell all rolled into one. It certainly felt magical, enchanted even.

'You all right, Beth?' Harold asked, when he realised I wasn't following.

My mouth closed with a snap.

'I had no idea,' I breathed.

Harold and Freya exchanged a look.

'It's quite something, isn't it?' beamed Freya.

I nodded mutely, knowing whatever I said wouldn't do the spectacle justice. Mum would have been in her element.

'And this is just the entrance,' said Harold, clearly keen to keep moving. 'Come on.'

I came to my senses and followed on just a few paces behind. Freya peeled off to the left when the path split and Harold and I carried on to where I could hear voices on the right. A loud cheer went up as Harold eased his scooter through yet another gate and rather than feel more jittery, I felt my nerves abate.

I was comforted to discover that I didn't feel upset at all, as I for so long had presumed I would when faced with a beautiful garden, but instead, I was soothed. And I just knew there couldn't be anything to fear from anyone who greeted my friend with such warmth.

The only niggle I really felt was with myself. I'd assumed I wouldn't be able to handle the great outdoors until I was much further down the grieving line, and had finally stopped imagining Mum around every corner, but all I'd actually ended up doing, I realised as I looked around, was deny myself some wonderful days out and the pleasure of feeling my fingers in the soil and the sun on my back.

Still, I was getting on with it now, wasn't I? And combined with my freshly found determination to find a new home, it felt as though I was slaying my demons at last. Not that I was about to let music back into my life. That was next level and never going to happen.

'And this is only about half of them!' Harold quipped once he'd introduced me to everyone present.

I was feeling a little dazed after being bombarded with a long list of names and felt immensely grateful that some of the residents were still at work.

'Don't worry,' smiled Luke, who was every bit as handsome as everyone at work had maintained, 'I wouldn't be able to remember everyone's names either.'

'I've told you before,' said a woman who I thought was called Lisa, 'we need name badges.'

Everyone laughed and a young lad, with a French bulldog hot on his heels, carried out a tray of drinks from an impressive-looking bothy and began offering them around.

'How's that sister of yours getting on, Ryan?' Harold asked him, when he reached us.

'Oh don't,' said the lad, with a long sigh. 'She and Jacob are still loved-up. It turns my stomach to see them, but my new room is nice. Bigger than the one I had in Kate's house.'

My ears pricked up at the mention of the house which I'd considered the prettiest in the Square.

'Ryan's sister, Poppy,' Harold told me with a nod, 'has recently moved from Kate's place and into the house next door with her partner, Jacob.'

'So, I had to go too,' explained Ryan, 'because Poppy and I live together. It's all right though really. I'm only teasing when I say their canoodling makes me sick. I'm really pleased to see her happy and Jacob's a great bloke.'

'Jacob's a teacher,' Harold approvingly elaborated as Ryan moved on.

'So,' I said, taking a sip from the fruit-filled glass of Pimm's and wondering if it was as innocuous as it looked and tasted, 'does that mean Kate's place is empty?'

'It was for a while,' said Kate herself, who I hadn't realised was behind me, 'because I wanted to have some alterations made to the inside, but it's rented out again now.'

'Oh,' I said, unable to stave off the feeling of

disappointment. Though I knew that even if it had been empty, it would have been well beyond my limited means. 'Well, it looked lovely. Harold gave me a tour of the Square before we came over. It's a beautiful house.'

'It is,' Kate agreed, looking wistful. 'You'll have to let me know if you fancy a look inside. There's one room still available if you're interested.'

I could hardly believe my ears and was about to say that yes, I was more than interested, when one of the children took a tumble and she rushed off to see if a band-aid was required.

'How's that drink working out for you?' Ryan asked Harold as he came back with an empty tray.

'Champion, lad,' Harold said happily. 'I only hope it's not as strong as last time. I don't want to be caught drunk in charge of my scooter, do I?'

'Don't you worry, Harold,' said a serious-sounding woman who had caught the tail end of the conversation. 'I checked the measures.'

'Thank you, Carole,' said Harold, sounding chastened. 'We know we can rely on you to administer some common sense.'

'Yes, well,' she said, missing the wink my friend and Ryan shared. 'After last time I thought I'd better keep an eye on things. Anyway, I really came over to ask if I could show you around, Beth? Would you like a tour of here and the rest of the garden?'

'Oh yes, please,' I said so keenly that I even surprised myself. 'That would be lovely.'

I left my glass on the table, just to be on the safe side, and followed her back through the gate and into the main part of the garden.

By the end of the evening, more residents had arrived and I was feeling relaxed and a little hazy. Not drunk, nowhere near drunk, more like pleasantly chilled out. I had met practically everyone now and felt like I'd known them forever, even though their names were a blur.

I'd eaten pizza made by Lisa's husband, John, in the bespoke oven, munched salad that had been picked and dressed less than a metre away from where I was currently sitting, and enjoyed another couple of Ryan's delicious concoctions, as well as elderflower champagne made by almost everyone present.

'We'd better make a move, I suppose,' said Harold, who looked as replete as I felt. 'I need to be back before the drawbridge goes up.'

I glanced at my watch, amazed that so many hours had slipped by.

'Yes,' I agreed, stifling a yawn, 'it's getting late. I just want to have a quick word with Kate and then we'll be off.'

'All right,' he laughed. 'It'll take me at least another hour to say my goodbyes!'

'I shouldn't worry about that,' I told him. 'Anytime you want to come back and Sara can't come with you, just ask me.'

'You want to come again?'

'To tell you the truth,' I told him, meaning it, 'I can't bear to tear myself away. It's wonderful here, Harold.'

He looked thrilled.

'There's Kate,' he nudged. 'I'll meet you at the gate.'

If Kate was surprised when I asked her if I could look at the room, she didn't show it.

'Of course,' she said. 'How about tomorrow morning?'

Realistically, I didn't think I'd be able to afford it, but I knew I'd regret it if I didn't at least look and my life already had more regrets littering it than I could comfortably manage.

'Perfect,' I nodded. 'It's my last day off before I start a new block of shifts.'

'Will you bring Harold with you?' she asked, waving as he headed towards the Grow-Well gate.

'No,' I said, 'I'd rather he didn't know anything about it, if that's all right? I wouldn't want him worrying that I'm not happy where I am.'

'But I take it you're not happy where you are?' Kate asked, looking at me intently.

'No,' I told her, 'I'm not. Between you and me, if I didn't have to go back there tonight, I wouldn't.'

Chapter 3

The house was in chaos when I arrived back after seeing Harold safely to the care home and I was on the receiving end of more than one accusatory stare, but I didn't care. I might have secretly set my heart on Kate's empty room in pretty Nightingale Square, but even if it didn't work out there, I knew there'd be somewhere else for me to go. Not everyone could be as slovenly as the specimens I currently lived with and I was determined that I would be leaving them behind as soon as I could.

Financially it would be a struggle to afford somewhere nicer, but just like Mum, I was used to the challenge of juggling money. I'd had to work, as well as look after her, when she came home from the rehabilitation centre and it had been a real strain, but I'd managed it. Just. Now there was only myself to look after and I was capable of doing that. I would find a way to make this move happen.

'How did the inspection go?' I couldn't resist asking my current housemates.

I kept my tone light as I made for the stairs.

'It was a total disaster!' shouted Courtney from the kitchen, where she was clattering dishes in the sink. 'Haven't you seen the state of this place?'

'Don't go disappearing,' Rob said huffily, as I lifted my foot onto the bottom step and he thrust a grubby tea towel in my direction. 'We've got twenty-four hours to sort this, otherwise we're in big trouble.'

'I think what you mean is,' I said, carrying on towards my room and ignoring the pleading look the third mucky musketeer, Aaron gave me, '*you three* have got twenty-four hours to sort it. There's nothing down here that belongs to me and none of the mess is mine either. You're on your own.'

This time I did stop to take a mental snapshot. The look of shock on the three upturned faces was golden!

The house smelt considerably fresher when I ventured down the next morning and Aaron was standing in the lemony-scented kitchen and looking sheepish. There was no sign of the other two.

'I think I owe you an apology, Beth,' he said, as I worked around him to make my breakfast.

I knew he'd seen that I had carried down my mug, bowl and cutlery, but I didn't care.

'Do you?'

'Yes,' he said. 'I do. It took us forever to clean up last night.'

I already knew that. Not even my expensive earplugs, the pair usually reserved to try and block out their noisy return after a night on the tiles, had been capable of shutting out the sound of the three of them vacuuming, swearing and crashing about until well after midnight.

'And had you done it all for us, I wouldn't have given it a second thought,' Aaron admitted shamefacedly. 'None of us would.'

I knew that too.

'I'm sorry we've dumped on you in the past and I shouldn't have assumed that you'd cave this time either. It won't happen again.'

'That's good to know.'

It was too little too late of course and I wasn't naïve enough to think that the house wouldn't be a mess again in less than a week or that Aaron's apology would carry the same conviction. No matter how heartfelt he thought his words were, they were never going to make me change my mind about moving, not that he or the others were aware that's what I had made up my mind to do.

'No hard feelings then?' he asked, sounding happier.

'None whatsoever,' I smiled. 'In fact,' I added, realising that his and Courtney and Rob's former treatment of me had played a significant part in creating the turning point, 'I should be thanking you really.'

Aaron looked confused, but I didn't explain the meaning behind my words.

It felt much chillier than the day before, and there was a threat of rain in the air, so I dressed in jeans and a jumper and remembered to pick up my umbrella before excitedly setting out for Nightingale Square. I took a bus for some of the way, but hopped off a few stops before the Square to remind myself what this part of the city was like.

If, by some miracle, I was fortunate enough to secure the room, the path I took, avoiding Harold's historical tour, would form the quickest commute to and from the care home. I rather liked the idea of not having to get the bus, as long as the weather behaved, of course. It would be a few pounds saved each week and I'd clock up some extra steps too.

The most direct route took me down a narrow road towards a row of shops I suddenly realised I knew, but hadn't visited for years. The line-up included a couple of familiar places. A grocery store called Greengage's was first. I remembered Ryan mentioning the previous afternoon that his sister, Poppy, worked there and there was also Blossoms bakery. I knew Sara was as partial to a pastry from there as I had once been and given the delicious sugary smells wafting out the door, I wasn't surprised the locals were still being tempted.

There was also an upmarket-looking coffeehouse, a general store, bookshop, vintage emporium, florist, a couple of charity shops and last, but by no means least, the film and movie store, On the Box.

I felt my temperature spike when I spotted it. I had assumed the place where my old friend, Pete, had a part-time job and where I'd sometimes hung out, would be long gone, but apparently not. I ducked my head and quickly scurried by. I had no idea if he still worked there, though most likely not, given the dreams he'd had along with a steely determination to make them happen, but I wasn't about to peer in the window to find out.

After all, I'd had ambitions too, not so different from his and yet here I was, treading the same streets. For all I knew, in spite of his resolve, fate could have dealt him a duff hand too and he might well be in a similar boat to the one I was bobbing along in.

Pete had been on my mind a lot recently and as an image of his kind face filled my head along with the memory of his warm personality, I felt a huge surge of guilt. I knew childhood friends often lost touch when university beckoned, but I should never have allowed that to happen between us. But then, letting Pete slip off my radar had ended up being about a whole lot more than just the excitement of a new life away from home.

Lost in my thoughts, I arrived in Nightingale Square sooner than I expected. It was even closer to work than I had originally thought and that in theory should have made it even more perfect, but if by some chance Pete did still work nearby, I wasn't sure how I would handle that. Coupled with the stretch it would doubtless be to find the deposit and then pay the rent a room in Nightingale Square would command, I felt my former upbeat mood start to ebb away.

I spotted Kate already waiting and gave myself a mental shake. It wouldn't do to let her know I was wasting her time and besides, Pete had most likely moved on, and therefore for the next half hour or so, I should allow myself the luxury of imagining myself doing the same.

'Morning!' Kate called when she caught sight of me. 'It's a bit chilly, isn't it?'

'Yes,' I agreed, 'it's certainly not as nice as yesterday. Thank you for taking time out of your weekend to do this, Kate,' I added. 'I really appreciate it.'

'It's no bother,' she said, pushing open the gate. 'I spoke to Elijah last night, just to check he didn't mind us popping in.'

'Elijah?'

'Yes,' she said, slotting her key in the lock and turning it. The door was wooden, with a stained-glass panel over the top. 'He's the guy who has already moved in. He's at work today, but he said he was happy for me to show you around.'

I wasn't sure how I felt about sharing with another man, but then Courtney was no more house-trained than either Aaron or Rob. I realised I shouldn't make assumptions based on someone's sex and resolved to take onboard what I saw in the house (as well as in my bank account) before I finally made up my mind.

'Here we are then,' said Kate, stepping aside to let me enter ahead of her. 'Home sweet home. Or it was until I moved across the road.'

With the stairs directly in front, I noticed there was no tangle of abandoned shoes blocking our path like I'd become used to. There was just one tidy coat stand and two doors leading off from the roomy hallway. I stepped right, through the first.

'Oh wow,' I breathed. 'This is lovely.'

The large sitting room, complete with squishy sofa, ancient armchair, bookshelves and original fire, had a bay window which gave a view of the green and all the other houses in the Square.

'I really struck lucky with this place,' said Kate, who looked pleased by my reaction. 'Miraculously, there were lots of original fittings still here when I moved in.'

There were picture rails in the sitting room as well as in the room we headed to next, which was set up as a dining room.

'And this dividing wall was still in place too,' Kate told me, patting it. 'Quite a few of the house owners here have knocked the two downstairs rooms into one, but I prefer it separated like this.'

'Me too,' I nodded, wandering through the room and into the kitchen, which was at the back of the house and most likely a later addition to the original build. I imagined the bathroom would be directly above it. 'It's far cosier and practical too, especially now you're renting the house out.'

The only space I could go to to get away from my current housemates was my bedroom and I didn't always want to be confined to there. In Kate's house, the tenants could have a sitting room each if they wanted to. I reminded myself that luxury was bound to come at a price and tried not to get carried away. I had already imagined Aretha in the bay window in the front room, so needed to rein my enthusiasm in.

'I agree,' Kate nodded. 'I like the original layout, down

here anyway. Upstairs is a different story. I had that altered as soon as Poppy and Ryan moved next door.'

I followed her up the stairs.

'Originally there were three bedrooms,' she explained, 'and I know I've just said how much I like keeping the downstairs rooms separate, but it just didn't work up here.'

'How so?'

'There used to be one double room,' she carried on, 'and two singles, one of which you had to go through to get to the bathroom, so I couldn't rent that out because it wasn't walled off. It was a wasted space really.'

'I see,' I said, looking over her shoulder.

'So, we had this corridor put in which now leads to the bathroom and knocked the two smaller bedrooms into one big one.'

'That sounds much more practical,' I said, wondering which of the rooms Elijah had taken.

'It is,' Kate nodded. 'There are two roomy doubles now, which makes far more sense. You go and have a look at the bathroom. It's a bit of a squeeze for two, and then I'll show you the bedroom.'

The bathroom, just like the kitchen and the other rooms downstairs, was immaculate. There were no mould patches around the bath seals and no puddles of damp towels littering the floor. The only things missing, and I would soon be able to rectify that, were houseplants. The décor was clean and fresh, as was the air, and I could imagine it further enhanced by my collection. The ferns would revel in the shady space.

'So much for not getting carried away,' I muttered under my breath.

'So,' said Kate, as we stood in the big double bedroom at the front of the house, which was the one available, 'what do you think?'

There were two large sash windows which overlooked the green. Kate was looking out of one and I the other.

'I think it's perfect,' I told her, with a wistful sigh. Noting how wonderful it all was, I was pretty certain I wouldn't be able to afford to move in, but I couldn't deny how much I was in love with the place. 'To be honest, I can't believe you haven't had any takers.'

'Any takers?'

'For the room,' I said, turning away from the view to take the décor in again.

I had no idea why Elijah hadn't picked this room for his own, but I was pleased he hadn't because otherwise I wouldn't have been able to see it. The second I'd walked in, I'd imagined myself lying in the bed with the curtains open, watching the comings and goings in the Square. Wherever I ended up was going to come in a poor second to this place.

'I would have thought the first person to view it would snap it up.'

'You are the first person to view it, Beth,' Kate smiled. 'Since Poppy left, there hasn't been anyone else, other than Elijah of course.'

'Oh,' I swallowed, feeling guilty again about wasting her time. 'I see.'

'Luke and I have never advertised the houses or the rooms,' she explained. 'And we have no intention of doing so either. We both think a lot of the properties we own and we like to get a feel for a person before we decide if we want to show them around.'

'I see,' I said again.

'Freya turned out to be the perfect fit for Harold's family home and her occupancy comes as part of her job as head gardener,' Kate further elaborated, 'and Luke had known Elijah for a while before he moved in.'

'But you've only just met me,' I pointed out. 'This time yesterday, we hadn't so much as seen each other before and beyond what Sara and Harold had told me, I knew nothing about Nightingale Square or the Grow-Well.'

'That's true,' Kate smiled, twitching one of the curtains so it sat more evenly on the pole, 'but you gave up your day off to make sure Harold could come and see us and that was both kind and generous.'

'I couldn't bear the thought of him missing out,' I sighed, running my fingers lightly along the end of the brass bedframe.

'Exactly,' Kate firmly said. 'Kind people are our kind of people. Come on,' she added, 'let's go across the road and talk it all out properly.'

Once Kate had made us both tea, we sat at the large table in the equally large kitchen in Prosperous Place. I had briefly seen Luke and met Jasmine and Abigail, his and Kate's girls, before he took them upstairs for a bath after their Saturday morning swim.

'Don't forget to use the detangling conditioner on Abigail's hair,' Kate called after him.

He had stopped off at Blossoms on the way home and I was enjoying a lighter than air apple turnover along with my tea. It tasted reminiscent of happy Saturdays long ago.

'I always tell myself that these are so light,' Kate grinned, reaching to take a second from the plate, 'they can't possibly have any calories in them.'

'If only,' I smiled, then tapping the paper bag the treats had been wrapped in, added, 'the garden obviously isn't the only thing around here that Sara's smitten with.'

'You're right,' laughed Kate, licking her fingers, 'although according to Freya and the other volunteer, Chloe, she's been a godsend in the garden, so she works the calories off. And she's a writer as well as a carer at the Edith Cavell, isn't she?'

'Is she?' I frowned. 'I didn't know that.'

Kate's face flushed.

'Well, I thought she was,' she shrugged, 'but perhaps I'm wrong.'

I was intrigued.

'And you remember Mark, from last night?' she carried on.

I nodded as I chewed.

'He works in Blossoms too.'

The Nightingale Square community was sounding more close-knit by the second. I felt a warm glow develop as I imagined myself becoming a part of it. When Mum was alive, we had lived somewhere with community spirit and neighbours who looked out for one another and I realised I missed it as much now as I had when I'd had to leave it behind.

'Does everyone who lives in Nightingale Square help out in the Grow-Well?' I asked.

'Yes,' Kate explained. 'Access to the garden is available to everyone who lives in the Square and Graham now works part-time in the main garden too. It's all a great joint growing effort and we have wonderful working parties and get-togethers.'

'Like last night?'

'Exactly like last night.'

I couldn't help wishing Elijah had been there. It would have been good to meet him too.

'So,' said Kate, as the sound of squealing from upstairs met our ears, 'you really like the house?'

'I absolutely love it,' I said honestly. 'It makes my current place look like a total hovel. Not that that's down to me,' I quickly added, regretting the admission.

My current means might not turn out to be capable of funding a new life for me in the Square, but I didn't want Kate thinking I was anything other than the ideal tenant.

'I'm guessing your desire to move is more about your housemates than the house itself then?'

'I'd say it's about equal to be honest,' I told her, having mulled it over for a moment. 'The house isn't very big; it's a bus journey away from work and there are four of us in it with only one sitting room. It's beginning to feel claustrophobic, whereas your place in the Square is much better laid out, and there would be room for Aretha, too.'

The end of the sentence had popped out and turned Kate's smile into a frown.

'I'm sorry, Beth,' she said, looking upset. 'I should have said before. Unlike at Harold's house, I've got a strict no-pets rule in my house now. It's a new policy . . .'

I began to laugh and she looked confused.

'Sorry,' I apologised. 'You'll no doubt think I'm bonkers, but Aretha isn't a pet.'

'Oh?'

'She's a houseplant. A huge glossy leaved cheese plant.' Kate's expression brightened. 'Mum and I named her after Aretha Franklin because she's so strong. A real powerhouse of a plant. Unfortunately, she's not getting the respect she deserves at the moment. No pun intended. She's too big to keep in my room and my housemates have been using her as the sitting-room ash tray.'

I stopped talking for fear of further oversharing and it took me a moment to realise that I'd brought Mum right into the conversation. That was something I usually avoided doing at all costs, but I felt so relaxed around Kate it had just sort of happened.

'I daresay she'd look great in that bay window, wouldn't she?' Kate grinned. 'Aretha, I mean.'

'It would be the ideal spot for her,' I nodded and then, emboldened by the fact that she could also picture Aretha, I momentarily set my money worries aside and added, 'and

I could imagine the rest of my collection dotted about the house too.'

'Exactly how many houseplants make up this collection?' Kate asked, sounding amused.

'I've honestly lost count.'

'Ballpark then,' she shrugged, refilling our mugs with tea from the pot.

'Definitely less than would fill a ballpark,' I laughed. 'Do you think Elijah would mind if I greened the house up a bit and more to the point, would you, Kate?'

I was beginning to talk as if I was actually going to be moving in.

'No and no,' she firmly said. 'I think it would be wonderful and I've got a no smoking policy too, so you wouldn't have to worry about cigarette butts!'

I was delighted.

'And as you're such an expert,' she said, standing up, 'maybe you can tell me what's wrong with this poor specimen?'

She disappeared and then came back in carrying a less than happy-looking peace lily.

'I've been watering it every day since I got it,' she told me, 'but it doesn't look good, does it?'

I winced at the thought of all that water and then gave her the low-down on how, and how often, to water the poor plant that currently had very saturated soil, along with where best to put it to aid its recovery.

'Perhaps you'll have another look at it for me next week?' she hopefully asked. 'Maybe when you're working out where best to position the rest of your own collection across the road.'

I swallowed hard and focused on my tea again.

'I'm asking five hundred and fifty a month for the room,' she tentatively said.

I let out a long breath and felt the colour drain from my face.

'And a month's rent in advance as a deposit.'

That was way above what I was currently paying, but given how much lovelier the house was, and given that it was a houseshare for just two people, I shouldn't have been surprised. It was a reasonable rent, all things considered. Given the house was large, airy, clean and in a beautiful part of the city, it was very reasonable indeed.

'That includes all of the bills,' Kate added, when I didn't say anything. 'There would be nothing extra on top.'

Sadly, my time pretending to be Cinderella was up.

'Okay,' I sighed, before taking a deep breath, 'that sounds more than fair, and the house is stunning, but I'm really sorry, Kate, I simply can't afford it.'

Chapter 4

Kate was kindness itself and we spent a long time further chatting everything through. She was so keen for me to take the room that she was even willing to waive the deposit. Unfortunately, it didn't matter how hard or which way I crunched the numbers, I still couldn't find a way to make my salary stretch quite as far as I needed it to. I would have been able to pay the rent, but there wouldn't have been all that much left over to live on and as much as I wanted to move, I had no desire to find myself constantly fretting about my bank balance, like I had in the past.

However, in spite of the common-sense practicalities my financial situation had pushed to the forefront of my mind, along with my brief wonderings about whether Pete still had any connection to On the Box, there was space enough for a little daydreaming about what my life in the Square could have looked like during my lunchbreaks.

I hadn't forgotten how I had felt stepping into the gardens. The sense of serenity had been entirely unexpected and it made me realise that even if nothing else came from my acquaintance with the Square, it had gifted me the ability to realise that it was time to assimilate a few of life's triggers, rather than carry on avoiding them. Not that I was prepared to extend that train of thought to music. That would never happen.

'You've dropped something, my love,' said Harold, pointing his stick at the piece of paper that had fallen out of my trouser pocket as I helped get him dressed one morning that week. 'Looks like it says Nightingale Square at the top.'

'There's nothing wrong with your eyesight, is there?' laughed Sara who had joined us. She reached down and picked the paper up. 'Ow,' she winced as she straightened up and handed it to me.

I hastily shoved the moving to Nightingale Square pros and cons list I had written the evening before back in my pocket.

'Good holiday, was it?' Harold chuckled to Sara.

'I hope you're not being rude,' she scolded him, with a smile. 'But yes, it was very good, thanks. I got to be one of the warriors this time,' she further beamed.

'The mind boggles,' said Harold, but we both knew what she was talking about.

Sara was part of the Iceni re-enactment group which toured East Anglia recreating battles and lives lived long ago. Given her current aches and pains, I guessed the recent role had been physical and a bit full-on. I knew she had her sights on playing Boudicca herself one day.

'So why have you got a bit of paper with Nightingale Square written on it, Beth?' Harold nosily asked.

I shook my head and tutted, but as ever, he was not to be distracted.

'You're not thinking of moving into Kate's place by any chance, are you?' he blatantly asked.

'Are you?' Sara echoed; her gaze was inquisitive as it shifted back to me.

'What on earth makes you think that, Harold?' I snapped.

I was annoyed that he knew, especially as I'd asked Kate to keep my visit a secret, from him in particular.

'Luke let slip that you'd gone back again on Saturday and had a look at the house,' Harold explained. He looked a little rosy-cheeked, as was I when I realised both my annoyance, and the clipped tone which accompanied it, was misplaced. 'I wouldn't have mentioned it if I'd known it was supposed to be a secret.'

I sat down heavily on the edge of his bed.

'Sorry, Harold,' I apologised. 'Ignore me. I didn't mean to snap, but it's a bit of a touchy subject.'

'Didn't you like the house?' Sara frowned.

'Quite the opposite,' I admitted. 'I absolutely loved it, but there's no way I can afford it. It's wonderful, but out of my league . . .'

'Look sharp,' hissed Harold, but it was too late.

'Here you are,' said Sandra, the care home manager, striding in and addressing me and Sara. 'I might have known.'

I quickly stood up. Staff weren't allowed to sit on the beds.

'I've been looking all over for you two,' she tutted,

surprisingly turning a blind eye to where I'd been perched. 'I need you both to go and give Phil a hand, please. Greta's got into the garden and she hasn't got a stitch on.'

'Not again,' Sara groaned.

'Of course,' I said, trying not to smile. 'We'll go as soon as Harold's dressed.'

'I can wait. I'll want to stay put until you've got her covered,' said Harold, with a shudder, as he slowly buttoned his shirt. 'My eyesight's far too good to have to endure the sight of her streaking.'

Sandra shook her head in disapproval.

'And if you could come into my office for a quick chat before you head home today, Beth,' she added, 'that would be much appreciated.'

'You're in for it now, girl,' Harold muttered as she strode off. 'She must have seen you sitting on the bed.'

I'd thought I'd got away with it, but no doubt he was right. The last thing I needed was a telling off, but it was my own fault.

'Close the door,' said Sandra, once I had finally finished for the day. 'I was expecting you before now. I was beginning to think you'd gone home.'

Officially my shift had long since ended, but unofficially none of us left until we were happy our day's work was properly done. With one less staff member than we should have had due to family illness, we'd all had to pick up the slack but Sandra seemed to have forgotten that.

'If it's about me sitting . . .' I began, but she cut me off.

'It isn't,' she quickly said. 'It's not.'

I hoped I hadn't just shot myself in the foot. I'd been playing this conversation over in my head right from the moment she'd requested an audience and I thought that if I could get my apology in first then I might not be in for such a tiresome tongue-lashing.

'It's not that,' she said again. 'Although you shouldn't have done it. However, I want to talk about your job here, rather than that. About the part you play in the Edith Cavell Care team.'

'Oh,' I swallowed, panicking that I was in even more trouble than I had realised.

Mentally I skipped back through my shifts. I couldn't think of anything I'd done wrong. I was a stickler for filling out the endless paperwork and made it my mission to treat the residents with the same care and respect that I would have wanted anyone in my own family to receive. Not that I had any now, but I always took pride in clocking out knowing I'd worked a full shift well done.

In spite of being reassured by my positive work ethic, there was no getting away from the fact that we currently had more empty rooms than Sandra would have liked and we all knew, even though we were already stretched for staff, that she might have to let a couple of us go at some point. I hoped this unexpected meeting wasn't going to be that particular point.

'Would you say that you're happy here, Beth?' Sandra asked, steepling her fingers and making my stomach twist.

'Yes,' I said, my voice an octave higher than I would have liked. 'Of course.'

'You're happy with your role?'

'Yes,' I said again. 'I love it. Is there a problem with my work?'

'No,' said Sandra, 'absolutely not. You're one of the best we have.'

I felt my shoulders relax, but only a little.

'It would be a shame to lose you,' she continued, making them tense up again. 'From the care team, I mean,' she clarified. 'But I want to ask if you'd be interested in a change in direction.'

'How do you mean?'

Edith Cavell Care had homes across East Anglia and I wondered if she was going to suggest a transfer to work in another home, rather than letting me go completely. I hoped not. One bus journey across the city was enough for me and I couldn't drive, so . . .

'Another vacancy has become available,' she said, shifting in her seat and cutting through my thoughts. 'Quite unexpectedly and I think you'd be perfect for it.'

'Here you mean?'

'Yes, here,' she said impatiently.

'What is it?'

She took a deep breath and swallowed.

'Activities manager.'

'Activities manager?' I echoed, frowning. 'But I thought Karen . . .'

'Yes, well,' Sandra cut in, sounding put out. 'So did I. That's why I put her forward for it. That's why I invested in her training, but I was . . . wrong.'

I looked at her in amazement. Sandra *never* admitted to making mistakes.

'There was an incident a few days ago during a macramé session,' I wondered if she was referring to the near-strangulation or the almost lost digit but didn't ask her to clarify, 'and I had already been starting to wonder if Karen was actually right for the role, but today she resigned—'

'She's resigned?' I gasped.

That really was a turn-up for the books. She'd been like a cat with two tails since Sandra had singled her out and got her trained up.

'Um, with immediate effect,' Sandra winced, 'and since everyone had such a wonderful time when you were in charge of activities and haven't stopped going on about it since, I wondered if you'd like to consider taking the job on?'

I wondered if Harold and Ida had played any part in this unexpected turn of events.

'According to Karen,' Sandra pushed on, sounding almost scathing, 'it's not a job for the faint-hearted and having looked through the resources cupboard, I can see she never got stuck into the role, so there's plenty of . . . scope.'

By which she meant that if I accepted, I would be starting from scratch and most likely with no budget.

'But I'm not qualified,' I pointed out.

She let out a long breath.

'I'm beginning to think there's more to making someone suitable for a job than the certificates in their portfolio and the letters after their name. I know,' she continued, her tone warmer, 'how well you looked after your mum, Beth. You told me at your interview about all of the wonderful things you arranged for her to do. I think if you can apply those skills to the activities here, then the residents are going to be far happier.'

If she genuinely thought that, I couldn't help wondering why she'd picked Karen rather than me when she was originally recruiting but I didn't ask.

'Not all of them,' I pointed out instead.

'Well, no,' she smiled. 'We'll never please them all, but there are plenty who would benefit and you never know, it might even tempt a few more residents. It's imperative we fill those empty rooms.'

It was a wonderful opportunity and my head buzzed with all the things I would be able to do. Ever since Karen had taken the role on, I'd been thinking how I would do things differently, but did I want the responsibility? Would it be better to carry on in the groove I was comfortable in, even if staffing levels were precarious? Would anything I could do with the role really tempt new residents or make the current ones happier, and if not . . .

'It would mean no more night shifts,' Sandra enticingly said, 'and less weekend work.' That was tempting too. 'And of course, if you took it on, it would help to level out the care team numbers a bit.'

'So, you're saying that if I accept, then you won't have to let anyone go?'

'And you'd go up the pay scale,' Sandra added, refusing to confirm that everyone's jobs would be safe. 'Not by a huge amount, but the pay is definitely better.'

My heart thumped hard at the thought of a few extra coffers in the bank. Just a bit more money was all I needed to make the dream move, the potentially life-changing move, to Nightingale Square a reality.

I opened my mouth to immediately accept, but then took a breath as I remembered everything Ida and Harold had so recently said about the mess Karen had made of everything. This decision was about so much more than money. My head was telling me to snatch Sandra's hand off, but my heart was suggesting I exercised a little more caution. I needed to think realistically about this and not get carried away. Was it a job I could actually do in the long term, rather than for just a few days?

'Can I have a couple of days to think it over?' I asked, letting my heart and common sense get the upper hand. 'And is there a job description and remuneration details sheet I can look over?'

Sandra pushed back her chair and stood up.

'I copied both earlier,' she said, reaching for a folder on top of the filing cabinet. 'You can have a day, two at the most, but after that, I'll need to ask someone else. It'll be anarchy otherwise.'

My hands were trembling as I took the folder.

'Thank you, Sandra,' I said shakily. 'I really appreciate the opportunity.'

'I hope you'll do more than appreciate it,' she said meaningfully, before ushering me back out of the door.

The additional income accepting the job of activities manager at the care home would afford me was almost exactly the amount I needed to make the move to Nightingale Square happen.

It was the most fortuitously timed offer, and I would have been a fool not to take it; however, having experienced firsthand the impact of Karen's mismanagement of the role, along with the negative knock-on effect her ineptitude had on the residents' mental health and well-being, I was determined to think it through both carefully and rationally before I made a final decision.

I had no desire to let either myself, Sandra or any of the residents down and therefore I put my eagerness aside and, during yet another sleepless night, carefully measured up the weight of responsibility the role would press on my shoulders.

My phone constantly buzzed with notifications from the care team WhatsApp group, where speculation about Karen's departure was rife and I just knew the residents would be full of it the next day too. With the oblivion of sleep far beyond my reach, I once again reached for my box of treasures and delved deeper into the things I had kept and which I knew had the power to help me make up my mind.

Carrying on the hobby Mum had started when I was little, I had put together numerous scrapbooks recording our time together after her first stroke. They were full of images and notes of all the things I had inventively created to keep her stimulated and busy, as opposed to frustrated and bored.

Looking through them all again and seeing the details of what I had recorded, plus the activities I had photographed and logged, was creditable proof that I was more than up to the job Sandra had offered me.

As the clock next to my bed flicked to 3am, I decided that I was going to take on the role and I was going to move to Nightingale Square.

By the end of Wednesday, everything was arranged. I had officially accepted the job offer and Sandra and I agreed that it would be a great boost to the residents' morale if we kept my change of role a surprise. So, the plan was for me to take a few days' holiday, then go into work the following Monday, gather everyone together and make a big announcement.

After that, she suggested I could explain to her my vision and how activities would work going forward. I was thrilled and terrified in equal measure, especially as I also had a house move to arrange in-between.

I had already spoken to Kate, excitedly accepted the room and scheduled a second trip to the house. She was every bit as ecstatic as I was, which made me even happier. The next visit was going to be more about meeting the man I was going to be sharing a bathroom with than anything else.

I knew he would have to be a truly awful person to make me change my mind, and I also knew Kate wouldn't have him living in her house if that was the case, but once bitten and all that.

'I'm so pleased you're taking the room,' gushed Kate, the evening we waited outside the house for Elijah to join us. 'How did your landlord feel about you leaving a month before the end of your current tenancy?'

That had been the biggest surprise of all.

'According to the agency,' I laughed, 'he was more surprised that I had stuck out living there for as long as I have!'

'Oh, really?'

'Yes,' I nodded, 'he said it was obvious that I was the one holding the place together and after the last disastrous inspection, he'd guessed I'd had enough. I think he was half expecting me to jump ship and as long he gets his rent, he's not bothered when I go.'

He had even promised to return my deposit, which was more than generous and a huge boost because it meant I could give Kate what she'd originally asked for. Everything suddenly seemed to be coming up roses and I couldn't have been happier.

'I bet he won't be saying that when the others stop cleaning,' Kate smiled.

'Oh, they already have,' I told her. 'The sink is full of dirty dishes again and the bin is back to overflowing.'

I hadn't told my housemates I was leaving. They'd realise when they no longer had Aretha to stub their cigarettes out in – which reminded me, how on earth was I going to get her from there to the Square?

'They sound delightful,' tutted Kate as she quickly checked her phone. 'I hope Elijah hasn't forgotten about our meeting. I'm sure he would have let me know if he wasn't going to make it, but there's nothing from him so far.'

We'd already been waiting at least half an hour and it was starting to drizzle.

'Let's just go in,' said Kate. 'I daresay he won't be much longer.'

I felt a slight niggle that he hadn't even sent a text, but once I was over the threshold and looking at the lovely, and thankfully still tidy, rooms again, I forgot all about it.

'So,' said Kate, once we'd completed the second tour, and there was still no sign of Elijah, 'you're definitely happy to move in on Saturday, even though you haven't met your housemate?'

'I am,' I said.

It wasn't ideal, but it couldn't be helped. I wouldn't have time to come back again the next day, assuming he would be about then, because I needed to pack and start planning. I'd told Kate all about my new job and made it very clear that I wasn't going to tell Harold about the move until he knew about the job too.

He was a wily old thing and would doubtless work out that I'd been offered Karen's job if I'd moved into the Square because it was the only way I would have been able to afford it. Having revealed to him and Sara earlier in the week that money was the only thing stopping me, he would have immediately put two and two together. And with that in mind, we agreed not to tell Sara either. Fingers crossed the dynamic duo wouldn't show their faces in the Grow-Well until after the weekend.

'Great,' beamed Kate. 'Have you got a lot of stuff to pack?'

'Not really,' I said, thinking of the few things I'd already started to gather together. 'To be honest, I'm more concerned about safely moving my plants than anything else. I'm going to need to hire a van. Or a person and a van,' I amended, biting my lip.

I wouldn't be able to move Aretha single-handed and knew no one at the house would offer to help; as I couldn't drive, I'd need someone to jump behind the wheel of whatever I hired too.

'Oh, don't worry about that,' said Kate. 'We've got those in abundance here.'

'What do you mean?'

'Folk with vans,' she explained, pulling her phone out of her pocket again. 'John and Finn have both got one. I'll ask them if they can move you.'

I tried to object, but she wouldn't hear of it and by the time I left that evening, it was all arranged. I'd transferred the first chunk of deposit into her bank and signed on the dotted line. Kate insisted Harold's friendship with me and Sara's kind words were reference enough so she didn't need anything else and as I walked home in the rain, sheltered by my umbrella, I felt the biggest smile lighting up my face.

In just a few days I was going to have a brand-new job and a brand-new home and I couldn't wait! Finally, I had something in my life to look forward to again. Mum would have been so proud and indeed, so was I.

Chapter 5

'Morning, my love!' boomed the unexpected voice of my new neighbour, John, when I opened the front door early on Saturday morning, ready to depart. 'I know you were expecting Finn, but he's had van trouble after delivering one of his sculptures and didn't make it home last night. Will I do as a replacement?'

'What's going on?' scowled Courtney, from halfway up the stairs.

I couldn't work out if she was getting up or going to bed. Either way, she clearly didn't appreciate the early morning house call.

'Moving day!' John keenly announced, this time clapping his hands together. 'Are you going to give us a hand?'

Aside from Courtney's scowl, packing everything into John's van went remarkably smoothly and, as I watched him and a reluctantly press-ganged Aaron wrestle to find the most secure spot for Aretha, a sense of unease crept up on me. Everything had been going so well during the last few days – the jigsaw that made up my life morphing seamlessly into a spectacular new image — that surely it had to be too good to be true?

I had mourned the anniversary of losing Mum just a few short days ago and on that very date, a simple act of kindness on my part had evolved into a wonderful new home in an established community and a new job role as well. Surely it was too much good luck to be bestowed upon one person in such a concentrated dose? Either that, or I'd become a bit jaded and was going to need time to accept that this sudden dollop of blessed fortune might mean that my life could turn out better than I dared to hope.

Perhaps, I mused, as I attempted to push the unease to one side, I had finally reached the top of the universe's wheel and was now reaping the rewards. I would never forget everything Mum had struggled with, both before and after her stroke, but perhaps it was time for me to assimilate what life had thrown at me and turn my attention back to my present and future, rather than fretting over what had happened to shape my past.

'Is this it?' asked John, pulling me out of my reverie. 'Is this everything? There's not much aside from the urban jungle, my love.'

I moved to stand next to him at the back of the van and peered inside at my worldly goods. He was right. Apart from my multiple pots of plants, there wasn't much at all: a couple of boxes of kitchen paraphernalia, another from the bathroom and then half a dozen more filled with bed stuff and the like, along with a couple of suitcases of clothes and a bag of jumbled shoes. My box of memories, the one filled with the scrapbooks, photos, vinyl and a few trinkets, was travelling next to me in the front.

'Yep,' I said, shrugging off the memory of the house clearance I'd had to organise and which had carried off the bulk of Mum's and my furniture and possessions, 'this is it.'

We'd already downsized when we moved from the council flat into the even smaller bungalow and as I'd had to quickly make way for someone else in need after Mum's funeral, my living space was then reduced to a rented room. There was no money to spare for storage and consequently most of our things had had to go. However, thinking of the box on the front seat, I knew I'd kept the things that meant the most and that was all that mattered.

'Right then,' said John, slamming the doors shut. 'Let's get off, shall we? I daresay Lisa's arranged a warm welcome for you at the other end!'

I felt a bit jittery about that as I gave Aaron, who was lingering on the pavement, my house key.

'I really am sorry to see you go,' he said awkwardly, 'and not just because you've always been the one to clear up after us,' he hastily added. 'I hope you're not leaving because of what happened with the inspection.'

The incident had been the straw that broke the camel's back but I would be forever grateful for the nudge it had given me. However, Aaron looked and sounded so guilt-ridden that I couldn't say as much and with John waiting, there was no time to properly explain.

'Of course not,' I therefore said instead. 'It was just time for me to move on.'

'Well,' he said, taking a step back towards the house, 'that's all right then. Good luck.'

'You too,' I smiled, reaching for the van door.

He was going to need it living with Courtney and Rob, and so was the next tenant. I hoped they were made of sterner stuff than I had been and set their stall out right from day one. I'd hate to think of the mucky trio bending another victim to their will. Unless of course the new tenant turned out to share their attitude towards tidiness, then they'd be peas in a pod.

'All set?' asked John.

'All set,' I nodded, taking one last look at the house before tucking the box into my side.

'Get your belt on then,' he said, 'and we'll get you moved.'

Just as John had said she would be, Lisa was on hand the moment he parked the van. Thankfully, she hadn't rallied the rest of the neighbours but rushed over with mugs of hot tea and a plate of toast.

'I bet you were too excited to eat first thing, weren't you?' she said, offering me a slice of Marmite-covered toast.

'How did you know?' I asked, gratefully taking the slice and feeling dazzled by her intuition.

'She knows *everything*,' John said with emphasis as he reached for the plate and Lisa whipped it away.

'Hey,' she tutted, 'you've already had yours.'

'Yes,' he said, 'but I've loaded the van since then.'

She relented, but I bet she wouldn't have done if she'd known how little he'd had to lift. He winked at me, clearly thinking exactly the same thing.

'Morning, Beth,' said Kate as she came striding into the Square with her girls in tow. 'Sorry, I'm late. A certain someone didn't want to get out of bed this morning and with Luke away, I couldn't leave her behind.'

I could see the eldest girl, Jasmine, had a definite puss on.

'You're not late,' I quickly said. 'If anything, we're a bit early. I didn't have much to pack, so . . .'

My words trailed off as I realised that by reassuring Kate, I'd dropped John in it.

'Is that right?' said Lisa, shaking her head as John crammed in the last crust.

'Well,' said Kate, unaware of what was going on, 'here are your keys, Beth. One for the front door and another for the back, along with a card welcoming you to the Square, which has the code for the garden gate written inside.'

I took them from her, feeling my face grow warm.

'Thank you,' I said, turning to look at the house. 'Thank you so much.'

'It's precious that gate code,' said John with reverence, 'like being given the keys to the city.'

'I know,' I beamed. 'I'm very lucky. I'm so happy.'

Thanks to Lisa's timely toast, my nervous tummy butterflies had taken flight along with the last lingering concern that the whole chain of events was too good to be true. What I was feeling was happiness, pure and undiluted joy.

I hadn't felt it for a very long time and it was going to take some getting used to, but I was smitten with the sensation already.

'I'll take your two back over to mine, shall I?' Lisa asked Kate. 'I can give them breakfast while you help Beth settle in.'

Aware that John and Kate probably had better things to be doing on a Saturday morning than help me move, I hastily drained my tea, returned the mug to Lisa and rushed up the path. I held my breath as I turned the key in the lock and pushed open the door.

This was it – I finally felt that I was home.

Well before lunchtime, everything was inside and the majority of it was unpacked. There were plenty of empty cupboards in the kitchen, so I didn't have to worry about encroaching on Elijah's space.

I'd carefully spread newspaper over the table in the dining room and unboxed my houseplants too. Thankfully, there was no damage and Aretha looked right at home in her spot in the bay window. I would work out where to place the rest of the plants the next day. By then, I would have hopefully, finally, met my housemate and I would be able to ask him if he minded me putting them in the shared spaces rather than having to keep them in my room as I had before. Although if he did object, at least I had a much bigger room to accommodate them now.

I was just beginning to think about popping out to pick up some lunch when someone knocked on the door.

'Mum's made a picnic,' said a young boy who, if memory

served, was Lisa and John's son, Archie. 'We're having it on the green. She said you can come over, if you like.'

I looked over his head to where I could see a few people gathered. Lisa spotted me and waved.

'You must be famished,' she said, once I'd locked up and joined them. 'Moving's hungry work.'

'Don't mind her,' said Mark, as he rolled his eyes. 'She's a feeder. And so's Carole.'

My former garden tour guide, who was sitting on a fold-up chair next to her husband rather than on the blanket on the grass, tutted in response.

'What?' Mark shrugged. 'Am I right or am I right?'

'You're right,' everyone chorused, before laughing.

I ate and drank my fill, enjoying the company of the assembled group as I basked in the warmth of the sun. It was like no Saturday I'd ever experienced in my former abode. There had been no green space there, just a yard at the back for the bins and a path at the front which led straight to the road.

'Do you do this every weekend?' I asked.

'Not every weekend,' said Lisa.

'We usually congregate in the Grow-Well rather than here,' Carole's husband, Graham, expanded, 'weather permitting. We work for a couple of hours and then often share a meal together.'

'My dad's king of the barbecue *and* the pizza oven,' announced Archie.

'What he means is,' said Lisa, 'John won't let anyone else

near it. He's a total neanderthal where outdoor dining is concerned.'

John made no attempt to dispute that.

'And what about Elijah?' I asked. 'Does he generally join you?'

I'd found little trace of him in the house and was beginning to think he was actually a figment of Kate's imagination.

'When he's not working,' said Carole, quashing my theory.

'Which reminds me,' said Mark in full gossip mode, 'did you hear what happened . . .'

'Well, well, well,' said Luke, unknowingly cutting Mark off as he wandered up. 'Here you all are. I just looked in the Grow-Well expecting to find a few of you in there.'

'Daddy!' shouted his daughters, who were still in Lisa's care.

'Crikey!' gasped Mark, checking his phone. 'Is that the time? I'd better get back. Blossom will have my guts for garters!'

He rushed off and I felt pleased I had a few days off and didn't have to be anywhere other than in the Square.

'We thought we'd celebrate Beth moving in with a picnic closer to home today,' said Lisa, standing up and brushing the grass from her legs. 'How'd you get on?' she then asked Luke in a slightly quieter tone.

He picked up Abigail, the smallest of the girls, twirled her around and then shook his head.

'It's still a possibility,' he said, letting out a long breath.

'But not a sure thing . . .' Lisa frowned.

'No,' he said, sounding concerned, 'unfortunately not. Anyway,' he added, his tone lighter, 'I didn't come to break up the party, just to collect the girls and wish Beth a happy moving in day.'

'Thank you,' I smiled, 'I've had the warmest welcome. It's been wonderful.'

It was true. The only thing missing was my elusive housemate.

'It's not a bad spot, is it?' Luke grinned.

'It's a perfect spot,' I smiled back.

'Are you going to stay and at least have a drink, mate?' John asked, holding up a melamine cup.

'No thanks,' said Luke, 'I'd better not. I'm going home to get changed and then I'll see what Kate's up to. I've been gone ages.'

'You might as well leave the girls here then,' said Lisa. 'We're going to have some games in a while. That'll keep Jasmine happy. She was in a right grump earlier.'

'She's always in a grump in the morning these days,' Luke laughed. 'She's getting to that age. Just like Tamsin was when I first moved here.'

'Hey,' pouted Tamsin, John and Lisa's eldest. 'I wasn't that bad.'

The adults looked as though they would beg to differ.

'I'll bring them over before dinner,' said Lisa. 'And I'll pop over in a bit on my own, so you can give me the low-down.'

'All right,' said Luke. 'Just shout if you need anything, won't you, Beth?'

'I will,' I said, 'thanks.'

'Did Kate give you the house telephone number?'

'Yes,' I told him. 'Last week after I'd called her mobile to arrange a second viewing of the house.'

It was incredible to think that it was just a week ago that I'd seen the house for the very first time and now I was living in it.

'Excellent,' he nodded. 'Right, I'll see you in a bit, Lisa.'

'Yes,' she said, looking to my mind, a little concerned. 'I won't be far behind you.'

I wondered what the pair of them had to talk about. Clearly, given their expressions, it was something serious. I hoped life in Nightingale Square was going to be as sweet as I had imagined.

'Any takers for this last scone?' Carole asked the group as Luke crossed the road back to Prosperous Place. 'There's still a dollop of cream left to go with it.'

John quickly reached for it and I shrugged my apprehensive moment off. Life in the Square was sweet already.

With the sun shining, the sound of bees going about their business and the children playing, no one aside from Lisa, showed any sign of wanting to move. Abigail and Jasmine were more than content, so she left them in John's care playing a noisy game of quoits, and went to talk to Luke. I thanked her again for her generous welcome before she left and then settled back down to watch. The sound of the children laughing brought back some very happy memories.

'It's great here, isn't it?' said Graham, as he readjusted his hat after wafting away an eager bee.

'It is,' I agreed.

'It was wonderful before, but since Kate and Luke arrived within just a few weeks of each other, the place has really changed.'

I listened as he explained how the Grow-Well had evolved and how the more recent development of The Winter Garden and a seasonal celebration called Winterfest had proved to be successful too. I remembered Sara raving about that.

'And what about in the summer?' I asked, as I caught sight of Lisa already walking back from Prosperous Place. 'Is the garden open then too?'

'There are a few open days,' Graham told me. 'And we open the Grow-Well up to the public at the same time. We hope it inspires visitors to do something similar with their own neighbours.'

The sight of us set up on the green and the sound of ice-cream van chimes in a neighbouring road all reminded me of the many fairs and country shows Mum and I used to visit throughout the summer when I was growing up. We'd travel to nearby villages by bus to soak up the scenery and tradi-tional rural delights. Reclined on a blanket in Nightingale Square and replete from the picnic lunch, it was almost impossible to believe we were anywhere near a city, let alone in the heart of one.

'And what about a garden party or summer fair?' I asked, shielding my eyes from the sun as Lisa plonked herself down on the blanket next to me. She didn't look very happy. 'Have you ever hosted one of those?'

'No,' said Graham, 'nothing like that.'

'We're having the annual one at the care home soon,' I carried on, imagining the space where we currently sat lined with traditional stalls and stands and a waggiest tail dog competition being judged in the centre. 'The green and garden here would be perfect for you to hold one of your own.'

I realised I hadn't included myself in the suggestion; I daresay doing that would take some getting used to.

'Perhaps,' Graham said pensively, as Lisa stood back up again.

'It could be a country-type event in the city,' I dreamily added. 'With the Grow-Well and the hens and so on, you could easily play up the traditional element to make it a bit different. Homegrown and homemade and all that malarkey. Give it a proper rural in the city twist.'

The privacy and peace in Nightingale Square were already working their magic on me and my imagination and I could see why everyone loved it.

'Do you suppose something like that might raise a lot of money?' Lisa asked, sounding rather breathless.

I squinted up at her. There were bright roses in her cheeks that I didn't think had anything to do with the weather.

'Quite possibly,' I said. 'If it was pitched right and the weather behaved itself, you'd most likely attract hundreds of visitors. A "country in the city" summer fair would be quite a draw, I would have thought, wouldn't you?'

I was about to add that they probably took a lot of organising, but she strode off again before I had the chance.

'Was it something I said?' I asked Graham.

'Who knows?' he chuckled, watching her walk away. 'I shouldn't worry. I daresay we'll find out soon enough. Perhaps you've given her an idea for her next book.'

Chapter 6

Keen to settle further into my new home, I didn't wait for Lisa to appear again. I thanked everyone for the wonderful welcome and delicious picnic and headed back to the house. It was much cooler inside and I spent the rest of the day pottering about, getting to know all the nooks and crannies, including a hidden cupboard in my room, before making up the bed, taking a long, lazy bath and slipping between the cool sheets.

It felt a little strange to be doing it all, knowing that any moment a man I hadn't met before could walk into the house and introduce himself as the person I was now living with, but I was determined not to let anything mar the pleasure and comfort of the first relaxing evening in my clean, tidy and quiet new home.

Having locked the bedroom door, I lay in bed, listening to the unfamiliar sounds of the neighbourhood, which amounted to nothing more than a car door slamming and then a front door closing. As my eyelids began to feel heavy, there was still no sight or sound of Elijah.

I had no expectations that I would sleep any better than I usually did, having long resigned myself to being a terminal light and disturbed sleeper, but I went out like a light and probably would have slept much of the next morning away had I not been woken by the sound of music thumping up the stairs.

It took me a moment to remember where I was and after I had stretched out, I looked about me. The light was streaming into the room and I thought I could smell coffee. After such a restful night, I should have felt refreshed, raring to go, and enthralled to be living out the fantasy I had imagined when I first viewed the room, but the musical intrusion had set my heart skittering and had me wondering if I'd counted my chickens a little too soon.

After I'd pulled on my dressing gown, admired the view of the sun-filled Square and used the bathroom, I knew there was nothing for it but to venture downstairs. I had hoped my moving about above might have been noticed below and the music turned down, but it was being played so loudly I daresay whoever was in the house had no hope of hearing me. I took a deep breath and prepared myself to meet my new housemate.

'Good morning,' I said, but with no result whatsoever.

The guy, who I assumed to be elusive Elijah, was standing in the kitchen with his back to me, his head enthusiastically bobbing in time to the music.

'Morning,' I tried again, louder this time, but still to no avail.

I bit my lip, not sure what to do next as I got the measure of him. He was about a head taller than me, broad-shouldered and had sandy blond hair, which was attractively enhanced by a scattering of much lighter natural highlights. He looked tanned too, given the evidence of the colour of his legs below the hem of his cargo shorts and was barefooted.

I was still torn between either tapping him on the shoulder or walking away, when he spun around, spotted me and leapt at least three feet into the air, which resulted in him spilling his entire mug of coffee down his shirt.

'Shit,' he yelped, dumping the mug in the sink and pulling the soaked material away from his torso. 'Shit, shit, shit.'

'Oh my god,' I gasped, leaping forward, but with no clue as to what I could do to help. 'I'm so sorry!'

'It's fine,' he spluttered. 'I'm fine. Actually, I'm not. This is hot. Really hot.'

'You'd better take it off!' I shouted above the noise of the music, scared his skin was being irreparably scalded.

In one swift movement he lifted the shirt up and over his head and I felt my face start to burn far brighter than the mark on his impressively toned chest.

'Oh,' I swallowed, quickly looking away, 'I didn't mean . . .'

'Damn,' he said, catching his breath and looking at the swiftly spreading stain, 'that was my last clean work shirt. Oh, never mind,' he added, dumping it next to the sink. 'Hang on, I'll be back in a sec.'

I stood in the noise-filled kitchen feeling dazed, then came to my senses, grabbed the roll of kitchen towel and mopped up the little of the coffee that had made it as far as the floor. There wasn't a lot because the vast majority of it had ended up on him. I dumped the damp sheets in the bin just as the music was switched off.

'Beth?'

Feeling a little breathless, I turned around and returned the inquisitive gaze of the dark blue eyes I found trained on my face. The beguiling eyes were set in a tanned face, which also featured full lips and at least two days' worth of stubble. I opened my mouth to respond, but no words came out.

The silence stretched between us as we took each other in. I knew exactly what I was thinking, but I would have loved to have known what thoughts the guy now wearing a creased T-shirt was mulling over.

'You're Beth, right?' he eventually asked again.

'Yes,' I swallowed, feeling an idiot for not answering sooner. 'I am and you must be Elijah?'

His face broke into a smile that set my heart racing again.

'Yep,' he said. 'That's me.'

'I'm really sorry I made you jump,' I apologised. 'And I'm even more sorry about your shirt.'

He picked it up and bundled it into the washing machine.

'I've got an hour before I need to leave for work,' he said, reaching under the sink for the washing powder. 'I'm sure I can get it washed and at least part tumble dried in that time.'

I wasn't sure he could, but it was generous of him to try and make me feel better by saying it.

'It was my fault for playing my music so loud,' he further added, shouldering more of the blame. 'But who can resist an early morning session with the Foo Fighters?'

I could, but it would have been churlish to say as much.

'Quite,' I said instead. 'Can I pour you another coffee to make up for the one you've just ended up wearing?'

'I'll do it,' he insisted, stepping up, 'and then we'll have a proper chat, shall we?'

'That would be good,' I agreed. 'I know I haven't made the best first impression ...'

'Oh, I wouldn't say that,' he interrupted, and I felt my cheeks flame again. 'Do you take sugar?'

'Yes,' I said, 'just one, but I don't drink coffee, so I'll make myself tea.'

'You don't drink coffee?' he gasped.

I wasn't sure if he was genuinely shocked or was teasing me, but he did sound taken aback. Had I just unwittingly added another blot to my copybook by admitting my preference for tea?

'No,' I tentatively told him, 'I love the smell, but I can't stand the taste. It's fine though, I'm happy to make tea.'

'All right,' he said, standing aside so I could reach the kettle.

'So,' I said, trying to ignore the assault on my senses being so close to him seemed to have triggered, 'where do you work?'

'In the Castle Coffeehouse,' he said with a grin and I felt my mouth fall open. 'It's just up the road,' he added.

'But you've probably never been inside, as you can't stand the taste.'

I put my head in my hands and he laughed.

'So that's my first *and* my second impression ruined,' I groaned.

'It's all right,' he nudged, 'I won't hold your hatred of coffee against you.'

I shook my head and surreptitiously watched him while I waited for the kettle to boil. He certainly knew his way around a coffee machine and I imagined he was the kind of barista who could remember exactly what his regular customers came in for. Given how handsome he was, I'd bet there were plenty of regulars too.

'Shall we sit in the front room?' he suggested, once we'd finished making our drinks. 'There's not a lot of room around the dining table at the moment.'

'I hope you don't mind about the plants,' I said, looking at the table where my pots jostled for space while they waited for me to properly arrange them.

'Not at all,' he said, stopping to look.

'I'll have quite a few of them set up in my room by the end of the day,' I rushed on, not quite taking on board what he'd said, 'but I wondered if you would mind if I dotted some of the others about the place? The ferns would love it in the bathroom and the snake plant would too.'

'I wouldn't mind that at all,' he told me. 'I really like them. My grandmother was a huge houseplant fan. When I was little, my mum used to take me to see her at the weekends and I'd spend hours playing with the spritzer thing she had.'

I could imagine him running around spraying everything in sight.

'I've never actually thought to buy any of my own,' he added wistfully and I wondered if he was still thinking of his grand-mother. 'Feel free to dot them about wherever you like,' he beamed, echoing my words. 'I'm pleased we've found we've got something in common,' he then cheekily added. 'I was begin-ning to panic when you revealed your weird loathing of coffee.'

'It's not that weird and I don't loathe it,' I smiled back. 'I just don't like the taste.'

'Hmm,' he said thoughtfully. 'I bet I could come up with something to tempt you.'

I bet he could too, but my thoughts had nothing to do with cappuccinos or skinny lattes.

'Anyway,' he carried on, after plonking himself down in the ancient armchair in the sitting room, which I guessed was his preferred spot, 'feel free to put your plants wherever you like. This place is just as much yours as it is mine now.'

I was relieved he felt that way. I sat on the sofa and curled my feet up under me and noticed that Aretha was looking particularly glossy. When I looked back at Elijah, he was looking at her too.

'Now I come to think of it,' he said, 'plants are exactly what the house has been missing. They're all the rage again at the moment, aren't they?'

'There's been a definite increase in sales recently,' I

conceded, enthusiastically waxing lyrical about my favourite topic, 'especially among the rental generation, like us, but I've had some of my collection for years.' I wanted him to know my passion was more than a passing fad. 'They're like old friends now, definitely part of the family.'

'Just like my grandmother's were,' he added.

I wondered what had happened to her collection, but felt it too personal a question to ask. We'd known each other barely half an hour and there were things I wouldn't have wanted to talk about so soon.

'That's a cheese plant, isn't it?' he asked, nodding to Aretha.

'Yes,' I said. 'And she's called Aretha.'

Elijah looked at me and raised his eyebrows.

'Have they all got names?'

'Pretty much,' I admitted, 'and there's so many of them because I haven't had access to a garden for a while.'

'Well,' said Elijah, this time with a nod to the window and the view beyond, 'you've got plenty of green space now. Does that mean you won't be buying any more houseplants?'

'I can't commit to that,' I confessed. 'There's this great plant stall on the market. They've got these gorgeous moss balls in bottles and I'm sure there's one with my name on.'

Elijah laughed again.

'Have you seen much of the Grow-Well yet?' he asked.

'Yes,' I said, 'Carole gave me the grand tour last week. And Lisa arranged a picnic on the green yesterday. It's wonderful here, isn't it? I love it all already and I've hardly been here five minutes.'

My heart felt fit to burst as I thought about it all. If someone had tried to tell me how drastically and perfectly my life was about to change, even just a fortnight ago, I never would have believed them. I owed Harold a big hug, at the very least.

'It is wonderful,' Elijah agreed, his eyes trained on the view beyond the window. 'I love it too. It's been a real tonic since . . .'

He cut the sentence off and when I looked at him, I could see his face was as flushed as mine had previously been. I was curious to ask what had happened that meant he needed a tonic, but having already acknowledged there were things I didn't want to talk about, I bit the question back.

'It's really handy being so close to work,' he said, neatly changing the subject. 'And there's such a great mix of people here. Is it close to work for you, too?'

'Yes,' I said, 'it's much closer than where I was living before. I used to have to get a bus, but now I can easily walk the distance. I work at the Edith Cavell Care Home.'

'That's the place where Harold lives and Sara from the garden works there too, doesn't she?'

'That's right.'

'So, what prompted the move? Was it the distance to work or something else?'

'Definitely something else,' I said with a shudder as I compared the clean and comfortable sitting room to the last one I'd shared. 'My housemates were total sloths and I always ended up cleaning up after them. It wore me down in the end, and I decided to move.'

'Good for you,' he said, also casting his eyes about the room. 'I can't think of anything more selfish than having your stuff impinging on someone else.'

'I hope you won't be thinking that about the houseplants by this time tomorrow,' I said, pretending to wince.

'I won't,' he smiled again. 'I was thinking more about messy stuff. You won't have to worry about tidying up after me. I'm a bit of a neat freak, I'm afraid.'

There was nothing freakish about neatness. I found it an endearing and attractive trait.

'Don't apologise for that,' I grinned. 'I'm the same.'

'Something else we have in common,' he nodded.

He held my gaze and I was hard pushed to look away.

'I think we're going to get along just fine,' he said happily.

'Me too,' I agreed.

'Although,' he then teasingly added, 'I suppose I'd just better check, houseplants aside, you haven't got any other all-consuming passions I should know about, have you?'

'Nothing,' I shrugged.

'Well, that's all right then.'

'But,' I said thoughtfully, 'perhaps I should mention Star Wars Thursday.'

'Star Wars Thursday?' he asked, his eyebrows shooting up.

'Yes,' I answered, straight-faced, 'I like to dress up as an Ewok on a Thursday.'

'Damn,' he chuckled, 'now I really wish I'd made it back last week. I could have vetoed you before Kate had given you a key.'

'Well, you'll just have to put up with it now,' I told him.

As a result of our less than perfect introduction, I'd completely forgotten that he'd stood us up.

'I'm sure I'll cope,' he grinned. 'I bet you make a cute Ewok.'

I wasn't sure how to respond to that.

'You do know why I didn't get back to meet you, don't you?' he then asked, suddenly serious. 'Kate did tell you what happened, didn't she?'

'No,' I said, all ears, 'she didn't.'

'Oh god,' he said. 'I'm so sorry, Beth, I just assumed you knew. There was an accident just as I was about to leave work. My boss, the coffeehouse manager, was cycling in for the shift change and got knocked off her bike outside the bakery.'

'Oh my goodness,' I gasped. 'That's terrible. Is she okay?'

'She will be,' he told me. 'But she's a bit banged up at the moment. I'm surprised you didn't hear the sirens as it was so close. I would have called and let Kate know, but there was no time.'

'Of course, there wasn't,' I agreed. 'It must have been awful.'

'It was,' he said a little shakily.

A sickening thought suddenly landed.

'She wasn't coming in to work just so you could leave to meet me, was she?' I asked, feeling nauseous.

'No,' said Elijah, holding up his hand. 'Don't worry about that. She's always on the road at that time of day.'

I was relieved to hear it, although still very sorry about what had happened.

'She'll be out of hospital next week and then back to work a couple of weeks after that,' he explained, 'but in the meantime, I'm holding the fort.' He glanced at his watch and stood up. 'So, you won't see much of me while you're settling in. As well as working the extra shifts, there's the setting up and shutting down every day, so downtime's limited right now.'

'You'll have to let me know if you need anything,' I offered. 'If there's anything I can do around the house, just ask. I don't suppose covering you in coffee this morning was much help, was it?'

'Don't worry about that,' he smiled, 'and I should be fine, but thanks. Maybe we could draw up a rota and pin it on the fridge, so we know who is going to do what and when. Bins, bathroom and stuff.'

'Sounds good to me,' I nodded, following him back into the kitchen.

He sounded like a guy with a plan and I loved that. Organising bins, bathroom and stuff was my idea of heavenly and harmonious communal living.

'Great,' he said, taking his almost-dry laundry out of the machine. 'Oh, and by the way,' he added, as he pulled off his T-shirt and swapped it for his polo shirt, 'in case you didn't work it out earlier, you'll know when I am here because I've always got music playing.'

'Music?' I swallowed, feeling my knees go weak and

not as a result of the second glimpse of his impressive physique. 'Always?'

'Yeah,' he said. 'Tunes, melodies, songs and singing. You know the stuff.'

'Yes,' I said, feeling the colour drain from my face as I realised there was something in my new life that was far from perfect. 'I am familiar with the concept, Elijah, it's just . . .'

How could I explain that I couldn't live with someone who played music whenever they were in residence? I knew I'd go mad exposed to that amount of music. I'd spent the last few years shutting it out and it was the one trigger I would never be prepared to assimilate. I couldn't. But how could I express that without having to go into the whole of my history?

'It's Eli, by the way,' he said, before I'd even started to try and find the words.

'What?' I frowned.

'My name,' he elaborated. 'My grandmother used to call me Elijah, but pretty much everyone else calls me Eli.'

'Eli,' I repeated. 'Look, about the music . . .'

'Don't tell me you don't like it?' he laughed, making for the front door. 'The coffee embargo was a hard enough blow to handle; you can't object to music too?'

'Not object, exactly . . .'

'Thank god for that,' he said, pulling open the door and setting off down the path before I could utter another word. 'Have a good day!'

As I watched him stride off, I didn't think I stood much chance of that.

Chapter 7

As I closed the door, all of the joy and elation I'd been feeling right from the moment I'd accepted the room in Nightingale Square leached away and in their place were feelings of shock, surprise and disappointment.

My imagined perfect life had just turned into the worst possible nightmare and I was stuck in it, with no escape. I tried pinching myself, just to make sure I wasn't walking through some mad fever dream, but I was awake and had the mark on my arm to prove it.

This was my new reality. I was living with a music lover. And even worse than that, a drop-dead gorgeous one. I would not, could not, allow myself to develop a crush on someone who had a gargantuan fondness for the Foo Fighters *and* who I was now living with. If I unwittingly let slip to anyone, but especially Eli, that I thought he was a stunner, our harmonious cohabitating could be over before it had even started.

'Get a grip, Beth,' I told myself sternly. 'A new home and a new job are all you can handle right now. A schoolgirl crush is most definitely not part of the plan.'

I breakfasted, got dressed and then spent the day deciding where to put my plants, painstakingly checking they had enough light, warmth and water while also trying to mentally prepare myself for my new role at the Edith Cavell Care Home, but it was all to no avail. No matter how hard I tried, no matter how determinedly I pushed thoughts of Eli and my stirred-up memories away, they barged in, commanding the spotlight and tainting what should have been a perfect day.

No doubt some people would have considered my reaction to Eli's love of music over the top and they would have argued that song was good for the soul, a great healer, a universal language and a reliever of tension and stress and, had I been talking to those people a few years ago, I would have agreed with them wholeheartedly because back then, music had been my life. It had been my everything. Music had been my entire world and my hopes and dreams for my future were pinned on it.

My days spent at The Arches with Moira and the other kids who, just like me, didn't fit in with their peers at school were some of the happiest of my life. Mum always said she felt bad for leaving me there so often while she was at work, but I told her, time and time again, that I was actually in my element.

Located under the railway bridge on the outskirts of the opposite side of the city to where I now lived, that nondescript building was a place where dreams were nurtured, encouraged and honed. Within its walls so many of us had found our tribe and spiritual home.

It was there I met and formed a friendship with Pete, one that should have lasted a lifetime and it was Moira who helped me garner the courage to study for a vocal degree in London. I had taken a year out to work and save before I started, but I never had quite enough money to make ends comfortably meet.

The second-year digs I found myself in made my former houseshare in Norwich look like the Ritz. But of course, I didn't care. Mum had taught me how to juggle money and I was singing. I had my journey planned and I was going to forge a career doing the one thing I loved most in the world. I was going to make it.

Then disaster struck. I had just auditioned for a leading part in the university's winter showcase. It was a big deal, huge in fact. Important and influential industry professionals were going to be invited and I knew it could open doors.

'Everyone can go!' called the guy who had been put in charge of herding the nervous group of students about. 'Except Beth. You need to come with me.'

I had honestly thought I was going to pass out when he said that. Being asked to stay behind could only mean one thing: I must have been selected for the showcase. Why else would I have been asked to stay?

My legs shook as I again stood in front of the three people who had listened to my audition and were still seated behind a long table. They were chatting amongst themselves and it was at that moment that my phone began to buzz in my jeans pocket. I ignored it.

'Well, Beth,' said the woman who was sitting in the middle. 'That was quite an audition you treated us to.'

'Thank you,' I croaked, hoping that she meant it in a good way.

I had managed to shrug off my nerves, given it my all and thought it had gone well.

'You clearly . . .' her words trailed off as my phone began to noisily vibrate again. 'What is that?' she frowned, looking accusingly around. 'I thought we said phones off, people!'

'Sorry,' I swallowed, 'it's mine. I turned it on after my audition and forgot to turn it off again.'

It stopped buzzing.

'As I was saying,' she continued, her change in tone telling me that she was rattled. 'Your audition was faultless. Oh, for pity's sake.'

'I'm so sorry . . .' I flinched as my mobile buzzed again.

'Why don't you turn it off now?' suggested someone else at the table.

'Of course,' I said, inwardly cursing as I yanked it out of my pocket.

Mum's name flashed up on the screen. She knew what I was going to be doing that day and I couldn't think of any conceivable reason why she'd call and interrupt. And keep calling.

'I'm so sorry,' I apologised again to the agitated panel, 'but I really need to take this.'

'Really?' demanded the woman as everyone else's eyebrows shot up. 'You need to answer your phone now, do you?'

'Yes,' I said, turning away. 'It's my mother. There must be something wrong.'

Ignoring the shocked expressions, gasps and dark mutterings, I accepted the call.

'Mum?'

But it wasn't Mum. It was a neighbour ringing to tell me that Mum had been found collapsed and unresponsive in the garden. She'd had a stroke and was on her way to hospital.

'She looks bad, Beth,' the neighbour said tearfully. 'You need to come home, my love.'

'I'll leave now,' I said, the shock making my legs tremble even harder as sour bile climbed to the back of my throat. 'I'll get the train as soon as I can,' I gulped, trying to swallow it back down.

I turned back to the table.

'So, Beth,' said the woman, not waiting to hear my explanation of what had happened, 'in spite of your lapse with your phone, we'd like to offer you the starring role in this year's showcase.'

I bit my lip hard. I'd waited so long to hear those words. I'd even had dreams where I imagined myself graciously and maturely accepting such an offer while my insides were a whirl of heady excitement and my heart raced ninety to the dozen. My heart was racing but not with exhilaration. My stomach felt like lead and my head was spinning.

All eyes were on me and I felt the weight of their expectation of my response land heavily on my shoulders.

'Well?' said the one person there who had so far been silent. He was clearly confused by my lack of response.

'I'm so sorry,' I said, 'I've just had some terrible news. Could I possibly have some time to think it over?'

The woman looked outraged.

'I take it you are aware what this will mean for your career?' she hissed.

'I am,' I swallowed.

'And you do know that there are dozens of others desperate for the opportunity and who would kill for it?'

'I do.'

'And yet you still want us to give you some time?' She sounded incredulous.

I nodded.

'Are you sure you're cut out for a career in entertainment?' she scowled. 'This business is ruthless, Beth. Careers are made and broken on moments like this. Tough choices have to be made and there's no room for sentimentality. Whatever news you've just received during that inconveniently timed phone call can't possibly be more important than this. In this business, *you're* number one. No one else. I suggest you think about that.'

Needless to say, in spite of the fact that the opportunity was what I'd spent years working towards, I walked away.

'If you walk out that door, you won't get back in!' the woman called after me. 'Opportunities like this come along once in a lifetime.'

I knew she was right and I had just passed mine up. I rushed back to my digs, threw a few things in a bag and caught the next train back to Norwich.

Mum's first stroke was devastating and mind-bogglingly debilitating. She needed, and was going to need, round the clock care to aid her rehabilitation and for a very long time. When she was eventually allowed home, she said she would settle for being looked after by the care teams the local authority employed, but in the early days she had said she needed me and I never forgot that.

I never forgot the fear and vulnerability in her eyes and consequently, within weeks of starting the second term of my second year, I passed up the starring role in the showcase, dropped out and moved home for good.

Mum's needs were my priority and with the words of the audition panellist still ringing in my ears, I hadn't sung a note since. I hadn't contacted Pete or Moira either and I had no idea what was happening at The Arches. I didn't want to know. It was a world I was no longer a part of or, according to those in the know, cut out for. My dream was gone. The industry wasn't interested in someone who favoured family over filling venues. I had settled for a quiet life, in every sense, even packing up the vinyl Mum used to love to listen to, or I had until Eli walked into it.

I'd set my alarm, but I didn't need the blackbird chorus to wake me on Monday morning because I'd barely slept. I'd gone to bed, determined to block out my concerns about

Eli's handsome face and his love of music, but that had simply freed up some space for the new job jitters.

I hadn't felt nervous about going into work for a very long time, and as I got ready to leave, in the thankfully silent house, I ran through my plans and the extra online research I'd undertaken in lieu of sleep. I willed myself to embrace my fluttery tummy as a positive thing. It was proof that I cared, I told myself. My nerves were simply evidence that I felt passionate about doing right by the residents and that could only be a good thing.

'No, no, no, no, no!' Eli yelped as he came flying out of his bedroom and we collided in the corridor leading down to the bathroom.

'Morning,' I said, quickly untangling myself before my mind became even more befuddled by his aftershave, or was it simply Eau de Eli?

'Morning,' he responded, taking a step back and looking seductively like he'd just leapt out of bed. 'Are you in a rush? Do you mind if I get in the bathroom first? I've overslept and I'm *so* late.'

'Be my guest,' I said, backing off. 'I was just going to brush my teeth. But I'm early. You carry on.'

'Thanks,' he said, returning to his room and grabbing a towel.

The bathroom door had barely closed behind him before the strains of something with a heavy bassline could be heard pulsing through the house. I walked back to my room and firmly closed the door, turning my attention to what I was going to wear, now I didn't have a uniform to make life easy for me.

'What's going on here then?' demanded Greta as Sara steered her into the dayroom, and she noticed more of her fellow residents than usual were gathered together. 'Are we having an assembly?' she asked, excitedly bouncing up and down. 'I used to love assembly. I used to love anything that got me out of class.'

Sara looked at me and rolled her eyes and then, noticing I wasn't in uniform, enquiringly raised her brows.

'What's going on?' she mouthed at me, while settling Greta into a low, squishy chair she hopefully wouldn't be able to wriggle out of too quickly.

'You'll find out soon enough,' said Sandra, who I hadn't spotted behind me. 'Now,' she added, looking around, 'is this everyone?'

'Almost,' I said with a nod to the door as Harold came in, closely followed by Ida.

'What's all this?' Harold frowned. 'I've barely finished my cornflakes.'

'Assembly!' Greta called out. 'We're having hymns.'

'Are we?' said Bob. 'I'm not religious, you know.'

Sara laughed out loud and Sandra stepped forward and clapped her hands, before the impromptu gathering collapsed into further chaos. Sometimes it felt like we were herding cats.

'Now,' she patiently said, 'I know you all have lots to do.'

'Do we?' tutted Ida.

'So, I'm not going to keep you long,' Sandra carried on as if she hadn't heard. 'I just thought it would be nice for us all to get together to meet our new activities manager.'

Her announcement was met with silence as everyone's eyes swung to the door. Well, almost everyone's. Harold was looking at me, the biggest grin lighting up his face. Sharp as a tack, he was.

'We've already met her,' said Greta, scrabbling to get up. 'That Karen creature, isn't it? Useless. I'm not doing macaroni again.'

Sara laid a hand on Greta's arm and she quietened.

'Karen,' said Sandra, her tone ever so slightly strained, 'was our *last* activities manager. We have someone else for the job now and she's going to be with us much longer than Karen was.'

'Is it you, love?' Ida asked, her gaze swinging back to me as the penny dropped and her eyes filled with bright tears.

'It is,' I said, stepping forward and hoping she wasn't going to set me off.

It wouldn't take much and I didn't think Sandra would think much of that.

'I wondered why you weren't in unform,' Ida sniffed, as she reached up her sleeve for her handkerchief.

'Sandra offered me the job last week,' I said, loud enough to make sure everyone could hear, 'and I took some time to think long and hard about whether I was up to it.'

'Of course you're up to it,' beamed Harold.

'You can't be worse than the last one,' chimed in Greta.

'Can't she?' frowned Bob.

'Thank you for the vote of confidence,' I laughed, ignoring Bob. 'I hope you're still going to be as pleased that I've agreed to take the role on when we get started on the new schedule.'

I was deeply touched by the round of applause that followed my announcement, but I could have lived without Charlie's whistle. His teeth didn't fit quite as well as they should and he could reach a pitch only dogs could hear. Sandra looked dumbstruck. I didn't think the 'assembly' was going quite as she had hoped. She somehow always managed to forget that the residents could be every bit as excitable as pre-schoolers.

'That's champion news,' said Harold, still clapping. 'Now we'll definitely have something worth getting out of bed for.'

'Something worth waking up for,' grinned Charlie. 'I was beginning to lose the will.'

Sandra looked shocked, but Sara and I laughed, knowing he was joking.

'Are we going to do colouring again?' asked Ida. 'I loved those sheets you copied last time.'

I was about to confirm that yes, there'd be more colouring, but Sandra cut me off.

'Beth is going to outline her plans for me this morning,' she importantly said, 'and I'll come back to you with her ideas after lunch.'

She turned to walk away, but that wasn't how I wanted my first day in the job to work.

'Actually,' I said, pulling a chair out from under the table for me to sit on and then another for her, 'I thought I might as well address you and the residents at the same time.'

Sandra didn't seem to know how to respond.

'It'll save going through everything twice,' I carried on, 'and as my new role is entirely resident-centred, I'd like them to hear what I have in mind, first-hand.'

You could have heard a pin drop. Even Greta seemed to understand the magnitude of the moment and didn't interrupt it.

'All right,' Sandra said stiffly, 'I suppose that does sound like a good idea.'

I wasn't sure if she meant that or if she was just saying it to save face. The cheeky wink Sara gave me left me in no doubt what she thought. Aware that everyone was waiting for me to begin, I took a deep breath and dived in.

'Now,' I began, 'I know that a few of you haven't been taking part in the activities recently.'

'A few of us!' huffed Bob. 'More like about ninety-seven point five per cent, if you want to put a figure on it.'

There was a murmur of agreement and Sandra shifted in her seat.

'I've never been any good at maths,' said Greta, 'but does that mean pretty much all of us?'

'It does,' boomed Charlie from further back, making us all jump. 'Bloody macramé,' he muttered. 'How can I do that with my arthritis?'

'So,' I said, raising my voice again, 'with that figure in

mind, I've decided not to start the activities programme straight away.'

'You haven't got anything for us to do?' Greta frowned and Bob shook his head.

'I have a whole list of ideas,' I told her, while looking pointedly at Bob, 'but before I start scheduling any of them in, I want to come around and talk to you all, individually, and ask you what it is *you'd* like to do.'

Sandra shifted again.

'You might like to think about things you enjoyed doing before you moved in here,' I suggested. 'There might be something old you want to pick up or something completely new you want to try.'

Sandra shook her head.

'Within limits,' she said and I shot her a look. 'There's not much in the kitty,' she whispered, 'and I don't want you getting their hopes up.'

'There are always ways to make things happen,' I said determinedly. 'I can be thrifty and I don't mind shopping around. We can call on the good spirit of the local community if we need a helping hand with a few things too,' I added. 'There's no point in repeating the same mistakes Karen made and setting activities up that no one wants to do just because they're cheap, is there?'

'There certainly isn't,' said Harold, proving his hearing was still as sharp as his eyesight. 'And I for one would like our trips out reinstated again.'

'I'm not going to make any hasty promises,' I said firmly,

before Sandra had an attack of the vapours and began to regret offering me the job, 'but I'm going to take all of your ideas on board. This week is going to be all about collecting ideas and information. A sort of factfinding mission. I want you all to be involved.'

'It's nice to be included,' said Ida. 'I've missed having a say.'

'And I love a mission,' said Greta. 'I had one in the war . . .'

Her voice trailed off and rather than point out how young she would have been in the war, I thought I'd better stick to the topic in hand.

'These will be *your* activities,' I reiterated, 'so I want you to enjoy them and I'm going to ask for volunteers to help me sort through the resources cupboards and boxes too. I had a look in them earlier and found they're in a bit of a sorry state.'

'You can't ask residents to do that,' Sandra said sharply.

'Yes, I can,' I calmly responded. 'I want them to take ownership of this new phase in the home's development. Involvement at every level.'

The online research I'd read said it had made a huge difference to morale and engagement. I would make a success of this and if necessary, I would drag Sandra along with me until she caught up. She'd offered me the job and I was going to do it properly.

'But they're not all up to it,' she hissed.

'A lot of us are,' said Harold. 'I've been itching to get rid of those bloody jigsaws with the bits missing.'

'And the art supplies are grotty too,' said Ida. 'Some of the crayons are only about an inch long.'

'I'll sort those,' I told Sandra, before she flagged them up as a choking hazard. 'And I'm going to scour the charity shops and car boots for things too. Harold's right – those puzzles do need replacing.'

'You'll have to do that in your own time,' said Sandra.

'I'm happy to,' I smiled. 'I don't mind at all. I really want this to work, Sandra.'

She looked at me and then back at the faces of those residents still listening. There were a surprising number. Quite often they drifted off – either to sleep or by foot – but this hardcore crowd were a keen bunch and that filled my heart with hope and lifted my freshly found spirit, which had started to flag after Eli's lyrical announcement. Not even Bob's still-sceptical expression could dampen my enthusiasm.

'Given the number of empty beds,' Sandra said, turning to look at me again, 'so do I. A decent engagement level is bound to appeal to new residents and I know you're the right person for the job, Beth.'

I let out a breath I hadn't realised I'd been holding.

'I wouldn't have taken it on if I didn't think I could bring something new and worthwhile to the position,' I boldly said.

'I know,' she nodded, 'and I wouldn't have offered it to you in the first place if I didn't think the same. It's just going to take a bit of getting used to; you're obviously going to work very differently to Karen.'

'Thank goodness,' said Harold, still earwigging.

'Thank goodness,' Sandra smiled in agreement.

I pulled a new notebook out of my bag and clicked the pen that came with it.

'I've done my research,' I told her as she stood up and smoothed down her skirt, 'and I'm not going to let you down.'

'I know,' she said, making for the door. 'I know you won't. My heart is one hundred per cent certain that you're the perfect fit for the job, Beth.'

I held my breath again, waiting for Harold to say something about being surprised that she had a heart, but thankfully he didn't. She couldn't have been out of earshot before another, louder, cheer went up though and Greta, finally free from the confines of the chair, along with Ida and Harold, pulled me into a group hug.

'I knew it,' said Harold.

'*We* knew it,' Ida gently reminded him.

'Knew what?' frowned Greta.

'Didn't we say you were the woman for the job?' Harold crowed.

'You did,' I swallowed, feeling a little choked. 'Did either of you have anything to do with Sandra offering me it, by any chance?'

'No,' said Ida, and I believed her. 'This opportunity is all down to you, my love. We told you, you made quite an impact that time Karen was off. Thank goodness she was sick, or whatever she was off doing.'

'Yes,' said Greta, although I knew she wasn't really keeping up. 'Thank goodness.'

Sometimes I thought she just liked to join in.

'Hey, you dark horse,' said Sara, rushing over, having just escorted Charlie back to his room. 'Congratulations.'

'Thank you,' I said. 'I still can't believe it.'

'Well,' she said, 'you deserve it.'

'You wouldn't have fancied it?' I asked, wondering if the position had been advertised, she might have applied for it.

'No,' she said, 'it's not for me. I've got more than enough to keep me busy, what with my shifts here and my commitment to the Iceni group. There's as much to do behind the scenes there as at the actual events.'

And then there was the writing which Kate had unguardedly mentioned, but as Sara didn't list that, I didn't mention it either.

'Don't forget I said I'd help with sewing up your new tunic,' I reminded her instead.

'Hey!' cut in Harold, sounding even more excited. 'Does this mean you've jumped up the pay scale, Beth?'

Damn. He was going to guess, before I had a chance to tell him.

'Sorry,' he said, when I didn't immediately answer, 'I'm not being nosey. I just thought that if you had a few more pounds in your pocket at the end of every month, then you might be able to take Kate's room in Nightingale Square.'

'Oh yes,' said Sara.

'I'm going back to the Grow-Well with Sara this week,' Harold bowled on. 'Shall I ask Kate if you can take another look at it?'

I shook my head.

'There's no point, Harold,' I said, 'I happen to know it's already gone.'

'Oh bugger,' he muttered, looking upset and Sara's shoulders slumped too.

'Because I've taken it!' I squealed.

'What?' Harold gasped.

'I moved in on Saturday!'

'You crafty beggar,' he spluttered, as Sara gave me a hug.

'That's fantastic,' she beamed. 'How are you finding it?'

'Wonderful,' I said, refusing to acknowledge the bassline that had been playing on a loop in my head ever since Eli had disappeared into the bathroom earlier that morning. 'It's absolutely wonderful,' I blagged.

I would just have to find a way to drown out the music at home safe in the knowledge that at least it was something I wouldn't have to worry about while I was at work.

'I've just thought of something for that list of yours,' said Greta, sounding surprisingly lucid, as she clicked her fingers and pushed her way further into the group. 'I want a singalong!' she demanded. 'We never have a singalong anymore.'

Chapter 8

Thankfully, Greta seemed to forget her musical request almost as soon as she'd made it, but I had no such luck at home. Just as he'd previously explained, Eli wasn't in the house all that often, but I was in absolutely no doubt as to when he was in residence.

Unlike the Queen, he didn't need a flag to signify his presence, because music, of all kinds, filled the house and made me even more aware of his existence. It wasn't ear-splitting or anything, but it was loud enough to make me constantly mindful of it and as a result, the quiet of the care home was even sweeter.

'How's it going?' Harold asked one morning towards the end of the week. 'Are you getting there with the clear-out now?'

'I think so,' I said, looking at the piles of jigsaws I'd just deposited on the table and which were on the agenda for sorting through. 'I'm going to set up an ideas board today. Sandra has said I can use the empty pinboard in reception next to where she's advertising the garden party, along with the list of empty rooms.'

Harold nodded and gave a wry smile.

'What?' I frowned.

'Perfect placement,' he pointed out. 'Everyone coming and going will see it there, won't they? I bet she's keen to let the relatives know that you, and by association, she, has got everyone's mental health and well-being at the top of the agenda now.'

'You sound almost cynical, Harold,' I chuckled, but he was right. I hadn't thought about it before, but it was a strategic suggestion on the manager's part.

'Realistic, my love,' he said, 'not cynical. Anyway, I meant are *you* getting there? As in, how are you settling into your new job and your new home?'

I let out a long breath and took a few seconds to think it all through.

'You've had a heck of a lot of upheaval in the last few days,' Harold added, as if I needed reminding.

'I have,' I agreed.

'And all of it on the back of your mum's anniversary. You must be shattered.'

My mind tracked back over the week and, the unexpected and unwanted re-introduction of music into my life aside, I realised it had actually been pretty straightforward. I'd even managed to forget my thoughts about Pete by purposefully walking to work on the opposite side of the road to On the Box. Well, they were almost forgotten.

'I am tired,' I told Harold. 'But in a good way.'

He nodded in understanding.

'The house is absolutely lovely and I've enjoyed joining some of the neighbours on the green in the evenings, which is a wonderful way to wind down after working with you lot,' Harold smiled. 'But I haven't had the chance to spend too much time in the Grow-Well yet. I'm on watering duty this weekend though so that will rectify that and of course, getting stuck in with everything here has been brilliant.'

'I thought I'd see less of you, but actually I reckon you've been putting in more hours than ever,' Harold said with a smile.

'You're right,' I agreed, 'but that's not going to be the norm. I just wanted to throw myself into getting the new programme established so I know it's happening in the right way, right from the off.'

'No point going at it half arsed.'

'Exactly,' I said, my lips twitching into a smile to match his.

'Well, you've certainly made an impact.'

We both peered into the cavernous resources cupboard and I felt my smile falter. There was an awful lot of empty space, most of the shelves were bare now, but there had been no point hanging onto scraps and junk no one would ever use.

'I've only thrown away the rubbish,' I said, as much to myself as Harold.

I had said the same to Sandra who had looked horrified when I showed her the pared back results of mine and the residents' labour.

'But there's nothing left,' she had squeaked. 'How can you do activities with no resources?'

'There were no resources here to do activities with,' I said firmly, playing down the jitters the empty shelves were giving me as well. 'Half of the stuff was broken, run down or worn out. You can look through it all if you like. It's bagged, but not binned yet.'

'No, no,' she stoically rallied. 'I know you're right.'

She'd then taken me into the office and told me how much I could spend to re-stock. It wasn't much, nowhere near what I needed, but it would be a start and I had set my mind to trying to come up with ways to boost the activities bank account.

'I'm going shopping this weekend,' I told Harold. 'The charity shops are always full of puzzles and games and I thought I might try A Good Book for some more varied reading material.'

The current bookshelf was looking as sorry for itself as the one at the train station. A few battered paperbacks and some old copies of *Saga* magazine were hardly enticing everyone to peruse the shelves. I wanted to offer a bit of everything, fiction and non-fiction, to appeal to as many of the residents' tastes as possible.

'Perhaps you could put a sign on that new board asking relatives if they'd like to contribute,' said Ida, who had tottered up.

She had her slippers on the wrong feet, so I guided her to a chair to swap them over.

'I didn't think they felt right,' she tutted.

'I don't think Beth can ask relatives for money,' said Greta, also joining in.

'I didn't mean money,' said Ida, wiggling her toes. 'I meant she could ask if they wanted to contribute books and puzzles and things.'

'That's a great idea,' I told her and she looked well pleased. 'Do you fancy designing the poster?'

She and Greta settled at a table, companionably for the moment, making use of the few pens I'd salvaged that still had a bit of ink left in them. I'd sent off an order for all sorts of craft materials, including crayons and felt tips, but it wouldn't be arriving for a few days.

'So,' said Harold as he and Charlie began sorting through the battered boxes of jigsaws, 'work's all right and you love the house and the garden.'

'Yes,' I said, holding one of the jigsaw box lids together so Charlie could fix it with some tape. 'Everything's coming up roses.'

'But what about your housemate? You haven't mentioned him,' Harold pointed out. 'How are you finding life with Elijah?'

'Well . . .' I began.

Should I go into specifics or say something general? I certainly couldn't tell Harold that I fancied the pants off my housemate, could I? And I didn't want to bring up my feelings about his love of music either because that would risk exposing my aversion to it and potentially remind Greta of her request for a singalong.

'He's great, isn't he?' Harold smiled, before I answered.

There was no disputing that.

'He's lovely,' I readily agreed. 'Although I haven't seen all that much of him because he's working extra shifts at the coffeehouse.'

'Well,' said Harold, 'if you're on watering duty this weekend, he will be too. It's organised by household.'

'Is it?' I hadn't realised that when Lisa had explained what I would need to do.

'It is,' he said, 'so you'll have plenty of opportunity to see more of him this weekend, won't you?'

'Yes,' I said, feeling my tummy do a little flip, 'I suppose I will.'

'How's that?' asked Greta, shoving the sheet of paper I'd given her and Ida under my nose. 'Good enough?'

'It's perfect,' I said, moving the sheet far enough away so the words fell into focus. 'I'll pin it up straight away and ask Sandra if we can keep a box in reception for any contributions.'

'But not anywhere where we might trip over it,' said Ida.

'Of course,' I said. 'We'll keep it behind the desk.'

'I might trip over it there,' said Greta.

'You're not supposed to be behind the desk,' Charlie gruffly pointed out.

'I know,' Greta bristled, standing a full half a centimetre taller, 'but sometimes they need my help.'

Charlie snorted and I could sense Greta was getting annoyed.

'Why don't you come and give me a hand, Greta?' I said diplomatically. 'You can tell me if I'm putting it up straight.'

By the end of Friday there were already a couple of contributions in the box and some activity suggestions added to the list for me to mull over during the weekend. I'd stuck a piece of paper over the strip poker request, which no one would own up to adding. I was almost tempted to do the same to Greta's singalong idea. I had thought she'd forgotten about it, but apparently not.

'What do you reckon?' she asked eagerly, when she saw me writing the requests down in my notebook. 'That would liven them all up a bit, wouldn't it?'

I was amused that she didn't add herself to the contingent whom she felt needed livening up and looking at her mischievous expression, I knew she was right not to.

'Um,' I said, 'it probably would, but we might struggle for music.'

'But we've got the piano.'

'I know,' I sighed, 'but no one to play it.'

It broke my heart that she looked so crestfallen and I felt guilty too. I was supposed to be doing my utmost to give the residents what they wanted, not tailor their requests to fit my own agenda. We had a CD player somewhere, so I supposed we could use that at some point if it really meant that much to her. Perhaps I could convince one of the other carers to oversee it all. Preferably when I wasn't there.

'What about a pet?' Greta then asked, eyeing the list again and picking out the most improbable suggestion. 'Can we have a pony? Sandra's always moaning about the cost of keeping up with the garden. It could eat the lawn.'

I hated that Sandra talked about that sort of thing in front of the residents. I knew funds were tight and the empty beds were a worry, all of the staff knew that, but the people living in the home didn't need to be made aware of it.

'I'm hoping to find a way to get some of you doing a bit of gardening,' I told Greta, by way of equine diversion. I was going to talk to Sandra about introducing houseplants too. They would benefit everyone, but especially those who didn't feel inclined to, or couldn't, get outside. 'Would you like to grow some things, Greta?'

'Have you heard of naked gardening day?' she seriously asked, laying a hand on my arm. 'It happens at the beginning of May, so we've missed it for this year, but maybe next . . .'

'A pony might be a bit on the large side,' I interrupted, tracking back to her other idea and wondering if she was the strip poker suggester, 'and I'm not sure we could manage to have a pet full time. Do you know who added a pet to the list?'

Greta shook her head.

'I did,' said Charlie, who was waiting in reception for hospital transport. 'And you watched me write it, Greta.'

'Did I?' she shrugged, before wandering off.

Charlie shook his head.

'What sort of pet did you have in mind?' I asked him.

'I know we can't really have an animal here,' he said, 'but I do miss my old dog, Monty.'

'I'm guessing you had to leave him behind when you moved in?'

I knew lots of people had to part with pets when they moved into residential care. It was heartbreaking for both them and the animal they were leaving.

'No,' Charlie said, 'thankfully he passed away a couple of weeks before I came in. Oh dear, that sounds awful,' he tutted.

'No, it doesn't,' I told him. 'I completely understand and I promise I will think about what we can do on the pet front.'

As I walked back to Nightingale Square that evening, a broad smile lit up my face. Sandra had just acknowledged that the week had gone well, better than she had expected it to, in fact. She said there was a definite buzz about the place and she was looking forward to the following week and seeing a couple of the activities up and running.

I was looking forward to that too, but first I had a free weekend to enjoy. I had work plans of course, along with Grow-Well duty and some chores to catch up on, but it was an absolute joy to not be dreading time spent in the place where I lived, assuming I was home alone of course. If only I could have guaranteed two days' worth of silence, I would have really struck gold.

I did have the house entirely to myself on Saturday, once Eli had left for the coffeehouse and truth be told, I could have quite happily spent the whole day pottering about, enjoying the quiet and hanging out with my houseplants, but the shops beckoned. I wasn't an enthusiastic shopper when it came to buying things for myself, but I was itching to thriftily refill the resources cupboard and headed out optimistically, my pockets filled with reusable bags.

I hit the charity shops first and found a great variety of boardgames and jigsaws. Most of them looked as though they'd hardly been used and I was tempted to nab the lot, but settled for a selection which would suit all abilities. There was no point in splashing out on an intricate thousand-piece jigsaw when no one had good enough eyesight to put it together. It would have been too much of a stretch, even for Harold.

'My kids used to love this,' said the woman behind the till as she rang up my purchases. 'It's great for testing their memory.'

'That's why I'm buying it,' I smiled, carefully packing the shopping list game into one of my bags. 'But I'm working at the other end of the age scale.'

I explained who I was buying the game for. Greta was going to love it, as long as she could keep her competitive streak in check. I wouldn't allow any arguing over the trolleys.

'Hang on,' said the shop assistant, disappearing into the back. 'I seem to remember we had the extension game come in sometime this week. You might want to take that too.'

I did and already weighed down, I decided to drop everything off at the house before trying the bookshop. If I struck lucky in there too, I'd never be able to carry everything. I wondered if Sandra might come and pick me up Monday morning, otherwise I was going to be a bit stuck for getting it all delivered to the home.

It was busy in the bookshop, so I browsed for a while and helped myself to a cold drink which was on offer at the front of the shop, next to a seating area set aside for reading.

'Is there anything I can help you with?' the owner asked, once it had quietened down again. 'Are you looking for anything in particular?'

'I need a selection of books,' I said, a little unsure of what exactly to go for. 'Fiction and non-fiction.'

The shop owner, who told me his name was Colin, listened intently as I told him what I thought I needed and where it was for.

'I know I'm doing myself out of business,' he said, once I'd finished explaining, 'but you'd be better off borrowing from the library than buying from me.'

'I didn't even think of the library,' I flushed, embarrassed that I hadn't factored it into my plans. 'Do you think they'd lend to a residential home?'

'Of course,' he said, walking to the till and pulling a scrap of paper out from under the counter. 'You can sign up to the borrow box scheme and they'll select, deliver and collect for you.'

'They will?'

What a wonderful service.

'Yes,' he said, scribbling something down. 'If you ask the residents what sort of books they like, which genre and subject, then pass the info on to this lady,' he added, handing me the sheet he'd written a name on once he'd checked where the home was, 'then she'll sort it all out for you and exchange it every few weeks.'

'That's an amazing scheme.'

'It is,' Colin nodded. 'And they do it for schools too, especially if there's a student with a need that the school library can't cater for. I know someone whose daughter has a Lithuanian friend. She couldn't speak any English when she moved to the UK, so the library sourced books in Lithuanian to help ease her transition.'

'That's fantastic,' I said, carefully folding the paper and slipping it into my pocket. 'Thank you so much.'

'My pleasure. Let me know how you get on.'

'I will,' I promised.

I made a mental note to ask everyone what they fancied reading the following week and then bought three books for myself, to make up for the lack of sales Colin's kindness had made him miss out on.

With my shopping complete, I decided to treat myself to some lunch in the Castle Coffeehouse. I was sure they must serve snacks and would sell drinks other than coffee. I headed back up the street and was level with On the Box in just a few strides.

It was too late to cross the road and before I could talk myself out of the unexpected impulse, I opened the door and stepped inside. It was a shocking manoeuvre but my feet had bowled me over the threshold before I'd even had a chance to catch my breath. And talk about a blast from the past.

It all looked, felt and smelt so achingly familiar. In fact, I wouldn't have been at all surprised to see my younger self propping up the counter and hear Pete droning on about the newest sci-fi merch he was going to set out on display.

A lump formed in my throat as I wished I hadn't let our relationship slide off my radar. Pete might have been inexorably linked to The Arches and everything there I had wanted to forget, but he was the closest person I'd ever had to a brother. I knew that realistically it was far too late to start thinking it, but that didn't stop the regret forming and sitting heavy in my heart.

'Can I help?'

I spun around to find a sulky-looking teen staring at me from the other end of the aisle.

'No,' I said, clearing my throat. 'Thanks. I'm just browsing.'

She didn't look much bothered about whatever I was doing.

'Cos I don't know much about that lot,' she said, nodding to the display case of figurines I found myself standing in front of. 'My Uncle Pete's the expert. He'll be back in a minute if you want to wait.'

I felt as though all the air had been squeezed out of my lungs and I hastily burst back out of the shop and onto the pavement.

'Ouch,' I yelped as a woman with a buggy rammed my ankles.

'I'm so sorry,' she said.

'It was my fault,' I said, hobbling away as quickly as I could, 'I wasn't looking where I was going.'

My heart was still clattering when I got back to the house and my hand shook as I turned the key in the door. How was it possible that Pete still worked in the shop? How had his dreams reached no further than mine? And more to the point, now I knew he was in such close proximity, what was I going to do about it?

Eli rushed in, just as I was about to head over to the Grow-Well for my stint of watering. My nerves had only slightly settled since I'd spent the afternoon curled up in his armchair trying to work out what I was going to do about the Pete problem, but they were set off again as my housemate barged through the door and straight into me.

Clashing in corridors was becoming a habit.

'I'm coming!' he said breathlessly, once he'd righted me again. 'Just give me thirty seconds.'

I pointed to my ears and shook my head.

'Sorry,' he puffed, pulling out his earbuds. 'Was I shouting?'

'Just a bit.'

'Sorry,' he said again, quieter this time. 'Will you wait for me? You'll wait, won't you?'

'Yes,' I told him. 'Of course I'll wait.'

'Great,' he said, taking the stairs two at a time.

True to his word, we were out the door less than a minute later. He was wearing completely different clothes, but then I already knew how fast he was at getting undressed.

'I never thought I was going to finish today,' he said, as we crossed the green. He was still catching his breath. 'I'm knackered.'

'You're going to need a holiday by the time your boss comes back,' I acknowledged. 'How's she doing?'

'Well,' he said. 'Really well. She's home now and according to her best mate, bored witless so definitely on the mend.'

'That's great,' I smiled.

'And as of this afternoon, we've got another member of staff,' Eli carried on. 'He's someone who knows enough about the place to be left in charge which means I've been given tomorrow off and from next week, my schedule will be pretty much back to normal.'

'Well, that's even better,' I said.

He certainly looked as though he needed a break, but I hoped that didn't mean he was going to be playing music all of the next day.

'Has the new member of staff worked at the Coffeehouse before?' I asked.

'Yes,' he said, keying in the gate security code. 'He's a student but he's worked with Melanie, that's my boss, for years. He's back in Norwich on summer break and has taken the job on again.'

'That's a bit of luck.'

'You can say that again,' he smiled, holding the gate open and letting me in before closing it. 'But that's enough about my work. I want to hear all about yours. We haven't had a chance to chat this week, but Sara came in for lunch one day and said you'd started something new. You didn't mention a change in your role to me before, did you?'

'No,' I said, 'I don't think so.'

'We've hardly seen each other though really, have we?' he frowned. 'So, you wouldn't have had the chance.'

'No,' I agreed. 'We haven't. Although I have heard you.'

Eli looked a bit sheepish and ran a hand through his hair.

'You'll have to let me know if you want me to turn the music down.'

I wondered what he'd say if I asked him to switch if off completely.

'It's not that bad,' I fibbed, 'but maybe you could just dial it down a little.'

'Consider it done,' he said, opening up the bothy and setting out a couple of chairs. 'Let's have a breather before we start the watering, shall we? You can tell me what you're doing now and how it's going.'

It was so easy to talk to Eli, although a little distracting when he leant forward to listen and pinned me with his intensely blue gaze. He had a way of making me feel as though I was the only person in the world worth listening to and I knew my face was flushed. I hoped he assumed that was because of my excitement about the new job rather than the influence of his undivided attention.

'That's an amazing job,' he said, sitting back in his chair again when I had finished talking. 'And an important one too, isn't it?'

I was delighted he could see the value in and appreciate the importance of what it meant to be an activities manager.

'I think so,' I said, feeling my face grow even warmer. 'I'm taking it very seriously.'

'I can tell,' he smiled. 'It's one hell of a responsibility but it sounds like you've got off to a great start.'

'So far, so good,' I said, 'although naked gardening and strip poker are definitely not going to happen.'

He laughed as I explained about the two more risqué requests that had appeared on the suggestions list.

'And I don't think keeping a pet's very likely either,' I added, biting my lip.

'I feel sorry for Charlie,' Eli said sympathetically, 'even though old Monty passed on before he had to leave him.'

'Me too.'

'But you know,' he said, narrowing his eyes in thought, 'I think there is something you could try on that front.'

'Oh?'

He pulled his phone out of his pocket and began typing.

'Here you go,' he said, holding it out for me to take. 'This could be your answer.'

I read through what he'd found.

'This is perfect, Eli!' I said, scrolling down the page. 'And they're local.'

'I read about the group in a community magazine,' he told me. 'They'll jump at the chance to come and visit.'

He had found a pet therapy website and a group of local volunteers, all vetted, no pun intended, who visited schools and care homes with their dogs and a few other pets. They stayed anything between an hour or two to all day.

'We could have the benefit of canine interaction without the responsibility, couldn't we?' I said, my eyes flicking back to his face. 'There would be no squabbling or monopolising either.'

If I'd somehow talked Sandra into having a dog on site permanently, I could well imagine a couple of the residents trying to take over completely. Getting ahead of myself, I wondered if there was a charity who visited with Shetland ponies. Greta would be beside herself! Best stick to dogs, first. Assuming Sandra agreed to it of course.

'Exactly,' Eli said, standing up and stretching out his back and neck before rolling his shoulders.

I had another brief glimpse of his tanned tummy and hastily looked away.

'And the residents who don't like dogs, or who are allergic,' he carried on, 'won't have to worry about bumping into one all the time.'

Being a dog lover myself, I hadn't even thought about that.

'And,' he further added, clicking his fingers, 'if the residents have had to leave pets behind when they moved in and they're still in the family, maybe you could set something up so they can visit. Some sort of access programme.'

'Genius,' I smiled.

'Why, thank you.' He bowed.

'Conundrum completely solved,' I grinned, also standing up, and handing him back his phone. My skin tingled as his fingers briefly touched mine. 'I'll print some info off to show my boss on Monday.'

I was going to have to think of a way to increase the activities budget sooner rather than later if Eli kept coming up with such great ideas.

'Anything else I can help with?' he grinned, looking me straight in the eye.

'Just the watering for now,' I swallowed, handing him the hose and wondering if he felt the same flicker of attraction for me as I most definitely felt for him. 'But I'll keep you posted.'

Chapter 9

All the time I was in the Grow-Well with Eli, I had managed to block out thoughts of Pete, but once in bed, I spent at least an hour mulling over what I would have done if he, rather than his niece, had been in the shop when I indulged in my trip down memory lane. Consequently, I didn't expect to nod off at all, but I did.

I slept surprisingly well and woke early, eager to write up and print off everything Eli and I had discussed the day before, along with a couple of other ideas I'd come up with myself. I made an effort to be quiet as I moved about the house, so as not to wake him as I caught up with my chores.

By the time we had called it a night, he had slept through most of the film we had settled to watch, and I imagined he'd been out for the count ever since. It was all a far cry from the three musketeers I'd formerly lived with, drunkenly staggering in in the early hours and as a result ruining my Sunday mood. In spite of the soundtrack which accompanied it, everything about my new life in Nightingale Square was a million miles away from my previous houseshare and I felt exceedingly grateful for that.

'Hey,' croaked a voice from the dining room long after I'd eaten breakfast.

I was in the kitchen packing a few things for the picnic everyone was convening in the Grow-Well to share. As we were still on watering duty, Eli and I had decided we would walk over together.

'Hey,' I said back.

He appeared in the doorway, seductively ruffled from sleep and looking what I could only describe as apprehensive.

'What are you doing?' I asked as he hung back. 'Are you okay?'

'Yeah,' he said, 'I'm good. Are you on your own?'

'Of course I'm on my own,' I frowned, looking about the kitchen just in case we had a visitor I'd missed. 'What are you talking about?'

I wondered if he was sleepwalking and perhaps not awake at all.

'I thought I heard talking,' he said, finally stepping in and also looking around.

'Well, no one's phoned or called in,' I told him.

'It was earlier,' he elaborated, reaching for the kettle. 'I thought you'd maybe had a grown-up sleepover or something.'

I felt my face begin to flame as I realised what he must have heard. I had forgotten the dividing wall between the bathroom and his bedroom wasn't all that thick, but I hadn't realised he could hear me talking, even if it wasn't to another person.

'No,' I swallowed, refuting his assumption that a bedtime booty call had been made. 'No grown-up sleepover. It's been a very long time since I've had one of those.'

Why did I say that? I didn't want him thinking I was some sad single with no sex life. But then I didn't want him thinking I was the sort of person who just hooked up with someone on a casual basis either. But more to the point, why was I getting so hot and bothered about what Eli thought?

'Okay,' he said. 'Right. Well, I just thought I'd mention it because it would be fine if you had. Boys, or girls, are allowed to stay over. As far as I'm concerned anyway. What do you think? That's an all-right house rule, isn't it?'

'Yes,' I said, 'that's fine. Of course it is. We're both adults.'

'We are.'

'Right,' I further agreed.

'Not that either of us would want to wake up and find some random wandering about the house though,' he then added.

'We wouldn't,' I quickly confirmed. 'And you needn't worry about that on my part. That's really not my style.'

He ran a hand through his hair and smiled, looking far happier.

'Nor mine,' he said on an out breath.

I passed him his favourite mug from the shelf and our eyes locked.

'So, are you single then, Beth?'

'Ever so,' I said, trying to look away but finding I couldn't. 'You?'

'Terminally,' he said, finally breaking eye contact and banishing the smile that had made a brief appearance. 'I've had enough of love to last me a lifetime.'

Heartbreak bounced about the walls, but I didn't ask what had happened in his life to make him form such a resolute-sounding opinion.

'But you were talking this morning, weren't you?' he carried on, tracking back. 'I did hear you chatting to someone.'

'Sort of,' I mumbled.

'Either you were or you weren't.' He frowned.

'I was talking to my plants,' I said quietly, avoiding his gaze by stacking a few used dishes next to the sink.

I could have kicked myself. What I should have said was that I was on the phone. That would have made far more sense and easily explained the one-sided nature of what he'd no doubt heard.

'You were talking to your plants,' Eli repeated.

'Yep,' I said, my cheeks further flaming.

'Cool,' he grinned. 'My grandma used to do that.'

My gaze swung back to meet his.

'She did?'

'Yeah,' he said. 'All the time. She reckoned they were great listeners and she always won any arguments they had.'

I let out a snort of laughter.

'Well, your grandma was right,' I grinned. 'You should

give it a go yourself. I can thrash out all sorts of dilemmas and decisions talking to mine.'

'I might just do that,' he smiled back. 'Unless you've got an Audrey lurking somewhere?'

'An Audrey?'

'You know, from *Little Shop of Horrors*.'

'Oh,' I giggled. 'No, you're all right. There's no Audrey in my collection.'

'I'm pleased to hear it.'

'Although,' I admitted, 'I do think I get a response to what I'm saying sometimes.'

'You do?'

I nodded.

'Do you know who the response comes from?'

His tone was loaded with interest rather than ridicule. And of course, I had known it would be. I wouldn't have mentioned my imagined horticultural two-way chats otherwise.

'Yes,' I said, taking a deep breath. 'It's my mum.'

'Wouldn't it be easier to just give her a ring?'

'If only,' I sighed. 'She died a couple of years ago.'

'Oh Beth,' swallowed Eli, sounding mortified. 'I'm so sorry. That was a stupid thing to say. I should have realised.'

'No, you shouldn't,' I said, shaking my head. 'How could you have known?'

'What happened to her?' he asked. 'If you don't mind me asking. Tell me to shut up if you'd rather not say.'

'She had a stroke,' I told him. 'A life-changing one struck first, the result of an undiagnosed heart condition, and she couldn't garden anymore so I encouraged her to help me look after my houseplants instead.'

'I see,' Eli said softly.

'They enabled her to still connect with nature. Not in the same way as getting outside and mowing the lawn or walking in the woods, but it was a connection nonetheless. She could tend to them, with my support, and that provided a much-needed boost to her mental health. The sight of green things growing always lifted her mood. And mine.'

'Was it just the two of you?' Eli asked.

'Yes,' I nodded. 'Just us. She had me when she was very young and lost all contact with her family as a result. We never talked about my dad. I have no idea who he even was.'

Eli didn't say anything further and I carried on.

'We were adding to the plant collection right up until she died,' I said, feeling the familiar weight press down on my chest. 'She didn't survive the second stroke and once she'd gone ... well ... I know this will sound a bit out there ...'

'Go on.'

I looked at Eli's face. He was doing that thing again, making me feel like the only person in the world worth listening to. In spite of the topic of conversation, it was very seductive.

'Well,' I swallowed, 'I felt as though I could still talk to her, through the plants, and I fell into the habit of telling her things as I tended them. I started giving her a precis of everything that was happening in my life and I've never got out of the habit. That was what you heard this morning. I'm sorry if my rambling woke you up.'

Eli didn't say anything.

'You think I'm totally bonkers, don't you?' I self-consciously laughed.

I couldn't really believe I'd just told him. I'd known him no time at all and yet I felt comfortable enough around him to have said all of that. It was quite a shock.

'No,' he said seriously. 'Far from it.'

'Really?'

'Really,' he nudged. 'You and my grandma would have got on like a house on fire, Beth.'

'She sounds like she was a wonderful woman.'

'She was,' said Eli. 'And so does your mum.'

'She was the best,' I confirmed. 'I'm sorry if that was a bit of an overshare though. My head's all over the place at the moment.'

'It wasn't,' he said. 'Not at all. But I'm not surprised. About your head, I mean. You've had a house move *and* a promotion all in the same week – that's pretty full-on, you know.'

As was discovering my gorgeous new housemate was mad on music, but I didn't say that.

'I suppose it is a bit much to cram into just a few days,' I smiled.

I turned back to the sink to start washing the dishes.

'Have you added to the collection since your mum died?' Eli asked.

'A bit,' I said, 'but not in the same numbers as before. I've had to replace a couple that didn't survive when I had to move house after she'd gone.'

I'd really struggled with the guilt of that on top of everything else. It felt like I'd let Mum down.

'I think you should buy one of those moss ball things you talked about before,' Eli said, turning the kettle on again because it had been a while since it had boiled.

'You do?'

'Yeah,' he said. 'It would be something completely different. Kind of like putting your own stamp on the collection.'

'Are you actually encouraging me to buy more plants?' I laughed.

'Why not?' he grinned. 'They make you happy, don't they?'

'They do,' I blushed.

'Then go for it. You should do whatever makes you happy, Beth. Life's too short not to.' His words cut off and he drifted off for a second, before adding with a frown, 'Right?'

'Right,' I agreed.

I left him scrolling through his Spotify playlists looking for something that would make him happy and a short while later I heard the sound of gentle guitar strumming coming from his room. It didn't sound as though it was coming through a speaker and I wondered if there was more to Eli's love of music than I had initially realised.

'I've got one veggie skewer left!' shouted John from his station behind the barbecue in the Grow-Well. 'Who wants it?'

'I'll have it, Dad,' said Archie, who seemed to have hollow legs.

I'd eaten so much that I didn't think I would be able to move, but as the meal had been a vegetarian feast, I didn't feel anywhere near as bloated as I would have done if I'd been eating burgers squeezed between bread.

Looking at my neighbours, some deep in conversation and others gardening, while the children played and fussed Violet and Dash, the cats, I guessed they felt the same. Everyone had turned out to enjoy the sunshine and further welcome me and I finally felt that I was getting to grips with everyone's names. Although some of the kids were still a little hazy.

'How did your shopping trip for puzzles and things go yesterday?' Harold asked.

He and Sara had joined us, along with Chloe, who volunteered in the main garden, and her partner, Hannah. Consequently, there hadn't been a single spare seat around the table when we settled to eat, which was wonderful.

'Good,' I told him. 'I found loads and I've got more great ideas too, thanks to Eli.'

'Oh?' Harold eagerly said.

'I'm going to run them by Sandra before I tell you,' I told him. 'Just in case she says no.'

'She won't say no,' said Sara. 'You're flavour of the month with her now the relatives have been commenting on the board and dropping things off.'

'Is the box filling up?' I asked.

'It's bulging,' said Harold. 'You'll have loads to sort out tomorrow.'

'Excellent,' I said, 'and we'll be starting the new activities itinerary in a couple of days.'

'You're not hanging about then,' said Harold, with approval.

'No,' I told him. 'Now I have an idea of what everyone wants, I'm keen to capitalise on their excitement and enthusiasm.'

'Grand,' he grinned. 'And don't worry about Bob. He'll come around eventually.'

I hoped so. The last thing I needed was him dampening the spark I was working so hard to ignite.

'How did the Iceni meeting go yesterday, Sara?' I asked, before I started to fret.

I knew she had been hoping to be offered the role of Boudicca. As she hadn't mentioned it yet, I didn't think she'd got it, but I wanted her to know that I hadn't been so self-absorbed in the last few days that I hadn't taken on board what was going on with her.

'It was good,' she said. 'I didn't get Boudicca but I'm number one understudy if the woman who did can't do it for any reason.'

'That's great,' I said, because it was definitely a step in the right direction.

'It is,' she agreed. 'And not that I'll be ill wishing her or anything, but I hope to get at least one go at it before the end of the season.'

'And tell her the rest,' Harold insisted, giving Sara a nudge.

'Oh Harold,' she tutted.

'What?' I asked.

Sara shook her head.

'There's a fella who fancies her,' Harold carried on, regardless of whether she wanted him to or not. 'He hasn't asked her out yet, but it's only a matter of time.'

Sara turned bright red.

'Now Harold,' I scolded, 'I daresay that was meant to be private.'

'It's all right,' said Sara, giving him a hard stare. 'The cat's out of the bag now, but I don't think it's really going to come to anything. He's too shy. He stares a lot, not in a creepy way, but he never actually talks to me.'

'You could ask him out,' Harold suggested.

'Is he part of the group too?' I asked.

'Sort of,' she said. 'He takes the photos for us and does a few sketches. He doesn't take part in the re-enactment himself, but he's a very talented artist.'

If Kate was right about Sara's secret writing, then a creatively talented partner might be just what she needed.

'So,' she carried on, obviously eager to move on from the subject of her shy admirer, 'are you still going to have time to help me sew up my new tunic?'

'Of course,' I insisted. 'Absolutely.'

'But don't forget, it's only two weeks until the garden party at the care home.'

'We'll fit it all in,' I reassured her. 'You know I like to keep busy.'

'I hope the weather is going to be as good for the party as it is today,' she said, squinting up at the sky.

'Yes,' I agreed, also turning my face up to the sun, which

was shining in a cloudless sky. 'The rain last year really put people off, didn't it? From what Sandra told me, the profits were practically non-existent.'

The mention of the garden party made me think again about what I could do to raise more money to bolster the activities budget.

'We're going to be having a fundraiser here later in the summer now, aren't we, Luke?' shouted Lisa, who was within earshot and gathering the few last plates together for washing up.

I stood up to help.

'Are we?' I asked.

'Yes,' she said. 'We're planning—'

Luke rushed over before she could say anything else.

'Do you mind if we don't tell everyone just yet?' he said to Lisa. 'I don't want to say anything in case it doesn't happen.'

'It will,' she said firmly. 'It has to.'

Given her determined tone, I couldn't help thinking that whatever it was the pair were planning wouldn't dare do anything other than be a huge success.

'Even so,' Luke insisted, 'let's just get everything in place before we start shouting about it, yes?'

Lisa relented, but she didn't look as if she wanted to.

'In that case,' she said mischievously, to me, Sara and Harold, 'I'll tell you next week.'

I gave Sandra a call Sunday evening to ask if she might be able to give me a lift to work the next day. I told her I'd got lots to take in after my thrifty shopping trip and she eagerly agreed.

Given that I hadn't picked up any books from Colin, I might have been able to manage, but I had an ulterior motive. Sandra was often impossible to pin down at work, but if I could talk to her en route, then I might be able to get an answer to everything I wanted to talk to her about before the start of my working week.

'Is that the lot?' she frowned, as I slid the few bags and a covered box onto the backseat of her car. 'I thought you'd got more than that.'

'It's heavier than it looks,' I said, quickly jumping into the passenger seat and securing my seatbelt. 'And awkward too.'

'Well, yes,' she conceded, 'I daresay it wouldn't have been all that easy to bring in on foot.'

She drove out of the Square and joined the early morning traffic. The road seemed to be busier than usual.

'While we've got a minute,' I quickly began, not wanting to waste a second in case the road cleared, 'I might as well tell you what else I've come up with over the weekend.'

'If you don't mind, I'd rather wait until we get in,' she said. 'I need to concentrate on the road.'

Fortunately, the travel gods weren't on Sandra's side and we were going nowhere fast. She retuned the car radio and the local traffic news informed us that there were ongoing roadworks and a traffic light failure further around the ring road, which was responsible for the snarl up. She pulled on the handbrake and took the car out of gear.

'We're going to be late,' she muttered.

'And won't have time for a proper meeting,' I pointed out, capitalising on the queue.

'That's true,' she said. 'Go on then, tell me what you've been working on.'

The description of the new puzzles and games went down a treat, especially when I flagged up how little they'd cost and the library borrow box idea was well received too. I was beginning to realise exactly how budget-motivated Sandra was and, having wowed her with the bargains, I moved on to the potentially trickier terrain. I eased my way in with another economical idea first though.

'I've also added a couple of my houseplants to the stuff in the back,' I told her. 'So, they haven't cost anything either. I thought they might be nice in the dayroom.'

'Definitely,' she agreed, taking me by surprise. 'They're very en vogue at the moment, aren't they? And they'll cheer up the residents who can't get out in the garden.' She gave me a sideways look, before moving the car forward a few inches. 'I've been reading up online,' she told me. 'I found this website – houseplants for mental health. Apparently they're supposed to reduce stress, blood pressure and so on. I'm thinking of getting a couple myself.'

I was momentarily taken aback that she was so receptive to the idea, but quickly recovered and then spent the next few minutes preaching about plants and promising to help with her choices for her office.

'Well,' she said, as the traffic began to move more freely

again, 'you've certainly got me inspired and I know the residents will be too.'

I was delighted she thought so.

'In fact,' she said, biting her lip, 'they're pretty geed-up already.'

'There is just one more thing,' I ventured.

'What's that?'

'Charlie told me about his old dog, Monty, last week and how he still misses canine company.'

'We can't possibly have a dog,' she said briskly, back on high alert.

'I know that,' I soothed, 'and I wasn't going to suggest we could.'

'Good.'

'However,' I carried on, 'there are organisations which can bring carefully vetted,' I emphasised that point, 'dogs and other pets into the home. They can spend anything from an hour to all day with us, and,' I carried on in a rush because I knew she was itching to cut in, 'research suggests they might do more for us, both physically and mentally, than the plants.'

'But not everyone likes dogs,' she pointed out.

'And some people are allergic,' I added, before she could. 'I'm aware of that and so, when the dogs are visiting, those people could do something else.'

She was quiet for a moment.

'I'm not keen on dogs I don't know,' she said.

'That's fair enough,' I said, 'but with all due respect, this isn't about—'

'Me . . .'

'Quite.'

'I know,' she said, letting out a long breath.

'I've found someone who can bring in llamas, too,' I told her. 'And reptiles.'

'Let's start with the dogs,' she quickly said.

That sounded like the go-ahead to me. I resisted the temptation to high-five her.

'That's really sad about Charlie's dog,' she said, after stopping the car again. 'I know there must be lots of pets that get left behind, but I've never really thought about the implications of it before.'

'It must be such a wrench,' I agreed, 'and with that in mind, I've also been wondering if it might be possible to set up a visiting scheme for families or friends to bring in the pets that they've taken on, on behalf of their loved ones.'

'That's a really good idea,' she said, tapping the steering wheel as she mulled it over. 'We could use the conservatory for that, couldn't we?'

'We could.'

'Yes, I'd be up for that,' she told me, before quickly adding, 'as long as there aren't any snakes or llamas involved. Well done, Beth.'

'It was actually my housemate's idea,' I admitted, unable to take the credit.

'Well, they sound like a keeper.'

'Oh, he is,' I said, letting a sigh escape my lips as I

recalled Eli's kindness, understanding and unjudgemental listening ear.

'This is all going to cost money though, Beth,' Sandra pointed out, bringing me back down to earth with a bump.

'I know,' I said. 'And I am trying to think of what I can do to raise more funds.'

'I've been thinking about that too,' she said. 'How would you feel about taking responsibility for the garden party raffle this year?'

'The raffle?' I frowned. 'Isn't that Sheila's baby?'

Sheila was one of the carers. She was close to retirement, stuck in her ways and fiercely protective of the things she considered hers to organise. I certainly wouldn't want to be treading on her toes.

'It was,' Sandra said. 'But she's said she doesn't want to do it this year. She wants to enjoy the garden party without the responsibility as it's her last one before she retires. She's got a few of the usual bits and pieces for prizes, but it's not looking all that great.'

'You're really selling it to me, Sandra,' I laughed.

'Well,' she said, 'I was thinking you could perk it up a bit, perhaps ask some local businesses for contributions. I bet you could make it more than the talcum powder and tinned goods event it usually is.'

'In just a fortnight?' I pointed out. 'I don't think so.'

'You could keep all of the profits for the activities budget.'

'In that case,' I hastily said, 'leave it with me.'

Chapter 10

I had always managed to fill my time before, but now my life had vigour and purpose, and was a thrilling whirl of frenetic activity. No two days were the same and I was loving it. Aside from the music which filled the house whenever Eli was in it, it was perfect.

I was sleeping better, I felt better and as Harold was keen to point out and make me blush, I looked better. There had been times during the last couple of years when I could have cursed well-meaning folk when they had said time would help and that I would eventually pick my life back up again after losing Mum, but they had finally been proved right.

'The box is filling up again,' Greta told me as she wandered into the dayroom clutching to her chest the Fuzzy-Felt farm set someone had dropped off at reception.

I hadn't thought anyone would want it and when I emptied the donations box the Monday morning Sandra and I had been caught in traffic, I had immediately earmarked it to go with the basket of toys that were kept in the conservatory to amuse visiting children. Greta, however, had other plans for it.

She was loving creating different farmyard scenes and wouldn't be parted from it. No one minded her monopolising the set because she hadn't stripped off once since taking a fancy to it and I was going to buy more, just in case the lure of the rural idyll began to wane and she turned to streaking for entertainment again.

'Excellent,' I said, admiring the steadily filling shelves in the resource cupboard. 'This is looking better, isn't it?'

Greta nodded, as she settled herself at the last empty spot at the table and pulled the lid off the box she had been cosseting.

'Bingo!' shouted Charlie.

His opponents groaned and the rest of us jumped. The shopping game wasn't Bingo but it was proving just as popular.

'Let's have another go,' said Tony, shuffling the lists again. 'I only needed a loaf of bread that time.'

'And if you could keep it down . . .' tutted Bob, shaking out his newspaper with an air of arrogance. 'Some of us are trying to catch up with world events. We're not all interested in playing kids' games.'

Charlie pulled a face and I turned my attention back to the cupboard. Bob had moaned about everything I'd done so far, but I was determined not to let his belligerence get to me.

'Come on then,' said Tony, 'I'm feeling lucky this time.'

My eyes scanned over the colourful craft packs that had

arrived the day before. I couldn't wait to start running some sessions using those, but in the days leading up to the garden party, and knowing how much else I had to do, everyone, well almost everyone, was happy to work at putting together the jigsaws and trying out the new games.

'We've dropped off the lot,' panted Sara, as she and Harold joined us. 'And the woman in the library said the first borrow box will be delivered early next week.'

'You're absolute stars,' I told the pair. 'Thank you so much.'

Sara had finished her shift and gone out, with Harold riding his trusty mechanised steed, to deliver more of the flyers I'd printed off requesting raffle prizes. It was a competitive market in the run-up to the summer holidays, what with school fetes and church bazaars also happening, and there hadn't been much in the way of contributions so far.

It was all still a little too much like the raffle Sheila usually ran for my liking, but there was still time to pull off something spectacular if I could find a spare minute to put my mind to working out how to achieve it.

'You're welcome,' said Sara, ineffectively fanning herself with her hand as she blew her fringe away from her face, 'but now I'm going home. It's hot out there and all I want is a cool shower and my bed.'

'Will you able to sleep in this heat?' Harold asked.

'Oh yes,' she said, making for the door again. 'Don't you worry about that. I could sleep standing up after a night shift. See you later.'

'I'll make a start on your tunic tonight,' I promised her.

'You're a star,' she grinned, giving me a double thumbs-up and blowing me a kiss.

'I bet you don't miss night shifts, Beth,' said Harold, as Sara disappeared back through to reception.

'No,' I said, 'I don't. My body clock has quite happily readjusted to more regular working hours and it's nice to have the evenings to do other things.'

'Like sewing up Iceni re-enactment outfits?'

'Exactly,' I laughed.

'You're thriving, my love!' Harold beamed.

'I am,' I happily agreed. 'Now, who fancies helping me water these plants?'

Along with the new jigsaws, puzzles and games, the houseplants had been a big hit too. So much so that I'd bagged another lift in with Sandra the day after I'd set out the first two, so I could bring more in.

None were the originals from mine and Mum's collection, but the spider plants and few pots of ivy I'd donated had been grown from their babies and cuttings. They were easy plants to look after and their trailing habits meant they provided plenty of leaves and made an impact without taking up too much space.

'Me!' said Greta, abandoning life on the farm.

The raffle still wasn't looking all that spectacular when I finished work on Friday and I was beginning to think that I wasn't going to make any money from it at all, but what I didn't know was that someone had been secretly going out of their way to help me out.

'What's going on?' I asked Eli as we walked into the Grow-Well together early Saturday evening and everyone's eyes turned to us.

'No idea,' he shrugged, but I knew him well enough now to know that he had a bit of a clue.

I narrowed my eyes to try and make him spill the beans, but he wouldn't look at me.

'Come on,' he said, trying to hide a smile, 'let's eat before everything's gone. I'm starving.'

We had been harvesting and eating salads all week as the early summer heat had given everything a boost. Even some of the tomatoes were beginning to show a bit of colour and the early rows of rocket were starting to bolt.

'We'd almost given up on you two,' said Lisa, handing us a plate apiece.

'My fault,' said Eli, helping himself to a handful of leaves from the salad bowl. 'It took forever to shut the coffeehouse tonight. I couldn't let rid of the last few stragglers.'

'You're still coming to The Dragon though, aren't you?' Neil asked him.

'Definitely,' he said. 'Now I've made up my mind, I wouldn't miss it for the world.'

'Are you coming, Beth?' Poppy asked me.

'It's not Beth's sort of thing,' said Eli, answering on my behalf.

I gave him an indignant look and he grinned.

'It might be,' I pouted, even though I didn't have a clue what they were talking about.

'Believe me,' Eli whispered, leaning close, 'it's not.'

'I'll be the judge of that,' I said, pretending to sulk and ignoring the feelings his soft breath on my collarbone aroused.

'There's an open mic night,' Neil explained. 'All musical talent welcome.'

'Oh,' I said, 'in that case, no.'

'Told you,' Eli grinned.

'Have you decided if you're taking part, Eli?' asked Mark, which had the immediate effect of wiping the smile off his face. 'Are you going to play?'

'Nah,' he said, with a shrug that wasn't quite as nonchalant as I could tell he'd been aiming for. 'Not tonight.'

From this I surmised that it had been him playing the guitar on Sunday. He hadn't strummed for long, but the little I'd heard was lovely. I was almost tempted to mention it but then noticed how uncomfortable he looked.

'You can't put it off forever you know,' said Neil, not taking on board Eli's unease like I had.

'You know,' Eli shot back, sounding gruff, 'I think I can.'

'So,' I quickly cut in, 'what sort of week has everyone had?'

'All right,' said Poppy.

'Not bad,' added Lisa.

'But nowhere near as good as yours is about to get,' grinned Graham.

'Oh,' I frowned. 'Why? What's going on?'

Still my housemate refused to be drawn.

'Eli told us about the raffle you're running at the care home garden party,' said John, when Eli's lips stayed tightly zipped.

'I bet Sara and Harold mentioned it too,' Eli then interrupted, turning pink.

'Not as enthusiastically as you did, mate,' John teased.

'And we've come up with some donations,' smiled Lisa. 'A few things that we thought might help spice it up a bit.'

'Oh wow,' I said, putting down my plate and offering Eli a grateful smile, even though he was still trying to play down the part he'd played. 'Thank you so much. That's fantastic.'

His eyes finally met mine and I felt my tummy tingle.

'You don't know what we've come up with yet,' chuckled John.

By the time they'd reeled everything off, I was feeling even more thankful. There were food-based donations from Mark in the form of a selection of cakes from Blossoms; a variety of chutneys, pickles and preserves from Poppy; signed copies of Lisa's latest book; three hours of dog walking from Ryan; some needlefelt creatures from Heather and a huge box of plants and produce raised in the Grow-Well, which would be selected and delivered on the day, along with the cakes.

'I don't know what to say,' I said, feeling tearful and wondering how Eli would react if I gave him a hug. He'd really saved the day and wrapping my arms around him felt like the least I could do ...

'Hold on,' said Freya's partner Finn, who was an artist and made beautiful sculptures from scrap metal. 'We're not done yet.'

The pièce de résistance was going to be a small dragon sculpture he had cleverly crafted in his studio in the grounds of Prosperous Place. That alone would be worth a small fortune and I thought I might try and organise an auction for that, rather than include it in the general raffle.

'Now I'm even more lost for words,' I gasped, as Eli then handed me a collection of vouchers, which he'd gone around and talked the shop owners in the street where the coffeehouse was located into donating.

'There's one from Colin at the bookshop,' he explained, 'another from Lou who runs the vintage place, a third courtesy of the manager at On the Box and of course, one from the coffeehouse.'

'You did this?' I said, my eyes filling with more tears.

'We all did,' he said, looking sheepish as he ran a hand around the back of his neck. 'I knew it meant a lot to you and you were worried you wouldn't have time to source different things, so we all had a think about what we could do.'

Lisa wasn't settling for his selfless explanation.

'But it was you who got us all organised and then went around and collected from the shops, Eli,' she said.

'Yeah, well . . .' he stammered, looking awkward again.

Unable to resist a second longer, I threw my arms around his neck and squeezed him to me. He hugged me back just as tightly and as I held onto him, my warmth melded into his. It was in that moment that I knew. I knew that I was seriously starting to fall for my kind and thoughtful housemate.

'We were all involved,' he said huskily, slowly loosening his grip and looking down at me, but keeping his hands lightly resting on my waist.

His pupils were massively dilated and I wondered if he felt something too. Was he feeling the same spark that was currently lighting up my insides? Part of me was desperate for him to be feeling the sensation, but I was scared. I knew it was unlikely, but what if we did both feel the same way, then started up a relationship that went wrong? One of us would have to move on ...

'Well,' I said, pushing the thought aside. I didn't have time to worry about a relationship, even an imaginary one. I needed to stay focused on making my new job a success and Eli's act of kindness was going to go a long way to helping me achieve that. 'Thank you. Thank you all.'

I took a step away and then quickly hugged everyone else, so it didn't look like I'd singled Eli out. There was no denying that no one else's arms around me felt anything like his though. There had been sanctuary and comfort in his embrace and a whole lot of fizz.

'Thank you all so, so much,' I said for the umpteenth time, as I looked again at the vouchers on the table and imagined how wonderful the fabulous donations were going to look all set up at the garden party.

'And Graham and I have come up with something too,' said Carole, 'although it's not for the raffle and it will need approval from the care home manager if it's going to amount to anything.'

'Sounds dodgy,' laughed John.

'No, it doesn't,' I quickly cut in. 'What is it, Carole?'

'Well,' she said, ignoring John for what I guessed wasn't

the first time, 'we were wondering if we could offer our expertise. Graham's a great gardener and I'm a fairly decent baker.'

'You're a brilliant baker,' cut in Mark, which was a huge compliment, given his skill and talent level.

'Thank you,' she smiled, flushing at the praise. 'We were wondering, Beth, if perhaps Graham could set up a little gardening club at the home and I could run some baking sessions. Nothing fancy, just biscuits and angel cakes, that sort of thing. Minimal ingredients, maximum taste.'

'And we could possibly partner the gardening with a couple of trips here throughout the year,' added Graham. 'Harold told me that a few of the residents have been missing their away days. Granted, it's not far from the home, but it's still a change of scene.'

'What do you think?' asked Carole.

'I think you're all amazing,' I croaked. 'I honestly don't know what else to say.'

'And living with her,' said Eli, switching places and this time coming to my rescue, 'I can tell you, Beth's not often lost for words!'

Everyone laughed and I thanked them all again, somehow without shedding any tears. After that, we tidied away and those going to The Dragon prepared to head off.

'If any of you have time to spare tomorrow,' Luke said, just before the gathering broke up, 'Lisa and I have something to tell you.'

'Oh, let's tell them now!' Lisa shouted from the bothy

where she and Carole were finishing the dishes. 'You know I'm dying to.'

Luke shook his head.

'I think we've had enough excitement for one night,' he shouted back. 'Let's meet on the green, tomorrow at eleven, before it gets too hot.'

His words barely sank in as I finished the watering, made my way back through the garden, around the Square and into the house, the vouchers Eli had taken the time and trouble to collect clutched as tightly to my chest as Greta was inclined to hang onto her box of Fuzzy-Felt.

'Any idea what this is about?' I asked Eli, as we sat together on the green a few minutes before eleven the next morning.

It was set to be another hot day and I closed my eyes and tilted my face up to the sun, letting its warmth fill me up. Eli didn't say anything and when I opened my eyes, I found he was watching me. He hastily looked away and began pulling up handfuls of grass.

'No,' he swallowed. 'Not a clue.'

'Did you have a good time last night?' I asked. 'I didn't hear you come in.'

I guessed he must have had a great time as he hadn't appeared from his room until just a few minutes previously and the only breakfast he'd bothered with was a glass of water and a couple of painkillers. It was just as well he didn't have to start his shift at the coffeehouse too early.

'You missed a cracking night, Eli!' shouted Mark from the

other side of the road, shattering the peace while he waited for Neil to lock up.

'Didn't you go to The Dragon?' I frowned.

'No,' Eli said. 'I changed my mind just after we got there.'

'Oh?'

'How's your head?' Neil asked, much more quietly than his husband, as the pair joined us.

'Oops,' said Mark, lowering his voice. 'Sorry, I forgot about that.'

'It's all right,' Eli shrugged.

Clearly, his head wasn't all right and the painkillers hadn't been for a hangover.

'Did you come straight back?' I asked. 'I didn't hear you come in.'

'Morning everyone!' said Luke as he, Kate and the girls joined us along with practically everyone else who had now turned out.

The children began running around and chasing each other, perfectly safe thanks to the fact that the green was enclosed by railings so they wouldn't forget themselves and go bowling into the road.

'Morning,' Carole said briskly, sounding even more efficient than usual. 'I can't stay long as I've got a piece of brisket for dinner and it's going to need checking.'

'I keep telling you to do it in the slow cooker, Carole,' said Heather's husband, Glen.

'I know,' she said, 'I'll give it a go one of these days.'

I got the impression that Carole was a creature of habit.

'You can put it in and just forget about it,' Glen said impatiently.

'Right,' said Lisa, stepping up and interjecting, 'for the sake of Carole and Graham's Sunday dinner, we'll try and keep it brief.'

She looked to Luke for confirmation and he nodded.

'You can blame me for this idea if you think it sounds too much like hard work, and Beth actually,' she added, pointing at me. 'But really, I know you're all going to love it.'

'What have I done?' I gasped, eager to keep on the right side of everyone.

I'd been made to feel so welcome, and they'd all been so generous with prizes for the raffle, the last thing I wanted was to unwittingly ruffle anyone's feathers.

'Nothing,' she laughed. 'You should see your face! Nothing bad anyway.'

'As I understand it,' said Luke, offering me more of an explanation, 'you were the one who suggested that the green, and the grounds at Prosperous Place, would be the ideal spot for a summer fair in the city, Beth.'

'Oh yes,' said Graham, looking at me, 'we were talking about that the weekend you moved in, weren't we?'

I didn't think I'd expressed it *quite* as succinctly as that, but I had mentioned it.

'And as you all know,' Lisa carried on, sounding sad all of a sudden, 'now that the much-loved Arches have closed, we're trying to raise money to buy another site so the project can carry on.'

Suddenly the temperature on the green seemed to have shot up by at least a hundred degrees. I could feel my face was glowing and my ears felt warm too.

'We're desperate to continue the good work the late Moira Myers carried out for so many years,' Lisa further said, as I covered my mouth with my hand to stop a gasp escaping, 'and even though the things we've been doing in the wider community have been great, we're not quite there yet and time's running out.'

The grass beneath me began to undulate in waves and the sea of faces around me started to spin. I was either going to be sick or pass out. The Arches had closed and Moira had died. How were either of those things even possible?

Obviously neither the place nor the incredible woman behind it were a part of my life now, but I had always imagined they were still carrying on, helping and nurturing the talent of others. How had I not known, especially about Moira? It was devastating news and touched me deeply in spite of the fact that I had severed the connection a long time ago.

'With the bequest from Moira,' said Poppy's partner, Jacob, 'and a contribution from her son in the States, we're getting somewhere near enough to buy the chapel now. The council have said they'll pass consent for us to convert it so The Arches can re-form there, but we need a big fundraising push to make sure it happens before the building owners get tired of waiting and start to look for a buyer elsewhere.'

I couldn't really take in any of what he was saying.

'It was Beth's suggestion that got me fired up and think-ing,' said Lisa, pulling my out-of-focus gaze back to her, 'but we want to have something a bit different to a normal fair. Something that will appeal to everyone and that will help show off the wonderful creative talent that Moira spent so many years of her life nurturing.'

'So,' said Luke, 'at the end of August we're going to have a regular summer fair here on the green and in the grounds, with the usual stalls, fancy-dress competitions and so on, happening during the day but in the evening—'

'And most likely long into the night,' chimed in Lisa.

'We're going to put on a concert featuring the drama, music, dance and so on that The Arches is famous for. A sort of showcase if you will.'

'We're asking all the current attendees to take part,' said Lisa, 'and we're going to be appealing to faces from the past to contribute too.'

'So, if you know anyone who has ever been involved with the place,' said Luke, 'do please let them know. We really want to do Moira proud.'

'And continue to give the creative young people around here somewhere to go now that The Arches has sadly gone,' Lisa added.

Chapter 11

With the care home garden party just a few days away, I
should have had more than enough filling my head to block
out Lisa and Luke's announcement about the summer fair,
but it proved impossible. The chain of music-related events,
which had started to unfold practically from the very moment
I became aware of Kate's empty room in Nightingale Square,
had hastily taken up permanent residence in my mind and
all in a haphazardly orchestrated muddle.

First up, there had been my guilt-ridden thoughts about
Pete. They had increased tenfold since his sulky store assistant
had told me he still worked in On the Box, and now Eli had
secured a raffle voucher from the shop, he had unsuspectingly
deepened the connection.

Then there was Eli's obsession with music and his need to
constantly fill the house with it and finally, to top it all off,
came the biggest shock of all: some of my Nightingale Square
neighbours were involved with The Arches which no longer
existed, and Moira was forever lost to me too.

It was too much. The silent paradise, the one I thought Mum would have been so proud that I'd found, was fast turning into the noisiest place in Norfolk.

After everyone else had left on Sunday morning, Lisa took it upon herself to bring me up to speed with recent events at The Arches. She relayed the details as if I'd never heard of the place and I didn't say anything to contradict her assumption.

My head was still full of her suggestion that former attendees were going to be roped into performing at the fundraiser. I was fiercely determined that I would not be one of them. That said, it had been so long since I'd sung a note, I'd probably forgotten how to do it, so wouldn't have been of any use anyway.

Lisa told me that the original venue under the railway bridge had been lost thanks to a sell-off and subsequent huge rent hike and how, with Moira tragically gone, there was now a newly formed management committee looking after the project's interests to ensure that it could eventually get back up and running and carry on doing her wonderful work.

Lisa was at the forefront of it all, and very proudly so. All three of her and John's children had attended different classes at The Arches after my time there, and she herself had been running the new creative writing sessions that had been added to the schedule just before Moira's death. Jacob, a local teacher and keen supporter of the project, was jointly looking after the financial side of things with Moira's son, who lived in America.

'It was an amazing place, Beth,' Lisa had told me wistfully, her gaze drifting off as she imagined it. 'We can't lose the essence of it. It has to carry on.'

In my mind's eye, I could see exactly what she could see, but didn't dare say a word for fear of letting her know that I shared the same vision.

'The volunteers and instructors are still keen to keep teaching and supporting,' she said worriedly, 'but for how long? We can't lose too many months in case their time gets swallowed up by other commitments and we're terrified someone else will snap up the proposed new venue. Even though the current owners have given us a few months to raise the funds to buy it, that's no guarantee, is it?'

As hard as I tried to block it all out, as I sat at the dining table and drew up another poster advertising the garden party that afternoon, this time with a list of the much-enhanced raffle prizes, my thoughts kept tracking back to Moira and Mum, Pete, The Arches and the memory of myself singing my heart out on the stage.

It had never mattered to me whether there was an audience or not. I was happy to sing simply for the pure joy of it. Had been, I corrected myself. I *had* been happy to sing simply for the pure joy of it.

'Don't get drawn in,' I told myself, resolutely shaking the remembrance off and replacing it with the harsh words I'd been bombarded with after my audition at university. 'It's too late for you now. Your chance has long gone.'

After a restless night I walked to work, pinning up the posters and dropping others off in the shops which were already open as I went. I'd thanked both Blossom at the bakery and Lou who ran the vintage store, Back in Time, for their contributions, but I couldn't find the courage to stop at On the Box.

As Eli had so kindly collected the vouchers, perhaps I could coerce him into thanking Pete. The second the thought entered my head, Pete, the man himself, materialised from somewhere and strode along the pavement towards me. I stood rooted to the spot but was saved from his sight at the last second as he dropped his keys and I managed to find the wherewithal to scurry past as he bent to pick them up.

As I rushed on, I couldn't shake the feeling that there was a net closing in around me and I was going to have to face at least some of my demons if not in the immediate future, then pretty soon. Fate seemed determined to bring Pete and I back together and as I had discovered in the past, what destiny wanted, it got. One way or another.

'This is incredible,' said Sandra, as she read the list of raffle prizes on the poster that I'd pinned up on the activities board. 'I'm rather regretting my promise to let you keep the profits from this now.'

I hoped she wasn't about to change her mind.

'You're not letting Beth keep the money,' Charlie quickly pointed out. 'It's for our activities fund.'

'Don't worry,' Sandra smiled, 'I'm not about to claw it back for the pot, but I do agree about the sculpture, Beth. That definitely needs to be sold off separately to the raffle.'

'We need a better way to advertise it too,' frowned Harold.

'Not that your poster campaign isn't wonderful, Beth, but it needs a bigger audience than the few people who come through here every day and pound the city streets.'

I was thinking the same thing myself. Finn had shown me the exquisite metal figure and I'd photographed it and added it to the home's website, along with the local community events listings on Facebook, but it still wasn't enough.

'Maybe we could get something in the paper,' Charlie suggested.

'I'm submitting a few words about the party to a journalist friend of mine, so I'll add the photo to that,' said Sandra, 'and later this afternoon,' she added, turning slightly pink, 'I've got a spot on the radio to talk about all the good work we're doing here, so I'll definitely give it a mention on there.'

The rest of us exchanged glances. We all knew Sandra liked to be in the limelight and the centre of attention, but this was a whole new level, even for her. I daresay her worry about the empty rooms was the motivation behind the interview and she wouldn't wait long to give her hard sell. She'd doubtless put a spin on mentioning the rooms along with the updated and overhauled activities schedule and our good work, as she put it.

'You should take Beth with you,' said Harold, playing devil's advocate.

'No, she most definitely should not,' I quickly responded. 'Beth has more than enough to be getting on with here, thank you very much.'

Sandra eyed me speculatively.

'That might be a thought for the future though, Harold,' she said. 'When you start rolling out more of these wonderful activities you've got planned, we could get the media in, Beth. That pet idea . . .'

'Well,' I loudly interrupted, before Charlie heard. I hadn't mentioned it yet because I didn't want to get his or anyone else's hopes up, in case it didn't happen. 'We'll see. Let's focus all our attention on making the garden party a success first, shall we?'

'Yes,' said Sandra, checking her watch. 'And on that thought, I'd better get to the studio. I mustn't keep the presenter waiting.'

'Another friend, are they?' Harold couldn't resist asking.

'Yes,' Sandra said stiffly. 'He is, actually.'

Later that afternoon, we all sat on chairs around the radio in the dayroom. Both staff and residents were keen to listen in.

'This reminds me of the war,' giggled Greta, taking in our eager expressions.

Sara looked at me and winked.

'You can't be old enough to remember the war,' Bob belligerently said.

'Yes, I can,' Greta replied petulantly. She could bristle in an instant. 'I can remember sitting on my mum's knee and listening to—'

'Quiet,' said Harold, turning up the volume as the programme jingle finished. 'This'll be it now.'

'Winston Churchill?' questioned Greta.

'Sandra, you loon,' Ida hissed firmly enough to shut Greta up.

My boss did a great job of selling the rooms and the garden party, and the presenter was in raptures when she showed him the picture of the sculpture from Finn.

'You'll actually be auctioning the sculpture at the party, will you?' he asked.

'That's the plan,' Sandra said smoothly, although we hadn't thrashed out the finer details yet.

I could tell from her tone that she was thinking on her feet and wondered what she was going to come out with next. I didn't have to wait long to find out.

'If only we had someone talented to take the bids,' she sighed, and I could almost hear her fluttering her eyelashes. 'I'm sure we'd raise even more money then.'

The airwaves went silent, but only for a second.

'Well,' the presenter announced, using his very best radio voice, 'I was planning to pop in and visit the party myself at some point during the afternoon . . .'

'You were?' Sandra gasped.

'I was.'

'In that case,' she said, sounding so sassy I began to cringe and I noticed Sara was too, 'I know it's a cheeky request, but how would you feel about doing the honours and taking the bids for us?'

'Me?'

'Yes,' she said silkily, 'you.'

'Are they flirting?' Bob muttered, before we shushed him.

'Well,' said the presenter, sounding delighted, 'I suppose I could, couldn't I?'

'It would be very much appreciated,' Sandra practically purred and Greta started to make what I hoped were pretend retching noises.

'I'll see you on Sunday then,' the presenter said and I could tell he was smiling. 'Why not join us folks . . .' he then launched off, sounding all business again.

He wrapped the interview up with a save the date reminder along with the details of where in the city to find the Edith Cavell Care Home and we all clapped and cheered as he switched from the studio to the travel desk.

'Well,' said Harold, sounding impressed as he turned the radio off again. 'She really is a smooth operator, isn't she?'

'Disgusting,' sniffed Bob.

'Just a bit,' laughed Ida, ignoring him. 'This'll be a party to remember, won't it?'

'You're not wrong,' I laughed along, my worries momentarily forgotten.

Unfortunately, my good mood didn't last and neither did the sunshine. By the time Wednesday afternoon rolled around, it was chilly, wet and miserable. I hadn't thought anything would wipe the justifiably smug post-radio smile off Sandra's face, but the downturn in the weather had.

'I'll pick you up in the morning if you like,' she offered as I got ready to leave, selecting the biggest umbrella I could find from the stash in reception. 'We don't want the raffle prizes getting ruined in the rain, do we?'

'No,' I agreed, 'we don't. Thanks, Sandra. I'd appreciate the lift.'

I'd swapped mobile numbers with a few of my neighbours and Lisa had messaged to let me know she would round everyone up and drop her signed books, Heather's felted creatures, the potted-up plants from the Grow-Well, Poppy's bottles and jars, along with Finn's sculpture, straight to the house in her car.

She apologised that she didn't have time to bring everything to the care home, but I told her not to worry and that I could manage. Thanks to Sandra's offer of a lift, transporting the prizes was one less thing to fret about.

The fresh cakes and produce would be arriving on the day of the party, so I didn't have to worry about those just yet either and the vouchers, along with Ryan's dog walking promise, were only envelopes and therefore no problem to carry.

In spite of the unseasonable change in the weather, some things were at least beginning to come together and by the time I'd helped Lisa carry everything in from her car and looked it all over, I was in a more buoyant mood than the one I'd fallen into since The Arches revelations.

I set everything out on the dining table and took a couple of photos, with the sculpture as a centrepiece, from different angles. I didn't think I'd even seen better raffle and auction prizes and teamed with what had already been dropped off at work, I knew it was going to be spectacular, and hopefully, very beneficial to the activities fund.

Caught up in my thoughts as I set about making dinner, I didn't hear Eli come in, so had no idea how long he'd been watching me.

'Shit,' I swore, as I turned around and spotted him framed in the kitchen doorway. He was damp around the edges but had the biggest smile lighting up his handsome face. 'Shit, shit, shit,' I swore again as I realised I had pressed the hand which had been holding a wooden spoon covered in sauce to my heart. 'You scared me half to death.'

'Sorry,' he grinned, stepping into the room. 'And I've ruined your pinny, too.'

He tore off a few sheets of kitchen towel and handed them to me.

'I suppose you think this makes us equal,' I said, remembering the coffee he'd been covered in the day we first met.

'Pretty much,' he laughed.

I tutted and looked up to find he was still grinning.

'What?' I frowned, ineffectively dabbing at the stain.

It was tomato-based and would consequently be a brute to get out.

'You were humming,' Eli laughed.

My gaze momentarily flicked to his and then back to the stain again.

'No, I wasn't,' I snapped, instantly defensive and on high alert.

I hadn't been humming, had I? My heart was definitely racing but not to a specific tune.

'Yes,' he nodded, 'you were.'

'Rubbish.'

'You were.'

'Don't believe you,' I insisted, although *his* insistence was making me doubt my conviction.

'"Bloom", by the Paper Kites,' he said, looking me straight in the eye. 'Unmistakable.'

Given the hours he spent playing the track on a loop, it wouldn't have been any wonder if the song had become lodged in my head, but I still didn't want to acknowledge that he might have been right. I didn't do earworm. I was immune.

'I don't believe you,' I said again, turning away before he saw the tell-tale tears of frustration.

'I knew I'd get to you in the end,' he said happily, reaching around me for the kettle and sounding absolutely thrilled.

'You haven't *got* to me,' I swallowed, blinking the tears away before turning to face him again, 'because I wasn't humming, and even if I was,' I immediately countered, 'it wouldn't be any wonder if it was *that* bloody song because it's the only one you ever play.'

'No, it isn't,' he said.

'Yes, it is.'

His smile disappeared as I pushed on.

'That's all I hear coming from your room these days,' I said a little unkindly. 'The same tune, the same lyrics, the same volume. Oh, don't tell me,' I teased, meanly going way too far to cover how emotional he had made me feel, 'is it unrequited love? No, wait. It's a break-up song, isn't it?'

He banged the kettle down on its base.

'No,' he said quietly. 'It's not a break-up song.'

I should have stopped then, but I didn't.

'Is that why you don't play your guitar in public, Eli?' I asked cruelly.

'What?'

The mortification on his face proved I'd hit a nerve.

'Did you have your heart broken over a song?'

My attack was in no way justified, but unleashed, there seemed to be no way of squeezing my pent-up frustration back into the bottle.

'You and your stupid obsession with music,' I raged on.

Without another word, he turned around and walked out. He went right out of the house, slamming the door behind him and I was left standing in the kitchen, horribly aware that I'd just had a total overreaction and turned into the very worst version of myself and all because he said he'd heard me humming what was, in fact, a very lovely tune.

Chapter 12

I don't think Eli came home that night, I didn't hear him anyway. My week had been fraught with thoughts about Pete's proximity, my neighbours' connection to The Arches and my argument with my housemate. And just when I was beginning to think that this week, in spite of the wonderful selection of raffle and auction prizes and the thankfully sunnier forecast predicted for Sunday, couldn't get any worse, it did.

As promised, Sandra picked me up for work. The change in the weather forecast had restored her good mood and reminded her just how well she'd promoted the garden party on the radio. She was still justifiably thrilled that she had sweet-talked the presenter into putting in an appearance and I got the impression that they might well have seen each other since. She was also in a rush.

'We have a new resident moving in today,' she told me, as I hurried to fasten my seatbelt, 'so I hope the ring road isn't going to throw up any little surprises this morning like it did the last time I gave you a lift.'

She didn't usually worry all that much about being on-site for the arrival of a new resident so I had no idea why she was bothered about being there when this one crossed the threshold. That said, I knew she was keen to fill the empty rooms, so perhaps that was it, but her tone and the look on her face suggested there was more to it than just that.

I opened the window a little wishing she hadn't uttered the words 'throw up' because I had been feeling decidedly queasy ever since my uncharacteristically mean words to Eli. I dreaded to imagine what he must have been thinking of me. I'd sent him innumerable texts, but he hadn't responded to any of them and, to be honest, I couldn't blame him. If I were in his shoes, I wouldn't have wanted to talk to me either.

'Did you hear what I just said, Beth?' Sandra asked me impatiently.

'Yes,' I lied, looking out at the thankfully free-flowing traffic.

'So, you can understand why I'm in such a rush?'

'Uh huh.'

Having zoned out, I'd missed her explanation as to why she was in such a hurry.

'Are you all right?' she frowned. 'You look a bit peaky.'

I opened my mouth to answer, but she carried on before I had the chance.

'You're not coming down with anything, are you?' she demanded, her voice at least three octaves higher than it had previously been. 'Because I'm going to need you on Sunday. It's going to be all hands on deck; all stations manned all day.'

She sounded almost manic. I knew there was a lot riding on the event, especially now a local minor celeb was going to be in attendance to take the auction bids, but even so, her lack of sympathy was a bit jarring. I fought the urge to tell her to calm down and nodded along, all the while staring out of the window for the mercifully brief drive in to work.

The staffroom was fast filling up with all sorts of bits and pieces for the various stalls, games and events, so Sandra suggested we put Finn's statue in her office, which had more space and was locked when she wasn't in residence.

'Not that anyone's likely to run off with it,' she said, running her hands lightly over the smooth metalwork wings and neatly welded joints.

Having seen the glint in Greta's eye when she caught sight of the delightful dragon as I carried it in, I wasn't so sure about that and had Sandra spotted the covetous look, she wouldn't have been either.

'Tactile, isn't it?' she mused.

I was just about to warn her that Greta might be feeling the same way too, when an almighty shout went up in the dayroom and I almost jumped out of my skin. The outburst was immediately followed by a cacophony of whoops and further cheering.

'What on earth?' I gasped.

'He's here,' said Sandra, releasing the dragon and gripping my arm in an unexpected touchy-feely moment. 'He's early. Damn. I should have waited in reception, just in case.'

'Who's here?' I asked, following her out of the office and

locking it on her behalf because she'd forgotten. 'Who's early? What's going on?'

By the time I'd caught up with her, it sounded like all hell had broken loose. Someone was belting out Jerry Lee Lewis's 'Great Balls of Fire' on the dusty old piano, which hadn't been touched in years, and they weren't holding back. They were absolutely hammering the poor old keys and the residents were bellowing out the lyrics almost loud enough to match the music. The sight which met my eyes stopped me in my tracks.

'Oh my god!' I shouted, to myself because no one else was listening. In fact, and more to the point, no one else could have heard. 'Someone's going to break a leg.'

With walking sticks held aloft, hips were being gyrated, albeit creakily, heads were bobbing and vocal cords were being exercised more vigorously than they had been in years. Decades, in some cases.

'Isn't this wonderful?' shouted Sandra, looking every bit as excited as the rest of the rapt audience as she spun by, enthusiastically twirled by Charlie.

I couldn't believe my eyes. What on earth was she doing, and more to the point, who had run off with her consistently professional and often impersonal manner?

'Brilliant,' I muttered, craning to see who was responsible for the uproar.

The packed crowd meant I couldn't get a good look at whoever was perched on the stool, or close enough to bang the piano lid shut. All I could really see was the top of a jauntily angled, but slightly battered, trilby.

'I knew he'd liven the place up,' Sandra laughed as she flew by again, 'but I didn't expect him to start the second he walked in!'

'Who?' I shouted, but she didn't hear me.

For someone so obsessed with worrying about trip hazards and uneven floors, she didn't appear at all perturbed by the fact that some of the wobbliest residents had abandoned their wheelchairs.

'Rock and roll!' shouted Greta, as she sashayed past.

'Greta,' I said, reaching for her hand. 'What's going on?'

'We can have a singalong every day now!' she beamed. 'Live music, whenever we want it.'

'And even when we don't,' I muttered. 'That's . . . great.'

With a rousing flourish, the tune came to an end and the piano lid was finally snapped shut. There was a split-second silence and then the cheers started again. They didn't last as long this time, because everyone was, not surprisingly, out of puff. I could hear lungs wheezing even above the cracks and creaks of old bones. If they didn't all calm down, they wouldn't make them any older.

'Dear lady, dear lady,' said the man at the piano, who had spun around on the stool and was on his feet the second he spotted Sandra. 'I hope you don't mind that I announced my arrival.'

'Not at all,' Sandra beamed, looking more animated than I'd ever seen her, as she fanned her flushed face with her hands.

'Most people just ring the bell at the reception desk,' chuckled Ida.

'I let him in!' declared Greta, as she pushed her way

through the adoring crowd. 'I saw his taxi pull up and I let him through.'

She might have been keen to announce the part she had played in admitting him onto the premises but I knew deep down Sandra would be fizzing. We were going to have to keep a closer eye on Greta. Usually she was fighting to get out, not let people in. And really, this man could have been anyone.

'Well done, Greta,' I was therefore astounded to hear Sandra say. 'Without you, we wouldn't have had this wonderful introduction.'

So much for my assumption. If she was annoyed, the feeling was buried really, really deep down.

'But he could have been anyone,' I pointed out, stepping forward.

'Rubbish,' grinned Charlie.

'How can *he* be just anyone?' Greta indulgently sighed, turning doe eyes back to the object of her affection.

My own eyes met those of the great entertainer. I was surprised to find his were the brightest blue and twinkling mischievously. There wasn't a cataract or rheumy film in sight. I looked away again, feeling annoyed that I would have known he wasn't just anyone had I been paying attention to what had been said in the car when Sandra drove me in.

This man, this dapper-looking gentleman, with his coordinating shirt and cravat, and dashingly tilted hat, was doubtless the new resident she had been so keen to personally welcome into the Edith Cavell Care Home fold.

'I don't believe we've met,' the gent said to me, holding out his hand. 'I'm certain you weren't here when I came and did a recce of the place.'

'No,' I said, shaking his hand, which was cool, even though he'd just been bashing seven shades out of the piano, 'I don't think I was.'

'Beth,' said Sandra, 'this is—'

'Freddie Fanshawe,' said Greta and Ida together, before collapsing into giggles.

'*The* Freddie Fanshawe,' said Charlie, as if emphasising the 'the' made all the difference.

'Delighted to meet you,' said Freddie Fanshawe.

'Likewise,' I smiled tightly, thinking it was anything but.

'You do know who he is, don't you?' frowned Bob.

Even he looked happy for once.

'Um . . .'

'Don't embarrass the poor girl,' tutted Freddie. 'It was a very long time ago that my name was on everyone's lips.'

I couldn't decide if he was arrogant or just very self-assured.

'Everyone wanted a piece of Freddie, back in the day,' blushed Ida.

'As I recall, Ida Willis,' Freddie responded rakishly, 'you got more than a piece.'

Ida turned even redder and Greta looked furious. I was going to take bets that there'd be tears before bedtime.

'How about another song?' shouted someone from the back of the room.

'How about we get Mr Fanshawe settled in his room?'

I countered, holding out my hand, so the man of the hour could lead the way.

The sooner I parted him from the piano, the better.

'And perhaps have a nice cup of tea?' he suggested. 'I'm parched after that performance.'

'Of course,' said Sandra, stepping up and linking her arm through his. 'I'll see to Mr Fanshawe, Beth.'

'Call me Freddie, please.'

'I'll see to Freddie,' she amended, with a smile. 'I'm sure you have lots to be getting on with.'

'Let's start making a list of songs for the Friday singalong,' said Greta, plucking at my sleeve the second the pair were out of sight and as if it was a fait accompli.

She and Ida jostled to reach the resource cupboard first. I bit my lip as I watched them. Eli might have thought he'd heard me humming the Paper Kites, but now I had Nat King Cole singing *there may be trouble ahead* playing on a loop in my head.

'Did I miss him?' asked Harold, rushing in, looking hot.

He was closely followed by Sara.

'Steady up, Harold,' she said. 'You'll be doing yourself a mischief.'

'If you're talking about a certain Mr F,' I informed him, because there could only be one person he could possibly be talking about, 'then yes, you missed him. Well, his arrival, anyway.'

'Did he play "Great Balls of Fire"?' Harold asked, taking off his hat and fanning himself with it.

'Yes,' I said. 'Loudly.'

'I knew he would,' Harold laughed wheezily. 'That was always his party piece to get the crowd going.'

'Not Jerry Lee Lewis's?' I asked sardonically. 'Why did no one mention to me that this minor celeb was descending?'

I knew I sounded put out, and that Sandra most likely had, but my feelings towards Freddie Fanshawe had nothing to do with his personality. It was, as they say, all about the music. He'd already got Greta and Ida fired up for this so-called Friday singalong and it had very rapidly dawned on me, that not only was my home life now dominated by music, or at least it was when Eli was home, my work life was about to be, too.

'We didn't know until last night,' said Harold. 'Sandra told us after dinner.'

'Apparently,' said Sara, 'she smuggled him in to have a look around the place a couple of weeks ago.'

'Smuggled him in,' I scoffed.

'She didn't want to get our hopes up,' Harold said. 'Freddie could have picked anywhere.'

'But he chose here,' Sara beamed.

Not another one.

'Don't tell me – you know who he is too?' I frowned at her.

'Of course,' she laughed. 'Anyone local who has grandparents his age knows who Freddie Fanshawe is. He's the only entertainer they ever harp on about.'

'Hey,' said Harold, swatting her with his hat. 'We don't harp on. He's just very good, is all.'

I felt my face go red.

'Sorry, Beth,' said Sara, biting her lip, when she realised what she'd said. 'I didn't mean ... that is ...'

'It's fine,' I smiled. 'You're fine. Don't worry about it.'

Along with Harold, she was one of the few people who knew I had no family. No parents, grandparents, aunts, uncles or cousins, local or otherwise. The excitement of finding out the new guest of honour had arrived had just made her forget and given what had happened with Eli, I knew now that it was better to be in a forgiving mood than snap someone's head off.

'Right,' I said, rallying, as much to save her feelings as mine. 'I'm going to set up the table to make some bunting for the garden party. Who wants to help?'

'Me!' shouted Greta, shoving her list-making pen into Ida's hand. 'Can we have the radio on while we make it?'

'Why not?' I shrugged.

I was definitely fighting a losing battle.

It was with a heavy heart that I walked into work on Friday morning. For two pins I would have called in sick, but I didn't because that wasn't my style. We had the garden party to finish preparing for and if I was going to fake a bug every time Freddie Fanshawe sat himself down at the piano, then my condition would have been terminal and I would have been better off resigning.

My mood had been further darkened because mine and Eli's paths hadn't crossed once at home. He seemed to be going out of his way to be out when I was in and hadn't responded to any of my texts or the notes I'd left taped to the fridge. My downhearted reaction to his determination to avoid me left me in no doubt that my feelings for my house-mate were far more than friendly and that was yet another problem to add to the growing list.

I had been horrified to catch myself humming one evening, thus proving that Eli might well have been right about having heard me before. I needed to find a way to corner him and apologise. Not only for snapping, but also for the subsequently cruel words I had thrown at him. They were wholly unjustified and completely out of character but until I was able to pin him down, I would have no oppor-tunity to explain.

'I think that's everything then, don't you?' said Sandra, closing her file with a snap after our final Friday meeting ahead of the garden party.

I'd left every resident who wanted to be involved in the dayroom colouring in more paper flags for the bunting. I would have preferred to use fabric but scissors and needles needed constant supervision and my time was too stretched to be able to watch their every move. If the weather was as good as predicted, then paper would hold up fine and I had resigned myself to the slightly less aesthetically pleasing look.

'Signed, sealed and delivered,' I nodded, looking down the lengthy list in my notebook which Sandra and I had just finished checking off. 'Even the weather is apparently all arranged.'

There were sunny icons lined up as far as I could scroll on my phone, which was a huge relief all round. The Christmas bazaar was a squeeze because we had to host it indoors, but the garden party, as the name suggested, was a much grander affair and it would have been impossible to host that inside.

'Did Sandra tell you I've offered to entertain the troops on Sunday?' Freddie asked me after lunch that day as he flexed his fingers ahead of the inaugural singalong that was scheduled to start at two.

I'd noticed that some cheeky so and so had pinned a poster about it up on the activities board, which made it look as if it was a planned part of my new schedule. I had wanted to take it down, but resisted. I had started the job with the words *inclusive activities for all* ringing in my head, but I was finding the motto harder to live by, or should that be work by, now things weren't turning out quite how I had planned.

'She did,' I sighed, knowing there would be no escape from him tinkling the ivories. 'Apparently we're wheeling the piano over to the French doors so we'll be able to hear you right across the garden.'

Freddie dropped his hands in his lap and looked me straight in the eye.

'Why do I get the feeling that you don't like me, my dear?'

I felt my face blaze. His directness was shocking and the intensity of his stare most unsettling. His chin was raised slightly and I was in no doubt that he wasn't going to let me fob him off. I guessed, when you were liked, or rather, adored, by everyone you met, one less than enthusiastic groupie stuck out like a sore thumb.

'How can you think that, Freddie?' I nonetheless blagged, trying to smile. 'I don't even know you.'

'You don't get to be my age,' he said seriously, his eyebrows raised, 'without picking up a thing or two.'

I looked away.

'I'm not going to break Greta's heart,' he whispered, 'if that's what you're worried about.'

I was surprised to find a bubble of laughter fighting its way up and into my mouth, but I didn't let it out. How did he manage to do that? I'd seen the tactic work on everyone else, but this was the first time his magic had impacted on me. That said, I hadn't given him the chance to work it on me before.

'But what about Ida's?' I whispered back.

'No chance,' he winked. 'She broke mine years ago. It's never been the same since.'

That time I couldn't bite the laughter back.

'So, come on,' he pouted, 'out with it. Is it the cravat?' he quizzed. 'Or maybe the cut of my slacks. There's something, isn't there, and I'm rather hoping it's not actually *me* because I have this overwhelming need to be liked by everyone I meet.'

I could tell from his tone that this time he wasn't joking. He really did want me, along with everyone else, to like him. My gaze shifted, just for the tiniest moment to the piano. I barely registered the movement, but he spotted it.

'Good god,' he burst out, making me jump. 'It's the music, isn't it?'

'No,' I said, shaking my head and looking about to see if anyone was listening. Thankfully, they weren't. 'Of course not.'

'It is,' he said. 'It must be. You've turned even pinker than you were before. Is my repertoire a little too dated for your taste or are you one of those music-hating heathens I've heard tell of?'

He gave a shudder and again I found myself smiling.

'You are!' he shouted. 'You're a heathen!'

'Pipe down,' I said, laying a hand on his arm. 'For pity's sake.'

'You told Greta she couldn't have her singalong before because there was no one to play this thing, didn't you?' he pointed out as he ran his hands lightly over the keys. 'Was that the truth or was it because you didn't want to hear it?'

I didn't answer. What a traitor Greta was!

'I can't believe that you couldn't be bothered to organise anything,' he said, still lightly playing a tune I didn't recognise. 'From what I've heard, you're going above and beyond to spice up the activities rota and give everyone a go at something new or the chance to pick up something old.'

I was pleased to hear that the residents – Greta, and probably Bob, aside – were aware of the effort I was going to to make such positive changes and had quoted my words as I had spoken them. Perhaps Freddie wasn't the only one with a need to be liked. Was that extraordinary or just human nature? In return for his earlier honesty, I found myself matching it.

'The truth is,' I was shocked to hear myself say as I leaned closer in, 'music meant everything to me once. It was my whole life.'

It was a huge thing for me to admit, and to be honest, I couldn't believe I'd done it.

'But?' he asked, taking my announcement in his stride.

'But something happened and I had to give it up.'

He stopped playing.

'You had to give it up?' he frowned.

He sounded deeply shocked, as if the suggestion was preposterous and would be utterly impossible to see through. Loath as I was to admit it, I was beginning to think he might be right.

'Yes,' I swallowed.

'I think you'd better tell me the whole story.'

He budged along the piano stool and I sat wedged in next to him and told him everything. All of it. I held nothing back. By the time I had finished he had tears in his eyes and as everyone came in, he grasped my hand.

I felt every bit as moved as he was and I had no idea how he'd managed to make me reveal so much. Not that he'd forced me to say a single word, he just seemed to have this knack of listening. I wondered how many other people's secrets he knew.

I looked down at his hand grasping mine.

'You didn't have to give it up,' he said earnestly, squeezing my fingers. 'Just because your dream didn't work out the way you thought it was going to, that didn't mean you had to abandon it altogether. What that woman said to you was utter rubbish. You've let her words have far too much power over you, Beth.'

I looked at his face and saw tears were streaming down his cheeks. He made no effort to either wipe or stop them. Clearly, Freddie was a man who felt things deeply. Even though I couldn't bring myself to believe what he had said, I appreciated that my sad story had made an impact and that it hadn't been shared in vain.

'I mean,' he then smiled, 'why do you think I'm sitting here, getting ready to play for this lot in the Edith Cavell Care Home in Norwich, when I'd once had my sights set on living a swanky lifestyle in Los Angeles?'

I was intrigued and wanted to ask him why, but there was no time.

'Come on Freddie!' shouted Charlie. 'Give us a tune, mate!'

'It's almost two, you know,' added Greta.

He let my hand go, gently nudged me off the stool and cracked his knuckles.

'Right!' he said, back to his former suave self. 'Who rec-ognises this one?'

Chapter 13

By the time I got home that evening, I was feeling more than a little curious about the life and times of Freddie Fanshawe. His cryptic comment had left me wondering what his story was. Why exactly was he playing the piano in Norwich if he had once set his sights on life in LA? With no sound from Eli again, I fired up my laptop while I waited for the kettle to boil. I knew it was a long shot, but perhaps I might be able to find something out about Mr F online.

I went to the fridge for milk and discovered a new note stuck to the door. It was from my housemate, informing me that he wasn't going to be home at all that night. He had also scribbled that he was having trouble with his phone so couldn't message, which went some way to clearing up why he hadn't responded to any of my texts. His explanation didn't make me feel any happier though.

Since I had snapped his head off, Eli had gone out of his way to be out of the house and I didn't much like being the one responsible for causing the rift that had developed

between us. And now he was having a whole night away . . .
I couldn't help but wonder where he was staying, and
with whom.

In a bid to distract myself, I turned my attention back
to my quest. I typed Freddie's name into Google and
was amazed to find he had his own Wikipedia page and,
although not always the most reliable source, it did give me
a potted history before leading me down various virtual
rabbit holes.

There were even videos of Freddie's performances
uploaded to YouTube and it didn't take much scrolling for
me to realise that he'd always been attractive, charismatic
and a truly great entertainer, but I discovered there had been
sadness, loss and plenty of drama in his life too.

'No way,' I gaped, as my eyes scanned the details which
were sketchy in parts, but gave me the gist. 'Oh, Freddie.'

Freddie's professional music career had started out with
him forming one half of a duet. He and his partner, in both
life and on stage, Judy Hudson, had been quite the dynamic
duo in the early sixties. They had been hotly tipped as rising
stars after a stellar performance on a televised talent show,
but then Judy had met and fallen in love with entertainment
manager, Ted Hunter.

She had left the UK for life in the United States with Ted,
allegedly taking all of Freddie's original material with her.
A lawsuit ensued, but before a verdict was reached, Judy and
Ted were killed in a plane crash in Florida. The case was
dropped and, if what I read was correct, Freddie had never

reclaimed his intellectual property rights and I realised with a jolt that he had never played anything original since.

He had carved out a very different career for himself, opting instead to perform other artists' songs rather than write more of his own. He hadn't given up on music entirely, but rather found another way to still make it a part of his life, just as he had hinted to me. I couldn't decide if I thought his actions meant he'd succeeded or failed.

Weary and worn out from the week, I decided to have a bath instead of a shower and as I lay back and let the bubbles settle around me, I realised I was humming again. Eli had definitely been right. Music was making its way back into my life, whether I wanted it to or not. Up until that week, the house had been filled with it, and had felt surprisingly empty without it and now work was awash with it too.

I closed my eyes, took a deep breath and then quietly sang the first line of the song that had caused me to bite Eli's head off. It felt strange to hear my voice, alien even, and my eyes filled with tears as I sang the next line, a little louder and with more confidence.

By the time the bathwater had cooled, I had sung an entire repertoire. Songs Eli had played, songs Freddie had belted out on the piano, songs I remembered from memory, courtesy of Mum's treasured collection of vinyl. It was exhilarating, emotional and exhausting.

Freddie had told me that letting music go once it had filled your heart was impossible, but as I'd convinced myself that I'd been doing such a good job of exactly that, I hadn't believed him. However, as I began to shiver in the cooled water, I wondered if he was actually right.

For all these years, my love of music hadn't been permanently banished as I'd believed. Rather, it had remained stealthily buried within me, biding its time, and now the change in my circumstances had summoned it again. It had risen up, I had finally succumbed to it and it felt every bit as wonderful to let my voice flow and soar as it had before.

I had no idea what I was going to do with that knowledge, if anything, but I was certain that I had some wrongs to right and that most of them were bound up with music. I climbed into bed that night determined to right the first one on my list the very next day.

I tried not to obsess over what I was planning to do or say as I tended to my houseplants the following morning. The watering, misting and dusting routine was usually reserved for Sunday, but that Sunday I would be at work all day, setting up, helping to run and then clearing away after the garden party so I'd had to switch things about a bit.

My hands shook as I put the plants back in their allotted places and I decided for my sanity, and their safety, I couldn't put the moment off a second longer. Fate could only nudge me so far; it was up to me to push myself forward and take the final step.

I left the house and walked out of the Square and along the road at a pace fast enough to propel me straight through the door of On the Box again. I knew that if I dithered, even for just a second, I'd bottle it and turn back.

'Hello, Pete,' I said shakily. 'How are you?'

'Beth?'

Pete had his back to me. He looked taller than I remembered and definitely wider, but then it had been a while so it was hardly surprising that he had changed. That said, he still sounded exactly the same.

'Bethany Cousins!' he gasped as he turned around. 'It is you!'

He was in front of me in two strides and had scooped me up and spun me around by the third.

'Good god,' he said, setting me down again and hanging onto my hands as I regained my balance. 'I can't believe it. What are you doing here? It's so good to see you!'

He shook his head, tightly squeezed my hands, then released them. I didn't know what to say.

'Oh Beth,' he swallowed, tearfully filling the gap where my words should have been. 'You really are a sight for sore eyes. Are you back in the city to visit your mum?'

'Well ...' I began, feeling every bit as emotional as Pete looked.

'No,' he said, turning back to the shop counter. 'Don't say anything yet. Hang on. Stacey!' he shouted.

'What?'

'Can you come through to the shop, please? I'm taking an extended lunch.'

The teenager I'd met before sauntered through, with her phone in her hand and her eyes fixed on the screen.

'Lunch?' she scowled, never taking her eyes off the phone. 'It can't be that time already. We haven't been open five minutes.'

'Put that away,' Pete said irritatedly, 'and do some work, will you? Those shelves won't fill themselves, you know.'

'Yes, Uncle Pete,' she said sarcastically, slipping her phone into her pocket where I guessed it would remain just until Pete and I were out of sight.

'Though,' said Pete, 'if you need me, you'd better call. You might get a rush on and need me to come back.'

The girl looked at him witheringly and then at me with interest. I wondered if she remembered me from before.

'Right,' said Pete, marching to the door. 'Let's go. We've got a lot of catching up to do and my niece is more than capable of holding the fort if she puts her mind to it.'

The only thing she looked capable of putting her mind to was refreshing her TikTok feed.

Pete said he didn't fancy the Castle Coffeehouse, which was where I was going to suggest in the hope that I might catch sight of Eli, but there was an empty table on the pavement outside Blossoms, so we took that instead. Even though it was just to the side of the building, it felt a little public for the revelations I was about to try and make, but I decided to just go with the flow.

'What do you fancy?' Pete asked, clapping his hands together. 'My treat.'

As it was still early, we both opted for breakfast rolls and a pot of tea for two.

'I shouldn't really be having one of these,' said Pete as he bit into the sausage, bacon and egg-filled roll. 'The doctor says I've got to watch my weight, but this is a special occasion. A *really* special occasion.'

I was touched that he thought so, but then knowing how generous and kind-hearted he was, it shouldn't have been a surprise.

'A little bit of what you fancy every now and again never hurt anyone, my mum always used to say,' I said, offering him a wobbly smile.

'Problem is,' he grinned, wiping ketchup from his chin, 'I fancy one of these a damn sight more often than every now and again. How is your mum by the way? As lovely as ever, I'll bet.'

I picked up my roll, but put it back on the plate. I sipped my tea instead and took a deep breath. I let it out again, trying to calm the rapid beat of my heart and swallowed another sip, delaying the moment I would have to tell him.

'Beth?' Pete frowned. 'What is it?'

I forced myself to look at him.

'She's dead, Pete,' I said huskily. 'Mum died a couple of years ago.'

Pete's eyes widened over the top of his roll, which was halfway between his plate and his mouth.

'Oh my god, Beth, no,' he said, putting it down and reaching for my hand. 'What happened?'

In much the same way as I had to Freddie the day before, I explained the tragic chain of events, starting with how my first year at university had been such a success.

'I know that,' Pete quickly said, 'because we were still in touch then. It was the second year we began to drift apart.'

I felt my face flush.

'We didn't drift apart, Pete,' I said, squeezing his fingers and readily taking the blame. 'I stopped communicating. It was all down to me. Mum's first stroke was such a shock and there was so much to get my head around when it happened that I didn't have headspace for anything else. It was all so overwhelming that I didn't think to tell you. Or anyone really,' I added, thinking how I'd excluded Moira too.

'Of course,' he nodded, then frowned. 'A stroke ... but your mum was so young. I know you shouldn't assume, but ...'

'She had an undiagnosed heart condition,' I told him. 'It was responsible for kicking things off.'

'My god.'

'I had to drop out of my course to become her carer after the first one,' I carried on. 'She needed virtually full-time support.'

I didn't add that I had struggled to work part-time to make ends meet too. I wasn't looking for sympathy.

'Oh Beth,' Pete tutted. 'I'm so sorry.'

'Well,' I smiled ruefully, 'Mum had always put me first, hadn't she? So, it was only fair that when she needed me, I made her my priority.'

'But your dreams, Beth ...'

I shook my head.

'Pipe dreams as they turned out,' I said firmly.

'Why didn't you let me know what had happened once things had settled down a bit?' Pete then asked. 'I can understand why you didn't to begin with, but once everything had sunk in, why didn't you call me then? I could have helped.'

I bit my lip. I hated that he sounded hurt, but had the boot been on the other foot and he'd kept something so monumental from me, I would have been upset too.

'Our friendship . . .'

'I know,' I said, cutting him off. 'It meant the world to me too, but I also know you would have tried to make me go back to The Arches; you would have wanted me to carry on singing and I'd realised I wasn't cut out for it by then. I didn't think I could cope with the reminder of what I'd lost on top of losing the mother I had known and loved as well.'

I explained what had happened at the audition where I'd taken the call that had changed the course of my life. I could remember it word for word, like it had been branded onto my brain.

'I realised then that I couldn't have it all,' I whispered, 'so I decided to part with all of it.'

He looked as appalled as Freddie had.

'So,' Pete said sadly, his enthusiasm for his breakfast roll completely forgotten, 'you're not singing at all now.'

I shook my head. Aside from the bathroom session, I hadn't sung a note in years and that didn't count.

'No,' I told him. 'I'm not and I never will again.'

Pete opened his mouth to interrupt. I knew he was going to contradict me but I didn't let him.

'Mum's second stroke was a hundred times worse than the first,' I said quickly. 'She didn't survive and I've been on my own ever since.'

'You should have called then,' Pete said, sounding stung. 'A text would have been enough. I should have been there for you, Beth. I wouldn't have cared that we'd lost touch in-between. I could have helped you through it.'

'I thought it had been too long,' I choked. 'I knew you'd be upset that I hadn't told you what had happened right from the start and I thought I'd left it too late.'

We were quiet for a moment then, both lost in our thoughts. I could hardly blame Pete for looking so wounded. What had happened was huge, something best friends supported each other through and I hadn't given him the chance.

'And to think I thought you were flying,' he said quietly. 'I was expecting to see your name in lights and plastered across a billboard any day now.'

'No chance of that,' I sniffed.

'I should have called you . . .' he began.

'No,' I said firmly. 'This was all on me, Pete. You shouldn't have done anything.'

Pete nodded, but he didn't look convinced.

'So,' he eventually said, 'what's prompted you to find me now?'

I told him about my move to Nightingale Square. How I'd gone into the shop and his niece had told me that he still worked there.

'It was such a shock,' I smiled, imagining the look of utter surprise that must have flickered across my face that day. 'And I scarpered. I've been working my way up to coming back in ever since.'

'Well,' he said, 'thank god you found the courage! I envy you living in Nightingale Square. It's gorgeous.'

'It is,' I agreed. 'Where are you living?'

'In the flat.'

'The one above the shop?'

'Where else?'

It seemed like very little had changed in Pete's life, but what about his big dream?

'I'm so sorry about your mum, Beth,' he said, when we fell quiet again. 'I just can't get my head around it. I truly thought you were off and running and that you didn't need me hanging onto your coattails.'

'Oh Pete,' I gasped, feeling wretched.

'I didn't mind,' he shrugged. 'I was pleased one of us was living the dream.'

'Are you not then?' I asked, wanting to hear more about him. 'What about your dreams? Are you still writing and playing?'

'Beth,' Pete frowned, 'I still work in On the Box, I live above the shop and I let my niece run rings around me to keep my sister happy. Do you *really* think there's any possibility that I've hit, or come within fifty miles of, the big time?'

'I guess not,' I winced, mindful of his tone. 'But you're playing locally, right? You still gig, don't you?'

'I'll get us some more tea,' he said. 'This pot's stewed.'

When he came back, I asked him again.

'If I'd known we were going to have so much to tell each other,' he said, swilling the pot and avoiding my eye, 'I would have asked you up to the flat.'

'It's fine,' I said, looking about me and feeling grateful that the street was still reasonably quiet. 'So, come on, tell me. I've shared, now it's your turn. Are you playing or not?'

'I *was* playing,' he said reluctantly as he poured the tea, 'up until eighteen months or so ago.'

'Why did you stop?'

Whereas I had hesitated before, now it was Pete's turn.

'I was in a band,' he said finally, stirring sugar into his mug. 'There were just the three of us, but then the singer left and the other guy asked if his girlfriend could join us. She was a singer too. A pretty decent one as it turned out, and after her arrival things really began to take off.'

'So, what happened?' I frowned. 'What occurred that has stopped you playing now?'

Pete pushed away his plate, on which sat a huge custard slice he'd picked up with the second pot of tea.

'Let's just say, she turned out to be a bit of a bitch.'

'Oh,' I gasped.

She must have been really awful because Pete never criticised anyone.

'Go on,' I encouraged.

'Well,' he said, sounding uncharacteristically bitter, 'not to put too fine a point on it, she had big ideas for us and big dreams . . .'

'Just like you then.'

Pete snorted.

'Yeah, something like that,' he said derisively.

'I don't understand.'

'Let's just say, it didn't take me long to realise that *I* was too big,' he whispered.

'You?' I frowned. 'I don't understand.'

He fidgeted in his chair, looking uncomfortable.

'Apparently,' he said, making air quotes with his fingers, 'I didn't fit her vision for the band. I wasn't the right aesthetic and I was asked to leave.'

'You're kidding?'

'Beth,' Pete wryly smiled, 'I've just abandoned a pastry in order to be able to finish telling you this pitiful tale. Do you really think I'm kidding?'

'So ... she said, you were ...'

'Too fat.' He shrugged. 'In a nutshell.'

I didn't know what to say.

'And her partner, the bloke I used to call my best mate, sided with her and we parted company,' he said sadly. 'No more band and no more mate.'

'What's happened to the band?'

'No idea,' said Pete, picking up the pastry again. 'I've not followed them or the scene since. Although I did go to an open-mic at The Dragon a few days ago. Just to listen mind, not to take part. It was good. Really good and thankfully they weren't there. You should have come along.'

'You were right,' I readily agreed, ignoring the open-mic suggestion. 'She was wrong to do that and the guy must have been an arsehole to take her side.'

'Maybe,' said Pete, flinching at my words. 'I dunno. Maybe he was just in love. People do crazy things when they're in love.'

'Do they?'

I couldn't honestly say I'd ever been in love. Not the whole hook, line and sinker shenanigans anyway. I looked at Pete again. He'd turned bright red.

'Are you in love, Pete?'

'Me?' he blustered. 'God no. Well,' he added, 'sort of. A bit. But the woman doesn't know. I like her a lot, but . . .'

'Why haven't you asked her out?'

'I can't imagine she'd be very keen to go on a date with a fatty, would she? She's a goddess, Beth. Or she should be.'

I hated the fact that his confidence had taken such a battering.

'No, Pete,' I began but he reached across the table and grabbed my sleeve.

'Oh my god!' he gasped, scattering crumbs and drawing the attention of a couple walking by. 'You won't have heard what's happened. Oh Beth . . .' he then added, more quietly.

'If it's about The Arches,' I quickly cut in, sparing him, 'I do know some of it. My neighbours, Lisa and Jacob, are involved with the place and they've told me. Poor Moira.'

'Yeah,' he said. 'Poor Moira. And I know Lisa and Jacob of course . . . Hang on,' he then frowned, 'Moira and your mum were friends, Beth. She must have known what had happened. Why didn't she tell me?'

Thinking about it, I was surprised she hadn't said anything to him.

'Then again,' he carried on, his frown deepening as he worked the timing out, 'I did stop going to The Arches for a while, which is when it must have first happened.'

'And in that time,' I forced myself to admit, 'I did nothing to nurture Mum and Moira's friendship. In fact,' I shamefacedly added, 'I drove a wedge between them when I told Mum that keeping in touch with Moira was too painful when I wasn't in a position to carry on singing. She didn't see her again after that.'

I didn't feel good about that at all. At the time I had labelled my actions as self-preservation but with hindsight and some distance from the intensity of the situation, it felt straight up selfish.

'I can understand why you did that,' Pete said softly.

'I can understand why I did it too,' I responded, 'but that didn't make it right.'

We were quiet again then. I thought over all that had happened in the past and how much of it I regretted.

'Are you involved with The Arches now?' I eventually asked.

'Yes,' Pete nodded, further entwining the two previously pulled apart strands in my life. 'But only in an administrative capacity. And as you know Lisa and Jacob,' he then more excitedly said, 'I'm guessing you've heard there's going to be a summer fair and a musical showcase to raise funds for the new venue?'

'I have,' I confirmed.

'And that they're looking for current and former Arches attendees to perform.' He carried on with what he no doubt thought was a winning smile. 'You'd be perfect,' he said in a wheedling tone.

'No way,' I said, feeling my temperature shoot up. 'I haven't told them I know anything about the place and I've no intention of them ever finding out. I'm never going to sing in public again. You have to promise me, Pete,' I begged, beginning to panic. 'Please promise me that you won't say anything? I couldn't bear it.'

'It's okay,' he said soothingly, looking deep into my eyes. 'If that's what you want, of course I won't say anything. It's not like I'm playing either, is it?'

'You promise?'

'I promise.'

I knew Pete was someone I could wholeheartedly trust and as a result, I felt my heart rate start to level off.

'I'll help out with the event,' I told him when I was feeling calmer, 'but that's as far as it goes. I'm not going to do a Freddie Fanshawe,' I added.

'You're not going to do a what?' Pete frowned.

'Ignore me,' I said, shaking my head. 'We've got this new resident in the care home where I work now and he just popped into my head. It turns out he's a bit of a local celeb. Someone,' I added with a sigh, 'who found a way to incorporate music into his life even after he'd had his heart broken over it.'

'I know who Freddie Fanshawe is,' Pete grinned. 'What a guy.'

I was going to suggest that he should take a leaf out of the old man's book and find a way to keep his love of music alive but I didn't for fear that he might turn the argument around and suggest I do the same.

'He's playing at the care home garden party tomorrow,' I said instead. 'You should come along.'

'Do you know what,' Pete smiled and I felt my heart fill with familial love for my re-found friend, 'I think I will. What's the address?'

Chapter 14

After exchanging mobile numbers, Pete headed back to the shop to see what work, if any, his niece had done and I walked to the Grow-Well. I'd barely been able to visit during the week and wanted to show willing, especially as I was going to miss the Sunday session too. Not that I turned out to be much use when I got there.

I was so happy to have Pete back in my life, and I was so distracted by playing over our reunion in my head, that I could have been deadheading rather than harvesting and pulling crops up, rather than weeds. My old friend had been exactly as he had always been – warm, welcoming and above all, understanding.

I couldn't help wishing that he'd tell the girl he'd fallen for that he was smitten because her luck was very definitely in. As was mine. Pete was the best friend I had ever had and I was delighted to have made contact with him again and reforged our former connection. We wouldn't be losing touch again. Ever.

'Beth,' smiled Kate, 'how are you settling in? I've been meaning to come over to the house to see you, but haven't had the chance.'

She and Jasmine had been collecting eggs from the Grow-Well hen coop when I arrived.

'Good,' I told her. 'Really great. The house is wonderful and it's so close to work.'

'No problems, then?'

Aside from the fact that my housemate was music-mad and I'd upset him after he'd called me out for doing nothing more heinous than humming, absolutely none.

'Nope,' I said, keeping my eyes trained on the row of salad I was supposed to be thinning. 'None.'

'Super,' she said. 'I'm so pleased it's all worked out. I know Luke was worried about Eli being on his own so much. He's had a tough few months and it's good that he's got someone living with him now.'

'I'm sure the company is doing us both the world of good,' I replied, still avoiding her eye.

I didn't linger after that. Kate's words about Eli's 'tough few months' had cranked my guilt up another notch and as a result, I decided that I would walk down to the Castle Coffeehouse and force Eli to listen to my apology. I'd bared my soul once in public already that weekend, so I was sure I could do it again.

I had admitted to myself that my feelings for him ran far deeper than those you'd usually assign to a housemate, and even though there was no way I would ever further complicate things between us by admitting that, I wanted to clear the air and hopefully start our relationship afresh.

However, as luck would have it, I was gifted the opportunity to apologise in private because he was in the house when I got back.

'Eli,' I said, feeling breathless, 'you're here.'

'I am,' he said, leaning awkwardly against the kitchen cupboard.

He looked as tense as I suddenly felt.

'I've been trying to reach you,' I told him as my cheeks flushed red. 'But we've been missing each other here and I know you've had trouble with your phone.'

He didn't say anything.

'I want to say I'm sorry,' I bowled on. 'I had no right to talk to you the way I did and you most likely did catch me humming because I've caught myself doing it now,' I admitted. 'I really am truly, truly sorry.'

'I know you are,' he said, pulling his phone out of his shorts pocket and looking briefly at the screen.

'Did you get any of my messages?' I asked, feeling embarrassed because before he left the note on the fridge, I'd really bombarded his inbox.

'All of them,' he said, a faint smile playing around his lips.

'Oh,' I said. 'But I thought there was something wrong with your mobile. I assumed none of my messages had got through.'

'I just thought it would be easier to say that,' he said, running a hand through his hair.

'Easier than what?' I frowned.

'Admitting the truth.'

'I don't understand.'

'I know you don't,' he said, shoving his phone out of sight again, as he also turned red. 'Of course, you don't. Let me pour us some drinks, and then I'll try to explain.'

After I had freshened up, we sat together in the sitting room, him in his armchair and me on the sofa with my feet tucked under me. It felt achingly familiar but also a very long time since we'd done it. Considering I'd only recently moved in, we seemed to have established a whole pattern of comfortable habits and for the first time since losing Mum, I felt like I had a proper place to call home.

I very much hoped I wasn't about to lose it. I knew I was going to have to force myself to stop noticing how good-looking Eli was and ignore the silly antics of my heart whenever he was nearby if I wanted to stay living in Nightingale Square, but if that's what it took, I'd do it.

'Okay,' said Eli, leaning down the side of the armchair and picking up a plastic lidded tub. 'I have loads to tell you, Beth, and not all of it is going to be easy, so I'm going to kick things off with this.'

'What is it?' I asked, before my imagination could run amok and conjure up all sorts of horrible endings to our conversation.

The worst of which would be Eli telling me he had decided to move out. Dammit. Too late.

'Open it and see,' he said, reaching across so I could take the tub. 'Be careful. It's heavy.'

He was right, it was very heavy and as the weight of it moved from his hands to mine, the contents shifted and I almost dropped it.

'It sounds like money,' I said, my eyes flicking back to his.

'It is,' he nodded. 'Quite a bit. Have a look inside.'

I peeled back the lid and found it was half filled with one- and two-pound coins, along with a bundle of five-pound notes. There was a raffle ticket book on top of the haul, with lots of tickets torn out.

'They're raffle tickets for the garden party,' Eli explained. 'I've been selling them on your behalf in the coffeehouse. There's getting on for two hundred pounds in there.'

My breath caught in my chest as I looked from the money to him and back again. I'd upset him, we weren't even talking and yet he'd gone to all this trouble. Why had he done that? The incredible act of kindness, on top of what he'd already done to gather raffle prizes from our neighbours, did nothing to quash my feelings for him.

'I began plugging the garden party as soon as I'd put up the poster you gave me,' he carried on. 'Lots of customers said they wouldn't be able to make the event itself, but that they'd buy a raffle ticket if I had any available, so I picked up a book and started selling.'

I was genuinely lost for words. Given the way things had been between us, and given that I was the sole cause of the hiatus, I honestly couldn't understand why he'd made the effort.

'I hope that was all right?' he asked, when I didn't say

anything. 'I've written everyone's contact details on the stubs. That is right, isn't it? That's how it works.'

It must have taken him ages and caused quite a queue in the confines of the coffeehouse.

'Yes,' I swallowed, pulling myself together, 'that's exactly right. This is even more money than I thought I'd make at the party. It's a huge boost to the fund, Eli.'

'That's all right then,' he said, sounding relieved.

'Thank you,' I glowed. 'Thank you so, so much. It must have taken forever to take down everyone's details. Did your boss mind? Does she even know?'

Eli smiled.

'Melanie didn't mind at all,' he told me. 'She's back at work now, on light duties, and it turns out her grandmother was a resident at the home a couple of years ago and she loved the place, so the boss was all for it. She probably sold as many tickets as I did.'

'That's amazing,' I swallowed. 'Thank you. Both of you.' I rattled the tub. 'I can't believe it.'

'You'll be able to keep the pens and jigsaws stocked up for a while now, won't you?' Eli smiled.

'I will,' I smiled back, thinking of what this unexpected cash injection could mean for the residents.

At this rate, I might be able to arrange visits from the miniature donkeys I'd recently read about, as well as the dogs.

'I'm going to need every pound I can lay my hands on, to get things set up the way I want them,' I told Eli. 'So this extra money is a godsend.'

'That's great.'

I put the lid back on and tried to swallow away the words that were lined up on the tip of my tongue, but they poured out anyway.

'I'm not sure why you've raised it though,' I said. 'To be honest, given the way I spoke to you before, I thought you'd be asking Kate to turf me out, rather than further supporting my fundraising efforts. You've done so much already, Eli. I don't feel as though I deserve this, too.'

'I was upset with you,' he admitted, fiddling with a loose thread on the chair. 'That's why I've stayed out of your way, but the truth is . . .'

'The truth is what?' I asked, when he didn't carry on.

'The truth is,' he sighed, 'that some of what you said that day really hit home.'

'I'm sorry,' I whispered.

'No,' he said, 'don't be. It was high time I faced up to a few things and thought through them properly. You've actually helped me get my head straight.'

'Really?'

Was that a light at the end of the tunnel?

'Truly.'

There was such conviction behind that one word that I knew I could believe him. It was a huge relief. I felt as though a massive weight had been lifted.

'So why did you say you were having phone trouble when you weren't?' I couldn't resist asking him. 'And why have you headed out the second you've heard me come in? And you haven't been playing your music when you've been here.'

I wanted to ask where he'd spent the previous night too, but didn't for fear of hearing that it might have been with another woman.

'I just needed some space,' he said, picking up his drink. 'And some quiet.'

'Well, I never,' I gasped. 'That's something I never thought I'd hear you say.'

'I know, right,' he smiled sheepishly. 'I stayed at my mum's last night and she reckoned she'd never known me to be so silent.'

As delighted as I was to know his night-time where-abouts, I hoped I wasn't responsible for quietening him. Music and song were a huge part of who Eli was. It was too awful to contemplate that I might have turned his volume down for good.

'Does your mum live nearby?'

'She's up on the coast and she's always working, so pinning her down isn't easy,' Eli explained. 'It had been a while, so it was good to see her. I knew she'd be able to help me make sense of a few things.'

'Mums are the best for that,' I agreed, feeling a pang that I no longer had mine to turn to when I needed to talk some-thing out. 'You aren't thinking of moving out, are you?' I suddenly panicked.

'No,' Eli laughed. 'Don't look so worried.'

'And you aren't going to boot me out?'

Eli laughed again.

'It's not funny,' I squeaked.

'It is,' he said, wiping his eyes. 'Or it will be when you know what I needed to talk to Mum about. Or at least I hope you'll think it is,' he added, doing a complete U-turn and sounding deadly serious. 'Well, maybe not funny exactly.'

'Eli!' I scolded. 'What the hell's going on?'

'All right, all right,' he said, turning a peaky shade of pale.

'Will you please just put me out of my misery?'

He leant forward a little in his chair and stared deep into my eyes. I had to look away.

'The thing is,' he began, and I could tell he was still looking at me even though I wasn't looking at him. 'The thing is, Beth, I'm falling in love with you and I don't want to mess it up.'

My eyes snapped back to his face and the previously rolling wave in my stomach shifted and became a fluttery, butterfly feeling in my chest. Had he really just said that he was falling in love with me or had my ears morphed his actual words into something different?

'And I've been worrying that it's a rebound thing,' he carried on, confirming that I had heard him correctly. 'Because I had this horrendous break-up not all that long ago and my world turned to shit and I haven't so much as looked at another woman since. But then you and your million and one houseplants moved in and my heart began to beat again and my life became, well . . . perfect.'

I felt a bubble of something, possibly laughter, begin to

fight its way up and into my mouth, nudged along by the palpitations happening in my chest. I covered my lips with my hand and tried to turn the sound into a hiccup.

'I started to fall for you,' Eli carried on, 'the moment I set eyes on you but it's complicated, what with us living together and my heart having been so recently broken. It's complicated, right?'

'Yes,' I dumbly nodded, 'it's complicated.'

I wanted to add that it was also totally worth the risk.

'And that's why I turned to the song,' he explained, 'the one you reckoned was a break-up song. It was actually my way of trying to give you a hint of what I was feeling, without having to come out and say the words. I thought if you got the message through the lyrics, then what I was feeling had to be right and I wasn't going to mess anything up, because that's the last thing I want to do.'

I pressed my lips tighter together as I ran through the lines in my head.

'I should have known, given your aversion to music that it wasn't the right medium, but I didn't know what else to do,' he further said. 'Music has always been my go-to and that song, well, it just says everything I want to convey.'

He stopped talking and we stared into each other's eyes. His whole face radiated hope while mine must have registered shock, even though my insides were fizzing with pleasure.

'Oh, come on,' he said, making me jump, 'say something, will you, Beth? Mum told me to forget the music and just tell you straight, but now I'm beginning to wish I'd kept my mouth shut. You don't feel anything like that for me, do you?' he winced.

I knew I had to put him out of his misery, but it wasn't easy. I'd never experienced a forthright declaration of love before, and it had hit all the harder because Eli was someone I had deep, genuine and passionate feelings for. Like him, I didn't want to mess it up either.

'I think,' I began, then stopped as he leapt out of his chair and knelt in front of me.

'Or maybe you shouldn't tell me,' he said. 'Especially if it's not what I want to hear.'

I looked into his eyes again, leant forward and tucked a curl behind his ear.

'I wouldn't worry,' I smiled, 'it's exactly what you want to hear.'

'It is?' he gasped, wide-eyed.

I nodded, reached for the front of his shirt and pulled him closer.

'I think I'm falling in love with you, too, Eli,' I said softly.

When Pete had talked about love and being in love, I'd dismissed it as an emotion I'd never felt, but that was pure denial. Looking into Eli's eyes, I knew I had felt it, I was feeling it. The pounding heart, the lick of desire, the urge to be with someone all the time and the pain of not being with them when you were apart, these were all things I felt for and about Eli and they were growing in intensity with every breath. No matter how potentially complicated the situation was.

Before, I had conned myself into believing that my desolate feelings were the result of not having had the chance to apologise, but now I could be honest with him and myself. The heady feelings coursing through my system were all about the first stirrings of love and of course, a whole lot of lust.

'You really feel the same?' he asked.

'I really do,' I answered.

Our lips were just millimetres apart. I could feel the heat of him through his shirt. I could smell his aftershave. I could almost taste him on my lips.

'And you're sure you want to do this?' he whispered.

The gentle caress of his breath on my face was too much. I pressed my lips against his and kissed him and he kissed me back. My arms wrapped around his neck and as the moment deepened, he dipped the tip of his tongue into my mouth. It felt exquisite and I let out a gasp as the rest of my body tingled with freshly awakened desire and a pulse of pure pleasure.

By the time we came up for air, there was enough electricity coursing through my erogenous zones to light up Blackpool at Christmas. Eli rested his forehead against mine.

'You're sure,' he smiled.

'I am,' I told him, feeling rather out of breath.

'But ...'

'No buts,' I insisted.

'But,' he carried on, 'I want to take this slow, Beth. I've got baggage, and I get the feeling that you've got stuff you're sorting through, too.'

Mine was a very different collection of luggage to his, but he was right, there were still things I was having to process.

'I think we're about to begin something wonderful and I really want to get it right and do it justice. I think we both deserve that. We deserve the best relationship,' he carried on, 'so please, let's not—'

'Mess it up,' I finished for him.

'Exactly,' he said. 'Let's take it slowly, yes?'

'All right,' I whispered, dipping my head again. 'Slowly sounds good to me.'

Chapter 15

Eli and I spent a long time kissing on the sofa Saturday evening. We were hard pushed to stop long enough to eat the takeaway we'd ordered, but we just about managed it and chatted the whole time we ate. As we worked our way through the delicious feast, we discussed all sorts of things, but neither of us broached the subject of our heartbreak or the baggage from the past that we were lugging about in the present.

'Had it not been for your aversion to music,' Eli grinned, as he speared a mini spring roll with a chopstick, 'I would have fallen for you hook, line and sinker the first time we met.'

'Really?' I smiled back.

It turned out our feelings had been mirroring practically from the moment we had laid eyes on each other. Had it not been for Eli's love of music, I knew I would have found it impossible to resist my feelings for him from the off, too.

'Um,' he teased, biting the roll in half, 'I would. And in spite of the fact that you had soaked me in coffee.'

'I think you'll find you did that to yourself,' I laughed,

remembering the finer details of our less-than-ideal introduction.

'True,' he conceded. 'But it's a relief that my passion for playlists didn't scare you away.'

'It would have taken more than that,' I told him.

'Really?'

'Hell yes,' I giggled, as I nabbed the last prawn ball and dipped it into the bowl of sticky sweet and sour sauce. 'I really do love this place, so it would take more than a thumping bassline to make me leave.'

'You little minx,' Eli laughed as I popped the ball into my mouth. 'Are you telling me you're only in this relationship for the awesome digs?'

'The fabulous house might have a part to play in it,' I giggled as I chewed.

'In that case,' he said, laying down his chopsticks, 'I'll just have to find a way to switch your focus from bricks and mortar to me, won't I?'

'You will,' I laughed. 'And I can't wait to see what you come up with.'

My mind was dreaming up all sorts of seductive scenarios.

'And as well as applying some thought to that,' he then self-consciously said, 'I've decided I'm going to start writing songs again. As long as I can find somewhere other than my bedroom to try them out, that is.'

'You write your own material?' I interestedly asked.

'I do,' he said, turning endearingly pink. 'And it's time I started again.'

'In that case,' I said, 'you'd better try them out here, hadn't you?'

'I can't do that,' he said, a frown forming. 'You'd hate it. Even if I did stick to my room, you'd be able to hear me.'

Before, I would have been reaching for the noise-cancelling headphones at the mere mention of him playing in the house but having now experienced extreme aversion therapy at work and sung in private at home, I realised I could handle it. I had worked out that Eli, according to his Spotify playlist along with the occasional strumming I'd heard drifting out from his room, favoured a similar sort of sound to what I used to enjoy and, as a result, I was now intrigued to hear more.

'I wouldn't,' I insisted. 'I promise you – I wouldn't mind at all.'

He looked at me for a moment, no doubt trying to work out if I was being accommodating for the sake of our fledgling relationship or if I really meant it. I returned his gaze with heartfelt sincerity.

'Well, okay,' he smiled, letting out a breath. 'In that case, I'll play here, but only because you've admitted to the humming.'

'Excellent,' I smiled back.

'It would have been a very cruel twist of fate for me to have fallen for a genuine music-hater,' he further added.

'I definitely don't hate it,' I said, abandoning my plate and sitting further back on the sofa. 'I've never hated it. I just find it hard to listen to now.'

I knew I was trying to make light of something that was so much bigger, but I didn't want anything souring the start of this sweet new beginning, for either of us. There was no need for Eli to know anything about my singing past because it was going to have absolutely no bearing on my future.

'I'm guessing there's a reason why?' he asked.

'It's mostly to do with my mum,' I told him, trying to sound blasé.

'I take it she was a music lover as well as a plant lover?' Eli further probed.

'Yeah,' I said quietly. 'She was.'

We sat in silence for a moment. I was still stunned to admit that I had accepted that music was back in my life and it was going to be a permanent feature. But, given the circumstances, what other choice did I have?

There was Freddie at work and Eli at home, and of course, Pete, so it was a no-brainer really. If I wanted these men in my life, and I most definitely did, then concessions had to be made. I might have almost got my head around that, but there was still no way I was going to start singing again. Not in public anyway. I would carry on listening to music and maybe secretly singing in the bath, but that was as far as I was willing to go.

'Are you going to put yourself forward to play at the fund-raiser for the new Arches?' I asked Eli, my train of thought leading me in that direction. 'Will you have anything ready that you'd be happy to publicly perform by then?'

'I might have a couple of songs ready in time,' he said, his expression changing, 'but as I never had anything to do with The Arches, I wouldn't fit Lisa's criteria to perform. Though I was involved with a charity in the city I lived in before I came to Norwich and I really enjoyed helping out there. It was a similar sort of community-support project for kids.'

'In that case,' I said, 'I'm sure Lisa would make an exception and add your name to the bill.'

Eli shook his head.

'I might offer to help out a bit in the new place when it's established,' he said, 'but I wouldn't play at the fundraiser.'

'But—' I interrupted.

'There's no way I could bring myself to ever play in public again, Beth,' he then said, cutting across me. 'I don't deserve to.'

'I don't understand,' I frowned.

'I know you don't,' he said sadly, 'but if it's all the same, I'd rather not get into it all right now.'

'Of course,' I agreed.

I was curious to know why he wouldn't play in public again, but as I had secrets of my own that I wasn't ready to share, it wouldn't have been fair to push him to reveal his.

'I'll just stick to playing here in the house,' he said. 'For my ears only.'

'That's fair enough,' I nodded. 'As long as that's what you really want.'

'It is,' he responded. 'Now,' he said, sounding more like himself, 'are you going to fight me for this last spring roll?'

With the garden party happening the next day, I forced

myself to turn in early, even though what I really wanted to do was stay curled up on the sofa with Eli. As we had lingeringly kissed goodnight, we had agreed to keep our relationship under wraps for the moment, so there would be no hand holding and no kissing in public. I knew it was going to take me a little while to adjust to life as a twosome because I'd been on my lonesome for a very long time, so didn't mind about that at all.

'I really hope it isn't going to stay like this all day,' moaned Sandra, as she took in the cloud-covered sky late the next morning.

Everything was almost ready and the gardens and grounds at the Edith Cavell Care Home had been transformed and looked stunning. There were multiple stalls, games and a rather grand tea tent. I could also see that the piano had already been pulled into position for Freddie to entertain us. And talking of Freddie . . .

The paper bunting the residents had made and decorated was flapping in the gentle breeze and I'd noticed that a couple of 'I heart FF' flags had somehow made their way into a few of the garlands. I wondered if that was Greta or Ida's doing or perhaps even both. Where Freddie was concerned, they were neck and neck in the adoration stakes. Fortunately, he had enough about him to keep both of them sweet.

'I rather hope it does stay like this,' I said, steering Sandra away from the bunting. 'At least you're not going to have to worry about everyone getting heatstroke. This cloudy weather will help keep the temperature down.'

'I suppose that's true,' she said, biting her lip, 'and it will stop everything melting in the tea tent too, won't it?'

'Exactly,' I agreed.

The fridge in the staffroom, along with the table top, were full of the delicious cakes Mark had earlier dropped off from Blossoms for the raffle and he'd given me a pretty gingham-lined wicker hamper from Poppy too, which was now full of her mouth-watering chutneys and pickles.

I was absolutely thrilled with my stall. It looked very upmarket, thanks to the contributions from my generous neighbours and of course, Finn's sculpture, which was set on a separate table next to the raffle goods, added to the excitement. It was already attracting a lot of attention and the fete hadn't even opened yet. My heart skittered as I thought of the effort Eli had gone to to make it the best it could possibly be.

'I meant to tell you,' said Sandra, as we walked, her high heels struggling on the lawn, 'Mike has said he'll draw the raffle as well as take the bids in the auction, if that's all right?'

I knew now that Mike was the radio guy, the king of the local airwaves. I also knew he and Sandra had been out for dinner together the night before because she'd told me the moment I'd arrived.

'That's perfect,' I replied. 'And if he does both towards the end of the afternoon, it will hopefully keep everyone here right up until the end.'

'Yes,' she said, looking at her feet. 'That's what I thought.

Oh, and I spoke to those neighbours of yours yesterday after-noon – Carole and Graham.'

'Oh, yes.'

'They're going to liaise with you about getting the clubs going as soon as I've carried out the relevant checks.'

'That's wonderful,' I said.

'It is,' she agreed. 'You've barely started in the job, Beth, and you've already transformed the place. I'm pleased. Very pleased indeed. We'll be filling those empty rooms in no time. No wonder you're looking so happy.'

She was right in that I was happy in my work, very happy in fact, but I put my current level of joy down to the warm embrace and multiple kisses I'd received from Eli before, during and after breakfast. He reckoned that as we weren't going public yet, we needed to kiss in private *a lot* to make up for the lost opportunities and I was all for that.

'Right,' said Sandra, 'I'm going to change my shoes. These heels are getting ruined and they cost a fortune.'

She hobbled off and Sara took her place.

'You're looking very pleased with yourself,' she grinned.

For a moment I was thrown off guard.

'But then, looking at the raffle,' she added, 'I'm not surprised. You've outdone yourself, Beth. Sheila's already sounding sniffy about it.'

I'd spotted the former raffle organiser having a sneaky look at everything earlier, when she thought I wasn't about.

'It's all down to my housemate,' I quickly pointed out, feeling relieved that Sara had assumed my happiness was the result of the laden table. 'He asked the neighbours for contributions and they're such a talented lot. They've been so generous.'

Sara looked at me again. More thoughtfully this time.

'They are talented,' she agreed, then added, 'Have you done something with your hair? Or changed your make-up?'

'No,' I said, my hands checking my messy bun, 'I don't think so.'

I'd barely had time to give either my hair or face much attention after all the time spent lip-locked to Eli.

'You look different,' she said, 'but I can't put my finger on why.'

'Come on! Come along everyone!' called Sandra, clapping her hands together and saving me from having to come up with a response to Sara's astute observations. 'Team meeting and a quick bite before Mr Fanshawe cuts the ribbon.'

'Is Freddie opening the fete?' I laughed.

'Apparently,' said Sara. 'That'll put DJ Mike's nose out of joint, won't it?'

Freddie had barely snipped the ribbon before visitors started pouring in and the stalls were swamped with customers. I was selling raffle tickets wholesale, along with Harold, who was kindly helping.

Being such an authority on Nightingale Square, where the vast majority of the prizes had come from, he talked the talk and sold tickets like they were going out of fashion and there was plenty of interest in Finn's sculpture too. I could already tell that was going to make a mint. The auction was scheduled for four o'clock and lots of people had told me they were going to stay at the party to watch it happen.

I'd earlier heard a couple of the carers moaning about how much Sandra had splashed out on hiring the more elaborate than usual tea tent, but given the extra numbers of visitors, her investment was inspired and they were already eating their words. As well as the cakes. And Sandra was in her element; she'd rushed over to tell me she'd had enquiries about the empty rooms from three of the visitors, so her sales spiel was clearly working.

'Hey you,' said a voice close to my ear.

'Eli!' I gasped, spinning around. 'I didn't think you were going to be able to make it.'

'I can't stay long,' he said, 'but Melanie said I could pop down and spend a few quid on her behalf.'

'She's so kind,' I said. 'I can't wait to meet her.'

'You'll have to get over your aversion to coffee then, won't you?' he said, stepping tantalisingly closer.

I could smell the coffeehouse on his work shirt. It was a delicious aroma and as I gazed up at him, I wondered if my pupils were as wide as his.

'Perhaps I will,' I said breathlessly. 'I'm beginning to believe anything's possible since I moved into Nightingale Square.'

For a moment I thought I'd lost my charm because Eli suddenly wasn't looking at me, but gazing over my shoulder.

'Eli?' I frowned.

'Is this your young man, Beth?' came Greta's mischievous voice from behind me.

She really was the queen of the silent approach.

'Greta,' I smiled, turning around and taking a discreet step away from Eli as she eyed him with interest. Wasn't Freddie enough for her? 'I was wondering where you'd got to.'

'I've been turning pages for Freddie,' she said wistfully, 'but Ida's taken over now,' she added, with an acerbic edge.

'Who's Freddie?' Eli asked.

Had I still been close enough, I would have given him a sharp nudge in the ribs to shut him up. Greta could talk for hours on the subject of Freddie and I didn't want to get her started.

'Who's Freddie?' she theatrically gasped. 'Call yourself a local!'

'Not yet,' he said, 'I only moved to Norwich a while ago.'

Greta's expression softened.

'In that case, you're forgiven,' she twinkled at him. 'Why don't I fill you in while we have a dance? That is,' she said, turning her deceptively innocent-looking eyes to me, 'if you don't mind me purloining your young man, Bethany?'

She reached for his hand before I could answer.

'He's not my young man,' I called after them. 'He's my housemate!'

Eli turned and gave me a wink and I couldn't help but laugh as he and Greta began dancing along to 'I Can't Get No Satisfaction' by the Rolling Stones. They were on the receiving end of some very strange looks, but by the time I had finished selling more raffle tickets and looked up again, there was a whole crowd getting down to 'Mustang Sally' by

Wilson Pickett and singing along too. It was all a bit bizarre for a summer Sunday afternoon, but great fun.

'Beth, hi. How's it going?'

'Pete!' I said, rushing to give him a hug. 'Good, really good. I'm so pleased you've come.'

'You can hear the music out on the street,' he grinned, taking off his Fedora and fanning himself with it. 'I had no idea it was going to be such a lively event.'

'Neither did I!' I laughed. 'Can I interest you in a raffle ticket or two?'

'This must be the raffle Stacey gave the voucher for,' he said, spotting the envelope with On the Box written on the front.

'That was all right, wasn't it?' I frowned.

'Of course,' he smiled. 'I'm always happy to support a good cause.'

'Your young man had to go,' said Greta, who was back again and now looking very red in the face, 'but never mind, I see you've got another one.'

I wished Eli had had the opportunity to say goodbye, but I didn't begrudge Greta monopolising him. He was such a catch; I could hardly blame her. Although if she wasn't careful, she'd get a reputation for playing the field and Freddie might not appreciate that. Not that he was any better, of course.

'He wasn't my young man,' I told her again. 'And neither is this one,' I added, before she could say otherwise. 'Pete is a very good friend.'

'Would you care to dance, Pete?' she asked him sweetly. 'Only I'm without a partner at the moment.'

'I'm sorry,' he said graciously, 'but I'm not much of a dancer – perhaps I could interest you in a cup of tea and a slice of cake instead?'

'You know,' Greta grinned, 'I am a bit thirsty.'

I was pleased Pete had opted for refreshments over the twist. The last thing I needed was Greta getting overexcited and talking of overexcited . . .

'Hey,' Sara said breathlessly while plucking at my dress, the moment the pair were out of sight. 'Was that Pete taking Greta into the tea tent?'

'Yes,' I said, 'calm down. You'll do yourself a mischief.'

'Sorry,' she said, fanning herself and smiling widely.

'How do you know Pete?'

'How do *you* know Pete?' she countered.

'He's a mate from way back,' I told her. 'We've known each other for years.'

'Just a mate?'

'Yes,' I said, 'just a mate. So, where do you know him from?'

'Iceni, of course,' she said, as if I should have known. 'He takes photos for us and keeps the website updated.'

That sounded very Pete. As the penny dropped, I went to ask if he was the guy she had hinted had a crush on her, but she carried on talking before I had a chance to get the words out.

'Between you and me,' she confided, her eyes still fixed

on the tea tent, 'I reckon he wouldn't mind having a go at the re-enactment stuff himself.'

'Why doesn't he then?'

'Too shy,' she tutted. 'I reckon that's why he hasn't asked me out either. I'm sure he likes me.'

'So, he's your secret crush,' I smiled.

I thought back over what Pete had told me about the woman he was smitten with. Hadn't he said something along the lines that she should be a goddess? He must have been talking about Sara and her desire to be awarded the role of Boudicca. I knew Boudicca wasn't strictly speaking a goddess, but it was too much of a coincidence for him to have been describing anyone else.

'What would you say if he did ask you out?' I asked eagerly.

'Yes, of course,' she said. 'He's one hunk of a man.'

'Sara!' Sandra called and waved from the other side of the lawn.

She had a man with her. A guy in his forties, casually dressed and in possession of a very self-assured air. He was attracting almost as much attention as Freddie. It could only be Mike from the radio.

'Showtime!' giggled Sara, confirming my thoughts. 'See you in a bit.'

A few minutes later, Pete was back again. He looked red and flustered and I was about to ask what Greta had been up to, but it turned out she wasn't the reason behind his flushed face and nervous stutter.

'That woman,' he said, pointing to where Sara was now

tripping the light fantastic with Charlie and his grand-daughter, 'do you know her?'

'I do,' I grinned. 'She's a work colleague and a very good friend and from what she just told me; I know you know her too. Sara!' I called.

'Bloody hell,' said Pete, through gritted teeth. 'Don't call her over.'

'Hey,' said Sara, as she jogged over to join us.

'Sara,' I beamed, thoroughly enjoying playing match-maker as I knew both parties were wholeheartedly interested in each other, 'I believe you know Pete?'

'I do,' she said, smiling up at him. 'How are you, Pete? No camera today?'

'No,' he stammered, 'not today. And I'm good ... great, actually. I ... er ... I didn't know you worked here ... or that you knew Beth.'

'Well,' she said, seizing the moment, 'you do now. How about a dance?'

'How about a drink?' Pete suggested instead, having looked nervously at the geriatric dance party, which was fast running out of steam.

'After a dance,' said Sara, reaching for his hand and pull-ing him away.

By the time she'd got him settled among the throng she was wearing his hat and he was wearing the biggest smile. It was a sight which made me feel very happy indeed. They were the perfect match for each other and I wondered if Sara might be able to encourage him out from behind his camera and into a rustic tunic. If anyone could do it, she could. I'd make a point of offering to sew him an outfit to match hers.

At four o'clock the fete was almost as busy as it had been all afternoon. Mike had drawn the raffle with aplomb. He had turned it into quite an event, sprinkling the draw with a smattering of witty anecdotes that kept everyone amused. Given the wonderful selection of prizes, I was grateful that he had made such a big thing about it and not just bellowed the numbers out like Sheila used to.

'And now,' he said theatrically, 'it's time for the auction.'

'I tried to get Finn to come,' said Freya, who was by my side, 'but he said he didn't want the attention.'

'Bless him,' I said, 'it's such a generous donation. The money it's going to raise will make a massive difference to what I can get set up to offer the residents.'

'That's great,' she nodded. 'I'll tell him that.'

'No Nell today?' I asked, looking around her feet as Mike read out the information about Finn and the local significance of the sculpture. Norwich was famous for its dragons.

I wasn't really surprised the lovely dog wasn't in attendance. She was a nervy little thing and there was still quite a crowd.

'Oh, she's here,' Freya smiled. 'I didn't realise it would be this busy though, so a chap called Charlie is sitting with her in the dayroom. I hope that's all right?'

'That's fine,' I told her.

I knew Charlie would be made up to have some canine company now his family had headed home.

'Right,' boomed Mike in his best radio voice. 'Let's get the auction started. Who's going to kick things off? I have a bid here from a visitor who has had to leave and it's for seventy pounds, so let's start with that.'

A collective cheer went up.

'Do I hear any advance on seventy?'

By the time the bidding had finished, Mike and the rest of us had heard a lot of advances on seventy and when the walking stick, in lieu of a gavel, went down, the final bid had hit just over eight hundred pounds.

'I can't believe it,' I said, feeling rather overcome as I fanned myself with the book of raffle ticket stubs.

Sandra looked as dazed as I felt.

'Neither can I,' she gasped, before turning to address the crowd. 'All of the money raised from the raffle and auction,' she said loudly, 'is going straight into the activities pot, and given how very generous you've all been, I know there are some fun times to come. Thank you all so much!'

There was another cheer at that and I couldn't wait to get started, putting all the activities in place.

'Would you mind telling us where this beautiful sculpture is going to end up?' Mike asked the young woman who had stepped in at the last moment with the winning bid.

'Not at all,' she grinned. 'I work in The Dragon, just up the road, and the landlord asked me to come and bid on the sculpture because he wants to put it on display in the pub.'

'That's fantastic,' said Mike, starting another round of applause. 'Everyone will be able to enjoy it in there.'

I recognised the bidder. She was Hannah, the partner of Chloe, who volunteered in the gardens of Prosperous Place.

'You wait,' said Freya, giving me a nudge, 'you'll have a request to visit the pub written on your activities suggestion list by the end of the day.'

'I wouldn't be at all surprised,' I laughed.

I wondered if the landlord might be receptive to giving the residents a private viewing.

'We're leaving now,' said Sara, who had stayed along with the rest of the staff, whether they were on shift or not, to help dismantle the fete and settle the residents.

It had been a wonderful afternoon and now everyone, staff and residents alike, was exhausted. I was more than willing to accept when Sandra, buoyed up because she had secured reservations on two of the empty rooms, said I could take the next day off. That said, I wouldn't be sleeping in too late because, knowing what the raffle and auction had raised, I was keen to start researching and planning. If I took my time and struck a bargain or two, pretty much everything on the activities wish list would be able to happen.

'We thought we'd head down to the pub,' said Pete, who looked happier than I'd ever seen him as Sara linked her arm through his. 'Do you fancy it?'

'On any other day I would,' I smiled, 'but I'm dead on my feet, so I'm going to head straight home.'

Eli had sent a message telling me not to worry about

dinner as he'd got it all arranged, but obviously I wasn't going to tell Pete and Sara that for fear of blowing our cover.

'In that case,' said Sara, stifling a yawn, 'we'll see you next week.'

She gave me a wink as she wandered off. She looked every bit as happy as Pete did and I found myself wishing for the day when Eli and I would be able to go public, like them.

'All in good time,' I wistfully reminded myself as I carried on stacking the last few chairs and considered how much easier it was going to be getting used to being a couple without the scrutiny of our well-meaning friends and neighbours, 'all in good time.'

Chapter 16

My new life in Nightingale Square had so far been something of a rollercoaster. In the brief time since moving day,
I'd lurched from ecstatic to anxiety-ridden and stressed and
back again. However, when I woke the day after the garden
party, I just knew that things were finally settling down as I
had always hoped they would. A hundred times better than
I had always hoped they would, in fact.

My blessings were many and varied. Along with the
dream house and access to the Grow-Well, I also had a job
I loved and, thanks to the generosity of Eli, my neighbours
and the wider community, would now be able to excel at.
I'd also reforged the bond with the best friend I'd ever had
and to top it all off, I was right at the very beginning of
what I knew was going to be a wonderful and long-lasting
relationship.

'Morning, sleepyhead,' Eli grinned when I eventually
kicked off the duvet and went down to join him in the
kitchen. 'I thought you were never going to get up. I was

going to give you five more minutes and then come and find you.'

'Why do you think I waited up there for so long?' I purred, wrapping my arms around his waist and breathing in his fresh out-of-the-shower scent.

'Bethany Cousins,' he tutted, looking down at me with a mischievous glint in his eye. 'Were you going to try and seduce me?'

'Most certainly not,' I said, switching to a prim and proper tone, which made him laugh. The feel of it reverberated through his chest and into mine. 'I was just hoping for tea in bed, that's all.'

'Um,' he said disbelievingly, 'no time for that I'm afraid.' He planted a swift kiss on my lips and released me. 'I'm in serious danger of being late for work and that would not be a good start to the week, would it?'

'I suppose not,' I yawned.

'We can't all swan about the house on a Monday,' he teased.

'I'm not going to be swanning about,' I told him. 'I've got work to do.'

'In that case,' he said, 'I'll leave you to it. Come to the Coffeehouse for lunch and I'll introduce you to Melanie.'

By the time I'd remembered that I'd messaged and subsequently promised to meet Pete for lunch, Eli had gone. As I wasn't going to see Sara for a couple of days because she was working night shifts, I wanted to get all the goss from Pete on the other new relationship in my life. Theirs. The more I'd thought about it, the more I realised they were made for each other. What a clever matchmaker I was.

'Crikey,' said Eli, as he came crashing back into the kitchen. 'I almost forgot!'

'What?' I laughed.

'My second goodbye kiss,' he said, pulling me into his arms.

'Wow,' I gasped, when he eventually drew away, having made a very thorough job of it and himself even later for work, 'I hope you'll almost forget every day.'

'Bye!' he shouted, rushing off again. 'See you later.'

This time he really did go and I still hadn't mentioned my plans for lunch. I would just have to take Pete to the Coffeehouse instead of Blossoms.

With the incredible amount of money the garden party raffle and auction had raised fixed firmly at the forefront of my mind, I spent a productive morning plotting and planning the activities and events for the care home residents.

Thanks to Carole and Graham's generous offer to run both baking and gardening clubs and Harold having talked to Luke about the possibility of a trip to the Grow-Well, activities in the home were going to be very different from when Karen was in charge.

Macaroni (as Greta still called it) was officially banned and in its place, there was now a varied schedule and opportunities that were fit for purpose and would suit every taste. Sandra was going to be thrilled and hopefully the residents, both old and new, would be too. I wouldn't officially book anything until I'd got an idea of the potential uptake, but I thought I'd pretty much nailed it and found something for everyone. Perhaps even Bob might be tempted to join in and not moan for once.

A quick glance at the clock told me I was in danger of running almost as late as Eli had been earlier and I left the house in a rush, desperate not to keep Pete waiting.

'Sorry,' I puffed, when I caught sight of him standing on the pavement. 'I've been working at home this morning and I lost track of time.'

'Never mind,' he said, 'I'm not exactly rushed off my feet. I can close up for an hour.'

'What about Stacey? Isn't she working today?'

'Monday is a college day,' Pete told me, adding sceptically, 'allegedly.'

'In that case,' I said, linking my arm through his, 'let's go.'

Pete then set off one way and I went the other. We must have looked like the pushmi-pullyu in *Dr Dolittle*.

'Where are you going?' Pete frowned.

'The Castle Coffeehouse,' I said firmly.

Pete didn't look impressed and I remembered he'd turned the place down the day we were reunited.

'It'll make a change,' I told him.

'But I prefer Blossoms.'

'We went there last time,' I tutted, tugging him in the direction I wanted to go.

'But I like Blossoms,' he said, looking back over his shoulder towards the bakery.

'It'll still be there tomorrow.'

'But I always have my lunch there,' he said wistfully as I pulled harder.

'All the more reason to shake things up a bit,' I told him. 'And talking of shaking things up, how did your date with Sara go yesterday?'

'It was only a pint in the pub,' he said, his feet finally but reluctantly moving in my preferred direction. 'Not a real date.'

'All right then,' I laughed, 'how did your pint in the pub with Sara go yesterday?'

'Brilliant,' he said, ducking his head and looking about ten years old. 'Bloody brilliant actually. Tons better than a real date because the pressure was off.'

I was delighted to hear it. The pavements were packed, which shouldn't have come as a surprise as everyone was on their lunchbreak, but that meant the Coffeehouse was busy too.

'Are you sure you want to have lunch here?' Pete frowned, looking at the crowded space.

'Yes,' I said, giving him a nudge, because he was dithering on the threshold. 'You grab that table,' I pointed as one fortuitously became available, 'and I'll join the queue.'

'What if it's table service?' he asked, glancing about him.

He looked genuinely uncomfortable and I realised he really was a creature of habit.

'Queuing will probably be quicker,' I pointed out, looking at the number of customers streaming in.

'All right,' he relented, squeezing himself behind the table which was near the wall.

The chair he sat on squeaked loudly on the tiled floor and poor Pete turned bright red. Perhaps this wasn't the best idea after all.

'I won't be long,' I told him.

I quickly joined the queue, hoping that the staff, and one in particular, were efficient and I wouldn't be kept waiting too long. I soon realised, however, that there was no sign of Eli. There was a woman overseeing everything with one arm in a sling though and I guessed that had to be Melanie and the guy whizzing about making the machines gurgle and clatter must have been the student who was currently on summer break and had agreed to help out.

'What can I get you?' he asked, when I reached the counter.

It was only then that I realised that, having been so pre-occupied with trying to catch a glimpse of my beau, I hadn't asked Pete what he wanted.

'Oh,' I said, feeling a fool as I read the board, which listed many, many coffees but as far as I could see, no teas and not a huge selection of food either.

The guy looked at me and bit his lip and Melanie stepped forward, most likely to ask if anything was the matter, just as Eli appeared from behind the side of the counter, carrying a huge bag of coffee beans.

'Beth,' he grinned, setting the bag down, 'you came.'

There was a sudden rumpus at one of the tables, which caused a momentary distraction and I stepped to one side, to let the student guy carry on serving the people who were huffing in the queue behind me.

'Hey,' I said to Eli. 'Of course.'

I could tell my face had flushed red as a result of his enthusiastic welcome.

'So,' said the other guy, banging the milk jug on the counter as his attention returned to me, 'this is the Beth you've not shut up about, is it?'

This time it was Eli who turned red and Melanie shook her head. That said, I knew I'd turned an even deeper shade of crimson at the thought of Eli not shutting up about me. That was assuming he only knew one Beth, of course.

'I'm Melanie and we're delighted to meet you, Beth,' smiled the boss, taking over the bungled introductions. 'Eli's been like a different guy since you moved into the house.'

'Do you love his music as much as he loves your houseplants?' the student asked me, with a wink.

'Exactly how much have you told everyone about me, Eli?' I smiled.

'Too much probably,' he laughed, sounding embarrassed.

'Not at all,' said Melanie. 'You're every bit as lovely as he described.'

'Thank you,' I swallowed, feeling even more self-conscious.

'Are you staying?' Eli asked. 'I was hoping we could grab a few minutes, but it's hectic already. Lunchtimes are always busy, but for some reason, it's next level in here today.'

It was quite a contrast to the footfall Pete's place was experiencing, but then his stock was rather niche, while the coffeehouse was fulfilling a basic human need. That is, if humans really did need a latte macchiato or espresso con panna. It was all a different world and language to me, but given the rapidly growing length of the queue, I guessed caffeine provided a much-needed boost on a Monday lunch-time, even in July.

'That's all right,' I told him. 'I didn't get the chance to mention it earlier, but I'd already made plans to meet a friend.'

I looked behind me to wave at Pete but couldn't see the table through the waiting crowd.

'Was that because Eli wouldn't let you up for air?' grinned the student.

I didn't answer, but looked at Eli and frowned. So much for keeping our relationship under wraps.

'That'll account for the stubble rash then,' the student laughed when I didn't answer.

By the time I'd worked out he was trying to get a rise and that Eli hadn't said anything, I'd already rubbed my fingers along my chin and jawline.

'It's just as well you can do your job, James,' Melanie intervened. 'Otherwise, you'd be out on your ear. Focus on what you're doing and Eli, if you want to take a few minutes to talk to Beth, I'm sure we can manage.'

'No,' I said, aware that I had already eaten into a chunk of Pete's lunchbreak, 'it's fine. You get on Eli, and we'll catch up at home tonight.'

'Are you sure?' he asked. 'I'd like to meet your friend.'

I would have liked to have introduced him to Pete too. As they both had a passion for music, I was sure they would get along. That said, given that Pete knew all about my former aspirations and had played duets with me on many occasions, perhaps it was better if I kept them apart. At least until I'd primed Pete as to what I had and hadn't told Eli about myself. In the future, I could imagine Eli and me and Pete and Sara all going to the pub together, but for now I'd probably be better off keeping the past and present separate.

'Honestly, it's fine,' I insisted.

'In that case,' he said, 'let me get you some drinks. What were you going to order?'

'Look mate,' said an agitated voice over my shoulder. 'Are you serving or what?'

'It's fine,' I told Eli, knowing Pete would rather eat at Blossoms anyway. 'You serve this chap and I'll see you later. I'll cook for you tonight.'

'All right,' he relented, but he sounded disappointed. 'I might be a bit later than usual. I have a surprise to pick up first.'

'A surprise?' I asked, biting my lip. 'I wonder what that could be?'

'Well, if he tells you,' tutted the impatient customer, 'it won't be a surprise, will it?'

I blew Eli a kiss and left him to serve Mr Miserable.

'It's a bit crowded in here,' I said, pulling out my phone to check the time as I finally squeezed my way back to the table. 'We'll try Blossoms instead, shall we?'

I looked up to find two women sitting where I'd left Pete.

'Oh,' I said, looking about me, 'sorry. My friend was sitting here a minute ago.'

'Are you Beth?'

'Yes.'

'The young man said to tell you he had to get back to the shop and that we could have the table,' one of the women explained.

'Oh.'

'I hope that's all right,' said the other. 'You haven't got an order coming, have you?'

'No,' I said, pushing my way out. 'That's fine. I didn't order. Enjoy your lunch.'

The sign on the shop door was still turned to closed when I arrived back and I had to hammer for what felt like ages before Pete eventually appeared.

'What happened?' I frowned. 'Why did you take off?'

'Sorry,' he said, looking sheepish. 'I thought I'd left the gas on in the flat.'

I didn't believe that for a second. I didn't think the area was even connected to gas.

'Right,' I said, sensing Pete's unexplained awkwardness and deciding not to push the issue, 'well never mind. It was heaving in there anyway. How about I go and buy some bits from Blossoms and we eat them in the shop. That way, if you do have a rush of customers, you won't miss a sale.'

'Great,' he said, sounding relieved. 'That works for me.'

Rather than just the one, Pete and I spent a very pleasant couple of hours further catching up on what we had taken to calling *the lost years*. He also told me how Sara had convinced him to take part in the forthcoming re-enactment rather than hide away behind his camera.

'She's going to ask you to help make me a tunic and everything,' he said excitedly. 'And I'm not going to lie, I can't wait to get into it.'

'I was going to offer, but you've beaten me to it,' I smiled. 'Are the peasants going to be revolting?' I giggled.

'Something like that,' he grinned back.

'Did you really leave the Coffeehouse because of the gas?' I asked him.

The question had been prowling around my head and I couldn't fight it off, even though I'd previously promised myself I wouldn't make a thing about it.

'No,' he said flatly, 'of course not.'

'What was it then?' I frowned.

He set aside the Blossoms bag which was still full of cakes.

'Someone turned up who I didn't want to see,' he said eventually, screwing an empty bag into a tight little ball.

'Who?' I asked.

'I don't want to talk about it,' he said crossly.

I was taken aback. It took a lot for Pete to get annoyed.

'Fair enough,' I smiled. 'No worries.'

'Hey,' he shouted as Stacey sauntered in, 'shouldn't you be in college?'

'My lecture was cancelled,' she replied smoothly. 'Any cakes left in that bag? I'm starving.'

*

I felt a little nervous about the forthcoming evening with Eli. Not only because I didn't have a particularly extensive culinary repertoire, but also because a few questions had been forming in my mind as the afternoon wore on and the mental cogs had begun to whir.

I had earlier decided that a mix of past and present wasn't what our relationship needed as we got it launched, but something potentially important had been flagged up now that I needed to get to the bottom of.

'Honey!' called Eli in a faux American accent, at roughly the time I had expected, given that he had said he was going to be a little late. 'I'm home!'

'And about time too,' I said, playing along. 'Your dinner was very nearly in the dog.'

'Well,' he said, joining me in the kitchen and sniffing the air in appreciation, 'I'm pleased it's not because it smells amazing. What is it?'

'Risotto,' I shrugged, dropping the act, 'nothing fancy.'

'Exactly what I fancy though,' he said, pulling me into his arms.

I was pleased about that. It might have been an easy make, but I had gone to the trouble of splashing out on a decent bottle of white wine and the very best pecorino to stir through it, along with some fresh peas from the Grow-Well.

I had enjoyed a wonderful cottagecore interlude, sitting by the open back door shelling them into Mum's old, but much-loved, metal colander. I couldn't deny I'd popped as many of the tiny green treats in my mouth as had gone in the risotto. They were like tiny, sweet explosions of flavour on my taste buds. Utterly delicious and very moreish.

'It's just about ready,' I said, after we'd kissed hello and I'd turned off the heat and given the pan another stir. 'Shall we eat in the garden?'

There wasn't much of a garden behind the house, but there was a bistro set, comprising of a tiny table and two chairs and I was planning to ring the changes by planting up some shade-loving pots and containers as the aspect was predominantly north-facing. I rather fancied a banana, with its lush, tropical canopy, but that might have been a little too ambitious, given the space.

'That would be lovely,' said Eli, 'but first, close your eyes and come and see what I've got.'

'That's a contradiction in terms, isn't it?' I asked, taking the pan off the hob and setting it to one side.

'You know what I mean,' he laughed. 'Come on.'

Given everything else my head had been full of, I'd forgotten about the surprise he'd mentioned earlier and I was pleased he hadn't told me what it was. He carefully led me from the kitchen into the dining room.

'Okay,' he said, 'open your eyes.'

I took a breath and slowly blinked.

'What do you think?'

'Of the cardboard box?' I asked, wrinkling my nose.

'No, you loon,' he laughed, pulling it open. 'Look inside.'

'Oh my goodness,' I gasped. 'Where did you find them?'

Nestled inside and wrapped in newspaper were a collection of Sylvac and Withernsea Estate plant pot holders.

'They were in the loft at my grandmother's old place,' Eli told me, carefully lifting them out. 'I rang the current tenant and asked if I could pop round and get them. I haven't been there for a while and going back made me feel a bit funny, but the look on your face says it was worth it.'

'Is that why you didn't go there when you moved?' I asked, peering further into the packed box, 'because it felt wrong being there without her?'

I hadn't really had the chance to find out how the bungalow Mum and I had ended up in would have felt without her in it, because within a matter of weeks I'd had to leave.

'Not really,' Eli explained. 'I suppose I would have got used to it if I'd gone there, but the place is far too big for just one person. It's a proper family home and besides, it was already let when I started looking. Anyway,' he said, with a nod to the box, 'what do you think?'

'They're gorgeous,' I said, picking out a particularly brightly painted one and examining it. 'This little deer is precious.'

Eli looked a little teary.

'That was my grandmother's favourite,' he told me. 'Mum wanted to get rid of the lot when we cleared Grandma's house, but I put them all in the loft before she had the chance.'

I supposed they weren't to everyone's taste, but I adored them.

'What happened to this one?' I asked, selecting one with a rabbit on. The rabbit had an ear missing.

Eli laughed.

'Grandma swiped it with the duster,' he said, rolling his eyes. 'She wasn't the most careful cleaner. So, what do you think? Are they too kitsch for your houseplant collection?'

I looked at the rabbits, fawns and pixies that decorated the pots, many of which were made to look like tree trunks.

'No way,' I told him. 'My plants would be honoured to reside in such vintage splendour.'

'You really like them?'

'I love them!'

'I hoped you would,' he said, sounding well pleased. 'After dinner we'll fill them, shall we?'

'Yes,' I said, 'I can't wait.'

'Your plants and my pots,' Eli smiled, 'are going to be perfect together.'

'That,' said Eli, leaning back in his chair, once he'd completely emptied his bowl and mopped up the last few grains of plump cheese-coated rice with a crust of one of Mark's rustic loaves, 'was absolutely delicious.'

'You really enjoyed it?'

He showed me the inside of the bowl as evidence.

'Almost clean enough to go back in the cupboard,' I laughed, as he then poured out the last of the wine.

We hadn't rushed the meal, having spent as long chatting

about the plant pots and his grandma as we had eating and it was beginning to turn cool.

'Do you want to go in?' Eli asked, as I stacked the dishes and rubbed my arms.

'No,' I said, 'not yet.'

He carried everything inside and came back out with my cardigan, which I'd thrown off while I had been cooking.

'Thank you,' I said, as he draped it around my shoulders.

I felt a shiver of excitement as he bent down and lightly kissed my collarbone.

'Thank *you*,' he said, before sitting back down and picking up his wine. 'By the way,' he asked, 'how was your friend? The one you had lunch with.'

'He was good,' I nodded, as my heart began to skitter now the subject had finally been broached. 'We chatted for ages. He told me recently that he's been through a break-up. It was hard for a while, really tough, but he's getting over it now. Moving on with his life, you know.'

It wasn't a lie. The loss of the friendship Pete had told me about was a break-up of sorts. It had hurt him and he missed the person he had lost and now he was slowly moving on. Ergo, a break-up, just not a romantic one.

'Break-ups are hard,' said Eli, with a sigh. 'When I was going through mine, I honestly thought I would never love or trust anyone again.'

I didn't know what to say to that.

'But now,' he said, looking into my eyes, 'I'm not sure that what I felt before was even love.'

My heart raced harder and a lump formed in my throat. That really was quite a declaration.

'I'm sorry you had your heart broken,' I whispered, 'but I'm pleased I'm helping you put it back together again.'

'You most definitely are,' he said, reaching across the table for my hand. 'The feelings I have for you are in a different league, Beth, but sadly, there's one part of my heart that not even you will be able to fix.'

'Oh?'

Eli took his hand back and ran it through his hair.

'My ex broke my heart even before she had given any hint that she was thinking about taking off,' he said, his voice choked with emotion. 'She caused a rift between me and my closest friend and I ended up choosing her over him. I've never forgiven myself for that and I never will.'

My head spun with more than wine as the pieces of the puzzle I'd unexpectedly stumbled across slipped seamlessly, but horribly, into place. Deep down, all afternoon, I had known it was going to happen, but the reality of it hit me hard nonetheless.

'My behaviour was unforgivable,' Eli further added, shaking his head at the memory. 'I said and did some unspeakable things under her influence and now I can't take them back and I can't make things right.'

'But would you, if you could?' I heard myself asking.

'In a heartbeat,' he replied, even before mine had thumped again.

Chapter 17

I went through the motions of tidying away with Eli and filling up his grandmother's cool kitsch plant pot collection with my plants that evening, but my head was spinning with what I'd worked out. Eli was so excited about our collab, he didn't pick up on my shift in mood, which was a relief.

Later, I lay in bed, staring at the ceiling long after I'd turned off the light and mulled everything over. I dug deep to try and fathom another possible explanation for what I'd discovered, but it was all in vain.

The fact of the matter was, it was Eli's band that Pete had been a part of, Eli's girlfriend who had ousted my friend, dented his confidence and then disappeared, leaving a brace of broken hearts behind her. Eli was the person Pete was trying to avoid, as his fleeing from the coffeehouse earlier had confirmed, and Pete was the person Eli desperately wanted back in his life but didn't know how to, or even if he could, make amends.

There was no doubt in my mind that Eli was devastated about what had happened. Eli had felt Pete's loss so keenly and deeply, he had sacrificed playing his music in public as a result and knowing how much it meant to him, that was the harshest possible punishment he could have sentenced himself.

Seeing the two men I loved so scarred by what had happened, I desperately wanted to help heal their rift, but unlike the simplicity of pushing Pete and Sara together, this situation was far more complicated. Pete had no idea I even knew who Eli was, let alone that I was living with and dating him and Eli had no idea I was friends with Pete. As far as the two men were concerned, there was nothing to connect me to either of them.

As keen as I was for my musical past not to merge with my new life, that should have been a blessing, but if I wanted both men in my life, which I obviously did, I wouldn't be able to keep them apart forever and actually, I was amazed to acknowledge, I was prepared to risk Pete spilling the beans if it meant the pair of them could be friends again.

I hated the thought of letting Pete down for a second time and if I didn't initiate a stealthy and meticulously thought through plan of action, then there was every chance he could get hurt. There was no margin for error and there wasn't much time either. Pete was dating Sara and Sara knew I was sharing a house with Eli because of her connection to Prosperous Place, so the pressure was on. I needed to come up with something fast.

I spent a restless night tossing and turning and when I eventually got out of bed again, I was no further forward in trying to get the guys back together in a way that wouldn't upset Pete or risk damaging my fledgling relationship with Eli. I didn't want him thinking I had kept knowing Pete a secret – once I'd worked out their connection – for any dubious reason, but for the moment, and in spite of the time constraints, I had no choice but to set the situation aside.

I needed to focus my attention on successfully rolling out the new activities schedule and hope that in the meantime nothing happened to reveal that I was waving a flag for Team Eli *and* Team Pete.

'Good morning,' twinkled Greta, who was perched behind the reception desk bright and early on Tuesday morning. 'Who are you here to visit today?'

I looked at her and shook my head. She loved her role play, but sometimes it completely took over her mind, nudging out both reality and common sense. If I wasn't careful, I knew, convinced as she was that I was a visitor to the home rather than staff, she'd not let me in and start bellowing for security and the place would be in uproar.

'Please make sure to sanitise your hands before signing the visitors' book,' she said sweetly, turning the book so I could see it. 'I'll need your car registration, assuming you drove here, along with the name of the person you're here to visit.'

Apparently, Minnie Mouse was visiting the kitchen, Dr Indiana Jones was attending a patient on the second floor and Bob the Builder was somewhere in the building fixing a leak. I bit the inside of my cheek and decided to let her fictitious additions to the visitor book pass.

'I'm here to talk to the residents,' I told her, trying my best to sound important. 'I have some official news to share with them about their new activities schedule.'

'I see,' she said, clearly interested.

'I'm going to need someone to help gather everyone together in the dayroom.'

She continued to eye me eagerly, taking in every word.

'I'm holding a meeting at nine thirty,' I said, thinking that should be long enough for everyone to get through their breakfast and morning ablutions. 'Would there be anyone available to help me, do you think?'

Her hand shot up into the air, her elbow cracking in response, in a gesture reminiscent of how children implored their teachers to pick them for important tasks such as running letters to the school office.

'I could do it,' she said excitedly.

'But aren't you needed here?' I frowned.

'There'll be a shift change in ten minutes,' she said, craftily fixing the game to suit her need. 'I could start rounding everyone up after that.'

'Excellent,' I agreed. 'I'll see you in the dayroom at half nine then.'

With a new mission to accomplish, she let me pass without further commotion and I went to drop my bag off in the staffroom.

'I wasn't sure you'd still be here,' I said to a very sleepy-looking Sara, who I found sitting slumped at the table. 'But I had a feeling you'd need this, if you were.'

I handed her a bag containing a breakfast roll from Blossoms and a reusable cup filled with the strongest coffee the bakery sold. I don't know what I would have done with it had my friend not still been in situ.

'Oh, you are a love to go out of your way for this,' she yawned, gratefully receiving both. 'I've hung on to see you. I had a feeling you'd be in early today.'

'I've got loads to tell everyone,' I said, patting the folder which contained the list I hoped the residents would be keen on. 'Was there something in particular you wanted to see me about?'

I felt a prickle of unease crawl across the back of my neck. Had Eli's name already come up in a conversation where Pete talked about his former band breaking up? I hoped not.

'Yes,' she beamed, looking suddenly far less sleepy. 'I wanted to say thank you for pushing me and Pete together. We've been skirting around each other for months. Your nudge was exactly what we needed.'

'I'm so pleased,' I smiled, still thrilled for the pair of them in spite of the potential complication their togetherness had unexpectedly landed me with.

'He said the two of you go way back,' she carried on.

'Oh, we do,' I nodded, my anxiety prickling again. 'We've known each other forever.'

'We've got so much in common,' she said dreamily. 'Not many people know this, but I'm a writer in my spare time. I write children's stories about a community of magical creatures who live in the fern garden at Prosperous Place.'

So that's what Kate had been referring to all those weeks ago.

'Oh Sara,' I said, unable to make the connection to Pete, if indeed there was one. 'I love that.'

'I got the idea,' she further explained, 'when I attended this Winterfest event that Luke had organised. I've got a whole collection of tall tales now. I've shown a few of them to Pete and he's going to illustrate them for me.'

'Of course,' I said, finally joining the dots. 'He's a wonderful artist, isn't he?'

Sara's stories sounded right up his street too. Anything to do with magic and fantasy had him hooked. He was a huge Tolkien fan, which was probably the original reason behind why he'd got involved with the Iceni re-enactment group.

'He's amazing,' she agreed. 'Although like me, he's very private about it.'

'Will you ever publish your stories?' I asked.

'No, I don't think so,' she said, wrinkling her nose, 'but then again, it wasn't all that long ago that I plucked up the courage to start writing them and thought I'd never show them to anyone, but now I have, so never say never.'

I rather liked the idea of attending a book launch, surrounded by children dressed up as characters from Sara's imagination. Perhaps she and Pete could give each other the confidence boost they both needed to put their creative work out into the world. I knew Pete's was certainly accomplished enough and I'd bet Sara's was too.

'Anyway,' she carried on, bringing me back down to earth

with a bump, 'Pete and I have been talking about more than my writing over the last couple of days.'

'Oh,' I squeaked, my voice a few octaves higher than before.

'I hope you don't mind, but before my shift yesterday I happened to mention a few of the things the residents had written on the activities ideas list and Pete said if the quizzes come off and you need a hand getting them organised, he'd be more than happy to help.'

I took a deep breath and forced my shoulders to relax. If Sara had discovered Pete and Eli's shared history, she would have mentioned it by now.

'He loves that sort of thing and has so much knowledge,' she carried on. 'He said he'll put some question sheets together if you want him to. Themed as well as general knowledge. He's got quite carried away with it all already,' she added, with a laugh.

I was certain that the quizzes would be going ahead. So many people had put a tick next to the suggestion, and Pete would be the perfect person to come up with the questions. Putting him in charge would be a weight off my mind and save me loads of time.

'That's great,' I therefore said. 'I'm sure the quizzes will be happening and it would be a huge help if Pete did prepare the sheets, but only if he's sure he can spare the time.'

It would be quite an undertaking.

'He'll be in his element,' she laughed. 'I'm seeing him later today, so I'll ask him to make a start if you like?'

'Yes please,' I told her. 'Thanks. That would be much appreciated.'

We had just started talking about the re-enactment out-fits but stopped as our ears caught the sound of a laboured panting noise coming from the corridor. Sandra popped her head around the door, but it thankfully turned out that the sound wasn't coming from her.

'Who is that?' I asked, bypassing the traditional morning greeting as I spotted an elderly chocolate Labrador sidle up and sit at her feet.

'Morning Beth,' smiled my boss.

She looked more relaxed than I'd seen her in ages.

'This is Buster,' she said, patting the dog's head and making his tail thump. 'He's my parents' dog and from yes-terday, he's also my new office companion.'

I was flabbergasted.

'Mike and I were talking about some of your suggestions over the weekend,' she explained, 'and I came around to your way of thinking about pets. Mum and Dad spoil this fella rotten, so I thought, as long as everyone was in agreement, he could come into work with me and get a bit of exercise for two or three days a week.'

It sounded very much as though my host of new ideas had been the hot topic recently and I was delighted.

'As long as he's not around the dining room at meal-times anymore,' Sara laughed, 'he might even shed a pound or two.'

'We had a slight hiccup yesterday,' Sandra told me. 'I

caught a few of the residents feeding him titbits from the table, but we've had words and it won't be happening again.'

I wasn't quite as convinced about that as she sounded, but Buster was a very welcome addition to the team. I bet Charlie was delighted with his arrival.

'Excuse me, Sandra,' came a voice from behind her, 'I don't mean to interrupt, but is Beth in the staffroom?'

'Yes, Harold,' she said, stepping aside, 'she is. Is everything all right?'

'That depends,' he said, moving into view and giving Buster's head a quick rub. 'Morning, Beth.'

'Morning, Harold,' I replied. 'What's going on?'

'Greta's in sheepdog mode,' he said, rolling his eyes. 'She's got everyone penned in the dayroom, allegedly on your say-so.'

'It's all right,' I said, glancing at the clock. 'I did ask her to rally the troops. She's just got the time a bit wrong, but never mind. As the saying goes, there's no time like the present.'

'Do you want me to stick around?' Sara yawned.

'No,' I said, rearranging my folder and pulling my additional notes out of my bag. 'You get off home. If I have any trouble, I'll set Buster on watch.'

I quickly ran Sandra through what I was going to say to everyone and then walked to the dayroom with her. Buster wasn't quite hot on our heels, but he followed loyally on behind, panting again from the exertion. He really did need to go on a diet.

I don't know what Greta had said or done to get so many

residents gathered in such a short window of time, but the place was standing room only and felt stiflingly hot. I threw open the French doors at the end of the room, letting in the gentle and thankfully cool early morning breeze, while Freddie softly played a few bars of 'English Country Garden' on the piano. Listening closely, I realised Greta, standing on sentry next to him, and a couple of the others, were singing a rather ruder version of the lyrics than the ones I was familiar with.

'Thank you for getting everyone organised, Greta,' I said, joining her at the piano and quickly cutting the singing off. 'I'll take over from here.'

She graciously inclined her head and moved to the side; Freddie stopped playing and closed the lid over the keys to resist further temptation.

'Good morning, everyone,' I said, keen to get on. 'I hope you all had a wonderful time at the party on Sunday and are now looking forward to the new activities schedule I've been able to draw up as a result.'

'That'll depend on what's on it,' Bob said gruffly and his partner in crime, Wilfred, nodded in agreement.

Belligerent at the best of times, I'd never seen the pair of them join in with anything. To be honest, they were two residents I wouldn't have minded Greta missing out in her all-encompassing round-up this morning.

'Right,' I said, clearing my throat, 'without further ado, this is what I've come up with so far. I'll run through the plan, and then we'll discuss it all at the end,' I added firmly, hopefully heading off any interruptions before they began.

I glanced up and found the residents rapt as I began to run through the list.

'On Monday mornings, we'll be carrying on looking after the houseplant collection,' I started, 'which I can see has grown quite a bit over the last few days.'

'My grandson gave us the palm,' someone piped up. 'It had grown too big for his apartment.'

'And my daughter dropped the cheese plant off yesterday,' echoed someone else.

So much for staving off any interruptions, but at least they were positive ones. Tending the houseplants was a gentle activity, and scheduling it for Monday mornings would give me the opportunity to chat with everyone and find out if there had been any gripes or excitement over the weekend.

'Excellent,' I said, raising my voice a little as I pushed on, 'please pass on our thanks. They both look wonderful already.'

'Very exotic,' Greta agreed, channelling Monty Don as she twisted round to look.

'Monday afternoons,' I continued, 'there'll be the puzzle club and games. Both indoor and out. We've got some new quoits sets coming so we can set those up outdoors when the weather's nice.'

There was a murmur or assent. I knew everyone was keen to get outside a bit more and if I set the games up on the lawn just beyond the French doors I could, hopefully, oversee the two things at once.

'I'm partial to quoits,' smiled Freddie. 'Rather good at it, too.'

Why didn't that surprise me?

'I suppose that'll be all right,' sniffed Wilfred.

Wonders would never cease!

'As long as we've got someone to pick them up for us once we've thrown them,' Bob then added, spoiling the moment.

'Some of us can still bend down,' tutted Harold. 'You need to get moving a bit more, old fella. You'd feel much better for it.'

Bob looked outraged.

'The Zumba will help with that,' I grinned, throwing fuel on the fire.

Everyone gasped and Greta clapped her hands.

'But that's for Wednesday,' I said, before the meeting ran away from me, 'I'm getting ahead of myself.'

I glanced over at Sandra who was looking pleased and gave me an encouraging thumbs-up. By the time I'd finished, ending with a flourish as I described the pampering manicure, pedicure and hairdressing combo I'd penned in for Fridays, she was smiling even more broadly.

'Seated Zumba,' said Ida, gazing into the distance. 'I should be able to give that a go, shouldn't I?'

'Easily,' I told her.

'I want to hear a bit more about these special clubs, please, Beth,' said Sandra, her voice rising above everyone else's and restoring a modicum of calm.

I smiled at her, grateful for her timely intervention.

'There's going to be a proper baking club *and* an official gardening club,' I explained. 'They'll be run by Carole and

Graham, who are two of my neighbours in Nightingale Square. They're both experts in their field and will be able to offer you more in the kitchen and garden than I can.'

With any luck, I thought, they might be able to teach me a thing or two as well as inspiring the residents.

'A gardening club,' said Wilfred, sounding almost impressed. 'I might give that a go if the fella really does know what he's on about.'

Had I finally found something to spark dour Wilfred's imagination? If he carried on sounding so keen, he'd find himself turfed out of Bob's Miserable Old Man's Club for good.

'Oh, he knows what he's about, all right,' said Harold, winking at me. 'He's one of the team at Prosperous Place and Luke Lonsdale wouldn't have just anyone working there, would he?'

Wilfred, at long last, looked enthralled.

'I want to put my name down for Zumba,' said Ida, as she shuffled over with her frame.

'And I want to do scrapbooking and have my hair done,' said Greta, also stepping forward.

'Quizzes for me,' said Charlie and Harold in unison.

I looked around the room and took in the excited and happy faces. I didn't think my ideas could have been any better received. The place had almost erupted when I'd said we'd be taking trips again and that there would be visits from more dogs and perhaps even miniature donkeys if the waiting list wasn't too long. Bob was the only one still looking dissatisfied but I hoped that even he might soften once everything was underway.

If only my personal life could run as smoothly as my professional one, but then how often did anyone ever really end up having it all? I gave myself a shake and rooted myself in the moment, thankful that at least one thing was heading in the right direction.

Making a difference to the lives of the wonderful people around me had been my main reason for getting out of bed in the mornings for a very long time and, as I started handing out the sign-up sheets, I realised that I was very definitely succeeding on that front and now on a whole new level.

'Well,' said Sandra, once the chatter had finally settled and I'd got some crafts up and running in line with the new plan for Tuesday mornings, 'I don't think that could have gone any better.'

'I wish we were baking this afternoon,' said Greta, unashamedly listening in.

'Don't worry, Greta,' Sandra told her. 'Carole and Graham are coming to see me and Beth this afternoon. We'll get everything sorted and then within the next week or so, it'll be all systems go.'

'It's going to be brilliant here from now on,' Greta then grinned, adding a big dollop of pink glitter to the cupcake she'd been colouring in.

If there was one thing that I could be certain about, it was that.

Chapter 18

Rather than head straight home that evening, I first popped into the Grow-Well to help out for an hour and collect a few ingredients for mine and Eli's supper. The increasingly hot weather ensured everything in the garden was romping away and it was a huge and much-appreciated perk to have such an abundant seasonal larder right on my doorstep.

'Beth,' smiled Lisa, who, given her laden basket, was also enjoying the bounty, 'how's it going? I heard the raffle and auction made a vast amount on Sunday.'

'It did,' I told her. 'And the people who won your books were ecstatic to have signed copies. Thank you so much again for donating them.'

'It was my pleasure, my lovely. I would have liked to have been able to visit the party myself,' she added, 'but I'm on a deadline and don't tend to see the light of day until, well, the end of the day, at the moment.'

Looking at her more closely, I could see she did look a bit tired. It was hardly surprising, given the amount she had piled on her plate. There was the escalating success of her writing career, her large family to look after and, not forgetting, helping out in the garden. And there was the extra responsibility that came with trying to re-establish The Arches, too. It must have been quite a stretch, even for Lisa, the one-woman powerhouse. She was an inspiration and the ultimate example of someone leading as large a life as possible.

I'd been safely cocooned in a small life for so long, and there was absolutely nothing wrong with finding comfort in that, but now I was unfurling and stretching my wings a bit and it felt wonderful. The house in Nightingale Square, and my recent promotion, had landed in my life right at the moment when I needed them the most. And, I had Eli and Pete too, but they came with complications attached so I wasn't ready to wax lyrical about them in the same sentence together just yet.

'I hope the words are flowing,' I said to Lisa.

I could imagine there was nothing worse than being faced with a blank screen and not knowing what to write on it, especially when a deadline was looming.

'Oh, they are now,' she smiled, sounding relieved. 'Hence the state of my hair, lack of mascara and the disorganisation over dinner. I've barely had time to think of anything but this new book and we'd all be lost without this place to come and graze in. John usually cooks on a Tuesday, but he's had an emergency call-out.'

'Salad it is then,' I laughed.

'Yes,' she said. 'Salad *again* and a tortilla to go with it because there are loads of eggs.'

'That sounds wonderful.'

'Mine are never as good as the ones we have on holiday in Spain,' she said, sounding disappointed, 'but it's simple enough to make once you get the hang of it. You should give it a go if you haven't already. I bung in some potatoes and onions and everyone's happy.'

I didn't think I had either the skills or the know-how to make an authentic tortilla, but I could crack a few eggs.

'I'm feeding myself and Eli tonight,' I said, 'so I wouldn't inflict on him something I haven't tried before, but I could rustle up an omelette. If I added a handful of grated cheese and a few chives that would bulk it up a bit, wouldn't it?'

'That sounds perfect,' Lisa grinned. 'A very cosy meal for two. How are you both finding life under the same roof?'

I felt myself go red, which was the last shade I wanted to turn. Lisa's knowing tone left me in no doubt that she was willing to make a calculated guess as to exactly how Eli and I were finding life under the same roof.

'To be honest,' I said, aiming for breezy and most likely missing it by miles, 'we haven't seen all that much of each other. We're both so busy with work we're hardly ever in the house at the same time.'

'Well,' said Lisa, 'I hope you'll both be able to make it over here tomorrow night.'

'Tomorrow?' I frowned.

If we were meeting as a group, it usually happened over the weekend rather than on a week night.

'Yes,' she said. 'Tomorrow afternoon Jacob and I have got a meeting with the owners of the chapel that we're hoping to buy and we want to give them more of an idea about how we're raising the funds for it so they know we're serious contenders. We're getting together here afterwards to tell everyone how it went.'

'But I thought they'd already promised to give you enough time to come up with the money,' I frowned.

'Oh, they have,' she said, 'but we didn't think there'd be any harm in reiterating how intent we are on pulling it off, just in case someone else comes along with the right amount of money in a briefcase and tempts them.'

Given that the chapel had formerly been a religious building, I hoped the people responsible for selling it would have more morals than that, but then I supposed, business was business and it was more likely to be a legal team in charge of the sale than the former vicar. Or should that be reverend?

'I see,' I said. 'In that case, I'll come over as soon as I've finished work and had a bite to eat.'

'You can have a bite here,' said Lisa, handing me the secateurs so I could snip some salad. 'John's going to be making pizza for everyone.'

'Oh well,' I smiled. 'When you put it like that, I'll most likely be the first to arrive.'

I'd washed the salad, grated some cheese and was breaking eggs into a bowl by the time Eli got back.

'What a day!' he called from the hall, as he closed the door.

'Has it been busy?' I called back.

'Yes,' he said, rushing into the kitchen and planting a kiss on the back of my neck. 'Busy and hot.'

I felt a tingle run down my spine as his soft lips gently caressed my skin.

'I'm the last person you should be complaining to about the heat,' I reminded him as I abandoned the eggs and twisted around so he could kiss me again, this time on the lips. 'I work in a care home, remember? Constant temperature of at least one hundred and three, every month of the year.'

'Is that to match the average age of the residents?' he laughed.

'Near enough,' I laughed back.

'Anyway,' he said, his eyes locked on mine, 'how did you get on? What did everyone think to your new ideas?'

It was impossible to rein in the smile which lit up my face every time I thought about the meeting in the dayroom.

'It was a total triumph,' I grinned, turning my attention back to our meal and briskly beating the eggs before adding some salt and pepper to the mix. 'Even if I do say so myself.'

'That's fantastic,' Eli responded. He then made me glow all the more by kindly adding, 'And I'm not at all surprised. When word gets round of how engaged and inspired the residents are courtesy of their gorgeous new activities manager, you'll have a list of pensioners as long as your arm all wanting to move in!'

'Well,' I flushed, 'I don't know about that, although that

would make Sandra's year. I'm not doing anything ground-breaking though. Just setting up what should already be in place, really.'

Eli was having none of it and gave me a mild telling off. He said I needed to learn to accept credit and praise and that I should be aware that not everyone had the same work ethic as I did. He told me that the residents were lucky to have me, whereas I'd always considered myself fortunate to have them. Even minxy Greta had a certain charm and she certainly kept me, and everyone else, on our toes.

'So,' Eli then said, 'what's on the agenda for tonight?'

Given his tone, I wasn't sure if he was referring to the meal I was preparing, or some potentially seductive afters. I abandoned the eggs for the second time and turned to wrap my arms around his neck.

'I thought I'd keep it light tonight,' I told him, punctuating each of the words with a tender kiss. 'Fresh salad from the Grow-Well and an omelette, courtesy of the hens,' I sighed, melting into his embrace.

'Sounds delicious,' he murmured, pulling me closer.

I didn't know about Eli, but I'd never been so turned on by talk of such a simple supper. If we'd carried on as we were, we might never have made it to the table.

'I think,' he said, pulling away after a sultry few seconds, 'I'd better go and have a shower.'

'A cold one?' I asked, raising my eyebrows.

'Glacial,' he confirmed, 'if I'm going to stand any chance of putting out these flames, it will have to be ice cold.'

To further dampen our ardour, we ate outside in the little garden. With the sun long gone from the shady courtyard, it was cooler than the last time we'd done it, but I didn't mind that. After the heat of the July day and the tantalising temperature in the kitchen, it was a pleasure to feel the chill on my arms and face. I ran through my day at work in more detail, obviously avoiding mentioning Pete's generous offer to draw up the quiz sheets.

'And Lisa told me there's a meeting happening in the Grow-Well tomorrow night,' I said, once I'd finished relaying most of the particulars of my wonderful day. 'She and Jacob want to talk about the fundraiser for The Arches and fill us in on how their meeting with the current chapel owners goes.'

Eli nodded, pouring us both another glass of crisp and refreshing lager.

'Yes,' he said, 'I know all about that. She messaged me just as I was leaving work.'

Perhaps she had been fooled by my insistence that Eli and I didn't spend all that much time together after all.

'She also asked me if I wouldn't mind helping Archie with something he's struggling with on his guitar,' Eli further said, a frown furrowing his brow. 'Apparently, his teacher is on holiday for a couple of weeks and the lad's losing interest now he hasn't got The Arches to go to.'

'Do you mind?' I asked, wondering about the reason behind the frown. 'Helping Archie, I mean.'

'No,' he said, 'not really. As long as no one tries to rope

me into carrying on playing after I've helped. They all know I play a bit and you know how persuasive Lisa can be when she sets her sights on something.'

I didn't have much first-hand experience of that, but I could imagine she could be pretty convincing when she put her mind to it. I hoped she wouldn't try and cajole anyone into playing anything because it would be nice to keep the Grow-Well a tune-free zone, especially given that nowhere else was. Not even our garden in Nightingale Square, as it turned out.

I'd just realised there was music playing through the speaker Eli had set up on the kitchen windowsill. I couldn't believe I hadn't picked up on it before. How stealthily the musical tendrils were weaving their way back around and through my life . . .

'Your expression tells me you know exactly what I'm talking about,' Eli smiled, misinterpreting my reaction.

'No,' I said, 'it's not that . . .'

My explanation was cut off as both our phones pinged with incoming messages. Mine read . . .

Evening Beth. Thanks for giving me the go-ahead to set up the quiz sheets. I've got a whole batch of general knowledge ones ready. It's been a blast! Let me know when you need them. Pete x

Before I typed out my reply, I risked a quick glance at Eli, just to make sure he hadn't spotted Pete's name lighting up the screen. I needn't have bothered though because he was too engrossed in his own phone to notice who had popped up on mine.

*

As a thank you for getting the quiz sheets ready so promptly, the next morning I stopped en route to Pete's to buy a couple of fully loaded breakfast rolls from Blossoms. Pete had offered to drop the sheets at the care home later in the week, or even have Sara deliver them, but I was keen to get the new schedule started straight away and therefore said I'd collect them.

Even though I hadn't managed to book the Wednesday morning seated Zumba at such short notice, I could launch the quiz that afternoon. But in truth, that wasn't my only reason for wanting to call round to the flat.

After Pete's message had arrived, and Eli had read whatever had turned up on his phone, the evening had turned a little flat and I couldn't help wondering how much worse it could potentially be when my duplicity was revealed. It felt inevitable that Eli was going to find out about my connection to Pete, or vice versa, so I decided the best course of action was to face the situation head on.

There was only the tiniest smidgen of doubt in my mind that I might have made a mistake and jumped to the wrong conclusion about the identities of the two estranged friends, but I was going to talk to Pete to snuff that out and then work out how I was going to proceed and hopefully resolve the situation.

'Beth,' Pete puffed, when he finally opened the door after I'd repeatedly rung the bell. 'You're early.'

I was, but only by a few minutes.

'And you're in your bathrobe,' I unnecessarily pointed out. 'I'm not interrupting anything, am I?'

'Only my shower,' he said, pushing his wet hair away from his face. 'Sara's not here, if that's what you're suggesting.'

'I'm not suggesting anything,' I told him with a smile, before following him inside and then up the narrow stairs. 'I've picked up breakfast, from Blossoms,' I added, keeping my eyes on my feet because his robe was alarmingly short.

'In that case,' he said, 'help yourself to a drink, make yourself at home and I'll be no more than three minutes.'

True to his word, Pete was back in the kitchen and plating up the rolls in record time. I'd taken in the space in his absence – walls covered in Tolkien movie posters, a groaning action-figure display cabinet and his trusty guitar leant against the wall. It was the guitar that caused a lump to form in my throat and I had purposefully turned my back on it.

'What's this song?' I asked, listening to the tune which was quietly playing, before I took a bite from my egg and bacon-filled roll.

It was a sound I very definitely recognised, but couldn't for the life of me place.

'Fancy you remembering I prefer sausages to bacon,' said Pete, taking an even bigger bite than the one I had managed. 'How good is this?' he beamed, chewing appreciatively.

The rolls were good, but I was more interested in identifying the music. It wasn't an urge I had ever expected to experience again.

'So good,' I agreed. 'But the music, Pete. This song . . .'

'I'll turn it off,' he said, wiping his hand on a sheet of paper towel, before reaching for his phone.

'No, don't,' I said, 'leave it on. It's good.'

'I thought you weren't interested in music anymore,' he was quick to point out.

'I'm not,' I shrugged, 'not really, but this sounds familiar and I can't place it. It's bugging me, is all.'

'You won't have heard this before,' he said, turning it down a bit more but not off, 'it's one of the songs written by the guy whose band I was in.'

I began to choke and Pete rushed around the counter to slap me on the back. The moment he'd said that, I'd placed the melody which had drifted through, under and around Eli's door in an instant.

'I'm fine,' I gasped, keen to call a halt on Pete's enthusiastic back-slapping, 'but can I have some water, please?'

'Chew your food, Beth,' he laughed, when he handed me the glass and saw I really was okay. 'Don't inhale it.'

'Um . . . where have I heard that before?' I smiled, sipping the water and simultaneously tapping the side of my head Pooh Bear-style.

'Don't,' said Pete, rolling his eyes. 'She still says it now.'

It had always been one of his mum's favourite adages. Her son had always loved his food and she'd always highlighted the fact, both in company and when the three of us were eating alone. I wondered if that incessant flagging up had made the sting of his former bandmate's comments about his weight all the sharper.

'I find that very easy to believe,' I said, taking another sip before wiping my eyes on the paper towel.

'She'll never change,' Pete sighed.

'But what I don't find easy to believe,' I carried on, seizing the opportunity, 'is that you're still listening to this song, especially given who wrote it.'

Pete shrugged.

'I can't help it,' he said, putting the remains of his roll on his plate. 'I still love it, and this demo recording I've got is fantastic because it's all instrumental. No hint of that cow's voice to interrupt the flow and stir up the bad memories.'

His words confirmed that he did still feel her sting and that she wasn't forgotten. It was hardly surprising and I had to face up to the fact that it was bound to make any reconciliation I was going to attempt between him and Eli even harder.

'Well,' I said, fighting the urge to blurt everything out, 'it sounds great as an instrumental.'

'It is even better with the lyrics though,' Pete begrudgingly acknowledged. 'Depending on who's singing them, of course. From what I can remember,' he then pensively added, 'your voice would suit them perfectly, Beth.'

'*Would have* suited them perfectly,' I cut in, stressing the past tense. 'I don't do that anymore, remember? I probably wouldn't even know how to.'

'Rubbish,' he smiled. 'You'll never forget.'

The conversation was heading into territory I wasn't prepared to navigate. I quickly finished my roll, noticing that Pete had left most of his, and wiped my mouth free of crumbs.

'Funnily enough,' he said, with the biggest sigh, 'I've seen the guy I used to be in the band with three times in the last few days.'

'You have?' I gulped.

'Yeah,' he said. 'He works near here and somehow I've managed to avoid any sight of him for months, but now he's bloody everywhere.'

'That's a bit weird, isn't it?' I squeaked.

'Annoying and weird,' he said. 'I don't want to have to spend my life looking over my shoulder on the off chance that he might be coming up behind me.'

'Um,' I said, feeling my throat turn dry, 'I can see how that would be awkward.'

'I was on tenterhooks when we split,' he further confided as I drained my glass. 'I even considered moving, but then I thought, why should I? I was here first.'

I wanted to suggest that perhaps it was fate's way of trying to get them back together. That's what I'd believed when I'd found out Pete still worked in On the Box, which was just up the road from where I had moved to. However, there was something about his tone which suggested he wouldn't go for that.

'It was fine for a while,' Pete carried on, 'but now it feels like it's all getting stirred up again. I can't put my finger on why, but that song, for example, I hadn't listened to it for ages and now I can't get enough of it again.'

'You said, this guy works nearby,' I said quietly.

'Yeah,' said Pete. 'Funnily enough, in the Castle Coffeehouse where you wanted us to have lunch the other day.'

'Why didn't you say anything when we got there?' I asked, my heart skittering.

'I was going to,' he said, 'but the bloke, Eli, wasn't there when we walked in and I thought it'd be all right.'

'Eli?' I repeated, clasping my hands together in my lap.

'Yeah,' he said. 'That's his name.'

'Pete . . .' I began, the words lining up in my mouth, but the doorbell cut their delivery off.

'Yes!' he said, jumping up and punching the air. 'Quiz sheets in that folder,' he smiled, pointing to a plastic wallet. 'Help yourself.'

'Hang on,' I pleaded. 'Can we just—'

'No time,' he said, heading for the stairs. 'We'll talk about them later. I've been waiting for this shipment of Orc figures for ages. I really need to get the door, Beth.'

And with that he was gone.

Chapter 19

Pete's quiz went down a storm that afternoon. In fact, there were a couple of times when there very nearly was a storm, but thankfully he'd supplied the answer sheets as well as the questions so I was able to quell any disputes speedily and without too much disruption.

Whether it was my preoccupation with my recently confirmed discovery, the impact of the summer heat or sheer bloody-mindedness on the part of some of the residents, I couldn't be sure, but it was a bit of a relief when the scores were totted up, the winners were announced and equilibrium was restored.

It wasn't quite the calm start to the inclusion of quizzes I'd envisaged, but then I had endured more than my share of lessons to prove that life didn't always go according to plan, so perhaps I should have been better prepared for the occasional off-piste moment cropping up in the new schedule.

'So,' said Eli, when I met him in the Grow-Well for pizza

and the new Arches update early that evening, 'how did the first official session of the new regime go?'

'Good,' I said, wishing we'd made it back from work early enough to have a smooch on the sofa at home before meeting our neighbours. 'Really good.'

'Are you sure?' he frowned. 'You don't sound it.'

'Well,' I admitted, 'there were a couple of differences of opinion over a question about the 1966 World Cup, but beyond that, it all went smoothly enough. On the whole,' I said, for the moment setting aside the memory of what I had found out at Pete's, 'it's been a good day.'

'I'm relieved to hear it,' Eli smiled. 'You had me worried there for a minute. I thought you'd had a rebellion on your hands.'

If Bob had had his way, I might have done, but mercifully it hadn't come to that.

'No,' I laughed. 'No rebellion. Besides, Sandra told me just last week that she wanted the residents more animated, engaged and inspired and from what I've seen and heard today, I've hit all three targets already.' Eli grinned at that. 'How's your day been?' I asked him.

His fingers tantalisingly brushed mine as he handed me a plate and I found my gaze locked onto his. I hoped no one was watching. I was trying to keep our exchange casual, but the sudden lustful undercurrent felt glaringly obvious, to me at least.

'Getting better by the minute,' he grinned, completely giving the game away.

I shook my head and tried not to smile too widely.

'I meant how was work,' I needlessly pointed out. 'As you are well aware.'

I gave him a playful nudge but then took a step away in case Lisa was lurking somewhere and had her astute eyes trained on us.

'Oh, you know,' Eli said. His whole demeanour altered as he shrugged his shoulders. 'Same old, same old.'

I knew he generally enjoyed his shifts in the Castle Coffeehouse. It was a classy establishment and he took pride in his barista knowledge and his work. He often waxed lyrical about the ethically sourced coffee and then, more modestly, how as a trained professional, he could transform it, so his reaction rather took me by surprise.

Even though he had said he was going to start writing songs again, I wondered if he was missing performing them. Was he craving being on the stage with Pete and his beloved guitar or was I just letting my imagination run away with me along the path which was most attractive?

'Hey, Eli!' shouted Archie, as he wandered into the garden. 'You're here! Did you bring your guitar?'

'Ignore me,' said Eli, lightly laying his hand on my arm and making me tingle from head to toe. 'It's just been one of those days. I'm going to get it after I've eaten, mate!' he then called to Archie. 'I've only just finished work.'

He walked over so they could carry on their conversation without shouting and I waited in line for a slice of John's delicious vegetarian special.

'It's a full house tonight,' said Sara, who had arrived with Chloe, when I joined her at the table.

'I didn't expect to see you here,' I said to her.

'Lisa's messaged everyone, I think,' she said, looking around. 'Residents of the Square, staff, volunteers and anyone else who's ever had anything to do with the place. Pete told me today that he helps out with the admin. Did you know? Apparently, he's been involved with The Arches forever. What a coincidence is that?'

One that had me choking for the second time that day.

'Are you all right?' Sara frowned.

'Uh huh,' I spluttered, reaching for the water jug as my eyes scanned around for Eli.

Thankfully, he was still talking to Archie on the opposite side of the garden and out of earshot.

'He was supposed to be here, but has had to bow out,' Sara sighed. 'Apparently there's been some mix-up with this delivery of Orc figures and he's still trying to contact the overseas supplier. From what I could make out, he's been on hold practically all day.'

I thanked all the gods I could name for the supplier's ineptitude. This triangle made up of Pete, Eli and I, was a ticking timebomb and I needed to work out fast how to bring us all together harmoniously.

I knew that some might say it wasn't my problem to solve, but I knew how badly both men had been hurt by what had happened, and loving them both, I was determined to find a way to fix it. It felt vital that I made it happen given that I wanted to keep them both in my life and without the current clandestine sneaking about which felt both disloyal and discomfiting.

'I'm going to grab a slice,' said Sara, standing up. 'I wasn't going to give in to temptation, but the smell of that melting cheese is too much.'

She and Pete really were peas in a pod. I wondered if, when I'd worked out how to do it, she might be willing to help me, if needs be, mediate between her love and mine. But then I realised, given what had happened, she would be bound to take Pete's side. He was the wronged party after all, even if Eli was insistent that his behaviour had been the result of his ex's influence. I would just have to carry on trying to puzzle out an amicable resolution by myself.

'Now you've all got full bellies,' said Lisa, a little later, while John took a bow and the much-deserved credit, 'let's get down to business.'

Everyone set aside their plates and sat up straighter.

'We've made great strides with the plans for the fair,' said Luke, 'which is set to go ahead over the twentieth and twenty-first of August, so massive thanks to everyone who has been able to contribute so far.'

I felt bad that I wasn't one of those people. I'd had my hands so full with settling into the house, falling in love and finding my feet in my new job, that I hadn't had the headspace to come up with anything more than a bright idea. And I hadn't even shared that yet.

'It's not happening over the bank holiday weekend then?' asked Finn. 'I thought the original plan was to have it then.'

I'd earlier thanked him again for the donation of the dragon sculpture and he told me that it was already on display in the pub. He'd helped the landlord find the perfect spot for it and it had gained a lot of attention.

I was very much looking forward to finding the time for a pint in the much-loved local – as long as I could be certain that I wouldn't find Eli and Pete propping up opposite ends of the bar. The second that unsettling thought landed, so did another.

Pete had told me how much he'd enjoyed the open-mic night in the pub the other week and Eli had told me he'd ducked out of attending. I knew why now and it wasn't anything to do with a headache. He must have spotted Pete and legged it.

'So, that's why we've switched it,' I heard Lisa say with finality.

'What was that?' I whispered to Carole, who was sitting next to me. 'I didn't catch what Lisa just said.'

Earlier, Carole, Graham and I had discussed the baking and gardening club plans in more detail. Carole had already come up with a whole list of quick and easy bakes to tempt the residents with. Thankfully, she understood the need to keep it simple and appreciated that there would be limited time in the care home kitchen.

Graham also had the measure of things and had consequently planned a variety of gardening tasks based on physical

ability and skill. He knew there were some seasoned garden-
ers who had signed up and he had no desire to patronise or
undervalue their broad range of knowledge and experience.

I already knew that my kind and generous neighbours
were going to be valuable assets to the care home and the fact
that they were willing to give their time for free was hugely
appreciated. Bob's name hadn't featured on the gardening
club list, but I hoped that even he might be tempted to join
in at some point.

'The city is already rammed with bank holiday events,'
Carole whispered to me, 'and that's the reason why the fundraiser is now going to happen the weekend before.'

'Oh, that's a great idea,' I whispered back. 'Everyone will
be cash-strapped by the end of the month, so getting in
before the bank holiday should help add a few extra pounds
to the fund.'

'Exactly,' she nodded.

Lisa and Luke then ran through the exciting list of stalls,
games and competitions that would be happening. Ryan said
he was keen to enter French bulldog, Gus, into the waggiest
tale competition and I'd bet good money Heather and Glen
had plans for their three little ones in the fancy-dress stakes.

It all sounded very reminiscent of the traditional summer
fairs Mum and I had enjoyed and I was very much looking
forward to it. There was bound to be a stall I could help out
on and it might not be too difficult to bring a couple of the
care home residents along. I knew Harold wouldn't want
to miss it.

'The only spanner in the works—' said Luke.

'The ridiculously ironic spanner in the works,' Lisa amended, with the biggest eye roll imaginable.

'—is the trouble we're having to find acts to perform in the evening,' Luke carried on. 'As you know, this is a fundraiser to help reinstate The Arches and we wanted to add acts to the bill that have a connection to the place, but they're proving to be a bit thin on the ground.'

I was taken aback to hear that.

'But The Arches supports dozens of kids,' I heard someone behind me say. 'I would have thought they'd all want to sign up.'

'The vast majority of them do,' said Lisa, with a sigh, 'but quite a lot of them are away on holiday that weekend.'

'In that case,' someone else suggested, 'can't you change the date of the event to sometime in the autumn?'

'Absolutely not,' Lisa said firmly, but with no rancour. 'We need the money as soon as we can get it. The chapel won't be available forever. We need to act fast and if we pitch it right, this will be the best way.'

It had never entered my head that the timing of the event might be an issue. It would be fine for the over-eighteens, but there were lots of younger people enrolled in classes and their summer holidays weren't theirs to do with as they pleased. As youngsters, they had to be wherever their parents and carers happened to be.

'Does this mean you're going to have to cancel the evening performances altogether?' Carole frowned.

'No,' Lisa said. 'There's just about enough to make a line-up.'

'Thank goodness for that,' said Carole.

'But we need more,' Lisa further added, 'to make a really decent show of it.'

'The main focus of the fair has always been the evening entertainment,' Luke continued. 'That's the whole reason why we're putting it on. It's about showcasing the local creative talent, providing the acts with a platform and getting them some decent media exposure while The Arches is out of action.'

'Luke's already got his media contacts lined up to cover the event, haven't you?' Lisa explained.

'Yes,' he nodded. 'They're all for it.'

'So, what can we do to boost the number of acts?' asked Neil.

'We've decided to cast the net a bit wider,' Luke told us. 'We're now putting out feelers to find any artists, dancers, singers or bands with a local connection who would be willing to perform alongside The Arches attendees.'

'A collaboration would be great,' said Mark. 'Maybe you could even get some of them to perform together.'

'That would be fantastic,' Luke agreed.

'We know it's a bit of a cheek, asking folk to perform for free and at such short notice,' said Lisa, 'but we're going to appeal to everyone's philanthropic nature and play up the "it's all for a good cause" element.'

'And not forgetting Luke's fabulous contacts in the media,

which will guarantee the acts some wonderful exposure,' Kate threw in.

'Exactly,' Lisa nodded.

I looked over at Eli and found his gaze was trained as far away from Luke's as possible. I wondered if Luke had already asked him to perform and he'd said no. It would account for his unwillingness to engage in the conversation. Not that I'd said anything either.

I wriggled in my seat and stared at my lap, uncomfortable in the knowledge that I most likely had a stronger connection to The Arches than anyone else currently sitting in the Grow-Well. Had Pete been present, he could have claimed that title too, but unlike me, he was still doing something, even if it was just filing paperwork rather than offering to entertain the fair attendees.

'We're so close now,' said Jacob, adding weight to my discomfiture. 'If we can make a success of this event and get more money in, then the move will definitely be happening. We're all working hard to get these kids back into a space where they can truly be themselves, among like-minded peers, and we know that you're all already going all out to support us, but if you can think of anyone who might be able to help, then please give them a call, a nag, whatever it takes.'

'Does anyone have any further questions?' Lisa asked.

After a little more discussion, the meeting came to an end but I couldn't relax. Just as I had originally suspected it would, everything which had pushed music back into my life was causing chaos and mayhem. I loved my new home and I was madly in love with Eli, but this move to Nightingale Square, and this new phase of my life, was currently having a detrimental impact on my stress levels.

'Let me help,' I said to Carole, as I spotted her struggling with a heaped pile of plates. 'Many hands and all that.'

Between us, we cleared and washed the dishes while some of the others left to put children to bed and the rest enjoyed a beer while carrying on with the endless watering. Eli and Archie were set up in a quiet corner, their heads bent over their guitars.

They were still together when Carole and I had finished tidying away and they had drawn quite an audience, but I had no way of warning Eli. With his back turned, he had no idea that anyone other than Archie was listening to the beautiful tune I'd heard him playing in the privacy of his room back at the house.

The moment he strummed the final chord, everyone began to applaud and he twisted around. His face turned pale and he hastily set his guitar aside.

'I know I've asked before,' said Luke, unable to resist the opportunity that Eli had unwittingly offered him, 'but I really wish you'd change your mind about playing at the fair.'

'I know you do,' said Eli, sounding genuinely upset, 'but I've never had anything to do with The Arches, so it just wouldn't feel right.'

It wasn't my place to say anything, especially as he'd told me he would never play in public again, but knowing that he'd been involved in a community project somewhere else in the past, to my mind at least, made him an ideal candidate.

'But that doesn't matter now,' said Lisa, as she helped Archie slide his guitar back into its case. 'You know we're having to widen our net to up the numbers. You're local and that was a truly beautiful song.'

'Perfect summer evening listening,' Kate added hopefully.

'It's also not quite finished,' Eli bluffed. He was beginning to sound ruffled, rather than upset. 'And it needs the lyrics to really make it shine.'

'I can hold a tune,' volunteered John.

Lisa flicked his arm with the back of her hand.

'No, you can't,' she tutted.

'Well,' said John, sounding amused, 'maybe folk would pay me to stop singing. Have you thought of that?'

Eli tried to sidle away, but he wasn't quick enough.

'You're sure you won't reconsider?' asked Luke.

'I'm sorry,' Eli said firmly, 'but for my songs to really work, they need a strong female vocal and I don't know anyone who can provide one.'

Luke nodded. Given that he and Eli had known each other for a while, I thought he must have known what he had been through and if that was the case, then it was a bit off for him to ask Eli to play, and so publicly too. But then, given that Luke was such a considerate and thoughtful bloke, maybe he didn't know it all. It was clear that Lisa and Jacob hadn't connected Eli to Pete, so maybe Eli had kept the finer details of the horrible situation entirely to himself.

'Well,' said Lisa, 'don't look at me. I'm worse than him.'

This comment was accompanied with a nod in John's direction.

'I can't sing either,' Kate shrugged. 'What about you, Carole?'

'Afraid not,' she sighed.

I beat a hasty retreat back to the bothy before anyone asked me.

'What about you, Beth?' John shouted after me, before I could close the door.

'There's no point asking Beth,' I heard Eli reply gruffly. 'She's not a fan of music.'

I felt my cheeks flush as I recalled the list of songs I'd recently belted out in the bathroom, but I wasn't about to waste the opportunity Eli had just given me.

'Eli's right,' I said, stepping out again and trying not to notice the frowns his comment had prompted. 'But I have had a thought about the fair that doesn't involve music.'

'What's that?' asked Lisa.

'It's to do with your books,' I told her. 'They were so well received at the garden party that I was wondering if you might be able to do a reading followed by a question-and-answer session during the day. Maybe a signing too. You ran the creative writing classes at The Arches after all, didn't you? So there's definitely a connection.'

'Hey,' said Luke. 'That's not a bad idea.'

'Thank you,' Eli silently mouthed to me as everyone's attention turned to Lisa.

'You're welcome,' I mouthed back.

Chapter 20

'Thanks for that,' said Eli, throwing caution to the wind and reaching for my hand as we left the grounds of Prosperous Place and crossed the road into Nightingale Square. 'Luke really put me on the spot back there.'

Thankfully, my timely intervention had got us both off the hook.

'You're welcome,' I told him, squeezing his hand in return. 'My guess is, Luke just wants to make the fair as successful as possible; I don't think he meant to make you feel bad.'

'I know,' Eli sighed, 'but he's asked before and I feel rotten for saying no. He's cranking the guilt up whether he means to or not.'

I could totally relate to that. Keeping my connection to The Arches, as well as my singing, a secret, was playing havoc with my conscience, but obviously I couldn't tell him that. It was something else for me to feel guilty about.

'That said,' he carried on, 'I know Lisa will be a much bigger draw than I would be.'

'Well,' I nudged, 'I don't know about that, but her books are very popular. Someone at work is always reading one.'

'Have you read them?' he asked, letting go of my hand so he could open the gate which led to the house.

'No,' I said, 'I haven't, but then it's been ages since I had a book on the go. I'm either at work or thinking about work, or looking after the houseplants on a Sunday of course, so I don't have much time for anything else. And now there's the commitment to the Grow-Well to factor in too.'

It wasn't a particularly adventurous list of things which made up the routine of my new life, but it pleased me nonetheless. I was happy and comfortable in the knowledge that my formerly very small existence had been stretched a little, but not too much. Just as I realised I hadn't mentioned making time for Eli, he reminded me himself.

'Well, that's nice,' he laughed, as he followed me into the house, then lunged to tickle me, which made me squeal. 'Where do I figure on your list of priorities? I'd rather you were thinking about me than work. For at least some of the time.'

He closed the door and reached for me again, but this time I was ready for him and jumped out of the way.

'You're on my mind all of the time,' I told him, pulling off my shoes. 'I thought you'd know that.'

He held out his hands and this time I let him pull me into his arms.

'This is a brand-new relationship,' he said, kissing me on the lips. 'I'm not taking anything for granted.'

I kissed him back and then rested my forehead against his.

'Well, in that case,' I whispered, 'let me spell it out for you. You're the brightest star in my sky, Eli.'

He let out a long breath.

'Am I really?'

'You are,' I reiterated.

'Crikey,' he swallowed. 'It's a long time since I've been that to anyone. And for the record, just so you know, you're my waking and final thought each and every day.'

'And it's a long time since I've been that to anyone, too,' I said in return, feeling my heart flutter in my chest. 'What a poetic pair we are,' I smiled, leaning back a little so I could see the whole of his handsome face.

'Oh, I'm all about the flowery words,' he smiled. 'And I hope I don't come across as needy, but as I said right at the start of our relationship, I don't want to mess this up. I've done that before and—'

'You won't,' I told him. 'We won't.'

He nodded.

'Okay,' he said, letting out another breath. 'We're doing all right, aren't we?'

'We are,' I agreed. 'So far, so good.'

'So far, so *very* good,' he grinned.

I leant in and kissed him for the longest time.

'Thank you again, for the earlier intervention,' he said, when we eventually drew apart.

'You're welcome.'

'I know I *could* play at the fair,' he said, as we then made our way through to the kitchen.

Clearly, his thoughts, like mine, hadn't strayed all that far from the conversation back in the Grow-Well.

'I mean,' he carried on, 'I have more than enough songs to cover a whole set.'

'In that case,' I tentatively said, 'perhaps you should. Maybe you should put what happened with your mate and your ex behind you once and for all and give performing in public another go.'

Eli reached for the kettle and shook his head.

'Oh, ignore me,' he said sadly. 'I shouldn't have said anything.'

'Yes, you should,' I told him. 'Especially if that's how you really feel.'

'But even if it is,' he said, sounding choked, 'I don't deserve to, do I? I can't play those songs. My mate loved them as much as I did and my ex, and I, fucked him over so badly, I couldn't bear to play them without him.'

As hard as it was to hear the upset in his voice, they were exactly the words I wanted to hear. They confirmed he was the stand-up guy I thought he was. Even though he craved his music, he knew the part he'd played in letting his friend down over it, and he wasn't prepared to shrug it off and simply move on. The fact that he was still putting Pete's feelings ahead of his desire to play said a lot about the man he was.

'I know I'm writing again,' he added huskily, 'and I've got some great new stuff, but there are a few songs it's really hard to let go of.'

I wondered if one of them might have been the song Pete had been playing in his flat. I pulled Eli close again, not to kiss him, but to administer a hug.

'Perhaps,' I said, as he returned my embrace, 'you'll find a way through all of this and you won't have to let them go.'

Eli sighed, but didn't say anything, and I felt more resolved than ever to try and heal the rift that had torn my two favourite men apart. I desperately wanted to keep them both in my life and that meant I needed to find a way to get them happily back in each other's.

No matter how much brain power I applied to the Pete and Eli conundrum, I couldn't for the life of me come up with a satisfactory fix and it dawned on me that I was hanging onto it all a little too tightly. Mum had always maintained that putting a problem on the backburner and focusing on something else instead would guarantee it would untangle itself and so that was what I did.

'Good morning, everyone,' I said to the assembled crowd in the dayroom a short while before lunchtime on Friday.

Quite a few of the residents had spent the earlier part of the morning enjoying a little pampering. As I hadn't been able to book a mobile hairdressing and beauty team for that week, we'd opted for a bit of make-do courtesy of myself and a couple of the carers, in readiness to embrace the full experience from the following Friday.

I'd given manicures and polishes to lots of the ladies, and even Freddie. He said he liked his hands and nails to look their best when he was playing the piano, although he drew the line at the polish. Greta had said it felt nice to be touched when I gave her a hand massage, which made me feel a little sad because she wasn't being minxy at all.

The care staff had enjoyed playing their part in the morning's pampering and between us we agreed that we would, when time allowed, carry on in the coming weeks. Our efforts would help save some of the activities' savings and both Sandra and I were all for that.

The second item on the agenda that morning was a meeting with Carole and Graham to explain to the residents how the baking and gardening clubs, which would be starting the following week, were going to run.

'I'm delighted to see so many of you here,' I smiled, addressing the packed dayroom. 'Thank you all for signing up to take part in the clubs. Carole and Graham are going to be joining us in just a moment, but before they do, I would like to remind you to abstain from asking questions until they have both finished talking.'

Greta stuck her hand up, the pink nail polish she'd picked out catching the light.

'What does abstain mean?' she asked.

'Keep your trap shut,' snapped Bob.

'Oh,' Greta grinned. 'Right.'

I wasn't sure whether it was Bob's blunt manner, or the commanding way Carole addressed the room, but either way, it worked. All of the residents (aside from Trevor who was dozing at the back) listened intently to both her and then Graham, and the questions asked at the end were sensible ones.

There was very little which had to be repeated, which I thought boded well and there was a ripple of excitement threading its way along the line as everyone filed into the dining hall for lunch.

'Well,' said Carole, looking well pleased, 'I think that was a success, don't you?'

'A complete success,' agreed Graham. 'I can't wait to come back next week. The long-range forecast looks good, so hopefully we should be able to set up outside.'

'You and your weather forecasting,' Carole smiled, laying a hand on his arm.

'If it does change between now and then, Graham, we can always set something up in here,' I told him. 'It might be a bit messy, but that won't matter.'

'I'm so pleased you've got cold frames,' he cheerfully said, 'and that greenhouse is going to be a godsend.'

I had been rather embarrassed when Sandra said she'd shown him that. It was currently being used for storage and not in its proper way at all. Unfazed and without a word of criticism, however, Graham had said he'd get it cleared, sanitised and set up in time for the following week.

'Your idea to start by sowing the perennials is perfect,' I told him.

When he had ended his speech by telling everyone that sowing seeds, which would flower next spring and summer, would be their first task, Wilfred had quickly piped up.

'That'll be something to look forward to then,' he had said. 'I'd like to see a nice row of delphiniums at the back of the long border.'

What Graham had cleverly done was subtly sow the seed of the idea that everyone would still be here to enjoy the plants when they reached maturity and flowered. In my experience, optimism and long-term goals were sometimes lacking among the residents, so it was a clever tactic on Graham's part, whether intentional or not. Even Bob, who had been listening in, though pretending not to, had smiled at that.

'And those iced biscuits are going to be perfect to go with the afternoon tea, Carole,' I added.

Her well thought through list of recipes would provide almost instant gratification, which I knew would be appreciated every bit as much as Graham's long-term rewards.

'There really is nothing easier and quicker to make,' she told me. 'I wanted something simple to gauge how everyone would manage.'

She was wonderfully aware that it wasn't simply about skills and knowledge gathered over a lifetime; there were physical factors to take into account such as arthritis, which would impede some of the residents' abilities to mix and stir.

For the moment, I had completely forgotten my worries about Eli and Pete and revelled in the pleasure of knowing that my beloved care home friends were going to be in the very best of hands. Not only were they going to have their horizons broadened, they were going to be taking part in activities under the guidance of different people.

Having Carole and Graham come into the home would provide alternative conversations as well as new faces and I just knew that both the clubs were going to be hugely popular and immensely successful.

'Sandra has asked if you'd like to stay for lunch?' said Harold, who was as thrilled to see his former neighbours as I was.

Carole and Graham exchanged a quick glance.

'It's fish on Friday,' he added, 'and always very good.'

'That sounds lovely,' said Graham. 'Lead the way.'

I hadn't had the heart to further quash the pleas for a regular singalong now we had Freddie in residence and had therefore reluctantly given in to the idea. However, I had decided not to announce it until just before it was about to happen. Given a few days' warning, Greta would have been insufferable and I knew that with everything else I had going on, I wouldn't have had the patience to cope with her excitement.

Having subsequently given the idea some serious thought, I had settled on arranging it for after lunch on a Friday afternoon. There were a couple of reasons behind my planning.

First off, everyone involved in the pampering sessions would be feeling good about themselves and I thought hearing a few tunes would compound that lovely sensation and carry them through the weekend. And secondly, having it down as the last thing on my weekly to-do list would give me the whole weekend during which to recover.

'Are we all set?' Freddie, who had been in on the secret and was keen to get started, eagerly asked. 'I'm ready when you are. You know I love to entertain.'

It was right at that moment that an idea landed. Sadly, not one to sort out the Eli and Pete problem, but a good one nonetheless.

'Freddie,' I said, 'how would you feel about playing at a much bigger gig than this?'

He looked at me and raised his eyebrows.

'How much bigger?'

'*Loads* bigger,' I elaborated, 'and it's for a wonderful cause.'

'A charity gig,' he tutted. 'No fee then?'

'Afraid not,' I told him, and then quickly explained what it was all about.

I might not have been prepared to put myself forward to entertain the crowds, in spite of my connection to The Arches, but I could lessen my guilt about not stepping up by providing a genuine local star to take to the stage instead.

'It gave me quite a turn when I heard Moira Myers had passed,' said Freddie, looking dewy-eyed. 'I was always soft on her, but she never had much time for me. I think she thought I was a bit of a show-off.'

Obviously, I'd had no idea she and Freddie had known one another.

'She must have been a bit younger than you, Freddie?' I pointed out, indelicately.

'Yes,' he said, 'she was, although not by an inappropriate number of years.'

'No,' I quickly backtracked, feeling bad, 'of course not. I didn't mean . . .'

'You can tell the people running the show that I will be happy to perform,' he said. 'Providing they can get hold of a piano of course. I won't be much cop without that, will I?'

'Oh, Freddie,' I said, clapping my hands together and attracting more attention than I expected. 'That's wonderful!'

'What's going on?' asked Ida, who was the person closest.

'Are we having a singalong?' Greta gasped, also clapping her hands together.

'You know what,' I told her, my excitement over Freddie's agreement to perform at the fundraiser getting the better of me, 'I think we are!'

'Oh goodie!' she grinned. 'I knew you'd come round to the idea in the end.'

By the time Freddie had played a couple of songs, I was beginning to wonder why I'd ever been so averse to the idea of incorporating music into the new schedule. Looking at the smiling, happy and flushed faces, I realised my resistance had been extremely selfish. Just because I had cut music out of my life, it didn't give me the right to banish it from anyone else's, especially those I was working for.

Not that it really was banished now, because since I'd moved into Nightingale Square, I'd listened to more music than I'd heard in years. And I'd sung too. I turned my attention to tidying the dayroom, determined not to get sucked back into remembering how absolutely wonderful it had felt to let my voice lift and carry.

My dream was gone, and I would gain nothing from starting to yearn again for something which was now far beyond my reach. If I couldn't have the dream, I certainly didn't want to try and quench my thirst for it on the dregs.

I stiffened my resolve for all of ten seconds and then Freddie began to play 'That Ole Devil Called Love' and a lump formed in my throat. No one was singing, I realised. Greta was fanning herself and Ida with a magazine, Harold was tapping his fingers on the arm of his chair and had his eyes closed and Phil was waltzing Hazel gently about the room.

'Play something else, Freddie,' I croaked, swallowing hard. 'You're losing them. No one's singing.'

'We're taking a breather,' said Charlie.

'We need to get our breath back.' added Wilfred.

I wished they could have been reinflating their ageing lungs to the sound of anything other than Mum's favourite song. It broke my heart to hear it. Not only had it been the last song played at her funeral, it was also the last song she would have ever heard, but I couldn't bear to think about the circumstances of that. Of all the songs in Freddie's repertoire, why had he chosen that one?

'And anyway, no one can sing this,' Ida wheezily said. 'It's too difficult.'

'No, it's not,' I muttered, without thinking.

'You don't think it's a tricky tune?' asked Harold, opening one eye.

'Oh, it's tricky,' I conceded. 'Definitely difficult, but not impossible.'

'Unless you're Billie Holiday,' grinned Charlie, 'then it's a breeze.'

I guessed they were all a little long in the tooth to remember Alison Moyet's rendition, but I was in agreement – no one sang it better than Billie.

'Fancy giving it a shot?' Freddie asked, cocking a brow in my direction.

'No thanks,' I said, feeling my face turn red.

'Go on,' said Bob, with a snigger, 'we won't judge. I'll even turn my hearing aid off,' he added, pulling it out and fiddling with the setting which I knew he wouldn't be able to fix.

I resisted the urge to react to his goading.

'Go on, Beth,' Phil then winkled. 'You give this a bash and I'll do "I Will Survive", by Gloria Gaynor.'

'It's not karaoke,' said Freddie, sounding a bit put out.

He stopped playing and went to close the lid.

'Wait,' I swallowed.

'Wait?' he frowned.

'Yes,' I said, licking my lips.

What I was suddenly tempted to do was complete madness but Bob's mean tone had got to me even though I was determined not to let it, and I wondered if I had the capacity to make him eat his spiteful words. That man needed to be taught a lesson and I wondered if I had struck on the way to do it.

'Billie again?' Freddie asked quietly.

I looked at him for a second and then nodded.

'Yes,' I said. 'Billie again, please.'

'Here we go then,' Freddie smiled and then he began to play.

He played slowly, as the tune was originally intended, and I confidently matched his pace. For the next three minutes I forgot everything. I forgot where I was. I forgot who I was singing in front of. I forgot that I had vowed that I would never sing in front of anyone, ever again. I gave myself to the music. I surrendered to the words and it was some seconds after Freddie had played the final note before I opened my eyes.

With my back to the room, it was impossible to gauge everyone's reactions but the silence was deafening.

'Good god,' blustered Freddie, staggering to his feet and pulling me into a hug. 'I mean to say ... good god, Beth!'

It was then that the clapping and cheering began and I came back down to earth with a bump. I felt my lips curl into a smile, my eyes fill with tears and I began to laugh. I threw back my head and laughed and laughed.

'That's given you a shock, hasn't it?' I winked at Bob.

But when I turned around to face everyone else, I found the biggest shock had been reserved for me. Eli was framed in the doorway and he didn't look happy at all.

Chapter 21

By the time I'd managed to fight my way across the room and into reception, the only evidence that Eli had ever been in the building was the lingering scent of his aftershave.

'That guy who just came in,' said Sacha, one of the carers, who was thumbing through the visitors' book, 'left this for you. He said he thought you might need it.'

She held out the folder of receipts I was due to hand in to Sandra and which I hadn't even realised I'd forgotten. I must have left it on the dining table and Eli, up later than me because he had a day off, had spotted it and kindly made time to drop it in.

'Are you all right, Beth?' Sacha frowned, when I didn't say anything. 'You look a bit pale.'

'That's because she's exhausted,' said Phil, looking thoroughly flushed as he joined us and I heard Freddie play the opening bars of his Jerry Lee Lewis favourite. 'You're a dark horse,' he nudged. 'I had no idea you had such a set of pipes on you.'

'Has she?' frowned Sacha.

'Yes,' said Phil. 'Didn't you just hear her in there?'

'Was that you?' Sacha gaped. 'I thought you'd fired up the CD player.'

'No,' said Phil, looking at me in a completely different way, 'that was our Beth.'

'Well I never,' said Sacha, still agog. 'I had no idea either.'

Unable to appreciate either Phil's praise or Sacha's surprise, I tuned out wishing that I had kept the secret to myself. What had I been thinking? Damn Bob and his taunting tone. Although I couldn't really blame him, could I? It wasn't as if he'd frogmarched me up to the piano and forced me to sing.

No, this mess was all down to me and I felt sick to my stomach as I tried to imagine what Eli must be thinking. No doubt he now had me pinned as the second woman he'd been in a relationship with who had let him down. The acknowledgement that the secret I'd kept from him, when he'd always been so open with me, was wrapped up in music, just like the last time he'd been hurt, made it all the worse.

Music had long been ruined for me and now, I'd got swept along by its unexpected return and unthinkingly tainted it for someone else. Someone who had only so very recently been brave enough to re-embrace it.

'You'd better come back in,' said Harold, peering out of the dayroom door and pulling me away from my increasingly panicked thoughts. 'Greta's just asked Freddie to play "The Stripper".'

'I'm on it!' shouted Phil, rushing off before I had even moved.

'You should think about turning pro,' said Sacha, eyeing me speculatively. 'If I could sing like that, you wouldn't catch me chasing Greta about day in and day out.'

I didn't say anything, but reluctantly followed Phil and braced myself to once again face the music.

Part of me was desperate to get home that evening while the rest wanted to stay away for as long as possible. I didn't think I could bear to see that look on Eli's face again. I had given Sandra the receipts and heard her gushing praise after she'd called me into the office to reiterate how well the week had gone and expand upon how thrilled she was that there were two new residents moving in at the end of the month, but I hadn't really taken any of it in.

She didn't readily dole out compliments so I knew I'd regret my inattention later, but all I could focus on was the expression of hurt and bewilderment I'd seen on Eli's face before he had turned tail and fled. Buster padded across the office, rested his head heavily on my lap and looked at me with his soulful brown eyes. With a dog's sixth sense, he was obviously aware of my less than buoyant mood, even if his mistress wasn't.

'Eli!' I called, as soon I'd closed the front door. 'Are you home?'

I knew he wouldn't be, but I couldn't stand the echoing silence as I stepped into the hall. I dumped my bag and shoes and went to the kitchen to see if he'd left a note. During the last couple of weeks, we'd taken to regularly leaving each other little missives and drawings on the fridge door, but that evening there was nothing.

I reached for the kettle and flicked the radio on. It was only playing quietly, but it filled the void where our voices should have been, excitedly making plans for the weekend. It really had come to something if I was choosing to fill the silence I used to crave with a running commentary from Radio Norfolk.

I sat in Eli's armchair long after it had fallen dark, but he didn't come back and he didn't message either. I must have made at least a hundred attempts to text him, but I deleted every single one because I couldn't find the words. Not the right ones anyway. I wondered if he'd gone to stay with his mum, but as I had no real idea where she lived, it didn't make any difference to my ability to track him down.

With no word from him at all by lunchtime on Saturday, I was feeling forlorn. I had busied myself in the Grow-Well as soon as it was light and long before anyone else was up. I tried to convince myself that occupation would help and that I would just have to wait for him to come back, but by lunchtime, I'd had enough and switched to more direct action than waiting around.

'What can I get you?'

'Hey, James.'

I had walked down to the Castle Coffeehouse, determined to catch a moment with Eli, assuming he was there and even if it was the wrong place, and indeed time, to try and beg his forgiveness and talk it out.

'Beth,' said James, smiling broadly. 'Sorry,' he added, 'I didn't recognise you for a second. What can I get you?'

'Eli?' I requested, hoping he hadn't gone to his mum's or somewhere else entirely. 'I just need a very quick word with him.'

James looked at me and frowned.

'He's not working,' he said. 'He'd booked today and tomorrow off. I kind of got the feeling it was supposed to be a surprise.'

It certainly was a surprise. I'd had no idea Eli had planned some time away from work beyond his usual days off.

'He told me he'd got a whole romantic itinerary organised,' James blithely carried on, making me feel bilious.

Not only had I ruined Eli's Friday, I'd scuppered what plans he'd gone to the effort of putting in place for the weekend too. I hadn't thought I could possibly feel any worse than I already did, but James's words succeeded in pulling me down to a whole new level of self-loathing.

'A *secret* romantic itinerary,' tutted Melanie, who had just finished talking to another customer, but clearly overheard her employee's indiscretion.

'Oops,' winced James as his boss pretended to cuff him.

'You'll have to act surprised, Beth,' she added, rolling her eyes.

I didn't think that would be any stretch at all.

'Unless Eli's changed his mind,' James said, probing.

'If you thought he was here, Beth, then perhaps his plans have changed.'

'Yes,' I swallowed. 'Perhaps they have.'

'Trouble in paradise?' he asked, full of curiosity.

'No, no,' I said, backing towards the door and knocking into a customer in my haste. 'Sorry,' I quickly apologised.

'It's really none of your business, James,' I heard Melanie berate him as I rushed back out again.

I took a minute to try and gather my thoughts. It was hot on the street and busy too, and I could feel my fingers beginning to tingle as my heart started to race. It had been a long time since I'd experienced a panic attack and I was determined not to succumb to one on a busy city street. Not that I had all that much control as to whether it landed or not.

I moved out of the path of the people passing by on the pavement and rested my back against the wall of the coffeehouse. It was cool, and gave me the distance I needed to focus on my breathing.

I reminded myself that the feeling would pass and all that I had to do in that moment was pull my breath in and then slowly let it out. Had I been at home, I would have closed my eyes, but in lieu of a private and peaceful space, I trained my gaze on a fixed spot across the street – a bucket full of beautiful sunflowers in the doorway of the florists – and waited it out.

It was a few minutes before I felt ready to head back to the Square and my legs were a little shaky so I took my time. Within a few steps, however, I was almost level with the door to On the Box and decided to go in. I had to try and salvage something from the carnage that my brief music hall moment had created. Perhaps I could somehow use what had happened to bring Eli and Pete back together again.

The dreadful look on Eli's face had suggested that keeping my talent from him had potentially sacrificed our relationship, and I knew Pete was going to feel deceived when I told him who I lived with and who I loved, but maybe the fact that I had kept further secrets from both of them might be the trigger that pushed them back together. They could get together over a pint to moan about me and forget all about the sins of the past.

Admittedly it was a long shot, but I was prepared to give anything a go.

'Hi Stacey,' I swallowed, as she briefly looked up from her phone screen. 'Is your Uncle Pete about? I need to talk to him.'

'Nah,' she said, 'he's away all weekend. He's left me in charge.'

'He's left me in charge actually,' said a woman I vaguely recognised and who had been previously hidden by a display of Stranger Things merchandise. 'Can I help? I'm Pete's sister.'

Stacey huffed and rolled her eyes, still scrolling.

'No,' I said, disappointed to be thwarted before I'd even started, 'but thanks. It's okay. I'll catch up with him next week.'

I stepped out into the sunshine and walked slowly back to

the Square. Having glanced at the weekend care cover rota the day before, I knew Sara wasn't scheduled to work either so perhaps she and Pete had gone away together. Maybe they were living the romantic dream that James had suggested Eli had been planning. Perhaps if I hadn't been such an idiot, I could have been living it too.

I had no intention of breathing a word to Sara about what had happened for fear of ruining her weekend, but when a text from her arrived early Sunday afternoon, after yet another sleepless night and a morning spent pacing about the house and neglecting my houseplants, I fired back a message telling her I'd had a rough couple of days and was feeling low.

Within minutes of pressing send, there was a knock on the door and I rushed to open it. My heart thumped with the hope that it was Eli and that he must have misplaced his key. I yanked the door open, found Sara and Pete on the doorstep and burst into tears.

'Hey,' said Sara, as she pulled me into a hug. 'What the hell's going on?'

Her kindness made me sob all the harder. Not only was I upset that it hadn't been Eli, I was also angry with myself for feeling disappointed that it was my kind and considerate friends. What sort of person did that make me?

'I think we'd better come in,' said Sara, rubbing my back. 'I'll put the kettle on and you can tell us what's happened.'

I nodded and stepped aside. It was only then I realised they were dressed in their re-enactment gear.

'Were you in the middle of a battle or something?' I croaked.

'No,' said Pete, looking hot under his smock collar. 'We were engaged in combat this morning, but we were on our way back to the flat when Sara messaged you.'

Great, so not only was I having a miserable weekend, I'd also messed up whatever plans Pete and Sara had for the rest of the day.

'I didn't mean for you to come around,' I said to Sara, feeling even worse. 'I didn't plan to ruin your weekend as well as mine.'

'You haven't ruined anything,' she said sternly. 'Tell her, Pete, will you? I'll go and make some tea.'

'You have ruined it a bit,' said Pete, with a wink and in a mock whisper.

I knew he was trying to cheer me up, but he wouldn't be looking so happy once I'd plucked up the courage and explained what had happened and with who.

'So, what's up?' he asked, flopping down and filling Eli's armchair.

He looked completely wedged as he then tried to pull his tunic further towards his knees. I hoped he was wearing twenty-first century underwear.

I took a moment, trying to decide the safest and least explosive way to proceed.

'It's my housemate,' I tentatively began, perched on the very edge of the sofa. 'I haven't seen him since Friday and I'm really worried about him.'

Pete looked at me and blinked, clearly expecting me to say more, but I felt that was enough to be going on with.

'Do you usually keep tabs on each other's movements?' he frowned.

'Yes,' I said quietly. My throat felt tight, as if it didn't want me to speak and I had to force the words out. 'Yes, we do, a bit.'

'So, what's going on?' asked Sara as she wobbled in with the tea tray and tripped on the hem of her long dress. 'What have I missed?'

I quickly stood up and took the tray from her. Unfortunately, my hands were shaking so badly, I made more of a hash of carrying it than she had. I set it down with a bump.

'AWOL housemate, apparently,' said Pete, with a shrug. 'Not been seen since Friday.'

He sounded like a PC reading out of his notebook in a television crime drama.

'Oh?' said Sara, looking at me.

'We had plans for the weekend,' I told her. Courtesy of James I knew that had been part of Eli's arrangements. 'But he disappeared on Friday and hasn't been in touch.'

'You had plans with your housemate?' quizzed Pete. 'You obviously get on well with this bloke you share a kitchen and a bathroom with.'

Sara looked at me and narrowed her eyes and I took another one of those deep breaths extolled by counsellors across the globe as grounding.

'The thing is,' I began, but then had to swallow hard because my throat was painfully dry. 'The thing is,' I started again, 'he's a bit more to me now than *just* a housemate.'

Sara's eyes widened and her smile reached from ear to ear. Clearly, she'd momentarily forgotten that all was not as it should have been.

'I knew it!' she said, clicking her fingers. 'Didn't I say to you that Beth had the dishiest housemate, Pete?'

'You might have mentioned it,' he sniffed, sounding long-suffering.

I didn't think the fact that Sara thought Eli was dishy was going to be at all helpful now the truth was about to come out.

'How did it happen?' she demanded, settling back for a gossip. 'When did it happen? And more to the point, why didn't you tell me it had happened?'

'Bloody hell,' said Pete, struggling to free himself from the chair and giving us a bird's eye view of the top of his thighs. 'I think I'll leave you two to it. I don't need to hear the ins and outs if it's all the same.'

'No,' I agreed, 'you probably don't, but I think you need to hear the who.'

He stopped wriggling.

'Oh?' he said.

'Although,' I added quietly, 'I know you're not going to like it.'

'What's going on?' Sara frowned, leaning forward again. 'What have I missed?'

'Try me,' said Pete, narrowing his eyes.

I had reached the point of no return.

'Well,' I said slowly, 'this guy is a singer and musician. A huge fan of music, in fact.'

'We know that,' said Sara, sounding frustrated.

'Pete doesn't,' I swallowed. 'Unless you've told him?'

'Well, no,' she shrugged. 'I don't suppose it's come up.'

'Anyway,' I forced myself to carry on, 'this guy didn't know that I can sing.'

'Can you?' Sara asked.

'Er, yeah,' said Pete, adding weight to the secret I'd just revealed. 'She's got the most amazing voice.'

'Has she?' Sara frowned.

'No one around here, other than Pete, knows about my voice,' I told her, 'because I'd given up using it years ago, but then,' I added, the words catching, 'I stupidly got swept along and ended up singing at Cavell on Friday. My housemate turned up unexpectedly and heard me and took off before I could explain why I hadn't told him I could hold a note.'

'I don't understand,' said Sara. 'What exactly am I missing? Why would he even care that you can sing?'

'Because it's Eli,' said Pete, looking straight at me. 'That's who you're living with and going out with, isn't it, Beth? Eli's your boyfriend.'

I blinked hard to hold back the tears. Pete carried on staring and it felt like time stood still. The only sound was the ticking of the clock on the mantelpiece.

'I'm right, aren't I?' he said eventually.

'Yes,' Sara answered on my behalf. 'Yes, you are.'

I could imagine the cogs in her brain beginning to whir. It was only a matter of time before we were all caught up now.

'He only moved to the Square quite recently ...' I said quietly.

'Which is no doubt why I've seen more of him,' Pete cut in. He distractedly ran a hand through his hair.

'And to begin with, I had absolutely no idea the two of you even knew each other—' I carried on, but he stopped me.

'But you've worked it out since,' he snapped, as he began to wrestle with the chair again. 'Why didn't you just tell me?'

His voice was uncharacteristically loud and I felt myself flinch.

'I didn't know how to,' I insisted truthfully, as more tears sprang to my eyes. 'I've been racking my brains trying to figure out how to get the two of you talking again, but this happened before I'd figured anything out ...'

Pete shook his head.

'Can I just make sure I've got this straight,' said Sara, looking from one of us to the other as understanding dawned. 'Eli's the guy whose band you were in, wasn't it, Pete?'

'Yes,' he said angrily.

'The one whose girlfriend kicked you out?'

'Yep,' he said again, this time through gritted teeth.

'And you had no idea that was who Beth was living with?'

He looked at her witheringly and she didn't ask anything else.

'Did you do this on purpose?' he then fired at me as he began to pace up and down.

I'd never seen him so angry.

'Do what?'

'Sabotage your relationship with him?'

'No,' I gasped. 'Why would I do that?'

'Because maybe,' he scowled, 'maybe you thought I'd step in and sort it all out. Perhaps that was actually part of your stupidly misguided attempt to get us talking again.'

'I told you I hadn't come up with—'

'Good old Pete,' he carried on. 'He's a salt of the earth type, so he'll sort it. It'll be just like that time I made your day by tracking down a second-hand mic so you could pretend you were singing on stage at home. Or like the days I used to invite you for tea at mine so you didn't have to be home alone while your mum was still at work and you were scared of the dark. He won't be able to resist making this better too and then we can all live happily ever after.'

The only fairy-tale ending I could image, as I watched him march up and down, was a grim one.

'But it backfired . . .' he stormed on.

'No,' I said firmly, this time interrupting him. 'This wasn't part of any plan. Eli was never meant to hear me. I was never meant to sing. That was all a mistake. A stupid mistake.'

He continued to stride about the confined space.

'Sit down, Pete,' Sara urged him, 'for pity's sake.'

He ignored her and carried on.

'So where do you think Eli's gone?' Sara asked me then,

forgetting to keep calm herself, adding, 'God, if I'd known it was him, I would have given him a piece of my mind.'

'I have no idea,' I told her. 'Maybe his mum's.'

What a mess it all was. I couldn't believe Pete could possibly think that *this* was what I'd come up with to get him to talk to Eli again. But then, he was no doubt still in shock and incapable of rational thought. I was feeling a bit that way myself.

'So, if he's going out with you, Beth,' said Pete, coming to a sudden halt, 'the manipulative and conniving cow who took over the band is now his ex.'

'They split up ages ago,' I told him. 'And until recently Eli hasn't played any of the band's music. He only plays it in private now.'

Pete's scowl softened slightly.

'He told me he won't ever play in public any of the songs that you and he wrote together even though he still loves them,' I said hastily. 'And he has no idea that I know who you are but he did share with me that there's not a day that goes by that he doesn't regret what happened between him and his former bandmate and best friend. He said he'd do anything to make things right between you.'

Pete bit his lip and I felt a lump form in my throat.

Eli really had been open with me. He'd trusted me with his deepest thoughts, his darkest secrets and most intense feelings. It made what had happened on Friday feel even more of a betrayal. I'd pretty much told him I hated music and then he'd caught me singing my heart out. It was no wonder he'd taken off.

'If he feels that bad, why hasn't he just come and talked to me?' Pete tutted, as he started to pace again. 'He knows where I work and where I live. It's literally a stone's throw from the coffeehouse.'

'I think he's been like me in that respect,' I told him. 'He hasn't known what to say. He's heartbroken about what happened with you though, Pete. He really is.'

He stared at me and I realised his frown had completely gone and been replaced by a look of concern.

'I can't get my head around this,' said Sara, shaking her head. 'No wonder Eli was shocked to hear you sing. We all thought you hated music.'

I'd almost forgotten she was there.

'I guess she must have kept the flat,' Pete muttered, oblivious to what Sara was saying. 'I'm surprised she didn't try and take the music too . . .'

'Pete,' said Sara, raising her voice, 'please sit down. You're going to wear the pattern off the rug.'

'No, bugger this,' he said, making for the door. 'I've had enough.'

'Where are you going?' I asked, rushing after him.

'To bring the eejit back, of course.'

'But we don't know where he is!' I sobbed.

'I'll find him.'

'You better get changed first!' Sara shouted, as he wrenched open the door and marched back down the path still dressed in full regalia.

Chapter 22

'Come on,' insisted Sara, once Pete had driven off. 'Come and drink this tea before it's stewed beyond all recognition.'

I didn't much want to sit and calmly drink strong tea, especially when I realised how much she'd sweetened it, but I downed it anyway, trying not to think of the conversation which could soon be playing out if, by some miracle, Pete did manage to track Eli down.

'They both hate me now, don't they?' I shuddered, as I returned the mug to the tray. My throat still felt dry in spite of the treacly drink. 'I knew I'd lost Eli the second I saw his face on Friday, but now I might have lost Pete, too. I can't believe I've made such a mess of everything and just when my life had turned a corner.'

I didn't mean to sound sorry for myself, especially as the mess was of my own making, but I was devastated. I should have paid far more attention to the warning in my heart. It told me I was juggling a ticking timebomb right from the second Eli and Pete's tangled friendship had been confirmed and I should have come clean from the start, rather than waste time trying to work out how to patch things up.

'Hey now,' Sara said sternly, 'I know you're not usually prone to hysterics and melodrama, so I'm going to put your words and over the top reaction down to shock. I don't think you're actually going to lose anyone.'

'Pete will probably be okay,' I then sensibly conceded, 'but you didn't see Eli's face.'

'Well, he was bound to be a bit upset that you hadn't mentioned you can sing, especially given his love of music and your insistence that you're not a fan. He must be thinking that you've deceived him, Beth.'

'He was a whole lot more than a bit upset,' I told her, feeling worse again.

Sara was quiet for a moment.

'Had you not said how much he regrets what happened between him and Pete, I wouldn't have cared how upset he was,' she said, 'but I can tell that the whole situation has really taken a toll on them both.'

'Yes,' I agreed, 'it has. I've heard both sides of the story and from what I've deduced, Eli's ex was a real piece of work. Not that that excuses the fact that he went along with what she wanted regarding Pete.'

My hands shook as I realised that Eli was going to think I was a piece of work now, too. He had made his past an open book and I hadn't reciprocated. It was little wonder he'd taken off.

'Look,' said Sara, 'let's just forget about them for a minute. I want to talk about you.'

'Me?'

'Yes,' she said, 'if that's all right.'

'I suppose,' I said hesitantly. 'What about me?'

'Well,' she said, 'I can't help thinking now that I don't know you very well at all.'

'What do you mean?' I frowned.

'For a start,' she reeled off, 'I had no idea that you can sing.'

'No one knew that,' I said quickly.

'Except Pete.'

'Except Pete,' I agreed. 'But he only knew because we practically grew up together. And I'd recently sworn him to secrecy not to tell anyone because I never had plans to do it again.'

I wanted to be clear that he hadn't mentioned it because I'd made him promise not to.

'So,' Sara frowned, 'what happened on Friday to make you break your vow of silence?'

'It was Bob,' I told her. 'You know how he likes to wind everyone up.'

Sara looked at me and shook her head.

'That was it?' she frowned. 'One old man's teasing was enough to make you do the one thing you'd told Pete you'd never do again and that he could never so much as even mention?'

She was right to be confused. There had been so much more to it than Bob's goading. Music had been weaving its way back into my life practically from the moment I set foot in Nightingale Square and my Billie Holiday rendition wasn't the first time I'd warmed up my vocal cords, in spite of my former conviction to never sing a note again.

'It's a long story,' I told her with a sigh.

'Well, I'm not going anywhere,' said Sara, sitting further back and making herself at home.

'And the story doesn't matter, because singing on Friday was a one-off mistake,' I told her. 'I should never have done it.'

'Well,' she sighed, 'whether you meant it to or not, that one-off mistake has achieved something. Things might not have happened in the way you hoped they would, but your impromptu crooning has got the guys back in each other's lives.'

I winced at her words, knowing them to be true but not all that comforting.

'I only wish it could have been a far less traumatic coming together,' I murmured, wondering how Pete was faring in his search for his former friend.

'I know now's not the time,' Sara continued, 'but I really would be interested to hear more about your musical past. Pete hasn't breathed a word about any of it, but my guess is the pair of you met at The Arches, didn't you?'

I neither confirmed nor denied her deduction.

'You do know that you can talk to me, Beth, don't you?' she said, sounding frustrated.

'I do talk to you.'

'I'm not talking about whether Greta's kept her clothes on, or if Wilfred's refused his medication. I mean *real* stuff. Life stuff. Hopes, dreams, the whole shebang. I know that you came to work at the home after your mum died, you have a passion for houseplants and that you hated your former houseshare, but that's pretty much it.'

'But that *is* it,' I shrugged. 'That's my life in a nutshell.'

'Of course, it isn't,' Sara tutted. 'I want to know about the Beth before she became her mum's carer. What was she like? What did she want out of life? What was her childhood like and her school days?'

'The truth is,' I struggled to say, 'I packed those memories and that version of myself away within days of Mum's first stroke. I pushed away practically everything about that Beth a long time ago and besides,' I added, 'I don't know any of that stuff about you either.'

'You know some of it,' she said gently. 'I tell you things about my family and life outside of work, but with you, it's like you walked into the home to work that first day and before then you didn't even exist.'

'Self-preservation,' I told her. 'It's just too painful to look back to that time.'

'What about Eli then?' she tried. 'Why didn't you tell me you'd made the move from housemates to couple?'

'Because the two of us had agreed to take things slowly,' I explained, trying to be a more open and honest friend. 'I've never had a serious relationship before and he's still getting over the trauma of his last one. We didn't want to make some big declaration and then find ourselves being scrutinised while we were trying to find our way.'

'That makes sense,' she nodded. 'See,' she then nudged, 'it's not that hard, is it?'

'What?'

'Letting friends in and sharing stuff.'

'Like I said,' I reminded her, 'it's self-preservation. After I lost Mum, I stopped letting people in for fear of feeling that level of pain when I lost them again.'

'I hate that you think you're going to lose everyone.'

I didn't have a response to that.

'Although,' she then said, sounding happier, 'I think that mindset is changing.'

'You do?'

'Yes,' she said. 'You've got Pete back in your life now and Eli's managed to wedge himself into your heart too. If you thought you were going to lose them, you wouldn't have let them in at all, would you?'

'I suppose not,' I agreed.

It was both a surprising and comforting thought. Assuming the whole Pete and Eli situation could be happily resolved, of course.

'Right,' Sara said, puffing out her cheeks. 'I'm going to make some more tea.'

'Good,' I said, 'anything to take away the taste of the last one.'

'Hey,' Sara pouted and I heard myself laugh for the first time in days.

After a much nicer mug of tea and a tour of the tiny back garden, we returned to the sitting room and while she was still wearing it, I sewed up the hem of Sara's tunic which had come undone after she'd earlier tripped over it.

My eyes flitted continuously to the clock. Pete had left hours ago and even though Sara had tried to keep me talking, my thoughts had constantly veered back to what was potentially happening between him and Eli.

'Oh,' Sara gasped, jumping off the sofa just as I'd snipped the thread, 'that's my phone.'

'Hurry up,' I urged, 'before it rings off!'

'I *am* hurrying!' she said, hoisting up her dress to reveal the whole of her cotton leggings and a velvet pouch tied to the internal waistband of her dress. 'I bet Boudicca never had this trouble,' she muttered, as she struggled with the drawstring opening.

'Probably not,' I tutted. 'But then she never had to find somewhere to keep her phone and keys, did she?'

Sara let out a bark of laughter before pulling out her phone with a flourish.

'Quick,' I said again and she shot me a look.

'Hey, Pete,' she said, confirming it was him. 'How are you getting on?'

I couldn't bear to listen to the one-sided conversation so I went to sort out the tea things.

'He's found him!' shouted Sara, rushing into the kitchen the second the call ended.

I felt my entire body wilt with relief.

'Where?' I asked.

'He didn't get to say because the signal cut out, but they're together and Eli's going to stay at the flat for a bit.'

I bit my lip.

'That's good, right?' Sara asked.

On the one hand, it was wonderful because it meant the two men were getting along well enough to stay under the same roof but on the other it meant that I had driven Eli out of his home and that was not a nice feeling.

'Pete said they've been talking loads,' Sara carried on. 'Which sounds really hopeful.'

'It does,' I agreed. 'Did he say anything else before you got cut off?'

Sara grimaced and I got the impression she'd got to the part of the conversation she didn't want to relay.

'Just that Eli's still processing what happened on Friday,' she said, with a sympathetic head tilt. 'Pete reckons he needs a bit more time to get his head around it all, feeling that maybe you haven't been entirely honest with him.'

'But he won't be able to process it if he doesn't let me explain,' I burst out.

'I know,' Sara said, 'but if you turn up, all guns blazing—'

I put up a hand to stop her.

'I get that,' I said, feeling a tidal wave of tears starting to build 'It's just . . .'

The torrent of tears broke through my defences before I had uttered another word. I felt so relieved that Pete had found his friend but I was also frustrated that I couldn't explain why I'd kept my talent a secret. It was a heady and emotional mix.

'I'm sorry,' I sobbed noisily, as Sara steered me into the dining room.

'Don't apologise,' she scolded, returning to the kitchen for some paper towel.

'I just never meant to hurt either of them, you know,' I sniffed.

'I do know,' she said, handing me the towel, 'and they know that, too. And you know what?' she smiled.

'What?' I hiccupped.

'There's no doubt in my mind that once they've sorted things out, their relationship will be even stronger than it was before.'

'But what about ours?' I sniffed. 'I know Pete will forgive me, but what about Eli? What about my relationship with him?'

'Well,' she said, 'maybe you should just let Pete tell him. He'll be able to explain and make him understand.'

I knew she was right. Pete was practical and level-headed. If anyone was able to fight my corner, it was him. Although there were things that had happened that not even he knew about, so explaining some of it would still be down to me.

'I'm just going to have to let them get on with it and wait it out, aren't I?' I sniffed again, forcing myself to rein in the dramatics.

'I think so,' she said, tearing me off another sheet of paper towel. 'We just need to give them a couple of days.'

It was going to be agony but I wouldn't do anything that might jeopardise snapping the slender threads the men were using to stitch their friendship back together.

'A couple of days,' I repeated.

'Pete said Eli's asked if I would mind taking a few bits from his room to the flat,' Sara further said. 'Do you mind if I go and grab them? Then I should get going.'

'Of course not,' I sniffed, only just realising how late in the day it was. 'I'm sorry I've messed up your day.'

'You haven't,' she said. 'You really haven't.'

I wasn't sure Pete would agree, but then perhaps it was worth sacrificing an afternoon of passionate role play if it meant repairing his friendship with Eli.

'I'd better find some clothes for you too,' I tutted. 'Now Pete's taken the car, you can hardly walk the streets dressed as the warrior queen, can you?'

Once Sara had gone, I returned to the sitting room and curled up in Eli's armchair to mull everything over. Another lump formed in my throat when I considered again everything Eli had so openly shared with me. It was little wonder he was feeling so hurt. I'd held back about something that was deeply important to both of us, something which I was now able to admit, defined who we were, even though it pained me to do it.

As late afternoon turned to early evening, I worked my way through my houseplant routine but it didn't supply the same succour as it usually did. In fact, when it came to watering the plants in Eli's pots, it made me feel quite wretched. We were supposed to be looking after the plants together, after all. As I carefully watered, I clung to the hope that he was as understanding as Pete had been and we could simply pick up where my rendition of Billie Holiday's hit had forced us to leave off.

Chapter 23

I slept better than I expected to that night and it was all thanks to a timely and considerate text from Pete. As I read what he'd thoughtfully typed, I acknowledged that there really was no one kinder or more forgiving than my oldest friend.

> I know you'll be fretting, but please try not to.
> Eli and I are working things out and it turns
> out people really do do crazy things when
> they're in love! I understand why you didn't
> say anything when you rumbled us but, given
> everything else that's happened, it might take
> Eli a little longer to come around. Would you
> like me to explain a few things on your behalf?
>
> Love, Pete x

I thanked him for setting my mind at rest but turned down his offer to explain why I had insisted I disliked music along with why I hadn't mentioned to Eli that I could sing.

Even though I had talked to Sara about Pete telling Eli about it all, and in spite of the fact that I was desperate for him to know, I knew it would be better coming directly from me. Therefore, I decided I would have to wait to explain until Eli came home and, in the meantime, keep my fingers crossed that he would give me the chance to bare my soul then.

Monday dawned with none of the excitement I had been predicting. It was the first full week of the new activities schedule and I had wanted it to all play out perfectly. However, as I had so recently been reminded, no matter how hard I tried to keep things under control, life had a habit of going off kilter whenever it felt like it and I needed to learn the lesson, embrace the tumult and go with the flow.

My carefully planned scheduling of the home's houseplant maintenance was a prime example. I had figured that first thing Monday morning would be the ideal lead-in to the week and give me the opportunity to catch up with everyone and find out if there had been any highs or lows over the weekend, but all it did that first week was provide everyone with the chance to bombard me with questions and berate me for not 'singing up sooner'.

'You wouldn't think it to look at her, would you?' I heard Ida say, not so quietly, to Greta as I gathered up the plants and set them down on the paper-covered table. 'She doesn't look the type at all.'

'That's what they used to say about that Susan Boyle,' winked Greta, 'and she can belt out a really good tune.'

'We can't wait for Friday,' joined in Bob, including me in the conversation. 'Best thing I ever did was tease you, Beth!'

He sounded extremely happy about what had happened and had his smile been the result of anything else, I would have revelled in the unusual sight of it.

'Shame we can't have a singalong every day, hey Freddie?' called Greta.

Freddie, I noticed, was sitting reading the newspaper a little distance away and hadn't commented at all.

'I'm not sure my finger joints could cope with that,' he said mildly. 'Best to stick to once a week, I think.'

Greta didn't argue. For once.

'And you'll have to make your own entertainment,' I said, turning towards the door and trying not to imagine Eli standing there looking distraught. 'That was definitely a one-off from me. I'll just go and find the Baby Bio.'

I escaped to the staffroom, but not for long, because Harold was hot on my heels.

'I know it's none of my business,' he said.

'Oh, Harold,' I frowned, 'why do people always say that right before they try to make something their business?'

I knew I sounded waspish, but I had been hoping the weekend would have been long enough to put a bit of distance between what had happened on Friday and the new week.

'As I was saying,' Harold carried on, 'I know it's none of my business and as such, I haven't mentioned to anyone at the Grow-Well that we have someone so musically talented living in the Square, because I'm pretty certain that if I did, then they'd be on at you to sing at the fundraiser.'

I felt my knees buckle a little.

'And for some reason,' he added, 'I get the feeling you wouldn't want to do that.'

I looked at him wide-eyed. So preoccupied with worrying about Eli, I had overlooked Harold's connection to the Square. He could have easily and innocently ratted me out, and so, of course, could Sara.

'And before you fly off into a tailspin,' Harold continued, having most likely noticed the colour drain from my face, 'I've said the same to Sara. If Lisa does find out, it won't have come from either of us.'

'Thank you,' I said, letting out a long but not particularly steadying breath. 'Thank you, Harold. I'm sorry for being so rude.'

'That's all right,' he smiled kindly. 'By my reckoning you must have some pretty good reasons for not telling anyone about your talent, but I am surprised that you haven't done anything with it.'

I shook my head and sighed, my cheeks turning pink again.

'Oh, or perhaps you have . . .'

'Beth!' I heard Ida shout. 'Greta's cutting the leaves off the ivy.'

I raced back to the dayroom, grateful to find it was more the usual tit-for-tat playing out between the two women who pretended not to rub along, but would have actually been lost without each other, than anything more sinister.

'Where did you get those?' I frowned at Greta who had thankfully only snipped off the less healthy-looking leaves with the tiny pair of nail scissors she'd purloined from somewhere.

'They were in a manicure set I won at the tombola at the garden party,' she told me. 'No one said I couldn't keep them.'

I hastily confiscated them and set her to work gently wiping the leaves with a pack of horticultural wipes instead. It was a large ivy plant and would hopefully keep her out of mischief until at least lunchtime.

'Shall we try and get them all outside?' Phil suggested later, after everyone had eaten. 'It'll be easier to keep an eye on them if they're all in one place.'

The sun had disappeared behind a thick blanket of cloud, so it was much cooler. I had planned to set the quoits up on the lawn, and as it was easy enough to carry out the fold-up tables and set the rest of the games up on the large patio area, I wholeheartedly agreed.

'That's a great idea,' I told Phil. 'Will you be able to give me a hand?'

'Of course,' he said. 'I'm planning to thrash Charlie at Connect Four.'

'No chance, lad,' Charlie sniffed. 'I'm the king of Connect Four.'

There wasn't a breath of wind, which meant there was no danger of the snap cards or the treasured shopping list game blowing away and by the time Sandra came to find us, with a panting Buster in tow, there was a lovely summer party feel to the afternoon.

We had covered jugs of squash and plates of biscuits, which Ida said would do until the baking club the next day. I tried to ignore the flutter in my chest when I thought how easy it would be for any of the residents to let slip about my performance the week before. I would just have to hope for the best and bank on Carole and Graham keeping everyone so busy that they wouldn't have time to think about anything else.

'How lovely is this?' smiled Sandra, even though I could see her high heels were, as usual, sinking into the lawn and she seemed to have something stuck to her jacket sleeve.

'It was Phil's idea to move everything outside today,' I said, keen to give credit where it was due.

I sidled closer and discreetly removed the fuzzy felt cow from the back of her arm. I frowned at Greta, but she refused to meet my eye. I had noticed Bob had had a pig stuck to the seat of his trousers earlier in the week. What a mischievous woman she was! I refused to let my mind imagine how she'd got the sow to stick to Bob's backside.

'An inspired idea,' Sandra said to Phil.

Phil looked thrilled.

'Thanks,' he beamed at us both.

Popping the cow in my pocket, I looked around and felt immensely grateful that, for the time being at least, everyone had stopped talking about Friday. If I didn't allow myself to be goaded into singing again, and stopped humming along to the radio at home, then hopefully I'd be able to put the recent fall from grace completely behind me and move on with my life as I had previously planned.

'You all right, Beth?' asked Freddie. 'You've gone a bit of a funny colour.'

'I'm all right,' I said shakily. 'I'm fine.'

But truth be told, I wasn't fine. My head was awash with sudden thoughts of the possibility of carrying on with my singing and not stopping at all. I realised with a jolt that there was now a very large part of me that didn't want to stop, even though finding my voice again had so far led to nothing but trouble.

As hard as my head tried to churn out the old, well-worn argument that there would be no point in carrying on when I couldn't pursue the superstar dream I'd had as a younger woman, and that songs such as the one I'd sung on Friday stirred up nothing but bad memories, my heart was beating fast and to a very different tune. One which suggested that simply singing for pleasure would be far better than not singing at all.

I looked up and found Freddie was still watching me. He didn't say anything further, but given the knowing expression on his face, he didn't need to.

'Who wants the last lemon chicken skewer?' John shouted in the Grow-Well the next evening and everyone laughed as Archie and Ryan scrambled to claim it.

It had been another busy day and I hadn't planned to come over to the garden but the evening before, home alone and spent missing Eli, hadn't gone well. I'd opened and drunk the best part of a bottle of wine, which wasn't like me at all, and then ended up downloading Spotify and singing along to everything from Bon Jovi to Billie Eilish. I'd spent the last few years in silence and now my voice had broken free it was hellbent on staying that way, especially when lubricated by so much wine and so many appealing lyrics.

I was grateful the evening hadn't ended in any drunken texting and now, in the company of my neighbours, I endeavoured to find a different outlet for my rediscovered creativity.

'I've been meaning to ask,' I said to Lisa, once she'd made Archie share the skewer with Ryan, 'is there anything I can do to help out at the fundraiser?'

'Thanks, Beth,' she said, smiling broadly and wiping her hands, 'I really appreciate you offering. I haven't wanted to ask because I know how busy you've been, settling into your new role at work. How's it going by the way?'

'Great,' I said, thinking back to the success the baking club had been and how Carole had kept everyone on their toes and thankfully distracted from the events of the previous Friday. 'Really well.'

'Are there any biscuits left?' Carole asked, once I'd explained to Lisa that the baking club had started that day.

'Not a single one,' I told her. 'And I reckon it will be early nights all round.'

What with the crafting in the morning and cooking in the afternoon, I'd got practically everyone involved in something. Even Wilfred had abandoned grumpy Bob and donned a pinny when it was time to do some icing. He'd then proved himself to be surprisingly skilful with the piping bag.

'Mission accomplished then,' Carole smiled.

'Absolutely,' I agreed. 'And it's Zumba in the morning.'

'Bloody hell,' laughed John. 'I thought the poor sods were retired.'

'Actively so apparently,' Lisa responded. 'And I'll have a think about the fundraiser, Beth. If I come up with anything, I'll let you know.'

I was disappointed that she didn't currently have anything I could take on. With Eli still absent and my desire to sing getting the better of me in unguarded moments, I really needed something, besides work, that I could throw myself into.

'Okay,' I said, trying to sound more buoyant than I felt. 'Great.'

'Actually,' said Jacob, stepping in, 'there might be something.'

'Oh?'

'Yeah,' he said, 'you're the ideas person, aren't you, Beth?'

'Am I?' I swallowed.

'Yes,' grinned Poppy. 'You are. It was you who came up with the summer fair idea in the first place, remember?'

'And my book signing,' Lisa added. 'What have you got in mind, Jacob?'

'Our trip to the chapel tomorrow,' he said. 'I know it's not direct involvement with any of the fundraising stalls and so on, but we could do with a fresh pair of eyes at the venue, couldn't we?'

'That's a good point,' Lisa said. 'We're getting a bit jittery that the place might not be quite right, Beth. How do you fancy coming and taking a look?'

Taking a trip to the building which was set to replace The Arches was the last thing I wanted to do.

'I'm not sure I'm qualified to help with that,' I said hesitantly.

'You are actually, Beth,' Carole said thoughtfully. 'You probably don't even realise you're doing it, but you manage the space at the care home wonderfully. You're the ideal person to size the chapel up. You'll be able to visualise what will work and what won't.'

'And you did say you wanted to help,' Lisa winningly added.

I wasn't sure I agreed with Carole It sounded a bit of a stretch to me, but with everyone looking so keen, I didn't like to say no.

'All right,' I conceded. 'In that case, I'll come along and take a look.'

Lisa messaged the next morning with the chapel address and directions to it from the Square. She and Jacob had a meeting to attend prior to our viewing, so I agreed to meet them there.

She also sent more details about the evening fundraiser, which included a list of the acts they'd got lined up so far. It was of a reasonable length and a varied selection, but they were right, there was definitely room for more. It was then I remembered that in trying to banish the traumatic memory of the singalong, I'd also ended up forgetting to mention that I'd asked Freddie to take a turn on the stage. Perhaps he would be able to fill the gap the entertainment programme currently had.

Having paced out the journey from the Square faster than I needed to, which helped to quell the urge to turn back, I arrived at the chapel a while before the others. The building was far larger than I had been expecting and there were plenty of parking spaces and a rough patch of overgrown garden around the back. Compared to what The Arches had had, they were both plus points in the potential new venue's favour.

Parking had always been a contentious issue at The Arches as the only outdoor space was shared with a mechanic and a small parcel-sorting depot. The people who ran those were forever arguing, and reasonably so, that their need for vehicular access was greater than Moira's. I wondered if their businesses had survived the recent rent hike.

I sat on a low wall, facing the entrance and took a swig from my water bottle. It was early evening, but still very warm. I'd just pulled out my phone to consult the weather app to help me decide if it would be too hot to hold the gardening club outdoors the next day, when Jacob and Lisa pulled up, in Jacob's car.

'Are we late?' Lisa asked, jumping out before he'd cut the engine.

'No,' I said, 'don't worry – I'm early.'

'Well, I'm thrilled you're keen,' Lisa laughed.

She didn't know the half of it.

'Come on then,' said Jacob, tossing Lisa a bunch of keys, 'let's get inside. The keyholder's given us an hour, then he's coming to lock up again.'

I held my breath as I stepped over the threshold. I might not have wanted to be there, but having been an attendee of The Arches, I knew exactly what a lifeline this sort of place could be. I had everything crossed that the chapel would prove to be every bit as adequate as the special place under the railway lines had been.

As it turned out, I didn't need the hour the keyholder had gifted us. Within five minutes, I had my answer.

'This is perfect,' I said, rushing back into the main area and turning in a slow circle, my previous misgivings about looking completely forgotten. 'It's absolutely ideal.'

Lisa and Jacob looked well pleased. Not that I was an expert or anything, but even my amateur eye could see that the space was spot on for what they needed to do with it.

There was a small lobby with a corridor leading off to the right and big double doors directly in front. Through those was the main chapel area. The space could easily seat a hundred and there was already a stage in place too. It wasn't particularly high, but it was far larger than what The Arches had had.

There was also a spacious kitchen, loos and another four smaller rooms, each plenty big enough to hold drama, creative writing, singing classes and anything else the managers came up with. I knew Moira would have loved the flexibility of a building like this. The Arches had been great, but there wasn't much separate space if you wanted to have more than one thing happening at the same time.

'This is so much more adaptable than The Arches,' I gushed, rushing back into one of the smaller rooms again. 'You're going to be able to have several things running at once here, and there's a decent kitchen space too.'

Lisa and Jacob exchanged a look.

'And the stage is fantastic,' I said, walking over to it and hopping up again. 'You could probably have a full-scale production here.'

'Oh Beth,' said Lisa, looking tearful with one hand pressed to her heart, 'you've absolutely made my day.'

I looked at her and grinned, delighted to have contributed something.

'I don't know why you'd got it into your heads that it wouldn't work,' I frowned. 'It's absolutely perfect.'

Expert I might not be, but I knew a good thing when I saw it.

'I think we've just been getting jittery about making the commitment,' Jacob said. 'This will be make or break for Moira's legacy.'

'Make!' I insisted with the benefit of my fresh eyes and no knowledge of the tight financials. 'Definitely, make.'

Lisa and Jacob exchanged another look and I wondered if I might have missed something.

'We're both delighted that you think so,' said Lisa, her attention returning to me, 'but I have to ask, Beth, how come you know so much about The Arches?'

'Yes,' frowned Jacob, 'I was just about to ask that too. I didn't think you'd even heard of the place before you moved to the Square.'

I turned away, cursing my enthusiasm for getting the better of me.

'I did a bit of googling last night,' I blagged, focusing my attention on the window that was set high in the wall, rather than on their curious faces. 'There were loads of photos online.'

It was true. I had spent an hour reminiscing online. Thankfully, I hadn't spotted myself in any of the performance images, but then I hadn't looked that closely. There had been plenty of Pete though. Lots of recent ones of him helping out on the sidelines and I'd felt a pang of regret for what I'd lost as I scrolled through them.

'Well, that's great,' said Lisa. 'I'm even happier now, knowing that you've done some research. It makes your opinion even more valid. It's good that you've got some idea of what we're comparing this place to.'

I was pleased she'd accepted my answer but felt bad about not coming clean, but how could I possibly tell them now?

'Me too,' Jacob agreed loudly, clapping his hands together as if it was all decided.

The sound of his voice echoed around the walls and I looked around again, wondering what the acoustics were like.

'Oh bugger,' Lisa groaned as she checked her phone, which had started to buzz.

'What's up?' asked Jacob.

'John has just been called out and Tamsin's not at home to keep an eye on the others.' She sighed.

'I'll run you back,' offered Jacob.

'But then you won't be here to return the key,' she pointed out.

'I'll stay,' I shrugged. 'I don't mind waiting.'

'Are you sure?'

'Of course,' I said, 'but before you go, I must just tell you that I've got another act lined up for the fundraiser.'

I quickly explained about Freddie, whose name was met with genuine affection and enthusiasm and the second Jacob's car was out of sight, I rushed back into the building to look around again.

I completed my second tour and ended it by climbing up onto the stage. Without overthinking I started to hum and then sing. This time I didn't go for something from my recently created Spotify list, but picked the one song I had missed hearing more than any other since Eli had left home. It was his song and I sang it wholeheartedly and a cappella, the words as well as the tune imprinted forever into my heart.

My voice trembled as it gradually filled the high ceilinged and cavernous space. I glanced at my phone and saw I had enough time to sing it again before the keyholder arrived. Second time around I didn't hold anything back. I let my voice lift and soar, and so focused on the lyrics, I didn't hear someone walk in.

I let the last note linger and when I opened my eyes, I found my audience of one staring up at me with tears in his.

'Oh Beth,' he swallowed.

'Pete,' I gasped, my hand instinctively flying to my chest to protect my hammering heart. 'You scared me half to death. What are you doing here?'

It was wonderful to see him, but he had given me one heck of a scare.

'More to the point,' he said, sounding choked, 'what planet were you on when you decided abandoning your voice was a good idea? You still sound incredible. That performance was enchanting, bewitching . . .'

'You know exactly which planet I was on,' I interrupted. 'It was planet shock and grief,' I reminded him nonetheless. 'And it was all-consuming.'

I quickly jumped off the stage and smoothed down my clothes. Still struggling with the sudden and surprising desire to start singing again, I couldn't let Pete catch even a glimpse of what I was thinking. If he worked out my resolve was crumbling, he wouldn't be able to resist applying some pressure and, in spite of my changing feelings, I wasn't ready for that.

'I'm sorry,' he said, biting his lip. 'That was insensitive of me. It was just so wonderful to hear you again.'

'It's fine,' I told him. 'I know you didn't mean anything by it.'

He looked at me and smiled.

'That's kind of you, Beth,' he said, 'to be so forgiving.'

I couldn't help but laugh when he said that.

'What?' he frowned.

'Compared to you,' I swallowed, 'and what you've for-given, it's a drop in the ocean.'

He stepped forward and pulled me into a hug.

'God, it's good to have you back in my life,' I said, from the depths of his embrace.

He kissed the top of my head, gave me a tighter squeeze and then let me go.

'It's good to have you back in mine, too,' he beamed.

I was desperate to ask if Eli had mentioned coming home, but afraid to hear what the answer might be, I bit the words back.

'Come on,' I said instead, 'I'd better check everything's shut up. Aren't you wondering why I'm here?'

'No,' he said, following me through the rooms, 'I know why you're here. Lisa told me that Jacob had asked you to take a look at the place. That's why I've come along. I was as keen to hear what you think as they were.'

'I still don't really get why they wanted me to come,' I told him. 'Carole thought I'd be ideal as I organise the space at work, but I've only recently started doing that.'

'Maybe it's fate stepping in and lending a hand,' Pete sug-gested. 'Especially given how well you knew The Arches.'

I didn't comment on that. Fate seemed to have had more than its fair share of a say in my life of late.

'Anyway, where are Lisa and Jacob?' Pete asked.

'Lisa needed to get home,' I told him. 'So Jacob drove her and I said I'd stay and lock up. They told me they'd started to worry that this wasn't the right place to carry The Arches on. You haven't been feeling like that too, have you?'

'Absolutely not,' he said vehemently. 'I know it's right. I can feel it.'

'I can feel it too.'

'And now I've heard you singing here, I'm even more convinced. The acoustics are incredible and there's so much scope to do more here than we ever did at The Arches.'

'That's what I told them.'

'What did they make of that?' Pete frowned. 'In view of what you told me, I assumed you would have made out that you didn't know anything about the place.'

'I did,' I confirmed, 'but then I got carried away as we looked around here and I ended up having to say I'd seen photos online. Which I had,' I added quickly.

Pete nodded. His expression suggested my continued duplicity didn't sit any better with him than it did with me.

'Well,' I said, 'I'd better finish locking up. The keyholder will be here in a minute. You can go if you need to. I'm sorry you've had a wasted trip.'

'It wasn't entirely wasted,' he smiled and knowing he was referring to my vocal moment, I kept quiet again. 'I'm in no rush,' he said. 'I'll hang on and we can walk back together if you like.'

'Okay.'

Once we'd checked everywhere was secure, we sat outside on the wall.

'While we've got a minute,' Pete said, giving me a nudge, 'I want to say thank you.'

'Oh?' I frowned, reaching for my water. 'What for?'

'You know what for,' he tutted. 'Getting me and Eli back together, of course.'

I nodded, fighting back the emotion I felt at hearing Eli's name.

'Are you really getting on all right?' I asked.

'We are,' Pete smiled. 'Our coming together might not have happened how you wanted it to, but it's done the trick. We've thrashed everything out and we're friends again now. We're back on the path we were before and I never in a million years thought that would happen.'

I wondered if that meant they were thinking about reforming their musical alliance as well as their friendship.

'At least some good has come out of me buggering everything up then,' I said quietly.

'You haven't buggered anything up,' Pete insisted. 'In fact, Eli wants to talk to you.'

My gaze leapt to Pete's face.

'He does?' I asked shakily, struggling to screw the lid back on my drink.

'Yes,' he said, taking the bottle and doing it for me. 'He said he'll meet you in the pub when you finish work tomorrow.'

'Not at the house?'

'No,' said Pete, handing the bottle back. 'I was surprised about that too, but he insisted it had to be the pub.'

'Oh my god,' I gasped. 'He's going to dump me, isn't he?'

'What?' Pete frowned. 'Why on earth would you think that?'

'Because meeting in a public place guarantees less of a fuss,' I panicked. 'Everyone knows that.'

'Rubbish,' Pete tutted. 'He's not told me he's thinking about binning you off.'

'What a wonderful way of putting it!' I virtually sobbed.

'Well, I'm not getting that vibe from him at all,' he added in a more placatory tone.

'Very reassuring,' I sighed.

'I promise you,' he said, putting an arm around my shoulders and pulling me close, 'everything's going to be fine. Trust me.'

I clung tightly to the hope that he was right about that.

Chapter 24

I must have missed the weather report which announced that storms were due to roll over Norfolk that night, but the drumming rain and rolling thunder ensured sleep was hard to come by. Giving up on counting sheep, I laid instead and listened to the crashes and bangs and ran through my Eli apology script, mulled over everything Pete had told me and wondered how it would all turn out.

Pete had said that he and Eli were back on the right path and that obviously meant they were friends again – Eli wouldn't have been sleeping on his sofa if that wasn't the case – but what about the music?

I already knew that Eli was writing again, so perhaps he'd convinced Pete to play too. And, if that was the case, and he wasn't going to bin me off (as Pete had so eloquently put it), given what he'd heard at the care home, I wondered if he might be gearing up to ask me to sing in their reformed band. I was shocked by the frisson of excitement that this possibility triggered and as I finally drifted off to sleep, I fell headlong into the most wonderful dream.

It started out with four of us jamming in the empty chapel. I was singing Eli's favourite song, Pete was grinning like the Cheshire cat and Sara was doing something slightly out of sync with a tambourine. I was front and centre with Eli and happily so. Then, when I looked down again, I saw the place was packed and Mum was there, right in front of the stage. She was smiling up at me, laughing and clapping. She looked fit, happy and healthy and as I continued to sing, she gave me the biggest thumbs-up.

I woke with a start as a particularly loud rumble shook the house. Surely that lucid dream had to be a sign? My waking mind hadn't been able to reach a final decision, but the nudge from my sleep state had provided both a sensation and an answer.

I felt the once-familiar rush of excitement and euphoria and I wanted it back in my life. In spite of what I had been told at my last audition and what I had felt after losing Mum, I wanted to experience it all again and if I could find the confidence to accept Eli's potential request, then I would.

Although dry, the weather that Thursday had turned chilly and having cleared away the crafting and scrapbooking equipment, I decided that it would be better to launch the gardening club indoors.

There was a keen post-storm breeze which wouldn't be conducive to helping arthritic fingers sow seeds, so I covered the tables in the warm dayroom with layers of newspaper and phoned Graham to let him know. He was in complete agreement and I was grateful that he'd thought about the weather and was happy to go along with the contingency plan. Given everyone's excitement, if we'd had to cancel I would have had a mutiny on my hands!

'Could you please pass me that seed packet, Beth?' asked Freddie. 'I'm not sure I can spell aquilegia.'

I reached for it and handed it over.

'Oh,' he said, sounding chuffed, 'I have got it right.'

Freddie hadn't been too keen to get his fingers in the compost so had been assigned the role of writing the labels which would go in the seed trays. He had beautiful copper-plate handwriting, so they looked rather fancy.

'What about delphinium?' asked Greta, waving the packet in Freddie's direction.

'Delphinium's a doddle,' he said, flashing her his best smile.

Greta blushed and went back to filling her tray. If everything germinated, the borders were going to be a riot of colour. Even Bob had pulled up a chair and sowed some seeds. I hadn't commented on his participation for fear of breaking the spell, but I was quietly thrilled he was finally taking part. Harold had tipped me a clandestine wink when he noticed, too.

'If everything comes up,' said Graham, practically reading my thoughts about the blossoming borders, 'you'll be able to sell the excess at the garden party next year. I'm sure folk would be prepared to pay extra for plants which have been raised on site.'

'That's a great idea,' I agreed. 'We might be able to take some houseplant cuttings and sell those too.'

Perhaps we could also have a marathon baking session with Carole, on the same premise. I wondered if Sandra would let me keep the profits to plough back into the activities fund pot again. With the garden party now behind me, I'd soon have to turn my thoughts to money-making ideas for the Christmas fair. Festive cookies might not be a bad idea.

'Spider plants have babies, don't they?' Harold frowned and I left Graham to answer that one.

'Are you all right?' Freddie asked me quietly as I let out a long breath.

'Yes,' I said, 'I'm having a wonderful time.'

'I meant generally,' he said, waving a label about to make the ink dry faster. 'You've not seemed yourself this week.'

I had tried to be myself, but it had been hard when my head was full of Eli and what was going to happen between us. It had taken superhuman strength to give him the space he had asked for and I thought I had succeeded in carrying on regardless, but apparently not.

'That's because I've been focused on making these first few days of the new schedule a success,' I said, dredging up a smile.

'Oh right,' said Freddie, as he checked that he'd written enough foxglove labels, 'and there was me thinking it was something to do with last Friday and the look on that poor young man's face when he walked in and heard you singing.'

None of the other residents had mentioned Eli, so I wasn't

sure if anyone had taken on board what had happened, but as sharp as a packet of pins, Freddie hadn't missed a trick. I wondered why it had taken him so many days to say anything.

'Oh,' I airily said. 'No, nothing to do with him.'

As the day had progressed, my vivid dream had drifted further into the background and my response to it had changed. I recalled the old pre-performance nerves, the churning stomach and the fear that I would open my mouth and no sound would come out, more vividly than the sight of Mum's happy face and encouraging thumbs-up. I might have been able to sing my heart out in the bathroom, but I wouldn't be venturing back on the stage, whether Eli asked me to or not.

'I know it's been said many times during the last few days,' Freddie carried on, 'but you really did take us by surprise last week, Beth.'

'Yes,' I said quietly, 'I know.'

'Have you really never thought about singing profession-ally again after what happened at that audition?'

'You know I haven't,' I reminded him. 'What that woman said was right and I had to let the dream go.'

He gave me a sympathetic look and I remembered what he'd been through, too.

'I know you know what that feels like, Freddie. It's hard, isn't it?'

'I suppose,' he said, his face breaking into an unexpected smile and I realised the sympathy had been solely expressed for me, 'but you have to remember, I never let my dream go. I simply let it lead me down a different path.'

'Well,' I shrugged, 'I wasn't prepared to compromise.'

'Right,' he said. 'I see.'

'No offence,' I quickly added.

'None taken, my dear,' he said, still smiling. 'I'm very happy with the choices I've made.'

'That's all right then,' I smiled back, relieved that I hadn't hurt his feelings.

'But can you say the same?' he then pointedly asked. 'Are you happy that you gave it all up rather than sought out a different way to make it happen?'

I felt my face begin to colour.

'Because from what I've seen of you this week,' he then added, 'I can't say your decision looks as if it's working out all that well for you. No offence.'

I bit my lip and forced back the rude reply I felt rising up.

'Music is clearly in your soul, dear girl,' he more kindly carried on, reaching out to give my hand a squeeze. 'And if I had a voice like yours, I wouldn't give it up, not even for a winning lottery ticket.'

I set out a few more labels and blinked back tears of frustration.

'Find a way, Beth,' he urged. 'There's always a way and believe me when I tell you, you'll soon realise that the compromise will turn out to be the path you were destined to take all along. It's all fate, my dear.'

*

With Freddie's timely words ringing in my ears and after a quick change of clothes, I left work and set off for The Dragon. I was a little later than I wanted to be, having taken a few minutes to have a debrief with Graham as we'd transferred the seed trays from the dayroom to the greenhouse and watered them.

'If you and some of the club members can check them and open and close the glasshouse on the days I can't come in,' Graham had requested, 'then we should see some seedlings in no time.'

I loved that there was now a rolling routine attached to the club, which would extend its reach beyond the few hours on a Thursday afternoon and I knew a lot of the residents were keen to embrace that too; even Bob had said he would carry on with it.

'I can't wait to see all of these come up,' I told Graham. 'And again, thank you and Carole so much for setting these new activities up with me. The home is beginning to feel very different to how it was even just a fortnight ago.'

Graham was delighted.

'We must sort out the trip to the Grow-Well soon,' he reminded me.

'Definitely,' I replied.

I was feeling a little nervous about that.

'Don't worry,' Graham smiled reassuringly. 'With everyone helping out, it'll be fine. We'll do it in relays if needs be. Just bring a few residents at a time so it won't be too overwhelming.'

I thought Greta might need a slot of her own so all eyes could be trained on her, but didn't suggest it as I had other more pressing matters on my mind.

I dithered on the pavement outside the pub for a minute or two, wondering if Eli was already inside. I fumbled through my bag for my phone so I could message him.

'Beth.'

I looked up to find him striding towards me, wearing his Castle Coffeehouse polo shirt and shorts. He appeared hot and flustered, but looked just as wonderful as ever.

'Hey, Eli,' I croaked, resisting the urge to fling myself into his arms.

'I'm sorry, I'm late,' he said, sounding every bit as nervous as I felt.

'I got held up at work, so I was late too,' I admitted. 'I've only just arrived. I was about to message you.'

'Well, we're both here now,' he said, stating the obvious. 'Let's go in, shall we?'

'Okay,' I said, stepping awkwardly around him and through the door. 'I'm looking forward to seeing the dragon.'

I'd never been inside the place before but it was immediately obvious why it was Pete's favourite pub. The low ceiling, tiny windows and cramped space put me in mind of The Prancing Pony from *The Lord of the Rings* and the dragon sculpture, cleverly lit to show the intricate detail on the wall opposite the bar, was the perfect fit.

'Look at that,' laughed Eli, making my heart melt. 'Smaug's in residence.'

'Indeed,' said Hannah, from behind the bar. 'Isn't he wonderful?'

'He is,' I agreed. 'And he looks right at home.'

'All the customers love him,' the guy next to her said.

He looked too big to squeeze behind the bar and I wondered if he was permanently wedged.

'This is Beth,' Hannah said to him. 'She organised the auction at the care home.'

'Pleased to meet you at last,' he smiled. 'I'm the landlord, let me get you and your fella a drink on the house.'

I wasn't sure if he was my fella anymore, but with a local pint of bitter apiece, we stepped out into the tiny beer garden and I braced myself to find out.

'So,' said Eli, once we'd gone through the palaver of settling at a table during which time my nerves had plenty of time to multiply.

'So,' I echoed back.

It was just the two of us in the garden and I was grateful for that.

'I know I owe you the biggest apology,' I quickly began, for fear of letting the ensuing silence grow into something insurmountable, 'and I've been going over and over the words in my head all week, but now . . .' I faltered. 'Now I need to say them, I'm not sure where to begin.'

I was starting to regret my decision to not let Pete fill in the gaps about what Eli didn't know about me.

'How about I kick things off then?' Eli suggested.

'No,' I said, pulling in a breath and finding my courage,

'I will. I'll most likely make a mess of it, but as this is all my fault, I think I should go first.'

Eli sat with his pint in his hand. I couldn't read him at all, which was most unsettling.

'So,' I swallowed, 'obviously you know now that I can sing.'

'Yeah,' he said gruffly, 'last Friday kind of gave the game away.'

'It's never been a game,' I said quietly.

'Tell me what it has been then,' he countered, shifting in his seat, 'other than the biggest bloody shock.'

I could read him then no problem. He sounded angry and I could hardly blame him. He'd told me so much about himself and his history and I hadn't reciprocated. His upset was wholly justified and even more painful to observe because I was the cause of it.

'It's a long story,' I sighed.

'Well, I've got all the time in the world,' he said, before taking a drink. 'I'd like to hear the whole of it. I had thought we knew everything of significance about each other, but apparently there's a few gaps in your history.'

'I'm so sorry.'

'Just tell me, Beth,' he said, 'because the thought that I've read you all wrong has been tearing me apart. I need you to convince me that you are the woman I fell in love with and that I can trust you.'

I wanted to cry when he said that.

'All right,' I whispered, 'I'll tell you.'

361

I took a deep breath and began.

'When I was growing up,' I started, 'it was just me and Mum. She'd been a teen mum, cast out by her family, and as a result we didn't have a lot, but that didn't matter because we were happy. Mum had her garden and I had my love of singing and we were content enough.'

'You sang when you were a kid?' Eli asked.

'I sang as soon as I could talk,' I told him. 'It was my dream to turn myself into a singing superstar. Saturday nights were all about the *X Factor* and Tuesdays and Thursdays after school and any other time Mum had to work . . .' I swallowed, 'were all about The Arches.'

Eli's eyebrows lifted but he didn't say anything.

'Mum couldn't afford private singing lessons,' I carried on, 'but her friend, Moira Myers, gifted me the best training in the most supportive environment for a fraction of the cost.'

'And that was where you met Pete?'

'Yes,' I nodded. 'Yes, it was. We clicked the first day he turned up, looking shy and self-conscious.'

Eli smiled. I daresay he knew that look.

'At eighteen,' I carried on, encouraged by his reaction, 'I left for university to study music. I had no intention of taking a risk on a reality TV programme. I wanted singing to be my career for life and I had firmly fixed ideas about how I was going to make that happen.'

Eli nodded.

'It was hard,' I admitted. 'Money was tight and I had to juggle two jobs, but Mum had spent her life showing me how to make ends meet and it was worth it. Totally worth it . . .'

My words trailed off as I pictured my nineteen-year-old self, working evenings in a bar and weekends in retail. I had no idea how I'd managed to fit in studying as well, but then I figured, I had wanted it so badly, I had kept my eyes on the prize and made it work.

'So, what happened?' Eli asked softly.

My gaze refocused.

'Mum had a stroke,' I said, forcing the words out. 'A huge one, just as I was settling into my second year. She needed me and I came home to look after her.'

A moment of silence settled before Eli spoke again.

'Geez, Beth, I'm so sorry,' he whispered; his tone even softer than before. 'Did you ever go back? To university, I mean.'

'They held my place for a year,' I somehow managed to say. 'But it wasn't an option. I'd been warned it would be hard to get back into the industry if I stepped away,' I told him, thinking of that awful audition which I'd allowed to have such an impact. 'I knew there were thousands like me trying to get a break but Mum was so debilitated. I couldn't leave her care to anyone else. She'd always looked after me, and suddenly, decades before I had expected it to be, it was my turn to be there for her.'

Eli bit his lip.

'I'm so sorry,' he said. 'I knew you'd lost your mum, but I had no idea you'd been through something like this. I can't imagine what that must have been like.'

'It was hell,' I said quietly. 'Especially in the beginning.'

'Did you have support?'

'Some,' I shrugged.

'Pete?'

'No,' I said, feeling ashamed. 'He had no idea. As soon as I realised how different my life was going to be, I cut Mum and myself off from everything and everyone associated with my dream. I didn't need the constant reminders of something I had wanted so badly but that was beyond my reach.'

'You didn't go back to The Arches?'

'I almost did,' I admitted, fighting back the tears.

'I don't understand,' Eli frowned.

I pulled in a ragged breath.

'Apart from the hours I had to work, I barely left Mum's side,' I choked, 'and as time passed, and we settled into a routine, she began to worry that my life was too limited. She knew I missed singing and so she suggested I go back to The Arches to try and salvage something.'

I took a moment to compose myself.

'I'd practically forced her to cut Moira out of her life and she'd gone along with it because she knew it was painful for me to have her visit.' I was so mortified about that. 'I'd also made her swear not to somehow get word to Pete about any of what had happened. I know now that I shouldn't have done that. Moira and Pete could have helped her.'

'And you,' Eli said. 'They could have helped you too.'

I didn't need to acknowledge that because I knew it was true.

'Mum kept asking,' I carried on, 'and in the end, I agreed to go back. I hoped it would alleviate some of the guilt she felt that I'd had to drop out of university and also some of mine because I could perhaps make amends with my old friends, but ...'

'But?'

'I didn't make it through the door,' I whispered.

'Why not?'

I knew Eli deserved to hear the whole story, but I would have given anything not to have to say the words.

'What happened?' he asked again.

'I walked there,' I struggled on, twisting my fingers together, 'but the very second The Arches came into view, I felt this all-consuming sense of foreboding wash over me. I just knew something was wrong and rushed home.'

The image played out in my head, like a scene from a horror film you want to forget but can't. Seeing the look on my face, Eli leant over and reached for my hands. I laced my fingers through his and looked down at our hands entwined in my lap.

'When I arrived home,' I whispered, 'I could hear music playing in the house, the very same song you heard me singing last Friday, in fact.' Given the circumstances of the last two times I'd heard it, I was still amazed I'd found the courage to even listen to it, let alone sing it. 'I opened the door and found Mum collapsed in the hall. She'd had another stroke. A catastrophic one and she'd already gone.'

Eli quickly pulled me into his arms, but I didn't stop talking.

'Everyone said that even if I had been with her, it wouldn't have made any difference,' I told him. 'I didn't believe them, of course. I'd failed her, and all for the sake of a trip down memory lane. There was no way I was ever going to go back to The Arches or sing again after that.'

Eli squeezed me tighter.

'Until I moved into the house in Nightingale Square, music and song had been forever banished, along with our much-loved friend, Pete.'

Eli released his grip and leant back to look at me and I felt something shift deep within me.

'Obviously, things have changed quite a bit since then,' I said, showing him a very wobbly smile and sounding more like myself.

'Oh Beth,' said Eli.

He sounded forlorn but I had found the outpouring sur-prisingly cathartic. The sad story had been told to the two men I loved most in the world and I had been responsible for both tellings. I was proud of myself.

'I knew I needed to make some changes in my life,' I told Eli. 'But I didn't expect singing to feature in those changes until . . .'

'Until,' Eli jumped in, picking up the thread, 'you found yourself living with a man obsessed with music and your old mate working just around the corner.'

'Exactly,' I agreed. 'Neither of you were part of my plan, and to begin with, I thought I'd be able to carry on blanking everything out. I had my new role at work to throw myself into and the Grow-Well to fill my non-working hours, but then . . .' I hesitated.

'But then?'

'But then,' I said, looking directly at him, 'I made the decision to make amends with Pete and I went and fell in love with you.' Eli looked choked again. 'And no matter how hard I tried to stop it,' I continued, 'music found its way back into my head, my heart and eventually out of my mouth.'

'Oh Beth.'

'I told you it was a long story,' I laughed, aware how long we'd been sitting there as I fumbled in my bag for a tissue. 'And it was one hell of a shock when I realised that your ex was the person behind Pete's heartache.'

'I was behind it too,' Eli quickly said. 'I should never have allowed it to happen.'

I wiped my eyes and remembered what Pete had said about people doing crazy things when they were in love.

'That's as maybe,' I said, 'but from what I've heard, you're working it all out now.'

'Yes,' he nodded, 'we're getting there. Thanks to you.'

'I'm so pleased,' I said, feeling relieved that some good had come from my musical mishap.

'And I'm truly sorry about everything you've been through, Beth,' Eli said, reaching for my hand again. 'I can completely understand why you didn't want to bring your musical past into your present.'

'I can't tell you how relieved I am to hear you say that,'

I said, leaning into him. 'But it's caught up with me now anyway, hasn't it?'

'Well, you know what they say,' Eli smiled.

'What?' I asked. 'What do they say?'

'*Without music, life would be a mistake.*'

'Who says that?' I frowned. 'You?'

'No, I think it was Friedrich Nietzsche actually.'

'Smart-arse,' I muttered.

'Me or Nietzsche?'

'Both,' I smiled.

'I'm sorry I didn't hang around last Friday,' he then said. 'If I had, we would have got to the bottom of all this far sooner.'

'But then you probably wouldn't be talking to Pete,' I pointed out.

Had I not been caught out, I'd most likely still be trying to fathom out how to push the pair of them back together.

'Though,' I admitted, 'part of me is wishing I'd let him tell you my life history because I'm exhausted now.'

'No,' Eli disagreed, 'it was better that you told me, Beth.'

'I'm sorry if you thought I was another woman you couldn't trust,' I apologised.

Eli shook his head.

'I had been thinking that,' he confessed, 'but when Pete tracked me down at my mum's and told me the pair of you were mates from way back and that you had a good reason for keeping your secret, I soon changed my mind.'

'He's a firm friend, isn't he?'

'The best,' Eli said vehemently.

We were both blessed to have Pete back in our lives.

'I bet your mum doesn't think much of me now,' I sighed, imagining Eli turning up on her doorstep and telling her what he'd been through.

'She doesn't know anything about all of this,' Eli said. 'She was away from home with work for a few days, which is why I bolted there.'

'Well,' I said, feeling relieved, 'that's something.'

'She's going to love you, Beth,' he said reassuringly. 'But can I ask you something?'

'Anything.' I swallowed and my heart began to beat faster again.

Was this the moment he was going to ask if I'd turn his and Pete's duo into a trio? With my past now fully revealed and feeling assured of Eli's understanding about it all, I really hoped it was. My post-dream thoughts had been yo-yoing and driving me to distraction all day, but in that moment, I was finally certain what my answer would be. I wanted to sing again and I wanted to sing with him and Pete.

'Mum's place and Pete's flat are both lovely, but if you're happy to have me back,' he said with a smile, 'I'd love to come home.'

I stared blankly at him for a moment and then realised that wasn't perhaps the reaction he was hoping for.

'Of course!' I quickly said. 'I'm desperate for you to come back.'

I threw my arms around his neck and held him close until my heart stopped skittering.

'The place isn't home without you,' I told him, desperate to make up for my former hesitation. 'I miss you and the plants miss you. It's just not the same.'

'That's all right then,' he said, pulling away and pretending to wipe his brow. 'For a second there, I thought you were going to say no.'

'Sorry,' I said, shaking my head. 'I just thought you were going to ask me something else.'

'What?'

'It doesn't matter.'

'What was it?' he insisted. 'I'd like to know.'

I didn't want to tell him, but in view of the upset keeping secrets had already caused, I thought it best to be honest.

'I thought,' I said, my cheeks colouring, 'that you were going to ask me if I wanted to join you and Pete and reform your band.'

'God no,' he said, tenderly kissing my lips. 'Pete and I have no plans to play again, and given everything you've been through, Beth, that's the one thing I would *never* ask you to do. Not in a million years.'

I felt my heart drop like a stone.

Chapter 25

After Eli had told me how much he understood and respected my decision to permanently retire my voice, I didn't much feel like finishing my drink. We left the pub, hand in hand, which was a wonderful and very public declaration, but it didn't completely compensate for the disappointment I felt that we were never going to get to perform music together.

The emotion that disappointment carried with it, coupled with the exertion of explaining my history, left me feeling as though I'd had the stuffing knocked out of me. Just a short while ago, I would have felt elated that Eli respected my vow of silence but now I wanted to sing, with him, from the rooftops and I was floored by how sad I felt that it wasn't going to happen.

It was getting late and as neither of us felt like cooking, we picked up a takeaway and then carried on towards the Square, our fingers still laced together.

'Do you want to collect your stuff from Pete's?' I asked,

as we carried home our Korean feast. 'It won't take a minute to make a quick detour.'

'No,' said Eli, as he handed me the bag of food and pulled his phone out of his shorts pocket, 'I'll grab it after work tomorrow. If we stop at the flat now, we'll end up talking for hours, but I'll message Pete with an update because he'll be wondering where I've got to.'

I was already looking forward to Eli and I spending nights out together with Sara and Pete in the pub. I had been rather taken with The Dragon, and as I watched Eli type, I acknowledged that, aside from the singing embargo, my life was looking a darn sight rosier than it had been when I set off for work that morning. I should have been feeling grateful for that. Humming, he planted an affectionate kiss on my cheek, and I wondered if I might somehow be able to find a way around the musical restrictions after all.

'Is that a message back already?' I laughed as Eli's phone sprang into life.

Barely thirty seconds had ticked by since he'd pressed send.

'Yes,' he grinned. 'Look at this.'

There was a whole paragraph of perfectly typed text filling the screen.

'How has he typed all that so quickly?' I laughed.

'A misspent youth spent perfecting the art most likely,' Eli laughed along with me.

'A talent he's now passed on to his niece,' I giggled.

The gist of the message was that Pete was delighted that everything was finally out in the open and that he was exceedingly happy that we were back together. I couldn't help wondering if he was as happy about the decision not to reform the band as Eli was. I'd have to ask him when I got the chance.

'Welcome home,' I announced, as I opened the door to the house with a flourish. 'It's so good to have you back.'

Eli followed me over the threshold, closed the door with his foot and put the bag of takeout on the hall table. He then pulled me into his arms and kissed me deeply.

'It's good to be back,' he said, when we eventually stopped. 'I almost missed this place as much as I missed you.'

'Is that right?' I asked, punctuating each word with a kiss.

'It is,' he replied, doing the same.

I laughed, but he looked serious.

'I had thought this place was home already,' he said, looking deep into my eyes, 'but then you moved in and took the meaning of the word to a whole new level.'

'I was worried when I first moved in,' I told him, 'given that you'd been here alone to start with, that you might resent having to share.'

'No way,' he said, releasing me and picking the bag up again. 'You and your many, many plants were a welcome addition, right from day one.'

I was delighted to hear it and he looked so relaxed, I wondered if I could get away with asking a bit more about his and Pete's music. I didn't want to dim his excitement about being home, but I was desperate to keep the topic of conversation open.

'Can I ask you something?' I therefore said, following him into the kitchen.

'Of course.'

I began to lift the takeaway cartons out of the bag and peel off the lids. The food smelt wonderful and my stomach growled in response.

'Back in the pub,' I said, as I spooned sticky rice into the bowls Eli handed me, 'you said that you and Pete aren't playing music now and have no plans to.'

'That's right,' he confirmed.

'Well, I was wondering why?' I asked. 'You've settled your differences, haven't you?' Eli nodded. 'And you've told me there are songs you don't want to let go *and* that you're writing new stuff, too. Surely now would be the perfect time to start playing together again.'

Eli shook his head.

'Pete's forgiven you,' I pressed on, 'and you're both so incredibly talented. It's such a waste not to carry on, especially as you're creating new material. Why not collab properly and have another go at it?'

'We have our reasons,' he said, taking one of the bowls.

'I hope I'm not one of them,' I quickly cut in. 'I'd love it if you carried on and I don't mind having music playing in the house now either.'

To prove the point, I reached for the radio behind me and turned it on.

'I'm genuinely happy hearing it,' I said over the sound of it. 'I *want* to hear it.'

374

I couldn't make my desire not to drop music again any more obvious, but Eli wasn't to be swayed.

'It's not you,' he said, reaching around me and turning the radio off again. 'And just to be completely clear, I meant what I said earlier. Knowing what you've been through, I completely understand your decision not to sing again.'

I appreciated that he was being so respectful but I felt frustrated too. He was telling me now what I had wanted to hear a few weeks ago. Now, I felt completely differently but I couldn't seem to find a way to get that across.

'Let's eat before this gets cold,' Eli said, carrying the rest of the food through to the dining room.

'And Pete agrees with you, does he?' I asked, following behind with the kimchi.

'Pete's very happy with his life,' Eli reminded me as I handed him a pair of chopsticks. 'You know how much he loves the shop and now he's in love with Sara, too.'

'They are perfect for each other,' I smiled.

'They are,' Eli readily agreed. 'And now Pete's taking part in the re-enactments and getting ready to help convert the chapel and support the musicians there, his life is rammed. He doesn't need to try and recreate what we once had. He's perfectly content and I'm really happy for him.'

His voice cracked and I reached across the table and squeezed his hand. I guessed they were all good reasons to stop him and Pete picking their music back up again.

'He deserves it,' Eli said, looking bright-eyed. 'He bloody deserves it all. And more.'

'You're right,' I agreed, knowing that we had both been guilty of not treating Pete well in the past. 'He really does.'

We stopped talking and greedily emptied our bowls. As always, the fried chicken was particularly delicious.

'Crikey, I needed that,' said Eli, once he'd finished. 'I haven't really eaten all week.'

'Same,' I smiled, as I wiped my lips which were tingling from the spicy gochujang. 'Sorting out your life builds up quite an appetite, doesn't it?'

'Just a bit,' he agreed, leaning back and rubbing his hands over his tummy. 'And I've had a *lot* to sort out.'

'Yes,' I said, 'I suppose you have. What with falling in love with me and sorting things out with Pete, you've had a hectic time of late. Oh,' I added, 'and not forgetting everything that's been going on at the coffeehouse because of Melanie's accident.'

'It's actually Melanie who's had the biggest influence over my decision to give music up,' he then surprised me by saying.

'Has she?' I frowned.

'Yes,' he said, sitting up straighter again. 'She's made me an offer I would be stupid to turn down and if I accept it, I certainly won't have time for music.'

'What sort of an offer?'

I already didn't like the sound of it if it put the final nail in his musical coffin.

'Let's go and sit in the other room,' he said. 'We can tidy up later.'

Rather than take his usual spot in the armchair, Eli sat next to me on the sofa and I resisted the urge to cuddle up to him. I wanted to look at his face as he explained what other monumental thing had happened in his life in the short time he'd been living at Pete's.

'So,' I said, unable to wait, 'what's this offer then?'

Eli ran his hands through his hair.

'Melanie's asked if I want to take over the business,' he said, with no preamble.

'Take over the coffeehouse?' I frowned.

'Yes,' he confirmed. 'She said a while ago that she'd been thinking about handing on the lease, but she wasn't entirely sure. She's on good terms with the owner of the building so it would all be pretty straightforward, but then she didn't mention it again so I just assumed she'd decided not to.'

'But now she has?' I surmised.

'Yes.'

'I wonder if it was because of the accident,' I mused. 'It was bound to be unsettling.'

'In part, I think it was,' Eli further explained, 'but she's got a daughter, Belle, who lives in America who she hardly ever sees. Now Belle's announced she's pregnant and Melanie wants to be with her. She messaged me a week or so ago to say she's definitely going ahead and we've been discussing it ever since.'

'I see.'

I wondered if that was the text which had landed the night Pete messaged me about the quiz sheets. Eli had been engrossed by her words, if it was.

'Melanie wants to go over to the States and stay for a while, with a view to making the move a permanent one. She says she wants to go without the responsibility of the coffeehouse at the back of her mind.'

'But surely that would be something to come back to if it didn't work out?'

'That's what I said,' Eli shrugged, 'but she says recent events have helped her decide. She's had enough of frothing cappuccinos. If I want the lease, it's mine.'

I didn't think he sounded all that excited about the idea, but maybe his lack of enthusiasm was more down to nerves about making the financial commitment.

'It's a good offer,' he said, his hands mussing up his hair again. 'It's a great business. I'd be a fool not to do it. It's time I grew up and took on a bit more responsibility. I need to start thinking properly about the future.'

I studied him for a moment and found the look in his eyes still didn't show so much as a hint of the exhilaration I would have expected and he didn't sound at all fired up either. I might still have had a lot to learn about him, but I knew enough to be able to see that his response to the offer was about more than nerves. This sounded more like something he was settling for rather than the thing he'd waited his whole life to grab with both hands.

'Have you told your mum?' I asked, not knowing how to say I didn't think it wasn't the right thing for him without causing offence.

'God no,' he said.

'Why not?'

He didn't answer straight away and I wondered if his mum's reaction and response would have been the same as mine – that taking on the coffeehouse lease was not something she could see benefiting her son's future.

'Melanie's asked me not to tell anyone,' he said, turning slightly pink. 'But obviously I wanted to tell you.'

I didn't think that was the reason why he hadn't told his mum at all.

'Has Melanie said when she needs an answer by?'

'No later than the end of the month,' Eli sighed.

'And do you think you'll take it?'

'I'm still not sure,' he shrugged.

Coupled with his lack of excitement, his indecision was all the motivation I needed. I had three weeks to help him see that taking on the lease wasn't right for him, but how was I going to do it?

Early on Friday morning, as I made my first cup of tea of the day, I found myself singing along to Pharrell Williams' 'Happy'. I was utterly immersed in my kitchen disco moment when I heard Eli's feet on the stairs and quickly flicked the radio off. I was still keen to persuade him that I no longer had any desire to banish music, but given the time constraints, I was more focused on making sure he turned down Melanie's offer first.

'Good morning,' he said, stretching in the doorway and treating me to a gorgeous glimpse of his tummy as his T-shirt rose up. 'How did you sleep?'

There was still one aspect of our relationship that we had agreed to take slowly, but we had been hard pushed to go our separate ways at bedtime. I didn't think either of us would be able to hold out for much longer.

'Considering one half of my bed was stone cold, not too bad,' I said cheekily as I stirred a little sugar into my mug. 'What about you?'

'Same,' he sighed, slipping his arms around my waist. I could feel the warmth of his breath on my neck. 'What time will you be home today?'

'The usual,' I told him, turning and wrapping my arms around him. 'You?'

'I'll probably be a bit late because I'm going to collect my stuff from Pete's.'

'Okay,' I said, kissing him softly on the lips.

'It's singalong day at the home today, isn't it?' he said, resting his forehead on mine.

'It is,' I swallowed.

'Will you be okay?' he frowned, all kindness and heart-felt concern.

'Sure,' I shrugged. 'Like I told you yesterday, I really don't mind it now.'

Eli nodded and I released him.

'That's all right then,' he said, sounding happier but I knew he still hadn't really taken my words on board, not in the way I wanted him to anyway. 'I'll see you tonight.'

'Tonight,' I nodded, picking up my tea. 'And tomorrow I'm going to the Grow-Well for an update on the fundraiser.'

Eli wrinkled his nose.

'I'm glad I'll be at work for that,' he said. 'And I wasn't going to say anything,' he then added, 'but I'm hoping we can book a weekend away somewhere when it's happening. That way, neither of us will have to endure it.'

I decided then wasn't the moment to tell him that I'd volunteered to help out.

Chapter 26

After such an emotional week I was exhausted and so, even though I was no longer worried about listening to music, I still had a plan to make myself scarce in time for the singalong at the care home.

I didn't think I could cope with the bombardment of requests I knew Greta and Ida were working on, so had asked Phil if he'd be willing to step up and oversee the event. Having been not so privately practising his Gloria Gaynor all week, he was thrilled. However, as it turned out, it wasn't the dynamic duo I needed to watch out for, but Freddie Fanshawe and he caught up with me when I least expected it.

'So, tell me Beth,' he said, within minutes of me announcing the running order for the manicures and blow drys that were scheduled for that morning, 'how's the whole compromising malarkey coming along for you?'

'The whole what?' I frowned, pretending I had no idea what he was talking about.

He rolled his eyes and shook his head.

'The different path,' he reiterated. 'I know you haven't forgotten our conversation, so don't even try and make out that you have.'

'Oh that,' I said airily. 'Nothing to report on that front, but I'll keep you posted.'

I tried to walk away, but Freddie was hard to shake off.

'Nothing to report,' he frowned, his white brows puckering. 'What's that supposed to mean?'

'Exactly that,' I said quietly, checking we weren't being listened to. 'And there's not going to be either. Honestly, Freddie,' I shrugged, my cheeks warming up, 'I'm happy to let it go. I love my job here, I'm very happy in my new home in Nightingale Square and that's more than enough for me.'

He didn't look convinced but I had no intention of letting on about my recent change of heart.

'I mean it,' I said more forcibly. 'Now can you please just let it drop?'

The look on his face broke my heart a little and if I was being completely honest, it fractured mine too. I would have loved to have bounded in that morning and announced that I was now part of a band. A band made up of my boyfriend, my best friend and me, but it wasn't meant to be.

Daydreaming over the details wasn't going to change anything and I couldn't bear the thought of telling Freddie that I did want to sing and then having to endure him trying to find a way to make it happen. I wasn't prepared to do anything which might damage mine and Eli's recently patched up relationship and Freddie's well-meaning interference no doubt would.

'Now, if you'll excuse me,' I said, looking everywhere but at his saddened expression, 'I need to talk to the lady doing Greta's nails today. She wants flowers painted on them and I need to make sure it won't break the budget.'

'If Greta's having flowers,' Ida piped up, 'I want them too. Pink ones to match my dress.'

I let out a resigned sigh, wondering what else she'd just been privy to.

For a while, it felt as though Saturday was going to end as stressfully as Friday had started, but then I took matters into my own hands and cleared the air. The day had started out well enough though, with breakfast in bed, provided by Eli, who sat on the edge of the duvet as I tucked into tea and marmalade toast. He'd got the toast just how I liked it – lightly done, almost cold, spread with butter and a generous layer of marmalade – delicious.

'What time are you heading over to the Grow-Well?' he asked as he checked his watch to make sure he wasn't going to be late for work.

'As soon as I'm sorted here,' I told him. 'I'm going to help in the garden before the meeting later on and then I think John's trying some new pizza toppings tonight. Will you come over when you've finished work?'

Given what he'd previously said, I could have guessed his answer, but still hoped he might have changed his mind.

'No, not tonight,' he confirmed, standing up and stretching. 'But I'll go over early tomorrow and do my stint.'

He was definitely doing his utmost to stay out of everyone's way until the fundraiser was over and I was still trying to work out how to tell him that, as wonderful as a weekend away would be, especially as he'd hinted at a cottage in Wynmouth on the Norfolk coast, I really wanted to stick around for it.

I might not have been assigned a specific task yet, but having seen the chapel, I knew it was going to be the perfect venue in which to carry on Moira's work, and I was determined to do what I could to help make that happen.

'I'll see you back here later then,' I said, disappointed that we wouldn't be enjoying the evening together.

'You taste of marmalade,' he grinned after he'd kissed me goodbye.

'Good,' I smiled. 'It's my favourite.'

'Mine too, now,' he laughed, coming back for another taste.

'Have you thought any more about taking over the coffeehouse?' I couldn't resist calling after him as he finally left.

He ducked back around the doorframe.

'I've thought of little else,' he frowned.

The continued lack of excitement in his tone further ignited the flame of hope I was carrying in my heart.

'I'll see you later,' he then added, before rushing off.

I spent a peaceful couple of hours deadheading, harvesting and watering in the Grow-Well before anyone else arrived.

It was pleasantly warm, but not stifling and I couldn't help thinking, just as I had when I first set eyes on the place, how much Mum would have loved it.

She had been in my thoughts a lot since I'd had the dream about her watching me perform on the chapel stage. Initially, I had felt guilty because it made me realise that she hadn't been on my mind anywhere near as much as before, but then I realised that was actually a good thing. It was positive proof that I was climbing out of the deep well of grief that I had been submerged in for so long.

That said, as I worked my way around the garden, I still kept up my internal chatter and I could sense her responses to everything I said, just like I knew what her smile and thumbs-up had meant when she came to me in my dream.

'Was that you singing, Beth?' frowned Tamsin, Lisa and John's daughter, as she walked through the garden gate.

'I don't think so,' I answered, feeling my face flush.

Had I been singing? I didn't think I had, but then I'd been caught out like that before.

'Here,' I said, noticing she was struggling with a packed cardboard box. 'Let me help. That looks heavy.'

'It is,' she said, as she gratefully transferred it from her arms to mine. 'Dad asked me to bring it over.'

'Whatever's inside?' I gasped, taken aback by its weight.

'No idea,' Tamsin shrugged.

'Perhaps it's the new pizza toppings he's been talking about?' I suggested.

Tamsin wrinkled her nose.

'I hope not,' she laughed, 'the weight of them would break the oven.'

It turned out the box was full of lidded bottles and jars that Lisa had collected for Poppy. She was going to be running one of her 'chuck it all in chutney' workshops in the garden soon and was gathering a stash of empty glass containers.

'You should come, Beth,' Poppy said encouragingly later in the day. 'You don't work weekends now, do you?'

'No,' I said, 'I don't. Put me down for a space. It sounds like fun.'

'And talking of fun,' said Lisa, shuffling a bundle of papers into a straighter pile.

'Is that your next book?' Heather asked hopefully. 'I'd love a peek.'

'No, it's not,' Lisa grinned. 'My editor would have my guts for garters if I was sharing that around.'

'What is it then?' Heather asked, sounding less excited.

'The fair details,' Lisa told her, passing the sheets around.

'Oh,' Heather smiled, perking up again. 'I've been dying to get a look at this.'

We read through the plans while waiting for Kate and Luke and then, when they arrived and the children were all happily playing, we pulled our chairs into the shade so we could talk through what had been arranged so far.

'It looks like it's going to be just like the fetes and fairs Mum and I used to enjoy,' I said happily, as my eyes scanned the details. 'Who's going to judge the fancy dress and waggiest tale?'

The fancy dress was happening in the Prosperous Place gardens, while the waggiest tale was being judged on the green in the Square. Luke and Kate had decided to make the gardens a dog-free zone, Nell and Gus excluded of course. Although Freya had said that Nell would be happier at home while the fair was in full swing.

'Me,' answered Luke. 'I'm doing both.'

He didn't sound very happy about it.

'Rather you than me,' laughed Heather's husband, Glen.

'Thanks, Glen,' said Luke, half smiling. 'I'm going to offend half the city, aren't I?'

'Can't be helped,' Lisa said briskly. 'Just go with your gut.'

She was back on her feet and handing round another list.

'And what's this?' asked Neil.

'Running order for the evening entertainment,' she tutted, rolling her eyes. 'It's written across the top – just read it, Neil.'

Neil grinned, but smiling was the last thing I felt like doing.

'Wow,' said Poppy, 'you didn't tell me it had filled up this much, Jacob.'

'Well,' he said, 'we hadn't had firm confirmations from a couple of these acts until very recently, so we've been hanging back before announcing them.'

'What do you all think?' Lisa asked, looking around.

I let the chat wash over me. Popular opinion was that there was a wonderful mix of performers and that Lisa and Jacob must have worked their socks off to turn things around in such a short space of time.

There was now everything from dance acts to performance poets, singers to comedians. It had the potential to be a hugely entertaining evening and it was going to be the perfect showcase to highlight the local creative scene. There couldn't have been a more appropriate launch for the chapel. And talking of the new venue . . .

'Have you decided yet what the new place is going to be called?' I heard Neil ask Lisa and Jacob.

They exchanged a smile.

'Funnily enough,' said Jacob. 'We have. We ran it by Moira's son earlier in the week and he was in agreement.'

'Pete, the guy who has been involved with The Arches forever, actually came up with it,' Lisa added.

My ears pricked up at the sound of his name.

'Can you tell us what it is?' asked Glen.

Lisa nodded.

'I don't see why not,' she said. 'The sooner it's on everyone's lips, the better. Do you want to tell them, Jacob?'

'Absolutely,' Jacob grinned. 'In keeping with The Arches,' he announced, 'the new venue is simply going to be called . . . The Chapel.'

'That's perfect,' I smiled, having already worked it out.

The ripple of chat that wove its way among my neighbours was all positive and everyone loved the name as much as I did.

'And you loved the venue, didn't you, Beth?' Lisa called to me, above the rising level of voices.

'I did,' I confirmed. 'It's an amazing space.'

'I wonder what the acoustics are like?' Tamsin asked, looking over at me.

She looked far from innocent and I felt my cheeks turn warm again. I had hoped she'd forgotten that she thought she had heard me singing, but evidently not, and, added to some of the names which had jumped out at me on the entertainment list, I began to think that Eli's idea to go away for the weekend might not be such a bad one after all.

I was fast running out of time and choices. The only options available to me now were to either have my talent exposed on the night or confess all as soon as possible. My body gave an involuntary shudder, clearly not keen on either.

'Don't forget to cast your votes, folks!' John's voice boomed later that evening.

He had created a mouth-watering array of pizzas and we were supposed to vote for our favourite three, which would become regulars on the Grow-Well menu. I was pleased to see that I wasn't the only one struggling to choose.

Everyone aside from Lisa and John, Jacob and Poppy and Carole and Graham, had gone home and I didn't want to be too far behind them, especially as I knew Eli would be back from work now and hopefully craving my company as much as I was his.

'Come on, Beth,' said John, shaking one of the lists under my nose. 'Look alive. Some of us have beds to get to.'

'Well, it's your fault,' I told him. 'You shouldn't have given us so many delicious options.'

'Beth's right,' agreed Poppy, who was still to pick her favourites too. 'It's impossible to choose.'

John took up the lists and frowned.

'They're all neck and neck,' he said. 'I'm beginning to suspect a conspiracy. How about I make them all on rotation?'

'Yes!' Poppy and I shouted in unison, then burst out laughing.

'Ladies and gentleman,' yawned Jacob, 'the votes are in and we *finally* have a result! Not the one we were expecting, but a result nonetheless.'

'In that case,' said Carole, standing up and smoothing down her skirt, 'I'm going home. Come on, Graham,' she added, nudging her husband who was snoozing in his chair and oblivious to everything. 'Time for bed.'

Graham didn't look as though he had a clue where he was and once Carole had steered him out of the garden, I took a moment to gather my thoughts.

'Before the rest of you rush off,' I heard myself saying to the remaining foursome, 'there's something I need to tell you.'

Prompted by the familiar names on the entertainment schedule and aware that considerably more people than Pete, Eli and Harold were now privy to my talent, I had mulled it over as I ate my pizza and knew the best thing I could do was confess my deception. My secret was inevitably destined to be revealed and the last thing I wanted was for it all to come out at the fair when I wouldn't have a chance to properly explain.

'You see, the thing is . . .' I began, but then faltered when I looked up and saw four sets of curious eyes trained on me.

Their attention caused the colour to drain from my face and John's interested gaze turned to one of concern.

'Let's all sit back down,' he urged the others. 'Come on, love,' he kindly said to me. 'What is it? It can't be that bad.'

'The thing is,' I said again, once they were all comfortable, 'and please believe me when I tell you that I did have, still do have, my reasons for not saying anything before, but I did know all about The Arches before I moved to the Square, even though I've always maintained that I didn't.'

'You knew about The Arches?' Lisa frowned.

'Yes,' I swallowed, 'I used to go there. I used to go every week when I was growing up.'

Looking at the confused faces and knitted brows which met my admission, I suddenly wasn't sure if my decision to confess was such a good idea, but it was too late to backtrack now.

'So,' said Jacob, his expression matching Lisa's, 'you knew Moira then?'

I nodded.

'I knew her very well, and Pete of course, and a couple of names on this list are familiar too,' I added, holding up the paper Lisa had previously handed out and which had further prompted my decision to tell all.

'What did you used to do there?' Lisa asked.

'Sing,' I said on an out breath. 'When I was growing up, it was my dream to be a famous singer.'

Lisa and Jacob looked at each other.

'Why didn't you tell us this when we were looking for former attendees?' Jacob asked. 'You're *exactly* the sort of person we've been looking for.'

That was *exactly* what I had hoped no one would say, but deep down I had known it was inevitable and the exasperation in his tone made me feel a bit nervous. I didn't want to have to explain more, but hearing Jacob's almost gruff enquiry, I knew I had no choice.

'Because I don't do it anymore,' I quickly said. 'I gave it all up to become my mum's carer after she had a stroke.'

For the moment, I was shying away from Freddie's insistence that somewhere there was a different path I could still follow.

'I looked after Mum for a long time,' I carried on, 'and that meant giving up my place at university, along with my ambitions. It was a terrible time and there were other things which happened too, but which I'd rather not share, and they completely quashed my desire to ever sing again.'

'Oh, Beth,' said Jacob, sounding shocked. 'That's terrible.'

'I'm so sorry, love,' John sniffed, as soft-hearted as ever.

'For years after Mum died, I banished music completely,' I told them, before I ran out of steam. 'I didn't sing, I didn't listen to music. For so long, I did everything I could to avoid it all, but then . . .'

'But then?' Lisa asked.

I took a moment and realised it was so quiet you could have heard a pin drop. There was no breeze and no traffic.

It was as if everything in the city had stopped to listen to what I had to say.

'Then,' I said, my voice slicing through the expectant silence, 'I moved into Kate's house, and only after I'd unpacked, I discovered that Eli was mad on music and a musician himself.' I shook my head at the memory. 'And, before I'd got my head around that, Freddie Fanshawe arrived at the care home and the Friday singalong was born.'

'Bloody hell,' smiled John. 'That must have been a bit overwhelming.'

'It was,' I nodded, encouraged by his understanding. 'For a while, it was really hard, but now it's turned out to be a blessing.'

'In what way?' he asked.

'It's made me realise,' I said, choosing my words with care, 'that my life is better with music in it. Not that I'm going to pick up my singing ambitions again,' I added quickly.

Had Eli told me he was reforming his and Pete's band it would have been a different story, but as he wasn't, I was keeping my desire to flex my vocal cords under wraps.

'You did sing at the care home the other week though, didn't you?' Lisa pressed me.

'That was a one-off,' I mumbled.

'A friend of mine has an uncle living there,' she elaborated, 'and he said he'd listened to a member of staff with the voice of an angel.'

'As I said,' I reiterated, 'that really was a one-off. A mistake I won't be making again.'

'So you're definitely not taking to the stage again?' Lisa asked.

'Very definitely not,' I said firmly.

'I daresay you didn't mention this before because you knew the missus would be cajoling you to take part in the fundraiser,' said John, before noisily blowing his nose.

Lisa gave him a hefty nudge and I was relieved to see that no one looked angry.

'To be honest,' I admitted, 'I didn't say anything before because I was trying to get used to what was happening. I never expected to let music back into my life in any shape or form, so the last few weeks have been heavy-going.'

'And all of that on top of moving, too,' Poppy said sympathetically.

'That's one of the top five most stressful things you can do, that is,' said John. 'According to a survey I read in one of Lisa's magazines last week.'

We all smiled and John winked at me. What a wonderful man he was.

'Not for me,' I said, feeling happier. 'You guys made moving as stress-free as it possibly could be and I've been reacquainted with my old friend, Pete, since then, so the move really couldn't have gone any better.'

'And you've started your new job,' John pointed out, highlighting yet another change. 'Now I think about it,' he added, scratching his head, 'I reckon that might have been on that list too.'

'The new job's a total joy,' I smiled. 'I love my role in the care home. In fact, now I've finally plucked up the courage to tell you about my musical past, everything feels perfect. I love my home, my work, this place, and . . .'

'Eli?' Lisa cut in.

'Eli?' Everyone else frowned.

'Well,' I said, turning pink again, 'I'm very fond of him, too.'

'Don't worry,' Lisa laughed, letting the cat escape further out of the bag. 'Your secret's safe with me.'

'Oh . . .' said Poppy, only just catching on, 'are you and Eli . . .'

I flashed her a smile and nodded. Given that Eli and I had recently walked home hand in hand, we were hardly keeping our relationship under wraps anymore.

'No wonder you were so keen on The Chapel, Beth,' Jacob said thoughtfully, side-stepping my acknowledgement. 'You knew exactly what was needed and how we could utilise what's already there, didn't you?'

'Didn't I say to you,' Lisa interrupted, clicking her fingers, 'that Beth seemed very knowledgeable about The Arches for someone who claimed to have only looked at photos online?'

'You did,' Jacob confirmed.

'And now you know why,' I said, biting my lip. 'I'm sorry I didn't tell you sooner.'

'We all understand why you didn't,' said John.

The nods and kind smiles his comment received told me everyone agreed and it felt like a huge weight had been lifted. Until that moment, I hadn't realised quite how heavy it had been.

'The only thing I'm sorry about,' said Lisa, 'aside from the not singing thing of course, is that you're so happy in your job.'

My gaze swung back to her. I must have looked shocked because she quickly clarified why.

'Only because Jacob and I have found out today that we've secured enough funding to employ a full-time manager,' she speedily explained. 'With your skills and experience, Beth, I reckon you would have been perfect for the role.'

'Yes,' Jacob agreed, 'you would. We really want someone with musical experience and an understanding of how these sorts of places work. You don't fancy another career change, do you, Beth?'

'No,' I said, 'not me, I'm afraid.'

'Shame,' Lisa mused. 'We had considered asking Pete but we reckon he's melded to that shop.'

She was right about that. Nothing would prise him away from On the Box.

'We'll just have to find someone else,' said Jacob, with a shrug. 'I'd rather it was someone local who we already know, but if we can't find anyone, we'll have to look further afield.'

My heart began to skitter as I realised that I knew someone who was ideal, if only I could convince him that cutting music out of his life wouldn't work out any better for him than it had for me.

Chapter 27

As excited as I was, I knew I had to temper my enthusiasm. Just because I thought Eli was the ideal candidate to take on the manager's role at The Chapel, it didn't follow that he would agree. I knew he had the experience and the expertise Lisa and Jacob were looking for, but given that he was hell-bent on leaving his own music behind, he might not want to spend his working life handling and encouraging the lyrical aspirations of others.

Nonetheless, I practically skipped back to the Square, my insides fizzing with a heady cocktail of excitement and relief. I was truly blessed to have such understanding neighbours. The fact that they had kindly accepted my explanation about The Arches and my singing with such good grace made my heart soar. I again felt immensely grateful that I had stepped up to take Harold to the Grow-Well that fateful day in June.

'Eli!' I called happily, as I crossed the threshold and closed the door behind me. 'Are you here?'

'I am,' he beamed, his face appearing around the door-frame, 'and I have food.'

He must have forgotten it was pizza night in the garden.

'Oh,' I said. I didn't think I could squeeze anything else into my already-full tummy. 'I ate at the Grow-Well.'

'I know,' he said, still smiling. 'This is pudding rather than main.'

'Oh well, in that case,' I smiled back, my tastebuds perking up as I eased my feet out of my Converse pumps, 'I'll grab a spoon.'

The pudding turned out to be delicious pastries from the coffeehouse, but supplied by Blossoms. They were topped with crème pat and fresh local strawberries which served to cut through the sweetness.

'If I take the place over,' commented Eli, as he cleared his plate, 'I'll definitely stick to stocking Blossoms' bakes.'

'I don't blame you,' I nodded, cheerfully noting that he had said *if*, as opposed to *when*, as I licked my spoon clean. 'I know I don't like coffee, but even I can tell cakes and cappuccino are the ideal amalgamation.'

Eli pushed his plate away and after a last delectable mouthful, I did the same.

'How were John's pizzas?' he asked.

'So good,' I said, licking my lips. 'Too good really. We couldn't decide which new toppings to vote for, so he's adding them all to the menu. The caramelised onion and goats cheese one was incredible.'

Had I been really pushed, that probably would have been my number one choice.

'Once all the furore over the fair has died down,' Eli then said, knocking the wind out of my sails a bit, 'I'll look forward to trying them, that one especially.'

I wondered if he was going to ask how the update had gone, but he didn't and as his comment didn't give me a lead into explaining the reason for my upbeat mood beyond the sugar rush, I just came right out with it myself.

'It was a great get-together,' I told him. 'And I enjoyed it all the more, once I'd come clean about a few things.'

'What sort of things?'

'Well,' I said, 'as I felt so much better after I'd told you about my connection to The Arches and the reasons behind why I'd given up singing, I decided to tell the neighbours too.'

'Oh right,' said Eli, 'I see.'

He sounded genuinely taken aback.

'They were very understanding,' I carried on, 'and I do feel better for telling them.'

'I'm surprised that you mentioned it at all,' Eli said, as he stacked our plates together, 'I mean, it's not as if you're going to have anything to do with this new place, so . . .'

'The Chapel,' I cut in. 'That's what they've decided to call it.'

'The Chapel,' Eli repeated. 'I think you could have quite easily got away with not saying anything.'

'No,' I disagreed, shaking my head and thinking of Tamsin, 'I couldn't and I didn't want to. Lisa had already heard that a member of staff at the care home had surprised everyone with their singing and I didn't think it was fair to expect you, Pete or anyone else to carry on with the pretence on my behalf.'

'What pretence?' Eli shrugged. 'There was no reason it would have ever come up.'

'It was bound to,' I insisted, thinking of Harold and Sarah and feeling frustrated that Eli couldn't see the situation from my point of view. 'And I think it was better coming from me. It gave me the chance to properly explain why I hadn't said anything before. I know for a fact that Pete would have felt awful if he'd let something slip and like I just said, I didn't want to put him, or anyone else, in that position.'

'Fair enough,' Eli shrugged.

'And there were names on the fundraising list I recognised,' I further added. 'I just know that if I hadn't come clean tonight then it would have all come out at the fair and I couldn't bear the thought of that.'

'But we're going away that weekend,' Eli said, sounding strained, 'so you won't be there to be recognised anyway.'

I wanted to point out that there would still be the threat of discovery after the event and that I had no intention of creeping about and carrying on with the subterfuge, but I didn't. Eli clearly wasn't in the mood to talk about anything music-related and I knew mentioning the manager's job would be a total waste of time. Far better to put a bit of distance between us before the increasingly tense conversation turned into an argument.

'Do you want to use the bathroom?' I asked him,

disappointed that the day had drawn to such a tetchy end. 'If not, I'll jump in the shower.'

Eli's mood was a little brighter the next morning. I had caught him chatting away to Aretha first thing, but he still wasn't sounding sunny enough for me to talk about the fair, any form of music or The Chapel. Overnight, however, I had made some headway in my determination to come up with a strategy to turn the tide, and once we had finished the houseplant routine and Eli had set off for the coffeehouse, I put the plan into action. It involved Pete and a very frank discussion.

'Hey, Beth,' Pete smiled, as I walked into On the Box the second he'd unlocked the door at ten o'clock. 'How's tricks?'

'Morning, Pete,' I replied. 'A bit of a mixed bag actually.'

'Oh?'

'Yeah, is there any chance we could talk?'

'I'm not usually inundated with customers on a Sunday,' he told me, 'but give me a minute.'

I perused the shelves while he rang Stacey to remind her that she was supposed to be working.

'She's on her way,' he huffed with an elaborate eye roll once he'd hung up. 'Allegedly.'

'Are you seeing Sara today?'

'No, she's working – I thought you'd know that.'

'I've not really kept up with shift patterns since I changed roles,' I shrugged. 'But after all this time, I do like not having to work at weekends.'

'Must be nice,' he said, as Stacey rushed through the door.

'There,' she puffed, pulling off her rucksack and clutching her side. 'I told you I hadn't forgotten.'

To be fair, she must have been practically at the door when Pete phoned.

'It's a miracle!' her uncle teased and she stuck out her tongue. 'We'll be upstairs if you get a rush on.'

'Oh yeah,' she said, massaging the stitch in her side as she looked back out into the street, 'it'll be bedlam in here in half an hour.'

'In that case,' I said, following Pete and flashing her a smile, 'I'll make it quick.'

With a cup of tea each, Pete and I sat in his flat and I realised that rather than make it quick, as I'd promised Stacey, I wasn't sure I would be able to make it at all.

'So,' said Pete, when I didn't say anything, 'what do you want to talk to me about?'

I let out a long breath. I had thought it would be easy to say, but when it came to it, it wasn't.

'It's a bit difficult,' I said, chewing my bottom lip. 'Delicate really and probably nothing to do with me, so I apologise now if you think I'm sticking my nose in.'

Pete put his mug on the little table next to his chair.

'It's Sara, isn't it?' he croaked, looking ashen. 'She's finding me too intense. She's sent you to tell me. I knew I was coming on a bit strong, but having wasted so much time . . .'

I put up a hand and shook my head.

'No, Pete, this is nothing to do with Sara. From what I've

seen and heard, she's every bit as smitten with you as you are with her.'

His expression was instantly transformed and the colour flooded back to his face as he picked up his tea again.

'Oh well,' he grinned, 'in that case, carry on.'

He put his mug to his lips.

'I want to talk to you about the band,' I quickly blurted out and he choked on his tea. 'Your and Eli's band, just to be clear. Or non-band . . . as the case may be.'

'I don't think there's actually anything to talk about, is there?' he spluttered, wiping the front of his T-shirt with his hand.

'Perhaps not,' I said, 'but can I say it anyway?'

'Be my guest,' he sighed.

'The thing is,' I began tentatively, 'I can appreciate that, given everything you went through because of Eli's ex, that it's really difficult for you to even consider reforming.'

Pete didn't refute that and I carried on.

'But now you and he are talking, and trying to put the past behind you, I thought you might want to make a go of it again.'

Pete's eyebrows began to slowly move towards each other.

'Eli's told me that it's too painful for you to reform,' I quickly added, for fear that he would think his friend hadn't fully grasped how he felt about it all and the depth to which his hurt extended. 'But couldn't you try and maybe just write some new stuff together? Even if you don't want to play it?'

Pete's mouth opened and closed like a trap door, but no sound came out.

'I know Eli's leaving music behind,' I said sadly, 'and he's assumed I'm going to do the same, but the truth is, now I've found my voice again, Pete, I don't want to lose it. How can I be in a relationship with someone who has banished the one thing I've just rediscovered a passion for?' I stopped to take a breath. 'Not that this is about me,' I quickly added, shaking my head.

My hands were shaking too. I was still getting used to the idea that I really did want to sing again, in spite of what I was going around telling everyone else, and the fact that I only wanted to do it when accompanied by the two men in my life who meant so much to me was a revelation too.

'Beth . . .'

'I know,' I grimaced, 'I know. I'm not explaining all this very well and I probably sound really self-centred.'

'It's not that . . .'

'And setting my selfish concerns aside,' I carried on, 'what I really want to ask is why you won't reconsider making a musical fresh start with Eli? Your friendship has survived, so why can't your band?'

Pete put up a hand to stop me.

'I don't know what Eli's told you, Beth,' he frowned, 'but I haven't once said that I won't play with him again.'

I looked at him and blinked.

'I don't understand.'

'Me neither,' he shrugged.

'So, you haven't said you won't restart the band with him?'

'No,' Pete insisted. 'I've never said that. We've never discussed it. I think the poor sod still feels so guilty about what happened that he's assumed that's what I would say. And just a couple of months ago, weeks even, I would have said no.'

'But now?'

He didn't even take a second to consider his answer.

'Now, I'd say that I was willing to let it all go and carry on,' he added seriously. 'And I wouldn't let some of the old tracks go either. They were far too good and with the right voice behind them—'

'So, let me get this straight,' I interrupted, 'you're willing to play?'

'Yes,' he nodded. 'And you're willing to sing?'

'I am,' I swallowed.

'So the only person who isn't willing to do anything, is—'

'Eli,' I sighed, 'and that's most likely because he's too scared to have the conversation, for fear of—'

'Kicking the upset with you off again.'

'Exactly.'

We drank our tea in silence and took a minute to allow everything to shift and settle into its new pattern.

'This is strictly between you and me,' I said, once I'd emptied my mug, 'but he's thinking about taking over the lease for the coffeehouse.'

This time Pete did properly choke. For a moment, I thought I was going to have to slap him on the back, but he righted himself eventually.

'He's what?' he gasped, still spluttering.

'Apparently Melanie is moving to be with her daughter in America,' I explained, completely breaking my promise not to tell anyone, but under the circumstances feeling it was allowed, 'and she's offered him the lease if he wants to take it on.'

Pete shook his head in disbelief.

'Eli's no barista,' he tutted. 'I mean, I daresay he can make a mean drink, but that job was only ever supposed to be a day job, the thing he did to make writing and playing music a possibility.'

'A job that paid the rent,' I murmured.

'Exactly.'

'Well, now he's talking about growing up and taking responsibility.'

'What the hell does he want to do that for?' Pete groaned.

'Beats me.'

We looked at each other and laughed.

'Seriously though,' I said, 'what are we going to do? I'm terrified he's going to come home and say he's signed on the dotted line and then he'll miss out on—'

'The job at The Chapel.'

Great minds really did think alike.

'You know about that?'

'Yes,' Pete said, 'Jacob rang me this morning and asked if I knew anyone who might fit the bill. Obviously, I immediately thought of Eli, but I didn't want to suggest him without talking to him about it first.'

'When Lisa mentioned it last night, my head went straight to him too, but in his current frame of mind, there's no chance he'd even consider it. We should have had this conversation days ago, Pete,' I said, my voice rising along with a sense of panic. 'I think we've missed the boat.'

'No, we haven't,' he said, jumping up. 'I know what to do.'

'You do?'

'Yes,' he said, puffing out his chest and looking into the middle distance.

He looked so much like a Tolkien hero that I almost laughed.

'Leave it with me,' he said, sounding incredibly sure of himself. 'I know exactly how to sort it.'

Chapter 28

By three o'clock the following afternoon, I was feeling jittery, but I should have known my friend wouldn't let me down, especially when he had sounded, and looked, so sure of himself. The residents and I were enjoying an afternoon of indoor puzzles and games when Sara came to find me.

'I don't know if this will make any sense to you,' she said, pulling her phone out of her pocket, which was strictly not allowed, 'but I've had a message from Pete asking me to tell you to meet him at The Chapel after work.'

I had no idea why he hadn't messaged me, but then my phone was in the staffroom so he might have done and I simply hadn't picked it up yet.

'Does that make sense?' Sara frowned. 'That's the place that's lined up to be the new Arches, isn't it?'

'Yes,' I nodded. 'But I have no idea why he wants to meet me there. Do you want to come with me to find out?'

'Best not,' said Sara, reading more of Pete's missive. 'It all sounds a bit cloak and dagger to me. I wouldn't want my unexpected presence to mess up his *quest*, as he's put it,' she added, squinting at the screen. 'And besides, he's promised to fill me in tonight if the *quest is a success*. You really don't know what's going on?'

'I don't know what he's got planned, but it sounds very Pete and I can guess who it's to do with ...' I began to explain, but then I spotted Sandra hovering in the dayroom doorway. 'Look out,' I warned, and Sara slipped her phone back into her pocket.

'Beth,' Sandra smiled, rushing over, with Buster close behind, 'just the person I'm looking for.'

I couldn't be certain, but I thought the old dog was puffing a little less and didn't look quite as rotund as he had before. The consistent warnings we'd given the residents about feeding the podgy pooch titbits seemed to have finally worked.

'I've got great news,' Sandra beamed at me. 'I've just taken a booking for the last empty room and the woman who organises the pet visits has rung to say she's had a cancellation for Monday. She can come for the afternoon, as long as that will fit around your plans, of course.'

'That's fantastic news all round,' I said. 'I can easily accommodate her then.'

I was grateful that Sandra hadn't announced the prospective visit to everyone. It would be nice to keep it under wraps and tell the residents on Friday so they had something to look forward to and talk about over the weekend.

'She said she can bring all sorts as long as there are enough staff to help out,' Sandra carried on. 'I said you'd ring her back so you can discuss it further.'

A bit of sleuthing was going to be required before I made the call. I'd have to discreetly find out if anyone had an aversion to anything before I confirmed what she should bring. Personally, I had a loathing of snakes, but the visit wasn't about me and if there were a few fans among the residents, then I'd just have to grin and bear them.

Sara wished me luck as I got ready to head to The Chapel after I'd finished for the day. I hoped I wasn't going to need it, but gratefully accepted it, just in case. It had been a hot day and as I walked along, I could tell it was going to be one of those nights where the warmth lingered. I was pleased I'd left the upstairs curtains shut at the house and keeping the wooden shutters in the bay window closed made a considerable difference to the sitting-room temperature too.

I tutted to myself as I strode out, aware that I was trying to think about mundane things to stave off worrying about what Pete had been planning. I hoped it wasn't anything too extreme. He'd really come out of himself since getting together with Sara and if he'd got any sort of death or dishonour battle re-enactment lined-up, then I would be turning tail and heading straight home.

He hadn't of course.

'Beth,' he said, jumping down off the stage when I walked in. The inside temperature of The Chapel felt wonderfully cool after the walk. 'You came.'

'I told you she would,' said Freddie, who appeared from the kitchen with a glass of water in his hand. 'I said, she'd come.'

I looked between the two men. One of whom I very definitely hadn't expected to see.

'What's going on?' I frowned. 'Does Sandra know you've left the home, Freddie?'

'Yes, yes,' he said, dismissively waving the question away with his empty hand, which wasn't entirely convincing. 'She knows.'

'Freddie's offered to help,' said Pete, as the man himself headed towards the stage.

'With what?' I asked.

Looking around, I saw that the stage had been set up with a microphone, two guitars and a keyboard.

'What's all this in aid of?'

'My master plan, of course,' Pete said with a flourish. 'A mate with a van helped me get it here and set it up and if this doesn't make Eli change his mind about picking up his music again, then nothing will.'

'So, what exactly is *this*?' I frowned.

'I've messaged him,' said Pete, offering Freddie a steadying hand as he climbed the steps to where the keyboard was located. 'And told him to meet us here. I reckon if he plays a few songs with us, he'll soon get into the swing of it again.'

I wasn't so sure; I feared that once he'd spotted the set-up, he'd be more inclined to walk straight back out.

'We've been practising all afternoon,' said Freddie, as he

corralled some sheets of paper together. 'It's not really my cup of tea, but some of it's not bad.'

I felt guilty for not questioning Freddie's absence back at the home and I was surprised that neither Greta nor Ida had flagged it up.

'Praise indeed,' I tutted, shaking my head. 'And what's my role in all of this?' I asked, looking about warily.

'Singing, of course,' said Pete, pointing at the mic.

I dropped my bag at my feet. I knew Pete had come up with the plan with the best of intentions, but was extreme aversion therapy really the way to accomplish this *quest*? I was genuinely concerned that the tactic was going to backfire and Eli would end up resenting us for pushing him in a direction he insisted he no longer wanted to be heading.

'It'll work,' Pete said firmly, picking up on my hesitation. 'Trust me, Beth.'

Given that he'd already messaged Eli, I didn't have much choice. I took a deep breath and joined him and Freddie on the stage.

'What time did you tell him to come?'

Almost an hour after the suggested time, I was sitting on the stage, my feet dangling over the edge, wishing I'd brought snacks. Three times Pete had taken me through the running order of what he had planned for us to play, but so far the three of us hadn't lifted an instrument or sung a note.

'I hope you got a late pass,' I said to Freddie.

'He did,' Pete quickly said, but the man himself looked a little shifty.

'Let's not waste any more time,' said Freddie, stretching out his fingers. 'Let's run through a couple of these songs with you singing, Beth, that way when the lad arrives, we'll be well warmed up.'

If he arrives, I thought.

'That's a great idea,' said Pete, reaching for his guitar and pulling the strap over his head.

The action was achingly familiar and I felt my throat tighten as he strummed a few chords and did a bit of retuning.

'What do you say, Beth?'

My heart skittered at the thought of releasing my voice again.

'It took me ages to get everything set up,' Pete said, 'and the bloke will be wanting the key back soon. I'm not going to let that stubborn sod make all this effort a total waste of time.'

I pulled myself back onto the stage and carefully took the microphone out of its stand. I didn't think much harm could come from the three of us doing what Freddie suggested and there was really no need for me to feel shy. Pete had heard me sing a million times and Freddie was familiar with what I sounded like now too.

'Are you happy with all of these, Beth?' Pete asked, handing me some sheets with lyrics printed on.

I knew most of the songs, thanks to Eli filling the house with music on a daily basis when I had first moved in, but I also knew my renditions weren't going to be perfect. A couple on the list I didn't recognise at all. I guessed those were the ones that had been set aside after Eli's ex had ruined everything.

'You'll have to bear with me,' I told him as Freddie played the intro to the first song. 'I'm familiar with most of them, but not these last three.'

Pete nodded and began to play along with Freddie.

'You'll soon pick them up,' he said confidently.

The next half an hour or so was a happy blur. The sensations and emotions I'd so recently dreamed of came back tenfold as we ran through the list and I became more familiar with the lyrics and melodies. Freddie had already picked everything up and I quickly matched him. By the time the keyholder arrived, we sounded as though we'd been playing together for far longer than thirty minutes.

'Any chance of another hour?' Pete pleaded with the guy.

'Strictly speaking,' he said, sounding put out, 'you shouldn't be here at all and I could hear you halfway along the street.'

'Half an hour then,' piped up Freddie, flashing his trademark smile.

'That might work on Greta and Ida, Freddie Fanshawe,' I laughed, 'but I think you'll find this audience a harder nut to crack.'

The man looked over at Freddie and his eyes widened.

'Are you really Freddie Fanshawe?' he asked, sounding awestruck. '*The* Freddie Fanshawe?'

His whole demeanour had changed and Pete looked at me and grinned.

'None other,' Freddie beamed again as he quickly banged out a bit of Jerry Lee Lewis on the keyboard.

'My mum used to love you,' said the guy, looking misty-eyed. 'I had no idea you were here, Mr Fanshawe.'

'Freddie, please,' Freddie said graciously.

'Freddie,' the man repeated, 'I suppose another hour wouldn't hurt. I'd better stay on site though,' he added. 'Just in case.'

He didn't say just in case of what and Pete looked at me again and this time winked.

'God bless Freddie's appeal with mums everywhere,' he laughed.

'Indeed,' I laughed back.

We carried on playing and I was facing Pete, singing the ballad that I knew was a particular favourite of Eli's, when his face changed. His smile faltered as his gaze flicked beyond me and the words he had been singing died in his throat.

'Carry on,' called Freddie, just as I was about to turn around. 'Just keep going.'

Pete nodded at me and started singing again and I felt rooted to the spot as the hairs on the back of my neck stood to attention. The next thing I knew, the guitar which had been left idle all evening was playing along with us and when I did then slowly turn, I found Eli by my side with tears in his eyes and a look of rapture lighting up his face.

Without a word we finished the song and then played it through again, this time without interruption. I kept my eyes focused on Eli's face and I was in no doubt that Pete's plan, the one I had been so sceptical of, had worked. Eli had reclaimed his music mojo, as well as his best friend, and I'd stopped denying myself what I loved most in the world.

For the first time since I'd received that call at university which had torn my world apart, everything felt right again. The harsh words which had scarred me for so long at the audition were healed and the course of my life was back in alignment. I might not have been rushing along the path to stardom, but Freddie had been right, this new one was no less valid.

As the song came to an end, I became aware that it was no longer just the five of us filling The Chapel. Crowded in the doorway were Lisa and John, Jacob and Poppy, and Luke and Kate. They started to applaud and rushed inside. It was Lisa who spoke up first.

'Ladies and gentlemen!' she shouted to the others, 'we've finally found our star turn!'

Pete, Eli and I exchanged a look and then Eli leant over to talk into the mic.

'Indeed you have!' he laughed.

Everyone clapped and cheered and he turned to look at me again. He cupped my face in his hands and kissed me with complete abandon. I realised the whoops and cheers had intensified even more when he eventually pulled away.

'I love you, Beth,' he said sincerely. 'With all of my heart.'

'And I love you too,' I said back, the words truly meant and spoken only for him, although I'm sure everyone else heard them.

'Thank you,' he said, kissing me again, 'thank you, and Pete, for giving me this back.'

'And thank you,' I sighed happily, 'for helping me find it again.'

'It has been my pleasure.'

'I only wish you could have heard more tonight,' I whispered, resting my forehead against his. 'We ran through practically everything on your playlist.'

'I did hear it,' he told me. 'I heard it all. I was late leaving work, but I arrived in time to hear you start playing. It just took me a while to pluck up the courage to come in.'

'You were here through the whole set?' I gasped.

'Through the whole set,' he grinned.

We could have stayed locked in our private world forever, but we needed to get everything dismantled and packed away.

While Eli and Pete sorted the instruments, with much back-slapping and animated chat about what we could perform at the fundraiser, I helped Freddie down from the stage. The Chapel keyholder, Kyle, had offered to drive him back to the care home and it turned out he had also been responsible for tipping our neighbours off about the impromptu mini concert.

'I suppose I should be getting back,' said Freddie, looking sheepish as he checked his watch. 'Someone's bound to have missed me by now.'

'Oh Freddie,' I said, appalled. 'You didn't tell anyone you were leaving, did you?'

'Yes, he did,' said Pete. 'I picked him up at the door and

there was a carer with him. Don't wind her up, Freddie. She's had enough to contend with for one day.'

'That I have,' I agreed, smiling at Eli and feeling my face colour.

Freddie gave my cheek a quick kiss.

'Thank you, folks!' he then called out. 'If you ever need an old entertainer, I'm available for birthdays, bar mitzvahs and even wakes!'

'You'd better be ready for the fundraiser, too,' Eli quickly said.

'I am,' he nodded. 'I promised Beth I'd play a tune or two.'

'We want you to do more than that, Freddie,' said Pete. 'We want you on that stage with us when we're playing too.'

Freddie looked absolutely flabbergasted.

'Do you really?' he gasped. 'Do you mean it?'

The emotion in his voice brought tears to my eyes. Clearly Eli's songs had grown on him over the course of the last couple of hours.

'Too right,' said Eli. 'And we'll be rehearsing every spare minute next week, so don't go double-booking yourself.'

'Well, I never,' Freddie chuckled. 'Wonders will never cease. I'll check my diary tonight and pencil it all in.'

'And you'd better check yours too,' Lisa said to Eli.

'Oh?' he frowned

She and Jacob exchanged a look and then Lisa carried on.

'We have a proposition we want to talk to you about,' she said.

'A proposition?'

I crossed my fingers, hoping they were thinking the same thing I was.

'There's a full-time manager's job going with this place,' Jacob elaborated. 'And someone mentioned to us that you've got the experience that makes you the perfect fit for the role. We're hoping you'll be the person to take it on.'

Eli's eyes widened.

'You're not serious?'

'We are,' Lisa and Jacob said together.

'In that case,' Eli beamed, whipping out his phone, 'let's get an interview date in the diary.'

Chapter 29

The days leading up to the summer fair were beyond busy. My entire life was suddenly all about changing, rearranging and of course, re-embracing. I had thought about the words of Friedrich Nietzsche that Eli had previously quoted to me and concluded that he was right: without music, life really was a mistake. Or mine was, at least.

Had I been thinking clearly when Mum had her first stroke (but given the circumstances I could appreciate why I hadn't been), and not taken the words spouted at me after my audition to heart, I would have realised that music was the very thing that would have helped me cope. It would have soothed and healed my broken spirit and I vowed to never neglect it or my dear friend, Pete, again.

Not that that was likely to happen now I was the voice of the band. Stardom might not have been about to beckon, but I had found something far more precious than that. Freddie had been right about the other path and I was grateful for his pearls of wisdom, gleaned throughout a life well lived.

He had generously agreed to play with Eli, Pete and I at the fundraiser, but after that we would need to look for a new keyboard player because he would be standing down.

'I can't have the girls at Cavell Care getting jealous about having to share me, can I?' he had said, with his trademark twinkle.

The girls, as he called them, seemed happy enough. In fact, I would go as far as to say that everyone at the care home was thriving. The new activities schedule was keeping them occupied and engaged and, perhaps most blessedly of all, it was keeping Greta fully clothed and out of mischief. Which was just as well because she had been awarded a very special role at the fair.

The inaugural visit to the home from Juliet, or the 'pet lady', as she was better known, had been a great success. The three dogs and two cats I settled for inviting had been calm and docile, which was more than could be said for a couple of the residents.

Juliet's visits were set to become a regular addition to the diary and so were trips to the Grow-Well. There had been one already and that had been a triumph. I put the success solely down to Carole and Graham. Carole especially. No one dared misbehave or cause mischief on her watch!

'So,' I demanded, the second Eli had rushed back into the house and slammed the door behind him on the morning of the fair. 'How did it go?'

He had gone out early to meet Melanie at the coffeehouse to explain that he wasn't going to be taking her up on her offer of the lease and why.

'Really well,' he replied, putting down a box, then scooping me up and spinning me around in the narrow hall. 'She was fine about it. In fact, I kind of got the impression she had offered it to me in the hope that it would make me think about what I really wanted out of life. She knew full well how miserable I'd felt about giving up my music.'

'Well,' I smiled as he set me on my feet again, 'her plan worked then, didn't it?'

'It did,' he grinned. 'Although it was Pete who pulled off the masterstroke.'

I couldn't argue with that. His quest had been an unmitigated success.

'And talking of Pete,' Eli carried on, 'he's been in raptures all week about something he'd spotted in the vintage shop and as soon as he told me what it was, I knew I had to buy it for you.'

'Oh?' I said, looking more interestedly at the box he'd carried in. 'More pots?'

'No,' Eli laughed, picking it up again. 'Come on.'

A few minutes later Eli and I were slow dancing in the dining room and I'd just about managed to dry my tears. Eli had spotted the box of Mum's much-loved vinyl in my bedroom and had instantly known the little second-hand record player in Back in Time would be perfect for playing them on.

They hadn't been out of their sleeves since Mum had gone and it felt wonderful to hear them again. Pete said he didn't mind Eli beating him to buying the player, although he might ask to borrow it every now and again.

Eli pulled me closer and I laid my head on his chest.

'Thank you,' I sighed dreamily. 'This is the best present I've ever been given. I wish we could stay here all weekend.'

The fair, along with the important part we were going to play in it, had for the moment been pushed to the back of my mind.

'Me too,' he said, kissing the top of my head as the record came to end, 'but we have plans, remember?'

'Oh crikey,' I said, glancing at the clock, 'you're right! We better hurry up or we'll miss the ribbon being cut.'

'Grab your sunblock then,' Eli laughed, as he took the album off the deck and slipped it carefully back into its sleeve. 'And let's go.'

'You haven't even finished telling me what Melanie said yet,' I pointed out as I pulled on my Converse.

The fair hadn't been the only thing I'd forgotten while we were smooching to Ella Fitzgerald.

'She was really great,' Eli grinned. 'Thrilled when I told her about The Chapel.'

The afternoon before, Eli had been interviewed for, been offered, and much to Lisa and Jacob's delight, immediately accepted the role of manager of The Chapel. Pete and I were thrilled about it too.

'We agreed that I'll stay working at the coffeehouse until The Chapel sale has gone through,' he further explained. 'That way, I won't end up stuck between jobs and penniless. Melanie was adamant that I hadn't left her in the lurch,' he also said. I knew he had been worrying about that. 'She told me she would easily find someone else to take the lease on.'

'That's all great,' I said, adding my purse to my bag along with the sunblock. 'Although you might want to think about taking a few days off in between jobs. The Chapel is going to be a full-on project, so you'll need to be rested for when you start.'

Lisa had kicked his interview off by telling him the wonderful news that more funding for the venture had been secured and it was now a given that Moira Myers' already incredible legacy had the potential to grow even bigger than it had been before.

'That's true,' he said, mulling over my suggestion. 'Maybe you could get a couple of days off too. We could book that getaway in Wynmouth that I'd originally been planning for this weekend.'

What a turnaround the last few days had seen. In both our lives.

'Sounds good to me,' I enthusiastically agreed.

I loved the quaint little village on the Norfolk coast. It was quiet and cosy, exactly the sort of place we needed to visit to recharge our batteries and not too far away from Eli's mum if the time felt right for introductions.

'Come on,' Eli urged. 'It's time.'

I had been worried that Lisa was going to call on me to cut the ribbon to open the fair as I was the one, as she liked to keep reminding everyone, who had put the idea for it into her head. Fortunately, I was spared that, although I did get a mention in her and Jacob's speech.

As I listened to them talk, I looked around the packed

green, taking in the stalls and games that had been set up early that morning. There were more in the garden at Prosperous Place, along with the stage for the evening's entertainment, and hopefully Greta was already installed over there with Pete and Sara.

The moment Eli and I had taken a look at everything on the green and he had managed to win me a Pooh Bear plush on the hoopla which, he jokingly said, proved his athletic prowess, we headed over the road.

'I'll feel better when I know she's behaving herself,' I said to Eli who, aware of Greta's former antics, was in complete agreement.

Spread across a large area of the lawn and quite close to the river which ran through the grounds, the Iceni re-enactment group had set up a part of their Celtic village. There were people dressed up in the same sort of outfits I'd seen Sara and Pete wearing, and they were all employed in some task or another.

I spotted Pete tending a fire and Sara was pounding something in a pot. She looked up and grinned when she spotted us approaching and Pete's face flushed.

'How's it going?' I asked, looking at what she was grinding.

'Good,' she said. 'We might have bread to go with the wild boar later.'

I wasn't sure if she was joking or not.

'And where's . . .'

The question died in my throat as I caught sight of Greta being led to a chair next to Pete's carefully contained fire.

'I'm the crow!' she shouted when she spotted me. 'That's very important apparently.'

'She means crone,' said Sara and Eli laughed. 'Or wise woman,' Sara elaborated with a grin.

'God help us if she tries her hand at healing,' Eli beamed and I whacked him in the ribs with the Pooh Bear plush.

'You look great, Greta,' I said, rushing over. 'How do you feel?'

'Regal,' she grinned. 'Apparently, I was a much-valued and respected member of the community in the past.'

The way she said it suggested that she wasn't now, but then given the amount of mischief and mayhem she caused us, she didn't make it easy. We did all love her though.

'Is Freddie here yet?' she eagerly asked. 'He won't know what's hit him when he sees me in this garb.'

'As soon as I see him,' I promised, 'I'll send him over.'

She wouldn't let us go until I'd handed over my cuddly toy and as we walked away, I looked back to see her in serious conversation with the funny old bear. It made for a very strange and not entirely authentic tableau.

'You can relax now,' said Eli, taking my hand and giving it a squeeze.

'Relax?' I gasped, my gaze swinging back to him. 'When we've got to perform tonight? That's the last thing I can do!'

We'd had multiple rehearsals since the impromptu concert in The Chapel and I knew every note, beat and lyric by heart, but that hadn't stopped my nerves steadily growing during the last few days. I only hoped they would dissipate when I picked up the microphone again and began to sing for real. That's how it had always worked in the past and that's what I was pinning my hopes on.

'You'll be fine,' Eli said softly. 'You're going to be amazing.'

'*We're* going to be amazing,' I amended, feeling marginally more confident, secure in the knowledge that I was going to have not two, but three of my favourite men performing alongside me.

'Are you two busy?' John's voice rang out as he beckoned us over to where Lisa had set up her table to sign books.

The waiting queue was long enough to wrap itself halfway around the lawn and Eli and I quickly rushed over to offer assistance.

'Slightly bigger turnout than anticipated,' John puffed. 'Any chance you could lend Lisa a hand, while I borrow Eli for a bit?' he asked me pleadingly.

'Of course,' I said. I was up for pretty much anything as long as it kept me occupied. 'Leave her in my capable hands.'

There was a sudden burst of excited applause as Lisa appeared, looking far smarter than I'd ever seen her. She was even wearing full make-up, which was a first. I stepped back while she addressed everyone, as best as she could without the benefit of a megaphone, and then helped keep the queue in order as everyone flocked to have their books signed.

'Has John done a runner?' she asked, as the first enrap-tured reader stepped up to place her book on the table like a holy offering.

'I think there was something he needed to sort out,' I

frowned, not actually sure what he'd gone to do. 'He's taken Eli with him.'

Lisa laughed.

'He gets in a right flap at this sort of thing,' she giggled. 'My readers are always asking if he's the inspiration for my hottest heroes!'

I'd read a couple of her books now and given how racy I knew some of her plotlines could be, I wasn't at all surprised to hear of John's blushes.

'Right,' Lisa grinned to her first adoring fan, 'let's make a start, shall we?'

Even though it was late afternoon, the Square and gardens were still heaving and I got the impression that a lot of people had decided to stay on for the evening's entertainment rather than go home in-between.

Mark, who had only just finished work at Blossoms, told me they'd had their busiest Saturday in forever thanks to people popping in and out for extra snacks between their time at the fair. And visitors had travelled from much further afield too.

Kate had introduced me to her brother Tom and his wife Jemma, who were staying with her and Luke for a long weekend. Jemma, Kate explained to me, ran a place called The Cherry Tree Café in Wynbridge, which was about an hour or so drive away.

'This is the first time I've been able to get her away for years,' said Tom, sounding amazed

'And we're child-free for the weekend too,' Jemma beamed, 'so I can't wait to party tonight!'

'No pressure then, Beth,' laughed Luke, before telling everyone that I was part of one of the bands which would be performing.

'No,' I said, feeling wobbly again, 'no pressure at all.'

'And there'll be more than a few press bods here,' he added, cranking my nerves up another notch. 'When I told them how you and Pete are two of the original Arches attendees and are now going to be involved with The Chapel and that Eli's the manager, they were even more keen to cover the event.'

I had been delighted to be asked to help out and was very much looking forward to making a start. Being on board with the new venture, right from its beginning, was a thrilling prospect.

'You'll be in the papers tomorrow, Beth,' grinned Kate.

'In that case,' I said, 'I'd better go home and start getting ready.'

It was a little early, but suddenly I felt I needed some time out. Eli was clearly feeling the same way too as we collided at the Prosperous Place gate.

'I thought you said you were feeling fine about it all,' I teased him as we walked back around the Square to the house.

'I was,' he said, looking considerably paler than he had been before. 'But then John told me how many people they reckoned were going to come.'

I didn't have a chance to extract the approximate number from him. Which, with hindsight, was probably just as well.

'Beth!' I heard someone shout and turned around to find Sandra rushing across the green and waving something in the air.

'Sandra,' I said, 'I didn't know you were here.'

'I've been here all afternoon,' she said, looking very happy. 'Look at this! Buster has only gone and won the waggiest tail.'

I realised it was a rosette she had been waving, with a number one emblazoned across it. On hearing his name, the lovely dog's tail thumped against the skirt of her dress.

'That's fantastic!' I laughed, giving him a fuss and noticing Sandra was wearing sandals, rather than her trademark heels, 'and very well deserved.'

I was about to introduce Sandra to Eli, but she was already turning away.

'I'm going to take Buster home and then meet Mike for an early dinner. We'll be back in time for the entertainment though.' She waved. 'Break a leg!'

'Now there's an idea,' Eli said. 'Would a broken leg get us out of performing?'

'No,' I said, feeling a curious mixture of excited and terrified. 'It most definitely would not.'

Just a couple of hours later and I was feeling more terrified than excited as we made our way back to Prosperous Place, but there was no turning back now.

'Eli?'

He dropped my hand and spun around.

'Mum!' he gasped. 'What are you doing here? I thought you were still at your work conference.'

I'd had no idea his mum was going to be putting in an appearance and given Eli's surprised comment, neither did he. I felt even more nervous than I had before. This was one introduction I had wanted time to prepare for.

'I was,' she mischievously smiled, sweeping her beautiful long hair over her shoulder, 'but I developed a mystery illness and had to leave.'

'Mum,' Eli pretend-tutted, 'are you playing hooky?'

Watching the pair of them together, and listening to her playful and relaxed tone, I felt my nerves settle.

'Something like that,' she winked, 'but I wasn't going to miss seeing you and Pete playing again for the first time and I was desperate to meet the clever woman who managed to get the pair of you back together.'

Eli reached for my hand.

'Mum,' he said, kissing my cheek, 'this is Beth. Beth, this is my mum.'

I didn't have time to ponder the protocol for meeting your boyfriend's mother for the first time because she stepped forward and pulled me into a hug.

'I'm delighted to meet you, Beth,' she said, when she finally let me go. 'You've pulled off quite a coup, getting these boys back on track.'

'I'm not sure I can take the credit for that,' I admitted, feeling a little taken aback by how comforting her embrace had felt.

It was an all-encompassing Mum hug and something I'd not had the benefit of in a very long time.

'Well,' she smiled warmly, linking her arm through mine, 'you can tell me all about it later, but now I think you're both needed backstage.'

'We'll see you later!' Eli called when we reached the garden and she headed one way and we went the other.

I'd only walked a couple of steps before I spotted how full the grounds were and my mouth fell open.

'Oh my god,' I squealed, squeezing Eli's hand perhaps a little too tight, given that he was going to need it to play his guitar. 'Where have all these people come from?'

I'd thought the place had been packed before, but it was nothing compared to the crowd standing in front of the stage and waiting to be entertained. I could barely see any of the lawns at all.

'The furthest reaches of the county, I reckon.' Eli swallowed, sounding as shocked as I was.

'And beyond,' I added for good measure, squeezing him again.

'Here you are,' said Pete, who had taken off his re-enactment outfit and was looking handsome, dressed in a black shirt and jeans. He had been waiting for us at the side of the stage, looking worried before he spotted our approach. 'I thought I was going to have to come and find you pair,' he scolded. 'It's almost time to start.'

'Sorry,' we apologised in unison.

'Are we mad to do this, or what?' Pete asked just a few seconds later as we prepared ourselves, as best we could, to go on.

His frown, I noticed, had been replaced with a broad smile.

'Totally,' said Eli.

'One hundred per cent,' I agreed.

'Come on then,' he laughed, grabbing both our hands in case we made a bid for freedom. 'Let's get closer to the stage. Freddie's there already.'

The only space backstage was one cordoned-off side of the lawn and there were lots of people already milling about so it was a bit of a squeeze. I spotted a few familiar faces, but there was no time to catch up with anyone yet.

'Just like I said,' Freddie grinned at me, as the time until our performance ticked down. 'A different path, but just as valid.'

'I'll never doubt you again, Freddie,' I told him. 'Harold!' I then shouted, as I spotted him weaving his way towards us, unchaperoned and on his mobility scooter.

He swerved sharply in our direction and came to a halt just inches from my feet.

'Phil said I could use it,' he said defensively.

'I'm sure he did,' I said, bending down to give him a hug.

'Oh,' he said, when I straightened up again, 'what have I done to deserve that?'

I bobbed down so our faces were level.

'Only set off the happiest chain of events to happen in my life for a very long time,' I told him, my bottom lip wobbling a little.

'Oh that,' he said, looking bright-eyed himself. 'That was nothing.'

We both knew it was but if I said too much more, I'd never be able to perform. I watched him trundle off to meet Sara, who was waving from the sidelines, and refocused on the other acts to try and stave off my nerves.

'Look up,' said Pete, nudging me in the back, what felt like mere seconds later. 'We're on.'

I reached for Eli's hand, took a deep breath and followed Pete and Freddie's lead towards the excited audience, most of whom were now on their feet. I picked up my mic as the guys played the opening bars of what had fast become my favourite song in our repertoire and let the lyrics express everything I was feeling. My voice held no hint of the former nerves I had been feeling and the applause that erupted when the song ended let me know that I had done the words justice.

I opened my eyes and drank the scene in and there, standing right at the front of the crowd, cheering and waving, were my new Nightingale Square family and the whole squad from Cavell Care. I imagined Mum standing among them and in that moment, I knew I was no longer alone; I had finally found my place in the world and on the stage.

'All right?' Eli asked, rushing to kiss me before the bright lights picked us out.

Everyone cheered even louder so we knew we'd been rumbled and we started to laugh, our eyes fixed on each other.

'You know what?' I smiled, revelling in the tingle of excitement that only Eli and singing on stage could ignite, 'I've never been better.'

Acknowledgements

So, my loves, this was our fourth trip to Nightingale Square. I hope you have enjoyed getting to know Beth, Eli and the Edith Cavell Care Home crew as much as I have enjoyed writing about them. There were a couple of characters in this book who weren't included in the planning at all. They simply waltzed on to the page and were such fun to write, right from the off. I bet you can guess exactly who they are!

I know I always say it, but as ever there are an extraordinary number of people to thank for helping to launch this book, my fourteenth, into the world.

Thank you to my wonderful editor, Clare Hey, and my fabulous agent, Amanda Preston, who laughed in all the right places when I sent in the first early draft and continued to do so throughout the editing process. Thank you also to Pip Watkins, Judith Long, Harriett Collins, Sara-Jade Virtue, Amy Fulwood and the entire Books and The City team for your incredible input and hard work.

Huge and heartfelt thanks to my wonderful friends Jenni

Keer, Clare Marchant, Rosie Hendry, Ian Wilfred, Mary-Anne Lewis, Claire Howard, Tracey Gant, Fiona Jenkins and Sue Baker. You've all, somehow, kept me smiling throughout what has been an incredibly challenging few months.

I'm delighted to report that the Swainette Squad is still going from strength to strength! Thank you to everyone who has made The Heidi Swain and Friends Facebook Book Club the loveliest place to be. Fiona and Sue have created such a supportive space, and it isn't all about books. The fabulous community there is both friendly and welcoming, just like the neighbours in Nightingale Square. Join us!

Thank you also to everyone sharing the book love on Instagram and Twitter. I've made so many new friends on both platforms in the last few years. I know some folk say online friends aren't real friends, but I vehemently dispute that. You all light up my timeline! Thank you to all the dedicated book bloggers who generously give so much time and thought to their posts and reviews, and to the library staff throughout the land who work tirelessly to keep us all borrowing and reading. You're all amazing and so appreciated.

A huge thank you also to everyone who has subscribed to my newsletter. This was a new venture for me last year and it's proving very popular, which is a lovely boost. You can find the details of how to subscribe on my blog if you haven't already but would like to.

And I'm adding in an extra squeeze for Lia here too. Our endless conversations, and mutual love of the man in the fedora, has made this book shine! Thank you, my darling.

And last, but by no means least, thank you dear reader, for taking another trip with me. I'm already looking forward to the next! Until we meet again, may your bookshelves – be they virtual or real – always be filled with fabulous fiction.

H x

Underneath the Christmas Tree

Wynter's Trees is the home of Christmas. For the people of Wynmouth it's where they get their family Christmas tree, and where Christmas truly comes to life.

But for Liza Wynter, it's a millstone around her neck. It was her father's pride and joy but now he's gone, she can't have anything to do with it. Until her father's business partner decides to retire and she must go back to handle the transition to his son Ned.

When Liza arrives, she discovers a much-loved business that's flourishing under Ned's stewardship. And she's happy to stay and help for the Christmas season, but then she has other plans. But will the place where she grew up make her change her mind? And can it weave its Christmas cheer around her heart . . . ?

AVAILABLE IN PAPERBACK AND EBOOK NOW

A Taste of Home

Fliss Brown has grown up living with her mother on the Rossi family's Italian fruit farm. But when her mother dies, Fliss finds out she has a family of her own, and heads back to England with Nonna Rossi's recipe for cherry and almond tart and a piece of advice: connect with your family before it is too late . . .

Fliss discovers that her estranged grandfather owns a fruit farm himself, on the outskirts of Wynbridge, and she arrives to find a farm that has fallen into disrepair. Using her knowledge gleaned from working on the Rossi farm and her desire to find out more about her past, Fliss rolls her sleeves up and gets stuck in. But what will she discover, and can she resurrect the farm's glory days and find a taste of home?

AVAILABLE IN PAPERBACK AND EBOOK NOW

booksandthecity.co.uk
the home of female fiction

NEWS & EVENTS | BOOKS | FEATURES | COMPETITIONS

Follow us online to be the first to hear from
your favourite authors

bc
booksandthecity.co.uk

@TeamBATC

Join our mailing list for the latest news, events and
exclusive competitions

Sign up at
booksandthecity.co.uk